be kept

D1121567

The District Nurse

The District Nurse

HUGH MILLER

860278

St. Martin's Press
New York

THE DISTRICT NURSE. Copyright © 1984 by Hugh Miller, Julia Smith, Tony Holland. All rights reserved. Printed in the United States of America. No part of this book may be used or reproduced in any manner whatsoever without written permission except in the case of brief quotations embodied in critical articles or reviews. For information, address St. Martin's Press, 175 Fifth Avenue, New York, N.Y. 10010.

Library of Congress Cataloging in Publication Data
Miller, Hugh, 1937-
    The district nurse.

    I. Title.
PR6063.I373D5   1984   823'.914   84-22875
ISBN 0-312-21359-X

First published in Great Britain by Arrow Books Ltd.
Taken from the BBC-T.V. series "The District Nurse."
First U.S. Edition

10   9   8   7   6   5   4   3   2   1

To
Julia Smith and Tony Holland,
who provided the spark

Part One

1

Her father's first cough brought Megan awake instantly, blinking in the dark at the dull red embers in the fireplace. She lay for a minute watching the steamy trace of her breath on the air.

She had been dreaming of mice, the little, round, dark-brown ones she saw in summer in the fields near the railway station. She hadn't wanted to hurt them, but in the dream they would only sit and watch her at a safe distance, timid among the corn stalks, black beads of eyes alert to the slightest forward movement as she coaxed them with lip sounds and bits of bread. One of them had begun creeping forward when Owen Roberts coughed. Megan saw them all scurry away, startled, a second before she woke.

She tightened her arms around herself and counted slowly to ten, as she always did on winter mornings, preparing for the wrench of leaving the warm hollow she'd made under the blankets with the old black overcoat on top.

'Eight, nine . . . *ten*.' The space between nine and ten got longer as the winter deepened. Megan slid out on to the cold brown linoleum and shivered. She stood still for a moment, listening. Her mother was up; Megan could hear her moving on the creaky floorboards. Her father coughed again, a long, rattling wheeze that tailed off to breathless silence. After long seconds she heard the muffled gulps as he sucked air back into his labouring chest. That meant he was up too, getting into his work clothes.

Megan went to the fireplace and eased back the front of the ash pan, letting air fan up through the grating. She waited until the embers flared bright, then she threw on half a dozen sticks from the bucket by the fender. While the fire got under way she went to the scullery and splashed cold water on her face and arms from the iron-hooped tub by the sink. She towelled her

9

numbed skin with the square of sacking hanging on the back door and went back to fold up her bedclothes.

Being able to sleep alone in a room was a luxury Megan had enjoyed for three years now, since her tenth birthday. Her mother and father had the room upstairs and her four brothers slept in the only other bedroom, across the lobby. Megan's bed was in the living room.

There were disadvantages to the arrangement. Six days a week she had to rise at a quarter-past five and put away her truckle bed to make space in the small room for the family traffic. Since she was on hand, she was expected to put tea in the pot and get the kettle on the boil too. After that she had to lay out the enamel mugs and sugar bowl for her father and for George, her eldest brother.

Her mother came down while Megan was getting into her clothes. 'You'll singe yourself one of these days, standing so near the fire.'

'It's that cold, Mam,' Megan said, buttoning her wool frock and taking her stockings from the edge of the fender where they'd been warming. 'There's ice all down the window.'

'No need to tell me, girl.' Jennie Roberts lit a paper spill from the fire and put it to the paraffin lamp on the table. She turned up the wick slowly, bathing the room in yellowy light. 'It's like an iceberg up there. Not helping your Da's chest, neither.'

'He didn't take his medicine last night.' Megan hoisted the big black kettle on to the hook over the hob, her thin arms trembling with the weight. She swung it in over the flames and threw on some more wood. 'He forgot, I expect. I was going to come up with it, but I thought he might be sleeping.'

'That stuff does him no good, anyway,' Jennie murmured. 'Makes his stomach bad.'

They took a moment to gaze at the bright flames licking up around the kettle. Jennie, forty years old, looked like a waxen wraith, her long grey hair hanging in lustreless tendrils on either side of her face. For eight years the pain of rheumatism had whittled at her energy and gradually stooped her shoulders; for more years than that anxiety, some of it well founded, had worked a change on her features and her manner. She was

10

known in the town to be a difficult woman, dour and rarely sociable. But people made allowances, because Jennie Roberts always looked so hollow-eyed and ill.

'Christmas Eve, Mam,' Megan said with an excited little grin. She risked an arm lightly round her mother's waist. 'We've lots to get ready.'

'It'll come whether we're ready for it or not.' Jennie moved back to the table, but not roughly, letting Megan's arm trail away from her. She lifted the edge of the oilcloth and pulled a knife out of the drawer. 'Get in the tea cans, and bring me that blue tin from the shelf in the scullery.'

Christmas Eve or not, the two men still had to do their ten hours at the slate quarry; to make the day a bit special, Jennie would give them a chunk of currant cake with their bread and dripping. There were some little biscuits too, the kind Owen liked, with bits of peel in them and burnt sugar on top.

Outside the sleet was starting, a slanting grey downpour that would sting the cheeks of the miners like needles as they made their way, in huddles of four and five, up Ruthin Lane to the tramped-shale slope that led to the open-cast workings, a mile north-east of the town. It was cruel, the sleet, but it was a sight kinder than the snow that had crusted the ground and frozen the slate for seven weeks the year before, the year when two children froze to death in Mostyn Wood, trying to find their way home from collecting firewood.

The sleet was the nearest thing to snow they would see in Drynfor that Christmas. 1905 had been a characterless year right through, half-hearted, without a positive mood in any of its seasons. There had been a damp, chilly spring, a tepid summer and scarcely an autumn to speak of. Now the winter was on them with its frowning dark days and its biting winds, the frost and the disheartening sleet.

'You've a job finding anything to laugh at, some days,' Owen Roberts said, peering out at the slush on the cobbles.

Megan came and stood by him, handing him his mug of hot black tea. 'You did a lot of laughing last Christmas,' she reminded him.

He looked down at her, grinning back at the impish smile on

11

the round little face. There had been beer in the house this time last year, two long-pulls in the big enamel jug, twopence a pull from the Lion, and Owen had drunk most of it.

'Not so much cause this Christmas, there won't be,' Jennie said from the fireplace, where she was filling the tea cans. It wasn't a warning to her husband, who only ever drank at this season anyway. It was a cold statement of fact. This year she would have no money over, not even fourpence for some ale.

'Oh, we'll manage something.' Owen touched Megan's face, closing his fingers for a gentle instant on the curve of her cheek. 'Special, this Christmas is going to be. Can't let it pass without a bit of something to celebrate it.' His face saddened a little, an instant before Megan's did. Special. The word wasn't the right one. Owen brightened again quickly, flashing his daughter some reassurance as he stepped over near the fire. 'Fit then, are you, George? Five minutes and we better be going.'

'Just finishing this.' By the scullery door, surly as always at that hour, George gulped down the remains of his tea and wiped his mouth on his coat sleeve. He would get a little more cheerful as the day wore on, but only a little. At sixteen George Roberts had the serious demeanour of a man who had put all the frivolity of the world behind him.

Megan brought her father his box-cloth work-jacket and his muffler. 'Button it up, tight and warm,' she said, standing on tiptoe to help him into the jacket.

'See you do the same,' Owen said. 'If you go over to Aunty Peg's, make sure your head's covered. It can tire a growing girl out, running about in this weather.'

'She'd get tired enough if she'd to put in some real graft,' George grunted.

Two years working alongside Owen had given him the appearance to match his grumpiness. Miners always kept their eyes half shut when they chipped the slate, for fear of getting blinded by a razor-sharp splinter; with some of them the frowning, mistrusting look became permanent, as it already had with George.

'That'll do now,' Owen chided softly. He put a kiss on Megan's cheek and another, more fleeting, on the brow of

Jennie, who didn't like him showing his affection for her in front of the children. 'Mr Hesketh's said we can knock off a half-hour early, if we're down the cleave by twenty-past.'

'A terrible generous bloke, our Mr Hesketh,' George muttered, jamming on his cap. He stumped to the table, picked up his tea can and dinner box, then stood at the lobby door, waiting. 'I'm ready, then.'

As soon as the front door banged shut Megan knelt on a chair by the window and waved at her father and brother going past, the pair of them bent forward against the driving sleet. She watched, craning her neck until they were out of sight round the corner of Conway Terrace, then she let the curtain fall back in place. She turned and smiled at her mother.

'What say you sit down at the fire for a while, Mam, and I'll make you some nice tea?'

Jennie looked at the girl, an automatic rejection already at her lips, then she stopped herself and nodded. 'That'd be nice.' She bent stiffly and pulled the old armchair nearer the hearth. 'A nice start to Christmas,' she added, forcing a little warmth, reminding herself this was going to be a hard time for the girl.

2

Daylight came on slowly, settling to a uniform greyness of sullen cloud. By ten o'clock the sleet had turned to rain. The wind had shifted by then, too, sheared high up by the sheltering hills to the north-west.

The respite was dubious. Smoke from tight-packed rows of chimneys, instead of being blown away to the south, drifted down walls and along narrow streets, griming the cracks on doors and windows. A thickening, sooty mist enshrouded the rows of cottages as wives and widows kept their fires banked against the dampness and the cold.

Drynfor was small, and it was bleak by any reckoning. It lay on the eastern tip of Pantmynach, a broad valley in the north-west of Wales, twenty miles inland from Cardigan Bay. There was a mainline railway, but the community was isolated nevertheless, being eighteen miles from Duglyn, the nearest town of any size.

Drynfor had grown up from a village in the early 1850s. It had been a rapid, though modest, growth that ceased abruptly in 1860 when the limits of the slate deposits had been determined. Since 1898 there had been a steady shrinkage in the population, as younger families went further east and contributed their numbers to the towns growing around the fresh slate workings in Denbighshire.

For the most part, Drynfor was a community of austere, squat miners' houses, built in unimaginative, clustered terraces that made three sides of a square around the town centre. Over the road from the school and the row of four shops there was a Methodist chapel; at a cautious distance, there was a smaller one for the Baptists. Near the chapels was the pub, which had survived their wrath for sixty-three years. Beyond the railway station to the south, broad fields sloped up over the hill that separated the body of the town from an area of more elegant dwellings which the children of Drynfor called *fachlach* – very posh.

Since eight o'clock that Christmas Eve morning, Olwen Phillips had been hard at it in her shop, getting the shelves stocked with the things folk always bought at the last minute. It was a good time for shifting the stuff that had moved slowly during the year, too. Olwen hummed softly to herself as she pulled out the big cardboard box her husband had labelled 'SEASONAL LUXURIES' and began stacking the contents prominently on both ends of the counter.

Spendthrift was never a word that could be applied to any of her customers, not even at Christmas, but long ago Olwen had noticed a tendency among certain women, however hard-up they were, to buy things at this season they would never dream of having at other times. They were items besides the usual extra Christmas purchases, things like half-pound bags of Nib's Trinidad Cocoa, jars of Viking Essence of Beef, tinned tomatoes, table jellies and big ninepenny bottles of Friar Tuck brown sauce.

It wasn't always things to eat, either. At Christmas Olwen could sell shilling bars of Wheen's primrose soap to folk who washed themselves, for the rest of the year, with Coulter's hard white at threepence a pound lump. There was even a woman who laid out two shillings every year for a box of fifty Player's Navy Cut cigarettes.

'Christmas time makes some folk prodigal,' Olwen's departed husband had told her, more than once. 'They often as not live to regret it, but they can't help themselves, all the same.' He had always underlined that piece of commercial wisdom with a slow wink.

'Prodigal,' Olwen murmured to herself as she set out three jars of quince marmalade. She pushed them well to the front of the display, since this was their third annual appearance. Her own perception of the customers, sharpened these past four years she'd had to run the shop on her own, was a shade or two different from her husband's. Prodigality never had a chance of flowering in a place like Drynfor. Not among women who had to keep a house running and a family fed and clothed on slate

15

miners' wages. It was Olwen Phillips's firm belief that at Christmas some bolder souls put themselves at a stretch just to make the season *different*. Making it carefree or even particularly jolly was too tall an order for most of them.

When the big box was emptied Olwen slid it across the floor with her foot and nudged it under the shelf by the window. She stepped back and ran her gaze along the shelves, checking for vital omissions. Now, as at no other time, it was especially important to have every item she was likely to be asked for right there, out in the front shop, where she could keep an uninterrupted eye on things. A trip through to the back to fetch something, even a swift trip, could result in some losses. It wasn't always the children who helped themselves, either. Hardship had a way of eroding people's morals; that was another of her husband's bits of wisdom, one that she agreed with completely.

The door opened, striking the bell on the spring. Olwen turned, smiling. The smile began to fade the instant she saw who had come in, but she held on to it.

'Well now, Mrs Roberts. You're about the place early. A terrible old morning, isn't it?'

Jennie nodded, brushing the wet from her coat sleeves. She remained by the door, leaving it ajar and letting in the draught. Olwen moved forward, hand outstretched to shut it, determined to keep in the warm. Then she saw Megan was coming, running down the slippery pavement, holding on to the sides of her woolly hood.

'Hello, Mrs Phillips,' she said breathlessly, hurrying up the step and into the shop. Her mother moved to the counter and Megan shut the door firmly behind her. 'Dropped my purse and all my ha'pennies came out. Soaking, they are.' She grinned, rattling the sopping leatherette pouche. 'Better spend them before they get rusty, hadn't I?'

Olwen went behind the counter, smiling without an effort now. She was a woman who'd had few occasions to regret being childless, the young ones being what they mostly were – noisy, troublesome, expensive. But young Megan Roberts! The sight of the girl always put a sharp little pang across Olwen's

16

heart. That Megan, she told customers, had charm and brightness enough for two. Which might explain what had happened to her mother's, Olwen occasionally added, though never out loud.

'Been saving up the ha'pennies, have you?'

Megan nodded. 'Since July. I get one every time I do washing for Aunt Peg.'

'I want to settle up,' Jennie cut in, fluttering her little tally paper at Olwen. Her face under the black folds of the shawl was frowning, as if there might be some argument in the offing. 'One and sevenpence to pay, I've reckoned it.'

'That sounds about right,' Olwen said brightly.

She took the paper and added the figures in her head. Two weekly instalments on the iced sponge cake with almonds: ninepence. Sixpence left to pay on the fancy biscuits. Twopence the nuts and raisins. Twopence for the savings club.

'Precisely right, Mrs Roberts. Your cake and the other stuff's made up ready.' She took the handful of change from Jennie and dropped it in the cash drawer. 'You've four shillings' worth on the club.' Olwen gestured to the display on either side of her. 'Got some nice Christmas specialities that might interest you, if you haven't decided what you'd –'

'I know what I'm after,' Jennie said sharply. 'Megan, where's that bit of paper you wrote the things on for me?'

'It's in your bag, Mam. You put it there before we came out.'

Jennie's frown darkened as she fumbled through the big handbag she carried on her arm. 'I don't see it. I'm sure I told you to bring it . . .'

'In the pocket bit at the side.' Megan smiled at Olwen Phillips. 'Mam's always getting things lost in there. Big as a cave, it is.'

Olwen saw the sharp, affronted glare Jennie shot her daughter and immediately leaned down across the counter. 'So what'll you be getting with all those ha'pennies, eh?'

Megan's lips tightened and her eyes flashed urgent secrecy at Olwen. 'Something special,' she said, glancing sidelong at her mother, who was still rummaging.

The Christmas feeling, which Olwen has thought wasn't

17

going to come to her this year, brimmed suddenly and all unexpected, taking her breath. 'You're a good girl,' she told Megan, feeling foolish at the way she must be looking, sad-smiling, mothering.

'Here it is.' Jennie put the scrap of paper on the counter. 'I hope you've got all this.'

'I'm sure I have,' Olwen assured her. She read Megan's careful handwriting, large and rounded: margarine, white flour, beef dripping, button thread, darning wool, wintergreen ointment, salt. A grimly practical list. Life went on, Christmas or no. 'I'll get this together for you, if you can wait a minute –'

'No,' Jennie said. She was moving to the door again. 'I just wanted to settle up. Megan will fetch it all in the afternoon, if that suits.' She pulled open the door.

'Mam . . .' Megan made a quick, conspiring glance towards Olwen. 'Can I catch up with you at the butcher's? There's something I want to get.'

Jennie paused, tutted softly, then nodded. 'Don't go getting no rubbish, mind. And be quick, there's things I want carrying.' She went out, shutting the door.

Megan was at the counter in an instant, leaning close to Olwen. 'I want something for Mam's Christmas,' she said, nearly whispering. 'A surprise, like.'

'What were you thinking of getting her?'

'Well . . .' Megan unfastened her purse and emptied her halfpennies on the counter. 'There's eightpence there.' She looked up at Olwen. 'What can I have for that?'

Olwen stared at the pile of damp coins. 'Well, now . . .'

To think of a suitable gift for Jennie Roberts was hard. The woman showed no tendencies, no preferences in life. She was just a pale, cheerless soul who seemed to be getting through her existence the quickest way she could, without trimmings. Olwen knew it was uncharitable of her, but she couldn't help imagining Jennie turning down any present she might be given, simply because she didn't like the idea of being beholden to anyone, even her own child.

'She's not got any jewellery,' Megan offered. 'Just her wedding ring, like. Would the eightpence –'

18

'Of course it would,' Olwen said at once. She had a mental catalogue of every line in the shop, even the failures that had lain neglected for years on the high shelves. As soon as Megan had said jewellery Olwen had recalled the very thing.

She pulled the folding stepladder to the corner where the dry goods met the shelves with the tins and bottles. 'Steady this for me, will you, Megan? I don't want to go breaking my neck. Not at Christmas.'

It took Olwen fully a minute at the top of the ladder to find what she was looking for. There were boxes of quinine toothpowder, some old fireworks that had got damp, packets of pearl shirt buttons, a card of gold-plated collar studs – a mad extravagance, she'd told her husband at the time they bought them in – half a dozen bottles of a perfume called Frangipanni, sundry button-hooks and a cartonful of small packets of saccharin tablets, another innovation that hadn't caught on in Drynfor.

'Ah. Here we are.' Olwen fished out a stout little cardboard box, blew off the dust and descended the ladder with it. 'Come over to the counter and have a look, Megan. There's plenty here for you to pick from.'

The box contained maybe a dozen twists of yellow tissue paper. With the unhurried style of a high-class shop assistant displaying her wares for a wealthy patron, Olwen opened them all and spread them in a fan around the box for Megan's approval.

'Oh, there's pretty.' On every piece of paper there lay a brooch, winking in the glow from the lamps around the counter. A little tag on each announced the name of the design: 'Remembrance', 'Sweetheart', 'Love Laughs at Locksmiths', 'Alpine Bell'. Megan looked up at Olwen. 'Are they eightpence?'

'Oh, yes.' Olwen smiled. 'Eightpence, every one of them.' Eightpence to Megan, or sixpence if that had been all she'd had. The brooches had been up on the shelf for about ten years. The selling price scribbled on the side of the box was two shillings.

'This one.' Megan put her finger on two small linked hearts,

19

matt silver, with a strange word across them. 'Miz. . .Miz. . .'

'*Mizpah*,' Olwen said. 'It's on the back, what it means.'

Megan turned the brooch over and read the tiny legend inscribed under the pin. '"The Lord watch over thee and me, when we are absent one from another."' Megan looked at Olwen again, her face suddenly very serious. 'I'll take this one, please, Mrs Phillips.'

'I've got a nice little box you can put it in,' Olwen murmured, turning away sharply.

She understood why Megan had picked that one, and now there was a big lump swelling in her throat. Feeling foolish again, she bent down and fussed in the cupboard under the counter. That lamb, she thought. Impulsively, she straightened again and picked up the prettiest brooch she could see. It was a simple bow shape in silver wire, with two little brilliants at the centre. She came round the counter with it and pinned it on Megan's coat.

'This is from me. Just a little thing for Christmas.'

'Oh, Mrs Phillips . . .' Megan's chin was tucked close against her neck as she peered down at the ornament. 'You shouldn't give me that.'

'It's for good luck,' Olwen said. 'And to show I'll be remembering you.'

They looked at each other in silence for a long moment, then Megan devastated Olwen Phillips by rising on her toes and putting a warm kiss on her cheek. 'That's kind, you are.'

Olwen was back behind the counter in a surge of briskness, dabbing her eyes with her apron before she reappeared from behind the stack of cartons at the end.

'I'll get you that box, then,' she said, red-faced, ducking down to the cupboard again. 'Mustn't keep you, your Mam'll be waiting . . .'

By one o'clock the Roberts boys' enthusiasm was running at its peak. They had had an exciting morning, an exhilarating time of preparation with lots of joking and laughter as they performed the little tasks Megan had given them to do while she and their mother were out at the shops. Megan was familiar with her brothers' random energy, and she knew how important it was to keep it channelled.

Over a period of an hour and a half they had made extra paper-chain decorations for the small tree – even though it had been covered in chains and garlands already – and added a few more cutout angels, coloured with wax crayons, to the walls on either side of the mantelpiece. They had polished their mother's most cherished ornaments, four stout brass candlesticks, and cleaned all the knives, forks and spoons from the drawer under the table. When Jennie and Megan got back, the boys were in the yard, unloading the bags of Christmas coke into the big bucket by the scullery window.

'Come in and wash your hands,' Megan called to them. 'Then you can have some cocoa.'

They came tumbling in, grimy and cheerful, elbowing each other to get at the sink.

'Our Billy's tore his sock, Mam!' Gareth called through to the living room.

'Couldn't help it!' Billy yelled defensively. He was nine, a year younger than Gareth and a whole head shorter. 'I caught it on that nail sticking out under the gate.'

By the table, unpacking the parcels Megan had carried from the butcher's, Jenny sighed and nodded absently. Billy was always having accidents. He was just going to be that kind of lad.

'And he's got mud all up his sleeve,' Tom chimed in, giggling. He was the youngest, seven, a boy with a fine capacity for laughter, even though he had less to laugh about than most children.

'Everybody's got to keep telling on me,' Billy wailed. 'I didn't *try* to get mud on me. I slipped with the coke I was carrying.'

Tom came through to the living room, still giggling, wiping his hands dry on his jumper. He walked with difficulty, half hopping as he came round the table and over to the fireside. His left leg was badly deformed at the knee, where the joint was permanently swollen and purple. In cold weather the swelling had to be bound or it caused him terrible pain.

21

Megan turned from the hob and frowned at the clump of grey bandage sticking out from under Tom's trouser leg. 'You just sit down for a bit,' she said. 'Keep that warm, like you've been told.'

An old doctor had looked at the leg when Tom was six months old. He had said there was no way of improving it. It was what he called a *genu valgum* – he had written it down and Jennie had sighed over the piece of paper many a night, seeing the black copperplate letters as an obscure punishment, stern and immutable, passed down by an authority she couldn't question. As Tom grew older, the doctor had said, he would have to start using a stick, for that leg would stop growing before the other one did.

Billy, the image of his mother, with big wary eyes and a small, tentative mouth, came in with the cocoa tin. 'I'll put it in the cups,' he said helpfully, and immediately had the tin snatched from him by Megan.

'We don't want it all over the floor.'

'Sorry,' Billy said. 'I was just trying to help, Megan.'

'You can help by putting the cups out and getting the sugar.'

As ever when the boys were all at home together, Megan took the active role of mother. The position had evolved as a result of Jennie's growing physical frailty and her daughter's instinctive, energetic sense of order. By stages Jennie was becoming a figurehead parent, dearly loved by her children but not at all adequate to the demands they made on her time and stamina. In the evenings and at holidays she could contribute little to the life of the family, beyond her presence. It was only Jennie herself who was unaware of that.

Major decisions, however, such as what they would eat, remained Jennie's province. She handled almost all of the money that came into the house. After giving her husband and her eldest son their pocket money – two shillings a week to Owen, a shilling to George – she paid the rent and insurance and set aside weekly amounts for clothing, fuel, shoe repairs and medicine. The rest, or most of it, went on food. Today Jennie had laid out half as much again as she would at a normal Christmas. As she began unwrapping the little packets the boys crowded round her, anxious to know what treats would be coming along at dinner-time tomorrow.

'We're having chicken,' Jennie said, showing them the eight pieces of boiling fowl which had cost her half a crown. 'Roasted proper, with potatoes and peas,' she added.

'Oh, Mam!' Billy poked at the meat, catching a smack on the hand from Megan. 'Chicken! We haven't had that for ages.'

Tom was frowning at the display. 'I'm not sure if I'll like it . . .'

'Of course you will,' Megan told him firmly. 'Chicken's lovely.'

'Not the way Aunt Peg did it at Easter,' Gareth said, making the other boys laugh.

'Listen, now.' Jennie looked at them sombrely, waiting for the hilarity to die down. 'You're not to make fun of Aunt Peg. She's old, she doesn't manage things the way younger folk can. She'll be round for dinner with us tomorrow and I'll expect you to –'

'Oh, no,' Billy groaned, slapping a hand dramatically on his forehead. 'Not *her*, Mam. She goes on at us all the time . . .'

'I'll expect you to behave right,' Jennie continued. 'She's not here often, so being nice to her once in a blue moon won't hurt you.'

Megan was standing behind the boys, staring at the food on the table and thinking about it all, the way her mother was making this Christmas special without saying why. Roast chicken, iced sponge with almonds, nuts; last year they'd had boiled brisket with mashed turnips, that was all. And company – they never ever had anyone else to the house when they had their Christmas dinner, not that Megan could remember. There were the brown-paper parcels in the corner of her parents' bedroom, too; for weeks and months they'd been piling up without a word from Jennie about what they were or why they were there. It was as if she didn't want to give voice to what was happening. Perhaps she truly didn't.

'Boxing Day we'll be having side mutton with suet dumplings,' Jennie went on, opening another parcel of meat. 'And some jelly for pudding, if you behave.'

23

The boys set up a small cheer which Megan suppressed with a call for order and some help with the cocoa. Gareth lined up the thick cups on the hob and Megan spooned in the brown powder. One level teaspoon of sugar was added to each and the boiling water poured in.

'There, now.' Megan handed round the cups and they all sat down, Megan and Jennie in the armchairs at either side of the fireplace, the boys on the floor between them.

'When can we do the ginger wine, Mam?' Billy asked over the steaming rim of his cup.

'Oh, I'd forgotten it.'

Megan saw the tiredness in her mother's eyes. Usually she rested at this time of day. 'I'll see to it while you have a lie down, Mam.'

'You know where the bottles are?'

'They're all ready,' Megan said. 'I washed them out yesterday.'

The two big jugs with the mixture of ginger-wine essence, sugar and water were under Jennie's bed, where they'd been standing for three months. The liquor had to be strained through cheesecloth, then transferred to old beer bottles. There would be enough to see them right through to the new year.

'And after we've done all that', Megan told her brothers, 'we can go down to Phillips's and pick up the stuff Mam's ordered.'

'Don't forget Aunt Peg,' Jennie murmured.

'I won't.' Before teatime, Megan had her aunt's washing to do. It was a job she had never liked, not the least bit, but today she didn't mind. There was something sad about knowing it would be the last time. Today she would make an extra effort to please the old woman. 'I'll go round when we've been to the shop.'

When Jennie went upstairs to rest, the boys went with her to fetch the ginger wine. Alone for a minute, Megan sat and stared into the fire. She was beginning to feel guilty. All the money her mother had laid out, the effort she was going to, just to make sure this would be a fine Christmas – it seemed a shame that any of it should be necessary. Megan would far rather have it the way it had always been: the closeness, the laughter and songs round the fire, just a time for them to be together. Instead, because of her, *because of her being a girl*, it was to be different. And no matter what, no matter what brave faces she and her father and mother put on it, it would be sad.

The boys came rattling down the stairs, bearing the jugs, arguing about who should hold and who should pour.

'Right now, bring it in here,' Megan said briskly, getting up from her chair. 'On the table there. Don't spill any.' The little hollow pain she had started to feel was gone at once. 'Gareth, get the bottles. Billy, you help him – they're under the sink behind the washing board.' She ruffled young Tom's hair as he hobbled over to the table and leaned on it. 'You can taste the first drop after it's strained, eh, Tom? And if you don't fall over drunk, we can all have a taste.' She ruffled his hair again, making him chuckle.

3

Christmas dinner was over by five o'clock. The living room had grown warm from the numbers round the table and from the big coke fire Owen had banked up before they sat down to eat.

'If I have any more chicken I'd go pop,' Megan told her mother. The portions, in fact, had been modest, and Megan could probably have eaten the same again. 'Really nice, Mam.'

To make room for everyone the two leaves on the living-room table had been extended. Owen Roberts sat at one end with Jennie opposite him; Gareth, Billy and Tom were at the side by the lobby door, while Megan, George and Aunt Peg sat with their backs to the fire.

'The best ever,' Owen sighed, pushing his plate away from him. He smiled warmly at Jennie, who responded by half standing and gathering the empty plates towards her.

'Just grand, Mam,' Gareth said.

Billy and Tom nodded their agreement. 'Grand.'

More appreciative sounds, scarcely audible, came from George as Megan rose to help her mother clear the things away.

'There's cake to come yet,' Jennie murmured, clanking knives and forks on to the stacked plates.

She was in her best dress, a dark-blue tea-gown trimmed with cream lace at the neck and cuffs. It had been brought out every Christmas for eleven years, but it still looked new. Jennie cherished the dress, but wearing it always made her self-conscious. Compliments coming at her from all around the table didn't make her feel any easier. Head bowed, she moved off to the scullery with the plates and cutlery. Megan followed with the serving dishes.

'I think', Aunt Peg said to Owen, 'that the chicken could have done with a bit less browning.' She pursed her wrinkled lips in an expression of mild pain. 'It takes a bit of skill, you know, to keep chicken moist and tasty.'

'I thought it was just right,' Owen told his sister. 'A lot better than what we had when we were young ones.'

The small blow landed squarely, widening Peg's tiny eyes. From the time their mother had died, when Peg was fifteen, she had done all the cooking for her brothers and sisters. She opened her mouth to issue a retort but closed it again as Jennie and Megan came back.

'Isn't that nice?' Megan set the iced sponge on the middle of the table. It had already been cut into eight slices.

'Oh, I never touch shop-bought cakes,' Peg grunted, her black taffeta sleeves hissing as she folded her arms. Her gaunt-mouthed little face jerked a warning towards the plate. 'Never know what they put in them.'

'More for the rest of us, then,' Owen said lightly. 'But I think maybe we should wait a little before we have it. Let our dinner sink a bit, like.' Smiling, he reached down by his chair and brought up a bottle, holding it before him to the applause of the younger boys. 'Just a little something special,' he said, addressing Jennie's sudden frown. 'For a toast. Have you got them fancy little glasses handy, Mam?'

Peg was squinting at the bottle. 'Is that spirits? Surely you've not brought spirits into the house . . .'

'Whisky, is it, Da?' Gareth asked. 'Are you going to give us some whisky?' The three boys laughed, nudging each other.

'Port,' Owen announced. 'Sandeman's old tawny.'

Jennie's frown hadn't shifted. 'I don't think the boys should be having any of that . . .'

'Oh, Mam,' Billy groaned.

'It's Christmas,' Gareth protested, his voice as plaintive as his brother's. Tom simply giggled.

'One small glass each,' Owen said. 'And only because it's for a special toast.'

Jennie went to the sideboard and got out the glasses. They were packed in wood wool inside a shoe-box. They had been her mother's, a wedding gift that had seen very little service.

Jennie wiped each one with her apron before she put it on the table. 'Just a drop for them boys, mind.'

Owen poured carefully, not spilling a drop, then set a glass in front of everyone. They all watched him, falling silent as Owen's lined forehead turned pink under his shock of silver hair. He stared at his hands for a moment, then pushed back his chair and stood up, holding his glass.

'What's Da doing?' Tom asked Billy in a hoarse whisper.

'Ssh!'

'This Christmas', Owen began, 'is an important one in our house.' He smiled across at Megan, and in the pause there was a heavy sigh from George, who had been silent for almost the entire meal. 'Our Megan here left school last week, and in another week, when it's her birthday, she'll be starting up a new life, away from here.'

Megan bowed her head, eyes closed. It's said, she thought. Now it's mentioned out loud. Although it was something she knew about, something that had been on her mind at one time or another every day for four months, the raising of the matter made her heart thump.

'Whatever happens,' Owen went on, his throat drying rapidly, 'things won't be the same from now on. Megan's leaving us, after thirteen years.' He paused, clearly meaning to say more but just as clearly unable. He blinked twice and held up his glass. 'To our little Megan. To wish her luck, to wish her well.'

Awkwardly they all lifted their glasses. Megan raised hers too. until she realized she shouldn't and put it down again. A memory came to her, as it did at bedtime occasionally, a neighbour's voice, out by the front door, hushed with sympathy for Jennie Roberts; 'It's hard, Lord knows, but what else is there for it? Five of them to feed, one who'll never work. It's always the girl has to go, isn't it? Sacrifices have to be made . . .'

'To Megan,' Aunt Peg intoned gravely and swallowed half her glassful. The others echoed her in overlapping mumbles and sipped. Except for George. He sat staring at his glass, then set it down. Owen frowned at him but said nothing.

The tight clamp of shyness came down again and remained

throughout the eating of the cake and the serving of ginger wine. In that region reticence was fiercely ingrained. People had no easy way of expressing their deeper feelings. Many children, Megan and her brothers included, had never even heard their parents call each other by their first name. Fondness, regret and sadness hovered at the table but remained unspoken. There were only the little signs, among them the growing mistiness of Owen Roberts's eyes as he drank a second and then a third glass of port.

It was Aunt Peg, in the end, who brought Megan's new life into open debate. Over the past weeks when Megan had visited her aunt's cottage to help with the chores and do the washing, Peg had said nothing about the forthcoming event. Even though she must have known about it, she had asked no questions, ventured no opinions. But now, as the table was being cleared and pushed back to make room for the boys to play on the floor and for the others to sit round the fire, Peg began to talk freely.

'Everything's going to depend on how you get on with your employer,' she told Megan. 'Your whole life can depend on that, girl. Service is a time of shaping. If you fit in proper, get yourself liked and work real hard, you'll shape just fine.'

'Our Megan's easy liked,' Owen murmured, pushing a chair close to the fire for Peg. 'And she's going to a good house, there's plenty that knows about the place. Fine people. They know how to look after help.'

Peg sat down, making a sour little face. 'I've heard tell she can be a tartar, that Mrs Pughe-whatsit.'

'Pughe-Morgan,' Megan said. 'Mam says she's nice . . .'

'Your Mam's not worked for her,' Peg snapped. 'Beth Lewis, now, she had a job over there. Lasted six weeks, she couldn't stand it no more. She said that woman was never off her top, always complaining at her, making her do jobs twice . . .'

'Beth Lewis is a lazy old article,' Owen said sternly. He sat down opposite Peg, loosening his collar. 'You and me, we've both known her all our lives, and we've known since kids what she's like. She a parasite, a thieving parasite at that. A saint would have a hard time being nice to that one. Besides, our Megan's not going over there to skivvy.' He frowned at his

29

sister. 'You're not to go taking away the girl's confidence before she's even got started.'

'No sense her going there with a lot of wrong-headed notions, neither,' Peg said huffily. 'The gentry can be a hard lot if they don't take to you.'

'But they *will* take to her, and that's an end of it.' Owen turned, smiling at Megan as she and her mother sat down. 'You're going to make us all proud of you, aren't you, *fach*?'

'I'm going to try.' Megan's smile was steady, an effort of will that kept her stiff-backed as she tried to settle in the chair. She wished now they wouldn't talk about it. She didn't mind what Aunt Peg said; she was always like that about anything, grumpy and full of foreboding. It was just that it hadn't felt nearly so sad when her leaving was something up ahead, something that was away in the future with no need to be talked about. Now there was only a week, one small week, and then her whole life would be changed.

'There's worse things than being in service,' Jennie ventured. 'A nice place to stay, regular meals, money in your pocket –'

'Plenty of kowtowing from morning to night,' George interrupted. He was standing by the scullary door, pulling on his jacket and glaring at Megan as if she was some stranger, a usurper of their fireside. 'Doing what the humble are supposed to do. Licking the boots of the rich, doing their donkey work and saying ta for the scraps from their table.'

'Now then,' Owen warned him, 'that'll be enough of that . . .'

One glass of port, swiftly consumed, had emboldened George and put red patches on his cheeks. 'They'll always be up there behind their piles of cash,' he grunted, 'as long as Megan and her like give them their place . . .'

Megan said nothing. She knew about George's moods, without having the words to express her understanding; she could tell when his jealousy had to be clothed as something else before he could spit it out.

'People like that keep you in work,' Jennie told George sharply. 'You've no call to go talking that way.'

'People like that keep me *poor*, Ma – me and Da and the rest of

30

us.' George went on glaring for a moment, then he turned to the lobby door and pulled it open.

'And where do you think you're off to?' Owen demanded.

'I told Mr King I'd drop in. He's on his own today.'

'Best way for him,' Peg mumbled. Idris King was a retired schoolmaster, a man with a passionate interest in politics. Twice he had been denounced from the Baptist pulpit as an iconoclast. Peg had no idea what that was, but it sounded bad. 'With your own family's where you belong at Christmas,' she added, addressing the bright flame in the grate.

'I'll only be a couple of hours or so,' George said stiffly. 'I did promise him.'

'See you're not back late, then,' Owen sighed. He waited until George had gone, then he leaned forward and patted Megan's hand. 'You're not to let it bother you,' he said. 'George has a head full of big notions just lately.'

'Doesn't know what he's on about, half the time,' Jennie said bitterly. 'And there's no respect in him, not a scrap.' The gulf between herself and George was one she had sensed widening over the last couple of years. It bewildered Jennie and at times it made her angry. 'If he doesn't start guarding that mouth of his a bit better, he'll find himself in trouble.'

'Let's be seeing your things, then,' Peg said, bringing the attention back to Megan. 'Your Mam told me she was getting them, a bit at a time.'

Megan went to the chest under the back window and brought across the brown-paper parcels, setting them on the floor.

'I got the list from Mrs Pughe-Morgan's housekeeper,' Jennie said, watching as Megan carefully folded back the paper. 'Every girl that goes to work there's got to take the same with her.' After a moment, and with a note of reverence, she added, 'It's a rule.'

Megan spread the garments one by one for her aunt to see. They were her Christmas presents for this year. She had two plain white feather-stitched nightdresses, four longcloth chemises, five pairs of white drawers, three pairs of black woollen stockings, a plain flannel skirt and six Irish cambric handkerchiefs.

31

860376

'I get the work-dresses and aprons given me,' Megan told Aunt Peg. 'And the shoes.'

Peg was shaking her head in wonderment. 'All that finery – and just to be a parlour maid.'

'She's got to be turned out right,' Jennie said. 'And these things'll last. I allowed for a bit of growth when I ordered them.'

'It's an awful expense, all the same,' Peg sighed. 'Still, a saving in the long run, I'm sure.' She leaned sideways in her chair. 'Young Billy! Fetch me in that bag I left in the lobby.'

Billy brought the canvas bag and stood expectantly by his aunt's chair. Beyond him, his two brothers were pretending to play with the new wooden lorries, the cart and the flat-bottomed battleship, home-made over many months by Owen; secretly they were watching too. Watching and hoping.

'Nothing for you here, boy,' Peg told Billy smartly. 'You can take your nose out of it.' As Billy glumly went back to the toys, Peg hauled two parcels out of the bag and handed one to Jennie and the other to Megan. 'Things you'll both need,' she said gruffly.

'Oh, thanks, Aunty Peg.' Megan started undoing her parcel carefully, because Peg usually expected paper and string to be returned.

Jenny got her present opened first. Three jars of preserved plums and a bottle of aconite liniment. Jennie nodded her approval and smiled at Peg. 'Just the thing.'

'I knew you'd used up the last of the rub for your legs and shoulders.' Peg stabbed a finger at the dark medicine bottle. 'That stuff's supposed to be very good.'

Jennie nodded again. 'It's kind of you, Peg. I've just been using the wintergreen. It doesn't seem to do much, besides making me itch.'

A small gasp came from Megan. 'Look, Mam,' she breathed, spreading the brown paper open on her knees. Folded neatly inside was a pale-green silk blouse, trimmed with coffee lace and little yellow ribbons at the bodice and shoulders. Megan held it up, eyes wide, unbelieving. 'It's *beautiful*, Aunty Peg! Beautiful!'

'You'll need something for Sundays,' Peg said offhandedly, but colouring a little. 'Something for best. . .' She frowned and tutted as Megan kissed her, then sat back, smiling openly as the girl stood up with the blouse held against herself and paraded with it for the benefit of her young brothers.

'That must have near bankrupted you, our Peg,' Owen said.

'Nothing of the sort.' Peg hesitated for a moment, as if she might leave it there, then she sighed. 'To tell the truth, it's been in tissue paper and shut in a drawer with camphor for more years than I can count.' Her eyes softened for a moment. 'My mother gave it to me when I turned fourteen.' She shook her head slowly. 'I never wore it, not once. Never had cause, saving one time, I suppose, and by then I'd grown out of it.' Her customary half-stern face came back as she wagged a finger at Megan. 'You look after it, mind. And I'll expect to see you in it before long.'

The gift of the blouse had worked a sweet magic; it cancelled the melancholy that had been invading Megan. It brought on the special, tingly pleasure of the season, too, the sensation that set this day apart. Christmas was suddenly what it had always been for her, a warm time, a time of closeness and gratitude and smiles – what she would call, years later, a time of reaffirmation.

Impulsively she went to the lobby door and opened it. 'I'll not be a minute,' she said, hurrying out with the blouse over her arm.

Everyone in the living room sat listening, the boys grinning at each other as they heard Megan moving upstairs in their parents' bedroom. They went on listening as she came back down the stairs and paused at the lobby cupboard, the place where she had her private cardboard box with her name on it in blue and red crayon.

The door opened again slowly and a small bundle of parcels, wrapped in tinted grocery paper, entered apparently on their own and were lowered on to the chair by the door. Then the door swung wide and Megan stepped in, flushed, resplendent in the new blouse.

'Oh . . .' Jennie put a hand to her cheek, out of herself for an instant, struck by the transformation in her daughter. Owen and Peg were silent, he with a hand furled at his mouth, Peg fighting to keep her delight under control.

'That's nice, Megan,' young Tom said, gazing up at her. 'Real nice.'

For Owen Roberts the sight was blinding. Standing there, soft-featured with her long dark hair shining, her small frame immaculately encased in the tailored silk, Megan was the embodiment of everything he called her in his heart – his angel, his jewel, his flawless diadem.

'Beautiful, my love,' he said hoarsely.

'You really like it? Mam? Aunty Peg?'

Jennie nodded and so did Peg, both speechless, both able to see what Owen saw, and more: they were seeing the woman Megan would be.

'Thanks again, Aunty Peg. I'll keep it good for as long as you did. That's a promise.' Megan turned to the chair and picked up the packages she had brought in. 'Right, now. It's time for your present from me, everybody.'

In a scramble the boys tore at their parcels as Megan handed them out. Her father made a great show of shaking his, weighing it, listening with his ear to the paper. Her mother knew what was in hers, but she was happy to put on an expectant face as she undid the string. Aunt Peg shook her head testily, as if such extravagance as she was about to uncover was more worthy of a rebuke than her thanks.

All of Megan's halfpennies saved from January to June had gone towards the presents. Tom had a colouring book, Billy got a wooden clown that danced when a string was pulled and Gareth had what he'd truly wanted, twenty glass marbles in a net bag. For her mother, as had been customary for three years now, Megan had knitted a little shawl in different-coloured wools. Owen let forth a cheer when he unwrapped a small tin of his favourites, hard-boiled fruit sweets.

Megan stood by, hands clasped, suppressing her glee as Aunt Peg fumbled open her own small parcel.

'Ah!' the old woman exclaimed, holding up a tiny bone-handled mirror, the duplicate of one which, months before, she

34

had dropped and smashed. She had been bemoaning its loss ever since. 'There's a thoughtful girl. Come here.' She enclosed Megan in a rough embrace, then released her and chided her, with a smile, for spending good money on fripperies.

For Megan Christmas was complete. It had fulfilled the expectation of other years, and the sadness had not been so overwhelming after all. Nothing had changed. They were still a family, solid in their kinship. Distance from them wouldn't alter that, Megan was sure of it now; she sensed the fine unity and glowed with it.

She had two more presents to give. She put the small packet for George – it contained a quarter-pound bag of chocolate caramels – on the mantelpiece. The other she kept in her skirt pocket for later.

She glanced expectantly at her parents. 'What are we going to sing, then?'

Jennie made her annual display of reluctance, and Owen said his breath was getting too short these days for him to squander it on songs. Aunt Peg declared she had no voice left. But in the end, after a lot of coaxing and cajoling from Megan and the boys, it was decided they would all sing a carol or two.

They sang for an hour. Every Christmas song they knew was lustily rendered and in some instances repeated. Owen gave a solo performance of 'Good Old Mary Ann' and followed it with his favourite comic number, 'Muddle Puddle Porter'. Encouraged by her mother, Megan stood in the middle of the floor and sang Handel's 'Angels Ever Bright and Fair', which she'd sung at the school concert the week before. To everyone's surprise and the boys' special delight, Aunt Peg sat back in her chair and rounded off the proceedings with a tremulous, heartfelt rendition of 'In the Gloaming'.

At ten o'clock, tired, elated and very happy, Megan sat with her mother by the fire, waiting for Owen to come back from seeing Aunt Peg home. The boys were in their room, tucked in their bed but still laughing and chattering over the day's events. George hadn't come home yet.

Jennie sat gazing at the fire, absently rubbing her right shoulder, which always ached more at night than at any other

35

time. Beside her Megan talked about the evening, reminding her mother of the funny moments, making her nod and smile. Finally, when she felt the time was as right as it could be, Megan took the small box from her skirt pocket and handed it to Jennie.

'You never get surprises from me, Mam. This year I've got you one.'

Jennie stared at the box for a moment, before cautiously opening the lid. She glanced at Megan, then lifted out the brooch. 'That's lovely, girl.' She frowned at the word across the two silver hearts. 'Foreign, is it?'

'Read the words on the back. They tell you what it means.'

Jennie had to peer very closely. She read the inscription twice, then without a word began fumbling with the pin.

'Let me do it for you, Mam.' Megan pinned the brooch to the front of her mother's dress, then sat back, smiling at her. 'It looks very nice.'

'Yes.' Jennie touched the brooch, drawing her fingers over the smooth metal. Very slowly her eyes filled with tears. She opened her mouth to speak but only a cracked little whine emerged. She buried her face in her hands suddenly, sobbing. Megan sat watching her, feeling distressed and helpless.

'I didn't give it you to make you unhappy, Mam . . .'

Jennie took her hands away from her face, shaking her head, looking at Megan with reddened eyes. 'We never wanted to,' she said, almost in a whisper. 'Your Da and me, we wanted you to stay . . .'

'Mam, it's all right, I understand.'

'It's hard, deciding.' Jennie took a deep steadying breath. 'Doing things for the best, Megan, that's terrible hard. We don't want you to have a bad time of it. Don't ever think – '

'I won't,' Megan promised. 'And it'll be like Da said – I'll make you proud of me.'

'I know, I know . . .'

Megan heard Owen's footsteps outside. 'Here, Mam,' she said hastily, thrusting her handkerchief into Jennie's hand. 'Don't let him know you've been getting yourself into a state.'

'No. Right.' Obediently Jennie dabbed at her eyes and snuffled, trying to calm herself.

Megan stood by the chair, watching, thinking how wrong it was that her mother should be worried for her, or feel so guilty about something that couldn't be helped. She leaned forward and touched the frail shoulder, squeezing it gently. How on earth, she wondered, was Mam ever going to cope on her own?

4

Two miles over the hill to the south of Drynfor and set half a mile back from the road, the Pughe-Morgan house faced south-east across the deep slope of the Pantmynach valley. It stood at the top of a driveway that wound upwards through lawned gardens overhung with elms and copper beech trees, spider-limbed at that time of year and restless in the steady winds.

The house was a long, two-storeyed structure of mixed Tudor and Gothic styles, built in 1840 by an Englishman called Cowper who had believed, mistakenly, that the people of the area would take to him. He sold it fifteen years later to the Welsh landowner Humphry Pughe-Morgan. For over thirty-five years the house served as an emblem of Pughe-Morgan's stature; he occupied it rarely, and then only when there were guests to impress.

When Humphry Pughe-Morgan died in 1892 the house passed to his eldest son, Robert. Since that time Robert's wife Gwendolyn had steadily developed the property, adding a large domed conservatory, several outbuildings and four extra acres of land at the rear, emcompassing a wood and a well-stocked fishing lake. Increasingly, as his wife became more involved in the management of the house and in the life of the region, Robert spent his time in London, overseeing his wine-importing business. Like his father, though perhaps for different reasons, he saw the house only on occasional weekends.

At eight o'clock on the first morning of January 1906, Gwendolyn Pughe-Morgan was already up, preparing to address her staff. As was customary at the beginning of a new year, she had assembled everyone in the big stone-flagged kitchen, where she usually delivered a summary of her hopes and expectations for the coming twelve months. Mrs Pughe-

Morgan was a believer in continuous progress; there was never room for complacency, she felt, no matter how well things were going.

'I want to begin by wishing you all a happy new year. Happy and fruitful,' she added, 'happy and fulfilling.'

She smiled at the assembly, knowing that her domestic evangelism tended to get a mixed reaction from them. She occasionally felt that everything she did, everything she *was*, invited at least a shade of mistrust in these parts. She was a tall, attractive woman of thirty-seven with dark gold hair and lively, intelligent green eyes. In Drynfor her naturally elegant deportment was taken by many people to be a mark of aloofness; her manner of speech, too, was inclined to set a distance between herself and the natives, who found the cultured, assured English accent disquieting, even unnerving.

'And a happy new year to you, ma'am.' Mrs Foskett, spokeswoman for the others, put on a tight smile and made the shadow of a curtsey. She had been the housekeeper for thirteen years and was well known for the firm control she exercised over the staff. Rhondda-bred, she enjoyed using her strident South Welsh voice like a cudgel whenever she thought it was necessary. 'We all extend our best wishes for the coming year to yourself and Mr Pughe-Morgan.'

'Thank you.'

Mrs Pughe-Morgan looked swiftly round them all, checking for symptoms of discontent. It was a habit, a useful one that had carried over from her childhood when she had been able to detect unrest among the servants long before her mother ever did. She had always found it best to anticipate staff problems, which showed most clearly when they were all together like this. Now, as she looked beyond the two gardeners and the kitchen and parlour maids, she saw a nervous little frown on the cook's face. That was no problem at all; Mrs Pughe-Morgan knew what was bothering the woman, and she would resolve the matter in short order when the time came.

'This year will see big changes for all of us,' she announced. 'In particular, the living-in staff will benefit from better accommodation when the renovations to the old ground-floor

39

quarters are completed in April. The workload will be lightened too. In a week's time a gentleman is coming to demonstrate the new mechanical carpet and curtain cleaners to us, and I have plans to install a proper laundry in the coach-house.'

She glanced at the cook again. As she had expected, the frown had deepened.

'Out of doors, we're making improvements to the gardens,' she went on. 'There will be a new toolshed, and I'm having an oil heater added to the gardeners' quarters. Before the summer, we should have another dozen or so wall-fruit protectors and a new lawn cutter – as I'm sure Mr Griffiths will be delighted to hear.'

Griffiths beamed as if he had been handed a sovereign. He was a short, rotund, mutton-chopped man who had worked in gardens since he was a boy. 'I'm obliged to you, ma'am. Either that old cutter's wearing out, or else I am.'

'A bit of both, likely,' his mate grunted, earning himself a sharp stare from Mrs Foskett, who disapproved of flippancy in front of the mistress.

Now it was coming, Mrs Pughe-Morgan thought. Mrs Edgar, the cook, was preparing to speak up. Her face had turned a deep pink and her lips were working; her stoutness was like a burgeoning threat, inching forward past the gardeners.

'Oh, I'd almost forgotten. Mrs Edgar.' The mistress's warm smile deflated the cook instantly. Her face remained red but she moved back, trying to unstiffen her mouth and put together a smile of her own. 'I have to admit to an oversight,' Mrs Pughe-Morgan continued. 'Twice in eighteen months the question of kitchen improvements has been brought to my attention. I forgot the matter the first time. The second time I didn't forget, but I forgot to *mention* what I'd arranged. I apologize for that.'

'That's all right, ma'am,' Mrs Edgar said meekly.

'I had to discuss the whole business with my husband, of course, but he's agreed to my proposals.' She took a sheet of paper from her jacket pocket and unfolded it. 'This is only an outline, Mrs Edgar, but it'll give you an idea of what's going to be done. First, we've obtained an estimate for a new brick flue over the stoves. The work should be carried out in the spring. Then there's the business with the leaking ice-caves – well, that's best solved by having new ones. The same goes for the big refrigerator; we're throwing it out and putting in an Alaska with an extra-large ice-store.'

'I'm very grateful, ma'am.' The cook's face was crimson now, the cumulative effect of embarrassment, gratitude and relief. 'There wasn't no rush, of course . . .'

'I'm sure you've been very patient. Oh, and, because I'm planning to do rather more entertaining this year, I thought you'd appreciate some new tools. I've had a list sent down from Harrods – it's got ladles, knives, dredgers, pots and pans, meat screens and all the other paraphernalia on it – if you'd like to go over it with me this afternoon and pick out what you think needs replacing . . .'

Mrs Edgar shuffled her feet and nodded, mumbling something.

'Fine.' Mrs Pughe-Morgan looked around them again. Apart from Mrs Foskett, who always looked sour as a matter of protocol, they seemed content. 'There's only one other thing. As you're aware, a new girl will be joining us today. I'm sure you'll all give her whatever help you can, but I want to remind you that she's very young and hasn't been away from her family before. She'll need a good deal of patience and understanding, until she gets accustomed to our way of doing things. Do please make her feel welcome.'

At half-past eight Mrs Foskett brought coffee to Mrs Pughe-Morgan in the morning room. It was barely daylight and rain lashed steadily against the windows. As the housekeeper set down the tray she glanced across at the fireplace and shook her head, emitting her breath sharply through her nostrils, which was one of her standard signs of disapproval.

'I told that Mary to put more coals on in here,' she muttered. 'I'm sorry, ma'am. You must be feeling the cold . . .'

'No, no,' Mrs Pugh-Morgan assured her. 'Mary did come in, but I told her to leave it.'

'But you could get a chill, it's so draughty . . .'

'Mrs Foskett, I don't like warm rooms. You know that.' Mrs Pughe-Morgan smiled to soften the rebuke.

"Just as you say, ma'am." Huffily the housekeeper snatched a duster from her pocket and drew it along the spotless edge of the table. 'Being attentive's a part of my job, that's all.'

'You mustn't fuss over my health. I'm robust as a horse.'

'Of course, ma'am.'

A fundamental problem with Mrs Foskett was that she had an undying urge to impose her notions of common sense on people. She would bank fires without being asked, simply because she believed that cool air in winter carried some special threat to human health. Similarly, she had often made the morning pot of coffee weaker than her employer liked it, because she was convinced that too much of the stuff was harmful.

At social gatherings, Mrs Pughe-Morgan would amuse friends with some easily recalled instances of Mrs Foskett's reforming streak. They ranged from attempts at having the gardeners kill off all the purple loosestrife growing around the gardens and in the wood, simply because she *knew* it was unlucky, to swilling buckets of a pungent, garlic-based antiseptic into every domestic sink, basin and bath, twice daily, to counteract poisonous gases seeping back from the sewers.

Now, as Mrs Pughe-Morgan poured the coffee, she realized the housekeeper was lingering. 'Was there something else, Mrs Foskett?'

'Ah, well, yes there was, ma'am. If you've a minute, that is . . .'

'Of course.'

The housekeeper cleared her throat and folded her hands at her waist. It was another sign Mrs Pughe-Morgan recognized; it meant Mrs Foskett was going to air a serious grievance. 'It's about the new girl.'

'What about her?'

'Well as I understand it, ma'am, you've told cook she'll be with her for a week or two.'

'That's correct.'

'From the start, that is . . .'

Mrs Pughe-Morgan nodded slowly. 'I think it's a sound idea. A good grounding in the running of the kitchen will make an ideal start for the child. She can learn something about cooking. Just as importantly, she'll appreciate cook's special problems and learn to accommodate them when she moves on to serving in the dining room.'

A sullen look was spreading over Mrs Foskett's broad features. She dabbed absently at her tight bun of grey hair. 'It's not the way things have been done in the past, ma'am . . .'

'No, it isn't.' Previously, new girls were assigned to Mrs Foskett straight away for supervision and guidance. 'I gave the matter plenty of thought, and I decided that this way is better.'

Now there was a trace of indignation. 'Am I to take it that I won't have any say in her discipline or her training?'

'Now don't go jumping to unwarranted conclusions,' Mrs Pughe-Morgan sighed. 'It's not like that at all. I want this girl involved with something practical right from the start. Something to distract her and keep her occupied. She's too young to take easily to the . . . well, shall we say, the tedium of general domestic duties. She'll need an understanding of how the cogs in the household relate to one another before she becomes one of them. So. She'll be with cook for a while.'

'And discipline?' Mrs Foskett prompted. 'It's very important to get them off on the right foot, ma'am. To put a proper respect into them . . .'

'That, as ever, will be your province,' Mrs Pughe-Morgan said patiently. 'That and her training.'

The housekeeper seemed placated. She gave a sharp nod and moved to the door. 'I'll bring the girl straight to you when she arrives.'

'Thank you, Mrs Foskett.'

For a minute after the door closed Mrs Pughe-Morgan stood by the window, looking out through the rain-smeared glass. Loneliness touched her at odd moments, a small sense of desolation that normally she would shake aside. This morning it was harder to do that. She was no great believer in portents, but it *was* the start of a new year and the weather *did* seem to isolate the house, making it solitary and somehow lost to the human warmth of the outside world. It was foolish, she told herself; she was a busy woman, her life was crammed with things to do, and there was scarcely time to catch her breath some days. Foolish, but it persisted, that little emptiness, that ache.

43

She sighed and turned away from the window. The feeling would go soon, and until it did she would drink her coffee and read through her correspondence. Loneliness wasn't a thing to give in to, she reminded herself as she sipped from her cup. 'Even when it's inevitable,' she murmured, as if another part of her insisted on arguing.

In her case it was inevitable, she knew, because no one truly required her to be busy. The housekeeper and the other servants could run the house without her. She had deliberately filled her life with duty to cover her solitariness, and occasionally the fundamental emptiness had to show through.

But it still wasn't a thing to surrender to.

She sat down by the fire and took up her correspondence case. On top of the papers was a testimonial letter from Miss Digby, the schoolmistress at Drynfor. She read the last paragraph.

Megan Roberts has always been a bright and attentive pupil. She works hard and shows a proper respect for her elders. I am sure she will prove a good, reliable servant.

She felt better at once. There could be no room for self-pity when she considered the plight of a thirteen-year-old girl who lacked the ordinary freedoms of childhood, a girl who had to leave home because her family simply couldn't afford to keep her. There was plenty of scope for bestowing pity and compassion outside of herself, where they might do some good. Nodding gently, her sense of proportion fully restored, Gwendolyn Pughe-Morgan drained her coffee cup and set to answering some letters.

In her Sunday shoes, tweed overcoat and the new woolly hat she had had for her birthday three days before, Megan arrived at the Pughe-Morgan residence five minutes before the appointed time. By prior arrangement she and Jennie had been given a ride by Forbes the carter, who passed that way on business and had taken them in his rumbling wagon as a favour to Owen Roberts, who was an old cronie. Favours were not lavishly bestowed by

Forbes, for cronies or anybody else. Jennie would have to walk back to Drynfor; there was no time, Forbes had pointed out, to sit idle and wait for folk, especially in weather like that.

Wonderment descended on Megan the instant they were shown into the hall. She stood dumbstruck for a moment, looking around her.

This was where she would be living!

She turned, and saw the look of reverence on her mother's face. Jennie had never been in the house before, either. All the arrangements for Megan's entry into service had been made between herself and Mrs Foskett, down in the housekeeper's little cottage at the rear, where she lived in her off-duty hours and dealt with tradesmen and other non-social callers.

'Oh, Mam.' The child's voice was the merest whisper. 'Isn't it nice?' She put down the old cardboard suitcase with her things in it. 'Isn't it just the fanciest place you ever saw?'

'Beautiful.' Jennie's eyes darted left and right, cautiously, as if she might not have the right to look. 'Like a palace.' She gazed at the opulent sheen on the curve-legged mahogany side-tables, took in the glint of brass stair-rods snug across Indian carpet, the inlaid ivory door-handles, the rich, prevailing scent of lavender wax polish. 'Like a palace,' she breathed again.

Mrs Foskett had gone striding ahead of them, rustling importantly in her bombazine as she told them to wait by the big wrought-iron coatstand. She tapped twice on a door halfway along the hall, waited, then disappeared inside.

'Where did she go, Mam?' Megan asked, a little anxiously.

'To tell the mistress you're here,' Jennie murmured. She was still eyeing the furniture. 'Must have cost a packet, just for one of them tables. And it don't look as if they even use them.' She pointed at a huge brass dinner-gong by the foot of the stairs. 'Indian, those things are. Your Da's got a picture of one in that big book of his.' A vase caught Jennie's eye next, blue-and-red porcelain and as tall as herself, standing on a plinth by the dining-room doors. 'Think of it,' she sighed. 'The cost. And all for show.'

Megan touched her mother's arm. 'Will I have to clean all this?' she whispered.

The door along the hall clicked open and Mrs Foskett reappeared. 'You're to come in,' she announced, making Megan's knees feel trembly. 'Both of you.'

The room they entered was even lovelier than the hall, Megan thought. It was less severe, more welcoming. There were easy chairs covered in figured green velvet, a matching couch and a low circular table with a big, broad-leafed plant set in an earthenware jardinière at its centre. Gwendolyn Pughe-Morgan was standing by the fireplace, smiling as Jennie and Megan were shown in.

'Thank you, Mrs Foskett. I'll call you in a few minutes.'

Megan hesitated at the edge of the green carpet, worried there might be mud on her shoes. Her mother stood close beside her.

'Do come in,' Mrs Pughe-Morgan urged them. 'Leave the bag by the door.' She shook her head at the window. 'Isn't this weather terrible?'

'Terrible,' Jennie agreed throatily. She met Mrs Pughe-Morgan's eyes only for a moment, then quickly glanced away.

'So.' The tall woman came forward and extended her hand. 'You must be Megan.'

Hesitating, Megan looked at the slim white fingers, then grasped them. They felt strong and friendly. 'Ma'am,' she murmured, and curtsied as her mother had told her.

'Mary will be bringing some tea in a minute,' Mrs Pughe-Morgan said, leading them across the room. 'Why don't you both sit down near the fire. You must be freezing.'

The next ten minutes were awkward for the three of them. Jennie was clearly awed by the mistress; Mrs Pughe-Morgan, for her part, found the woman's stiff-faced reticence difficult to penetrate, and she tried rather too hard to make her relax. Megan in her turn felt sorry for her mother, who always suffered in strange company.

When the tea was brought and served by the parlour maid in delicate china cups, Megan was sure her mother would drop hers. Mrs Pughe-Morgan kept talking steadily, explaining the training programme she had mapped out for Megan, reiterating details of wages, keep and free time – twelve pounds a year, accommodation, food and uniform provided, one day off per month – all the time graciously ignoring the rattling of Jennie's cup on its saucer.

In spite of her growing nervousness at the thought of staying behind, Megan felt relieved when it was finally time for her mother to go. Jennie seemed almost to hurry from the room, mumbling her thanks to Mrs Pughe-Morgan and telling Megan she was to be a good girl and do everything she was told. At the front door the girl stood on her toes and tried to kiss her mother, but Jennie was out on the step before even the briefest contact could be made.

'Now are you sure you don't want me to get the carriage round for you?' Mrs Pughe-Morgan asked, frowning at the swishing tree branches along the drive. 'It's a long way for you to walk back in all this cold and wet.'

'I'll be fine, thank you all the same.' Jennie tightened her shawl about her shoulders and head. 'Mind now, Megan. Do what people tell you.'

Megan nodded. 'I'll be back to see you in a month,' she said. Her voice sounded smaller than she had intended. She felt Mrs Pughe-Morgan's hand on her shoulder and made a brave smile at her mother. 'Go safe, Mam.'

Jennie glanced one more time at Mrs Pughe-Morgan, smiled thinly, then turned, ducked her head against the rain and walked off quickly down the drive.

Mrs Pughe-Morgan waved to the hunched, retreating figure. 'Goodbye, Mrs Roberts,' she called. She waited until Jennie had rounded the corner, then she steered Megan indoors again.

Tears, unbidden, stung Megan's eyes suddenly as she stepped back into the hall and heard the big door close behind her.

'You're going to be just fine here,' Mrs Pughe-Morgan said, her voice firm as she squeezed Megan's shoulder and led her back to the morning room. 'You'll feel a lot better when you get to know everyone.'

Megan swallowed very hard and nodded at the floor. 'Yes, ma'am,' she said dutifully.

Getting to know everyone turned out to be less of a pleasure

47

than Megan had anticipated. The introductions were made by the housekeeper, who took charge of Megan for an hour while the mistress finished dealing with her correspondence. Before they began their tour of the house, Mrs Foskett stood in the cloakroom with Megan before her and delivered an address which she had refined, over the years, into a small masterpiece of stern forewarning.

'You have to understand, Megan Roberts, that this household is managed by me, and me alone. The mistress is your employer, which is quite a different thing from being the person who gives you your orders. A soldier serves the king, but it's not the king who tells him what to do. Can you understand that?'

'I think so, Mrs Foskett.'

'Be sure you do. I expect everyone in the Pughe-Morgans' employ to understand it and to be obedient, hardworking and honest. I will not tolerate slackness. There are punishments for slackers. I'll be keeping a close eye on you, all the time, and I'll be seeing to it that you earn your wages and your keep.' Mrs Foskett leaned close, holding Megan with her severe brown eyes. 'So far as I'm concerned, you aren't a child any more. You stopped being a child the day you left school. You're a housemaid in training, and you'll be treated the same as any other servant here, young or old.' She straightened, smoothing the front of her black dress with broad, thick-knuckled hands. 'Do you understand everything I've said to you?'

Megan nodded. 'Yes, Mrs Foskett.' Her stomach was churning and she could feel herself shaking, but she held the big woman's gaze.

'Very well, then. I'll take you to meet the rest of the staff.'

Everything Mrs Foskett had said about her authority was evident in the way the others greeted Megan. The parlour maids, Mary and Agnes, glanced quickly at the housekeeper before they spoke, as if one wrong word, or one too many, would land them in trouble. It was even worse with the kitchen maid, Clara, a mousy little woman who said nothing at all. She nodded curtly and returned Megan's polite smile with a momentary flashing of her crooked teeth, then moved back to the sink and her pile of unpeeled potatoes. The cook, Mrs Edgar, was more self-assured, but she too seemed to be clouded by Mrs Foskett's glowering presence.

It was only the gardener, Griffiths, and his mate Jenkin who displayed any open warmth towards Megan.

'You'll like this place in the good weather,' Griffiths promised her, winking as he pointed out through the dusty window of the shed. 'Fruit trees we've got, a lake too, and nice lawns for strolling. Then there's the wood, the gazebo – that's a summerhouse, like – oh, a regular little paradise Jenkin and me have made it. You'll see.'

'She'll have no time for strolling about in the gardens, or any of the rest of it,' Mrs Foskett pointed out frostily. 'The girl's here to work. She's not a lady of leisure.'

Jenkin shook his head, smiling easily at the housekeeper. He was stooped and half bald, with a wily little face that put Megan in mind of a friendly goblin's. 'A soul has to have a bit of a break now and again,' he said softly. His smile widened. 'All work and no play – now you'd know the value of that old saying, wouldn't you, Mrs Foskett?'

Abruptly – angrily, it seemed to Megan – the housekeeper jerked open the shed door and stood to one side, gesturing for Megan to leave. She was glaring at Jenkin, her neck reddening. Mystified, Megan made a brief parting smile to the gardeners and stepped outside. Mrs Foskett followed her, slamming the door shut behind them.

'You're to go nowhere near that pair unless you're ordered to,' she snapped, striding past the girl.

'Yes, Mrs Foskett.'

'Don't ever let me catch you.'

The housekeeper stumped ahead of Megan up the path to the kitchen. Hurrying to keep up, Megan felt bewildered at the severity of the warning. Griffiths and Jenkin had looked and sounded like very nice men. There certainly didn't seem to be any harm in them.

At eleven o'clock, after receiving another lecture from Mrs Foskett – on hygiene this time, and the need for constant vigilance against marauding germs on her person as well as in her working environment – Megan was taken to the library. It was the grandest room yet, high and bright, with oil paintings covering two of the walls and book-filled shelves covering two others, all the way to the ceiling. Mrs Pughe-Morgan was at the table in the middle of the room, writing in a big red-bound ledger. She closed it and stood up as Megan came in.

'So,' she said, 'are you getting a little more familiar with us?'

'Yes, ma'am.'

'Good. Excellent. In that case, I think it's time we got you into uniform.' Mrs Pughe-Morgan nodded to Mrs Foskett, who was standing in the doorway. 'I'll take her along to Mrs Edgar a little later,' she said. 'You can get on with whatever you're doing now, thank you.'

Mrs Foskett nodded, and left without a word.

For a moment Mrs Pughe-Morgan stood gazing at Megan. The room was strangely quiet. Even the rain was muted by the heavy curtains and the room's padding of thick carpet and books. Megan could hear herself breathing.

'I hope you haven't found Mrs Foskett too strict in her ways,' the mistress said at last.

'No, she's fine,' Megan said, knowing she was blushing a little. 'Fine, ma'am.'

Again Mrs Pughe-Morgan was silent, not meaning to be, not at all intending to make the girl feel uncomfortable. When she had first seen Megan that morning, Mrs Pughe-Morgan had been struck by how small she was – *petite* was the word that had occurred to her. Now, without the bulk of her coat and hat around her, the new employee looked even smaller. Her thin little body was almost pathetic in its fragility. As she looked, Mrs Pughe-Morgan felt a powerful, protective surge. Thirteen, she thought; just a little girl . . .

'Well, now.' She clapped her hands, dispelling the sentimental swell. 'I don't think we'll trouble Mrs Foskett. I'll show you to your room myself.'

They went upstairs and along a wide corridor that let on to a narrower one. At the end of it there was a short flight of uncarpeted steps. At the top, Mrs Pughe-Morgan stopped by a plain, brown-painted door and turned the handle.

'It's rather tiny, Megan, but we'll find something better for you in the spring.' She pushed the door open and ushered Megan inside.

The child walked to the middle of the attic room and stopped. She turned, looked at her mistress, then at the small brass-framed bed, the chest by the arched window, the dresser, the bright-flowered wallpaper.

'Well?' Mrs Pughe-Morgan said, frowning, wondering why the child had become so flushed.

Megan looked at her again. 'Is it mine?'

'Oh, yes, it's yours. Not very much, as I said, but . . .'

Now everything was behind Megan, all the foreboding of days past and the daunting events of that morning. All gone, swept aside by this golden moment.

This room was hers, hers alone.

'It's . . . it's lovely, ma'am.' On an impulse she crossed to the window and looked out. She had a view into the garden and out across the lake and the wood. When she turned to Mrs Pughe-Morgan again her face was radiant. 'Thank you ever, ever so much. I've not had a room before.'

It was the first time Gwendolyn Pughe-Morgan had seen such rapture on a child's face. She didn't think she could trust herself to say much.

'Well, I'm pleased you like it.' She turned quickly to the door. 'Take your time,' she murmured, going out. 'Settle yourself in. I'll come back for you later.' She closed the door softly and hurried back downstairs, doing her best, once again, to keep her emotions in check.

5

The days wore quickly at the little traces of Megan's home-
sickness. From seven every morning until eight at night she was
enclosed by duty, diverted by it and glad each evening to tumble
into her bed and drift off to sleep, remembering all the new
things she had learned. Being carried on a tide of effort was
nothing new, but the setting was so different and the scale so
large that Megan found herself enjoying the hard work and the
long hours.

In a letter to her family she said that her life in the first three
weeks at the Pughe-Morgan house had been very happy. That
wasn't entirely true. She would have been much happier had it
not been for the persistence of Mrs Foskett's bad temper – most
of which, it seemed, was directed at Megan herself.

'The trouble is,' Mrs Edgar confided to Megan after one
outburst, 'she don't like getting sensible answers. That's what's
making her keep on at you, girl. You answer her back, and she
won't settle until she gets some silent obedience out of you.'

Megan understood that. She also understood that it was
impossible not to defend herself from the housekeeper. Mrs
Foskett hardly ever made a genuine complaint; on the few
occasions she did, Megan apologized and said nothing more.
But when the accusations were unfair the girl could never
swallow the injustice. It wasn't in her spirit or nature to do
that.

As time passed, however, Megan began to understand
something about the housekeeper. It was something that made
her reconsider her impulse simply to defend herself. She let the
awareness grow in her until it became a certainty that she kept,
very carefully, to herself.

On a bright, cold Sunday afternoon, the fourth Megan had
spent in the house, Mrs Foskett vented her worst torrent of
wrath so far. Megan was in the kitchen with Mrs Edgar. The

cook was putting trays of apple pastries in the oven while Megan scrubbed down the big baking table. It was a hard job but the girl worked at it methodically, scouring a quarter of the surface at a time and rinsing it thoroughly before going on to the next part. She had nearly finished when the housekeeper came in and stood silently by the door, watching her.

At first Megan simply worked on, her fingers gripped tightly on the back of the scrubbing brush, her elbow pumping the bristles in tight circles across the wood. After a time – Megan had known it would happen – she began to feel as if something was poised over her, ready to drop with a bang. It was the studied, frowning silence of Mrs Foskett that was doing it, the clear signal that she was waiting for her moment to pounce.

Megan's arm began to lose its rhythm. She paused for a moment, steadying herself.

'You're not paid to slack, girl!' Mrs Foskett barked.

Megan looked up, astonished. She was breathless from the effort of what she was doing – how could the housekeeper say a thing like that? 'I'm not – '

'Don't you cheek me!'

'But – '

'Didn't you hear me?' Mrs Foskett's face was twisted with sudden anger. She advanced on Megan, towering over the girl. 'You've been playing there, pretending you're doing work! I watched you!'

Mrs Edgar had stepped back from the oven, gaping.

'Slopping water all over the place,' Mrs Foskett raged on, 'then rubbing a brush about in it – that isn't *working*, Megan Roberts, that's larking about and I won't stand for it!'

'Now that isn't fair,' Mrs Edgar interrupted nervously. 'The girl's worked hard all day. And she does that table better than most, I might tell you.'

'Be quiet!' The housekeeper's voice was a harsh shriek. 'Hear me?' She glared at Mrs Edgar as if the woman had struck her. 'Who told you to interfere?'

'I'm only – '

'Well don't. This one here's got to learn her place and carry out her work proper, and seeing to it will be my doing, none of

53

yours.' Mrs Foskett was shaking as she turned her eyes slowly again to Megan. 'You get another pail of hot water with carbolic in it, and you do that table again. Every inch. And I'm going to watch you and see you do it right this time.'

For an instant Megan's eyes met Mrs Edgar's. The cook saw more than she had expected. The child was flushed and tired, her hair sticking in damp strands against her forehead. But there was a fierce energy in her look, a new, righteous defiance.

'Get on with it, then! Don't stand about!'

To Mrs Edgar's surprise, Megan did as she was told. There was no trace of resistance in her. Her actions were at odds with the way she had looked. She went to the drain and tipped away her wash water, then filled the pail from the kettle on the hob and poured in the disinfectant. When she came back to the table, carrying the heavy pail with both hands, Mrs Foskett jabbed her finger at the centre of the still-wet surface.

'Start there and work out to the edges. If you miss a bit you can just start over again.'

Without a word, Megan began working. Four times, even though she had covered every inch with the hot water and the scrubbing brush, Mrs Foskett made her start again. It took twenty minutes before the housekeeper appeared to be satisfied with the job. Even then she kept scowling and her movements were taut, as if the tension of her anger wouldn't leave her. She stood with her hands folded, watching as Megan tipped away the water and rinsed out the pail.

'Right then, my girl.'

Megan returned to the table, pushing back her hair with a red-knuckled hand.

'Any time I catch you slacking again, you won't be getting off so lightly.'

'Yes, Mrs Foskett.'

'And as for you, Mrs Edgar, I'll expect you to supervise this one a sight better from now on. There's just too much idleness in this house, all round. Nobody's going to get away with it, I'll see to that.'

The cook said nothing. She was watching Megan, still wondering at the child's docility. She waited until Mrs Foskett had turned and gone out, then she crossed and put a hand on Megan's shoulder.

'Terrible, that was, child. Terrible. She's no right treating you like that. I've never seen her go on at anybody the way she does with you.' She sighed. 'The mistress doesn't know the half.'

'I'm fine, Mrs Edgar.' Megan looked up, smiling. 'Just a bit tired, that's all.'

'Well, you go and sit on the stool. We'll try out one of my pastries in a minute.' She pinched Megan's cheek and waddled across to the oven, opening the door cautiously and peering in. 'Five minutes more, I'd say.'

She turned, her face growing solemn as she watched Megan sink on to the stool by the door. There were dark circles of weariness under the girl's eyes.

'I'm sorry for not standing up for you better.' Mrs Edgar's voice was soft, truly remorseful. 'That woman's got such a hold on us – it can make it hard to do what a body should do.'

Megan knew what Mrs Edgar meant. They all needed their jobs, and Mrs Foskett had the power to dismiss any of them.

'I don't think she has much hold on Mr Griffiths or Mr Jenkin,' Megan observed.

The cook looked at her for a second, then nodded thoughtfully. 'I've wondered about it a time or two. Still.' She wiped her hands on her apron and shrugged. 'It's not our place to wonder, is it, young Megan? We're just here to get on with our work and keep our noses tidy.'

Later, when Megan was sitting in her room, enjoying its cosiness and letting the tiredness wash over her, there was a soft tap on the door.

'Yes?'

The door opened and Mrs Pughe-Morgan came in. 'Am I disturbing you?'

'Not at all, ma'am.' Megan stood up uncertainly.

'No, no, do sit down. I just wanted to pop in with this.' She closed the door and crossed to the side of Megan's chair, stooping to show the girl what she was holding. 'Rather pretty, don't you think?' It was a small glass paperweight with china flowers embedded in a cluster at its centre. 'I thought perhaps you'd like it - to put on the window-ledge, perhaps.'

'It's very nice. Thank you, ma'am.' Megan handled the smooth, heavy sphere for a moment, then took it to the window and set it down. 'It'll look grand with the sun through it,' she said.

'Just what I thought.' Mrs Pughe-Morgan smiled, looking round the room. 'You're still happy in here, are you?' It was perhaps the fourth or fifth time she had asked that since the day Megan had come to her.

Megan gave her the same answer as usual - she was happy with the room, she loved it. 'I'm going to to buy a little picture when I have the money to,' she added now. 'One would look nice above the dresser.'

'Yes, I can imagine that.' The mistress smiled again. 'It's become quite the little house to you, hasn't it?'

Megan nodded, wanting the words to tell the mistress that the room was more than that to her. It was the enclosure of her dreams, the place where she conjured past and future, where sometimes she sat missing her family and at other times hugged herself at the thought of visiting them and telling them about her new life. It was the blessed gift of privacy; Megan's room was her retreat, where even the sting of Mrs Foskett's unkindness could never survive for long.

'I'll leave you to your peace and quiet, then.'

As ever, Mrs Pughe-Morgan gave the impression that she didn't really want to leave. She came to the room at least once an evening, either to ask Megan how she was faring in her work or to bring her something. Each time she would linger as she was doing now, with her hand on the door-handle, lost for an excuse to stay longer.

Megan remembered something. 'Didn't Mr Pughe-Morgan come down, ma'am?' The mistress had mentioned the previous evening that she expected her husband to arrive at the house early on Sunday.

'No. I'm afraid he couldn't get here, Megan.' She had averted her eyes suddenly. 'Business,' she added.

56

'He must be terribly busy. I've been here nearly a month and I haven't seen him yet.'

Mrs Pughe-Morgan saw no guile on the child's face, simply a trace of curiosity. 'He'll be down soon, I'm sure.' She drew open the door, then stopped and looked at Megan. 'Would you like to see some of our family pictures – Mr Pughe-Morgan and myself, our relatives and friends?'

'Oh, yes please, ma'am.' Megan was delighted. 'I love looking at pictures.'

'You're sure, now? You seem rather tired. If you'd prefer to leave it until another time . . .'

'Tonight'd be nice, ma'am.'

'Good.' The mistress looked almost grateful. 'Wait there, I'll be right back.'

They spent half an hour kneeling on the floor of the little room with Mrs Pughe-Morgan's albums spread before them. Megan had never seen such a collection. There were dozens of photographs, all carefully slotted into the pages with names and dates written alongside in indian ink. Every one was explained to Megan – its history, its later significance, its place in Mrs Pughe-Morgan's scale of treasured memories. Megan could detect a sadness in her mistress as she gazed, minute after minute, at faded sepia prints and fancy-edged hand-tinted portraits, smiling softly at some, almost frowning at others. In particular, the more recent pictures of her husband seemed to trouble her, as if they carried an intricate, concealed message that only she could read.

'He's a handsome gentleman, ma'am.'

'Oh, yes, he's that.'

Mrs Pughe-Morgan stared for a moment at the dark-haired man with his clear, steady eyes, gazing back at her from a postcard print. He was wearing a striped blazer and white trousers, with a straw boater perched on the back of his head. He looked very debonair and contented with himself. The legend beside the picture said 'Henley – 1902'.

'That was a lovely day, Megan. Warm and sunny and very, very long.' Mrs Pughe-Morgan went on staring at the picture for a moment, then abruptly she shook herself and closed the album. 'I think it must be bedtime for both of us.'

Megan helped her gather up the albums. With her arms piled high, Mrs Pughe-Morgan stood in the open doorway and wished Megan a good night's sleep.

'And thank you for looking at the pictures with me,' she said. The sadness was unmistakable now. It made Megan wish, dearly, that Mr Pughe-Morgan would come and see his wife more often.

Ten minutes later, tucked into her bed with the lamp turned out, Megan began thinking over the day, as she usually did before sleep overtook her. The first memory that came to her was a recent one, only minutes old; it was a picture of the mistress in a long white dress, fifteen years old and dazzlingly beautiful, smiling up at her mother. It had surprised Megan to learn Mrs Pughe-Morgan was Welsh – she had been born, in fact, only twenty miles from where she now lived.

'But she does *look* Welsh,' Megan said aloud. 'It's all in how she looks. None of it's in her voice.' Mrs Pughe-Morgan had also shown Megan a picture of her taken at school, in Cheltenham. 'And that's where the voice comes from,' Megan added. Speaking to the dark was a habit from long ago, when she had first come to believe that darkness was a kindly presence, not the absence of light and hope that they called it in chapel. 'It's a very nice voice. Nicer than old Mrs Foskett's.'

The memory of the housekeeper's scowling face made her sink a little further under the covers. That had been a bad part of the day, Megan reflected, but maybe not so bad as poor Mrs Edgar had thought. Because Megan had learned a little more about the housekeeper, and she had kept a promise to herself.

'Not the littlest bit sure of herself,' she murmured. Megan's father had taught her to notice that in people. The sure ones never blustered, they never lost control of themselves and they didn't ever act cruelly. Today she had seen Mrs Foskett blustering and losing nearly all of her control and behaving as cruelly as a woman could, short of torture. So Mrs Foskett wasn't sure of herself. That was one more thing of value Megan had learned, another thing to keep to herself. 'Know your enemy,' her father had said; 'soon you'll know all his weaknesses, and then he won't be able to hurt you.'

The housekeeper's worst weakness, the one that had taken time for Megan to guess at, was the one she had played on that day. She wondered, sleepily, if it had been bad of her to do that. After a moment she decided it probably hadn't. 'Scrubbing that big old table was my punishment, if I was bad,' she whispered.

It had taken her a couple of weeks to suspect the weakness. She would never have suspected it clearly at all if it hadn't been for Bella Lucas, an old woman down at the bottom of Conway Terrace who had the selfsame flaw in her. Bella liked to make children cry. Every child on the terrace knew it and passed it on to the ones who didn't: 'Keep out of Bella's road. She'll get you bawling, any way she can.'

That was a really evil old woman, Megan believed. As for Mrs Foskett – well, maybe it wasn't exactly evil that made *her* do it, but she did it all the same, and not just to children, either.

Megan had discovered that every female servant in the Pughe-Morgan household, past and present, had been brought to tears by the housekeeper. The fact had emerged, gradually, from little conversations with Mrs Edgar and the maids. Now Megan was sure that Mrs Foskett not only wanted to draw tears from people – she needed to. Megan had felt the need today, she had fought against it and she had won.

'She's never made me cry,' Megan yawned into the comforting dark. 'Not once. And she's never going to, either.'

6

At eight o'clock on Tuesday morning the elder of the two housemaids, Mary, came to the kitchen and told Mrs Edgar she was wanted in the library.

'Ma'am says it's an emergency,' Mary told the cook as they both hurried out again.

Megan was making the indoor staff's morning tea. She looked across at the kitchen maid, who was sullenly slicing the bone from a leg of mutton. 'Does it mean there's something wrong, Clara?'

'No.' The little woman shook her head slowly. 'It'll just mean more for us to do. Folk coming for dinner, most likely.' Clara looked eternally weary. This morning her eyes were more sunken than usual and her cheeks had the colour of tallow. 'Last time she said it was an emergency, eight of them turned up. Five courses, Megan, for eight big eaters.' The memory was stark on her face. 'It was bedlam in here. I wasn't right for days.'

'You don't look too right today,' Megan observed. It was the kind of thing you could say to Clara, she had learned. The woman appreciated the odd scrap of concern.

'Just a bit run down, Megan. I'm always better when the weather picks up.'

'A holiday's what you need.' Megan turned a spoon in the big teapot she had just filled. 'A bit of time away would make you a lot better.'

Clara's face cracked in a smile. 'Right old-fashioned worry-boots, aren't you?' With an effort she pulled the long bone clear of the meat. 'Holidays, indeed. Haven't had one of them since I was half your age – and then it was just an outing to Rhyl. Holidays isn't for the likes of us.'

'I s'pose not.'

Megan inhaled the aroma of the dark Indian tea, then put the lid back on the pot. She watched Clara start to slice the meat, realizing that the woman reminded her of her own mother. There was something defeated about her. For more than eight years, Megan knew, Clara had worked long hours in the kitchen, then gone home to spend the remainder of every day tending her mother, who had consumption. Some nights, Clara had admitted, she got no more than two or three hours' sleep, the old lady was so poorly.

'Ever been on a holiday yourself, then?' Clara asked, struggling to put the knife through the cold meat.

'Not really,' Megan said. There had been a trip to somewhere by the sea when she was two, but she couldn't remember much about that. 'We never had the money.'

'That's an old song in these parts,' Clara grunted. 'It's no wonder that man Keir Hardie goes on the way he does, about folk being ground down and kept down.'

Megan had heard the name before. Her brother George had used it once or twice when he was muttering to her father about the things he'd been learning from Idris King. Megan was about to ask Clara more about Mr Keir Hardie when Mrs Edgar came bustling back into the kitchen.

'Three,' she said breathlessly. 'All women.'

'As bad as having six men, that is,' Clara sighed. 'Fussy and picky. Always the same.'

'The mistress says to keep it plain. They're from the Maternity and Child Welfare place in London. They won't want anything fancy.' Mrs Edgar went to the larder door and pulled it open. She peered inside, shaking her head. 'Just as well, by the look of things. The butcher doesn't come till tomorrow.' She turned to Megan. 'Best pour that tea and we'll have it right away, my lamb. We're going to be busy.'

Mrs Edgar had decided on the dinner menu before her cup of tea was finished. She would serve mutton broth followed by pickled salmon, a main course of boiled leg of mutton and caper sauce with whatever vegetables the gardeners could muster, and thick slices of Bakewell tart for pudding.

'And we mustn't forget there's lunch to get ready. One guest, a clergyman of some kind or other.'

Mrs Pughe-Morgan's enthusiasm for causes was a steady

61

source of concern among the staff. She would be telephoned, sometimes at an hour's notice or less, to be told that one or other of her societies had representatives in the area who wanted to see her. In addition to her council membership of the Maternity and Child Welfare movement, she had active membership of three charity bodies, was on the board of two church schools and held an honorary position with Mrs Pankhurst's Women's Social and Political Union. What it all meant to the staff, in real terms, was that the mistress was forever entertaining at short notice and throwing their timetables into chaos.

'It seems pretty clear to me', Mrs Edgar observed, 'that the half of them come all the way out here just for the free meals.'

'I'll bet you old Mother Foskett's in a tizzy,' Clara murmured. 'She likes time to herself on a Tuesday.'

'Haven't seen her yet,' Mrs Edgar said, emptying the dregs from her teacup into the sink. 'But we will soon enough, I'm sure.'

By half-past nine preparations were fully under way. In addition to the lunch and dinner menus for the mistress and her guests, there were meals to be cooked for the eight members of staff. Since the servants' feeding was dictated by Mrs Foskett, no elaborate preparation was necessary, but nevertheless it took time.

'We're having tripe and potato stew for lunch,' Mrs Edgar said absently as she added the beaten eggs to her tart mix. 'Megan? Are you doing anything important?'

Megan came out of the pantry carrying a big enamel jug. 'Nothing too special, Mrs Edgar.'

'Well, do me a favour. Go down the garden and see if Griffiths can let you have some potatoes. Take a colander, that should hold enough.'

Megan immediately remembered Mrs Foskett's warning about going near the gardeners without her permission. However, she didn't hesitate in picking up the colander and going to the door. For one thing Mrs Foskett was unreasonable, and for another Mrs Edgar needed all the help she could have.

Griffiths was in the shed picking over the seed boxes. He looked up and grinned as Megan came in. 'Now there's some brightness for an old fella's morning, and no mistake.' He stood up slowly, brushing his hands on the knees of his trousers. 'How are you keeping anyway, lass? Haven't seen barely a sign of you since you got here.' Looking closely at her, he lowered his voice and said, 'That Mrs Foskett's been a bit rough on you, so I've been told. You don't want to let her worry you overmuch.'

'I'm just fine, thank you, Mr Griffiths,' Megan assured him. She held out the colander. 'Mrs Edgar sent me to ask if she could have some potatoes.'

'Oh, well now . . .' He scratched his head and frowned. 'Potatoes, is it? From a *garden*? Don't reckon you've come to the right place, my love. They come out of shops, is what I heard.'

He began walking round the shed, still scratching his head and peering comically in corners and under empty baskets until Megan began giggling.

The door opened and the stooping, goblin-faced figure of Jenkin came in. He nodded to Megan and stood watching Griffiths for a minute. Rakes and shovels were being overturned now and empty sacks were flying to left and right.

Griffiths stopped suddenly and turned to Jenkin. 'You ever see any potatoes hereabouts, boy? Lady here wants some, but I can't say as I ever – '

'*Potatoes?*' Jenkin looked appalled. He turned slowly and looked at Megan. 'You don't mean to tell me you want to go eating them things? Oh, they're terrible bad for you. Wouldn't let one near me no more.' He pointed to his threadbare scalp. 'See that? I had a plate of spuds once, only once mind you, and that's what happened. I grew right up through my hair.'

Megan started laughing helplessly as the two men took up the search, rummaging on hands and knees, Jenkin shaking his head sadly all the time. 'I'll give you one if I can find any,' he muttered, 'but don't eat it yourself, mind . . .'

The joke reached a point where Griffiths had his head inside a huge bucket while Jenkin struggled on his back, trying to disentangle himself from skeins of loose garden twine. When Megan dropped the colander and cupped both hands around her mouth to muffle her squeals, the gardeners stood up, laughing

63

heartily themselves, Griffiths holding his sides as his stomach wobbled uncontrollably.

'Oh, deary me,' Jenkin panted, leaning his elbow on the wall. 'We do enjoy a bit of pantomiming, him and me.' He took a faded blue rag from his pocket and dabbed at his eyes. 'We shouldn't have grown up at all, neither of us.'

When they were all three in control of themselves again, Griffiths picked up the colander and jerked his head towards the door. 'Come and I'll get you your potatoes, Megan, before Mrs Edgar thinks you've absconded.' He opened the door and led the way down to the vegetable store, still chuckling softly.

When they had filled the colander with plump Scotch Magnums, Megan thanked Griffiths and started back to the house. Halfway along the path she stopped and turned to the gardener again, pointing towards the fence.

'What's that flower, Mr Griffiths?'

He peered at the cluster of yellow heads on their slim green stems. 'That's shepherd's purse, Megan.' He stepped across the verge and pulled a flower. 'Look here, see,' he said, bringing it to her. 'The name comes from the leaves.' One thick fingertip traced the contours of a leaf. 'Like a little purse, isn't it?'

'It's nice. You don't see many things growing, this time of year.'

Griffiths nodded. 'But there's always something, if you look. Any time of year at all.' He sniffed the flower. 'You like plants and the like, do you, Megan?'

She nodded, swinging her hip sideways and resting the colander on it. 'I tried to grow some seeds in a pot at home. Didn't work, though. My Da said the frost got them.'

'That and the soot, most likely. These though. . .' He twirled the stem between his fingers. 'Hardy as they come. And useful, Megan, not just something nice to look at.'

'Useful?'

'Oh, that they are. You can boil up the stems and the leaves and it makes a grand tonic for the skin if you've got a rash, say. Crush them up if you've cut yourself and they'll stop the bleeding. And the young plants, they can be cooked in a soup – give it a lovely taste, too.'

64

Megan stared at the flower, fascinated. Growing things had always charmed her and made her curious.

'Everything that comes out of the ground has some magic about it,' Griffiths went on. 'Take the elder. Stews you can make with it, jam, syrup, and the wine's very nice when you get used to the taste.' He winked. 'Very comforting at times for a pair of old bachelors like Jenkin and me.' He was about to continue, then he suddenly stared past Megan. 'Bother, by the look of it,' he murmured, dropping the flower on the path.

Megan looked. Mrs Foskett was striding towards them, her gait purposeful and her face glowering.

'Oh dear.' Megan wrapped her hands nervously around the colander.

Mrs Foskett stopped near the gardeners' shed, ten yards away. 'Megan Roberts!' The girl's name was thrown at her like a rebuke. 'Here, this minute!'

'Yes, Mrs Foskett.' Megan cast one quick, worried glance at Griffiths and hurried along the path to where the housekeeper was standing, her hands spread-fingered on her hips.

'What's the meaning of this?'

Megan look up at the woman. 'I came for the potatoes, Mrs Foskett.'

'And what were you told?'

'When, Mrs Foskett?' Megan saw the immediate narrowing of the woman's eyes, heard the creak of tightening knuckles on bombazine.

'Don't play the innocent with me, young woman! You were told – *I* told you – never to come near the gardeners without permission. *My* permission, miss. Now explain why you defied me.'

'Cook needed potatoes, Mrs Foskett . . .'

'Then you should have asked me if it was all right for you to come down here.' The belligerence was feeding on itself, tightening the housekeeper's jaw as she bent a fraction closer to Megan. 'This is deliberate defiance.'

Megan set her own jaw and felt her head move once to the right, once left. 'No, Mrs Foskett.'

'Yes, Megan Roberts!'

65

'Now then, now then.' Megan heard Griffiths's voice behind her. 'There's no call to go growling at the girl like that – '

'Shut up!' Mrs Foskett's voice tore the air above Megan's head. 'You'll find yourself in trouble too if you don't mind your own business!'

Griffiths's boots scuffed closer. 'I'll be in no kind of trouble, woman. And this lass isn't in none, neither.'

'I've told you!' Mrs Foskett's tongue worked sharply across her palate, moistening it. Megan could feel the woman's unease, her small desperation to hang on to her authority. 'Get away from here!'

'It's where I work. You're the one's trespassing, as far as I can tell.'

The confidence in Griffiths's voice was too much for Mrs Foskett. Her face paled. Her eyes cast about wildly for an instant until they found Megan's and locked their malice on her. 'You're a conniving little devil!'

'I'm sorry if I – '

'Sorry's not good enough!' Mrs Foskett was losing control of herself. Her hands came up before her, blotchy fists trembling with her anger. 'You were warned, I gave my instructions – '

'But all I did – '

One large hand unballed suddenly and swept down across Megan's cheek with a crack. The impact sent her reeling against Griffiths, and the colander flew from her hands, scattering the potatoes on the path. For one instant, touching the stinging patch on her face, she felt the tears begin to surge forward. But then she remembered. She swallowed and set her teeth together tightly, staring at Mrs Foskett's demented face.

'Little *bitch*!' the woman snarled.

Megan heard Griffiths begin to say something, then the shed door opened and Jenkin stepped out on to the path. 'That'll be enough,' he said. His voice was soft, almost casual as he stood regarding the housekeeper. 'Get yourself back in the house, Rosie.'

'Don't you dare talk to me like that!'

Jenkin made a faint, derisory smile. He looked at Megan. 'Are you all right, chicken?'

Megan nodded, her hand still covering the weal on her cheek. Jenkin turned his attention to Mrs Foskett again. Amalgamated anger and outrage had made her face almost comical. She was twitching her eyes from one gardener to the other, her lips working uncertainly. 'The house is the best place for you, Rosie,' Jenkin said quietly. 'Fresh air makes you daft.'

'The mistress is going to hear about this.' The housekeeper's voice was lame now, shaky. 'My orders are to be obeyed. I'm responsible for discipline . . .'

'Discipline doesn't run to slapping kids about now, does it? Seems to me you could use some disciplining yourself.' Jenkin jerked a thumb towards Megan, who had begun gathering up her potatoes again with Griffiths's help. 'She's a good, hardworking little girl. There's got to be better targets for your spite.'

Mrs Foskett began moving away from him. 'I'm not standing here to listen to your babble,' she murmured.

'Well, just stay for this bit,' Jenkin said. He waited until the housekeeper had faced him again before he went on. 'You'll keep your hands and your tongue off young Megan from now on. She don't need no discipline, she's got enough built into her as it is.'

'I will *not* be ordered about by the likes of you!' Mrs Foskett's mouth was drying again, making her tongue click when she spoke. 'I'll deal with staff as I see fit!'

Jenkin shook his head sadly. 'Rosie . . .'

'And stop calling me that!'

'You're falling in love with who you think you are,' Jenkin went on calmly. 'A sense of proportion's the thing. Keeps you out of trouble. Carry on the way you're going and, next thing you know, you'll be back on the Cardiff cobbles.'

Mrs Foskett's face turned purple. Watching her, Megan wondered at the change. The woman could have been choking.

'Best you get back to the kitchen,' Griffiths said, cupping Megan's elbow and steering her past the housekeeper. 'If she asks, tell Mrs Edgar it was my fault you were kept. What you tell the mistress about the mark on your face is up to you.' He glared at Mrs Foskett. 'It's not going to happen again, anyway.'

'No, it's not,' Jenkin agreed. He stood watching until Megan was almost at the house, then he turned to Mrs Foskett and tilted his head at her. She was staring at the ground, like a chastised infant waiting to be dismissed. 'Next time you want to go causing that young one some more distress,' Jenkin told her, 'Just think hard about the proverb.' He moved closer, his voice very low and confidential. 'You know the one I mean – "Scandal travels faster than a bullet, and it spreads wider than buckshot." Well worth bearing in mind, Rosie.'

Without looking at either gardener, the housekeeper turned on her heel and strode off back to the house.

When she had disappeared around the corner, Jenkin turned to Griffiths. 'It was time that one got reminded how things stand,' he said.

'High time,' Griffiths murmured, and smiled.

7

It was a fine, bright Saturday morning when Megan stepped down from the carriage at the bottom of Conway Terrace. She stood by the roadside for a minute, waving to Griffiths as he moved off again, then she turned and made her way slowly along the narrow pavement, seeing curtains twitch as she passed.

At the front door of her parents' house she stopped and listened. She could hear the boys, tumbling about in the lobby. Further back, beyond their laughing and yelling, she heard her father's cough. Megan tapped the door and stood back.

The hubbub stopped and a second later the door opened. Young Tom was standing there, flushed and tousled. He grinned at his sister. 'Megan! Mam, it's our Megan!'

She went inside with the boys crowding round her, chattering, questioning.

'What's it like, then, Megan?'

'You look different.'

'They making you work hard, Megan?'

'Hush, now,' Megan told them, elbowing her way along the lobby. 'We'll have plenty of time to talk, after a bit.'

In the living room – *so small it seemed, so dark and tiny* – she found her mother standing tentatively by the table. Her father was beside her, smiling broadly.

'Hello, Mam. Da.' The tears she had learned to put under her control threatened for an instant to seize her. The sight of her parents was so different from what she had been expecting. Like the house, they looked smaller, sadder somehow in spite of their smiles.

'Come here, girl.' Owen Roberts stepped forward and drew her against him, closing his broad warm arms about her shoulders. After one long hug he stepped back, shaking his head.

'You look fine, Megan, just fine. I can see they've been treating you right.'

Megan nodded, not wishing to speak until she was sure her voice would be steady. She went to her mother and kissed her cheek, closing her fingers for a moment on the bony arms.

'Been a good girl like I told you?' Jennie asked. Her pleasure was evident, but as usual she was letting only some of it show, hiding the rest behind a little frown. 'Doing your work right, are you?'

'Yes, Mam. I've been working hard and learning all the things they've showed me.'

'Are they nice, Megan?' Tom wanted to know. He was still standing in the doorway with his two brothers, watching Megan closely, noticing the changes in her. 'Are they all toffs?'

'Listen, now,' Owen said, 'our Megan's going to take her coat off, have a cup of tea and take a minute or two to catch her breath. You lot go and play. You can come in after and ask her all the questions you want.'

Complaining, the boys went back out into the lobby. Owen closed the door and sat down by the fireplace.

'I'll make the tea, Mam,' Megan offered, but Owen shook his head.

'It's made and waiting for you. Take off your coat and sit down, love. Tell us all your news. We're bursting to know.'

For ten minutes Megan sat and delivered the summary of her first month in the Pughe-Morgan household. The night before, too excited to sleep, she had lain in her bed and rehearsed all the important things she mustn't forget. As she talked her parents sat listening in near-breathless silence, nodding, absorbing everything, wondering at how much could be crammed into just one month of a girl's life.

Megan told it with enthusiasm. There was the kitchen routine and how she had learned to make pastry and fancy things like damson pudding, gingerbread and seed-cake. She talked about Mrs Pughe-Morgan and how kind she was, always bringing little presents and asking if Megan was happy enough. She described her room, her own cosy little place with its nice furniture and its lovely view of the gardens. She went on at

70

length about Mrs Edgar, about Griffiths and Jenkin, and she talked about the elegance of the house and the posh-talking people who sometimes came to dinner. She said very little about Mrs Foskett, beyond mentioning that in the past few days she hadn't been bothering anybody very much.

'And they're feeding you proper,' Owen said. 'I can see that.' In four weeks Megan's pallor had shifted to a light pinkness, and she had gained weight. 'It's good to see you looking so well.' His pleasure had kept his eyes twinkling since Megan arrived.

'And how have things been here?' Megan asked her mother. 'You're both keeping all right, are you? The boys not getting on top of you?' Odd, she thought. I'm just like a visitor, asking my own Mam and Da about themselves.

'Your Da's been bad,' Jennie said, making Owen frown.

'Is it your chest, Da?'

'Oh, it's nothing much, Megan.' He tapped his breastbone. 'It always gets a bit rickety in the winter.'

'Never heard it so bad,' Jennie said sullenly. 'Been off work a time or two because of it . . .'

'It's nothing.' Owen pointed at the bottle of dark mixture on the mantelpiece. 'Been taking the medicine regular and it's clearing away nicely.'

'What about you, Mam?'

'The same as usual.' Jennie's eyes met her daughter's, showing the old dull, endless pain. 'Not any worse.' She looked away. 'Not much worse, anyway.'

Here, like a blot erased from a beloved picture, was a feature of their family life that Megan had forgotten, those dark moments when Jennie's illness could hang over them all like the spectre of hopelessness, stilling speech.

'Look, Mam.' Megan was determined to stay bright. She took her purse from her skirt and opened it with a flourish, holding it close so her mother could see.

Jennie looked and nodded solemnly. 'A lot in there,' she murmured.

'It's for you.'

Jennie looked startled. 'But you're supposed to keep some for yourself.'

'That's right,' Owen said. 'There's no sense working hard and giving away all your wages at the end of it.'

'I've got my pocket money,' Megan said cheerfully. 'Just like you get, Da.' She pushed the purse at Jennie again. 'Fifteen shillings there, Mam. Hold out your hands.' She tipped the silver coins in a cascade into Jennie's cupped palms. 'There, now. I hope that's some help to you.'

Jennie looked down at the coins, hefting them. 'Such a lot to part with . . .'

'Maybe you can get yourself something nice. A treat.'

'First off, I'll get your Da some real medicine,' Jennie said, putting the money carefully on the table.

'I'm fine with what I've got,' Owen complained softly. 'It makes no sense to go buying fancy-coloured cabbage water with a clever name on the label.'

Megan let the small argument spend itself before she said any more. Her father's cough had been with him for as long as she could remember, and in all that time there had been disagreement between him and Jennie over what medicine was best for him. The concoction he favoured, even though it gave him stomach pains and never appeared to do much to help the cough, came from Mrs Prewitt. She was a self-styled herbalist who sold her remedies from a smoke-black little cottage on the edge of the town. Jennie didn't like Mrs Prewitt or her medicines. Owen, on the other hand, argued that they were thick and rich and natural, and they were cheap – cheaper than the thin stuff you had to buy from the dispenser if you went to the doctor with your ailments.

As usual, Jennie sank into silence as soon as her point was made – the point, on this occasion, being that anyone as dirty and ignorant as Mrs Prewitt couldn't possibly make anything that would benefit anybody.

Megan saw her opportunity and changed the subject smartly. 'I thought I'd go over and see Aunty Peg later,' she said. 'Then I could take the boys down the road and treat them to some sweeties.'

'Peg's laid up,' Owen said. 'The woman next door's seeing to her. It's her legs again, the veins.' He sighed. 'Best not bother

her this time, Megan. She does nothing but moan at folk when she's like that.'

'Oh,' Megan said. 'Well, next time, eh? I'll bring her something nice from the garden. Mr Griffiths said I could always have a little something when I wanted it.' Piece by piece it was returning to her, the backdrop of pain in this family's life, in most of the lives around them. She had come into the house feeling bright, but it was fading. 'I'll take the boys out for a bit, then.' She stood up. 'Later on I'll help you with the dinner, Mam.'

For a time, an hour in the brisk air, Megan felt the brightness again. Walking along by the railway, with her little brothers chewing their sweets and chattering endlessly to her, she recalled times when they had all been smaller, romping over long grass and revelling in the openness and the smell of summer days. It was almost like that now, except that Tom's leg was worse these days and they had to walk more slowly. And there was something else, some other difference that was crystallized suddenly for Megan as they made their way back home.

'You're a lot different now, Megan,' Gareth told her.

She looked at him. 'How am I different?'

The boy shrugged. 'Don't know. But you are, all the same.'

One month away, she thought, and I'm different. But it was more than a month *away* – it had been a month in another world, a broader place, a place that made changes which couldn't be undone. With a little shock Megan realized it: she wasn't quite her family's shape any more; she had been altered, enough to make her not quite fit.

When they got back to the house Jennie was in the scullery, peeling the potatoes for their usual Saturday midday dinner of faggots and mash.

Megan took off her coat and rolled up her sleeves. 'I'll take care of that for you, Mam,' she said, edging into the space between the back door and the sink. 'I don't waste half as much of the spud as I used to.' She took the knife from her mother, then paused, peering back into the living room. 'Da gone out, has he?'

73

'No. He's upstairs.' Jennie dried her hands on her apron. 'Having a rest. He's not been good lately.' She hesitated in the doorway. 'He won't listen to me, though. I wanted him to see Dr Watkins, but he wouldn't hear of it, not even when it got so bad he thought he was going to choke.'

'But why doesn't he go, Mam? He pays his sick dues every week, like you told me. He's got a right to see the doctor.'

'But he doesn't want to. He says Watkins doesn't know what he's on about. That's a laugh when you think what Mrs Prewitt must know about anything. She's no better than a witch, but he swears by her.'

'Why doesn't he like Dr Watkins? I saw him at the school. He looks like a nice man. Sounds clever, too.'

'That's the trouble, Megan. Your Da doesn't like clever-sounding people much. They've only caused him bother in the past. That inspector they had up at the quarry, he was a clever-sounding one, told your Da he was doing his job all wrong. Then there was the English manager they had for a while, he was more trouble. Your Da only trusts his own kind.'

Megan nodded, concentrating on making a good job of the potatoes and promising herself she would talk to her father about seeing a real doctor, clever-sounding or not.

George arrived at the house five minutes before the dinner was due to go on the table. He had been working an extra half-shift at the quarry. When he came in he was grey-faced from the dust and red-eyed with weariness. He also smelt faintly of beer, Megan noticed as she came out of the scullery.

'How have you been, George?' she asked him brightly as he hung his cap on the back of the door.

He stared at her for a moment. 'Champion,' he grunted. 'I get a bit tired, like, but what can you expect with all the high living I get up to?'

His mother shot him a glance but said nothing.

'Got you a nice dinner ready,' Megan said.

'You cooked it, did you?'

'She's done the lot,' Jennie said. 'Made a real good job of it, too.'

'So long as it's nothing fancy.' George eased off his jacket and laid it on a chair. 'Plain's what we're used to round here. Don't need no high-class muck . . .'

'George!'

'Just making the point, like, Mam. Wouldn't want this one to think she could start infesting us with her new notions.' He went through to the scullery and sluiced his hands in the water butt.

'Pay him no heed,' Jennie murmured to Megan. 'Been in the Lion on the way home, I shouldn't wonder. The ale loosens his silly tongue a bit.'

Megan smiled at her mother as she started laying out the knives and forks. 'It's all right,' she said.

Something else had become clear to her and that was always a bonus, even if she couldn't see any way to do anything about it. Her brother George had the stamp of Mrs Foskett about him; his keenness to attack all the time was the same as the housekeeper's, and it carried the same hint that he was really trying, in a curious way, to defend himself.

At two o'clock, Jennie decided she should rest for an hour. The three young boys were out playing and George had gone off to Idris King's immediately after his dinner.

'We've just ourselves to entertain, then,' Owen said to Megan when her mother had gone upstairs. 'How do you fancy a walk, up on the hills?'

Megan looked at him dubiously. 'Are you up to it? You've not been well, remember . . .'

'I'll tell you, love, the best thing I know for these bellows of mine is a good long blast of fresh air. So what do you say?'

Wrapped warm against the winds, they made their way up Conway Terrace and out on to the rising ground beyond. As the hill steepened they walked more slowly, Owen panting steadily but taking strong, measured steps beside his daughter, his hand twined in hers.

They followed an old path that wound up to a solitary outcrop of rocky ground that Megan had always known as the Beacon. By the shelter of a clutch of stunted, wind-bent trees they stood and looked down at the ragged north edge of Drynfor, watching the chimney smoke snake low along its narrow terraces.

'I've been seeing that view for most of my life,' Owen said. 'It's never looked good to me yet, at any season. Funny that, when you hear all them songs about men pining for their homes, the places where they've got their roots. I don't reckon I'd ever pine for that.'

Megan turned and gazed at the scrubby, half-grassed hillside undulating across to Mostyn Wood. Even in a couple of months' time, she knew, it would still look bleak up here. Grey slate dust would cling to everything, muting the greens and golds of early spring. The hills would flower, but it would be a spiritless display.

'It traps people, you know,' Owen said. 'Something about it all just pares away at the spirit. You stop wanting to get away.'

Megan looked at him, aware of the new edge of candour in the way he spoke to her. *Another change.*

'Did you want away from here, then?'

'Oh yes, when I was younger, a lot younger. I wanted to get us all into a cottage on farming land, get myself a job in the fields. I used to dream about it, Megan.' He looked down at her and smiled. 'It makes me laugh when I hear folk call this *countryside*. This is what's left when countryside's been killed. Years and years of slate dust and neglect finished it. It's got no heart-beat.'

It was strange to hear her father talk that way. Megan wondered if her mother had ever heard these things. 'When did you stop wanting to leave?' she asked him.

The soft lines around his eyes deepened as he looked down at the town again. 'I think . . .' he began, then stopped himself, smiling. 'Maybe it sounds a bit fancy, Megan, but if you want, I'll tell you what I really think the answer is.'

'Tell me, Da.'

'Well, I think I stopped wanting to leave when I knew, just knew without thinking it out, like, that I'd come to belong here. Come to be part of this . . .' He waved a hand around him slowly. 'This deadness. It had withered something in me and I wouldn't belong anywhere else, even if I'd had the heart by then to try – to *want* to try.' He smiled again, shyly. 'Does that make any sense to you?'

Megan nodded. She tightened her fingers in his. 'It's terrible sad, Da. I'd have liked to live in the real countryside.'

'But you do, now.'

'Well, sort of . . .'

'No, no,' he contradicted softly. 'Real countryside, Megan. That hill there.' He pointed towards the humped, misty shape beyond the south fringe of the town. 'That marks the limit of this place. Drynfor and the hills round the workings, they end there. It's all farms and fine houses for miles on the other side. The deadness never touched that land.'

'It'd be nice for you to live there too,' Megan said. 'Do you good, I'm sure of it.'

'It'd be a waste now. And, like I said, I've no wish to move. Nor's your mother.' Owen removed his hand from Megan's and drew her head against the rough nap of his coat. 'I miss you, my love, but I'm glad you're out. It'll be the making of you, one way or the other.'

Strong and honest, Megan had always thought; that was her description for her father. Now she felt the sorrow, too, felt the power of it in him as he held her close. The single concern that had held her all afternoon was doubled suddenly.

'Da.'

'Mm?'

'Mam says you won't go and see Dr Watkins.' She waited for him to complain that there was no need, to start telling her he was all right. Instead, he remained silent. 'I wish you would, Da. I'm sure he's good at his job. He could maybe make you better.'

'No,' Owen sighed after a moment. 'He won't do that for me.'

'But how can you know?' She pulled away from him and looked up at his face. 'You can't know until you've seen him.'

'I've seen him, Megan.'

She blinked. 'What?'

'I went to see Dr Watkins. More than a year since.'

The concern tightened around her like something cold and damp. 'Did he say he couldn't make you better?'

Owen put his hands on her shoulders and looked down at her along the length of his arms. 'Listen, now. I'm telling you this because you'd keep on until I did, so it might as well be sooner as later. But promise me, Megan – not a word to your mother, or to anybody else. People don't always understand. Especially your mother, with her way of worrying over everything.'

'I promise,' Megan said, and now she felt a tiny ball of fear in her stomach.

'Dr Watkins told me that what I've got has no cure. That's not to say, mind you, that it's something terrible. As it stands it's more a nuisance than anything else. Pulls me down now and then, that's all.'

Megan considered what he had told her. 'Why didn't you tell Mam you'd been to the doctor?'

Owen smiled. 'Think about it, Megan. As long as I go on taking that horrible old medicine, your Mam's got something to hold on to – she goes on hoping that some day I might visit the doctor. That's not much of a hope, as far as she's concerned, but it keeps her away from the other thing. The despair. She's a great one for despairing when she thinks all the hopes have been used up.'

Megan nodded slowly, her face solemn.

'Remember now, not a word. It's our secret.'

She nodded again. 'What's it called, Da – this thing you've got in your chest?'

'I'm no good with long names,' Owen said. 'It sounded something like pneumonia-cosis. The doctor said a lot of the slate workers get it. Coalminers, too.'

'And there's nothing he can give you? Not even a bottle?'

Owen shook his head. 'With this, one bottle's as good as another, it seems. I told him straight I'd been taking Mrs Prewitt's mixture, showed it to him even. He said if it helped the cough in any way I should go on taking it. And it does help a bit, sometimes.'

The wind had shifted, blowing down cold behind them. Owen turned up his collar. 'Time we were getting back, I think.'

Megan tightened her scarf and buried her chin in its folds. For a moment before she followed her father down the path she stood looking at the town again.

Owen paused. 'What are you thinking about, my love? You've got your old-woman frown on.'

'I'm thinking about how things are changing, Da.' And she was thinking about fear, the ball of it inside her that wouldn't shift. 'I don't want it all to be different. There's things I'd like to stay the same.'

'Then do what my big book says, Megan. Work for what's called a mastery of life. I don't think it's very good Methodism, but it seems like good sense. You'll have a say in what's changed and what's not.'

Hours later, as Megan waited in the living room for Griffiths to come and fetch her, she took down the big book and put it on the table. The title was stamped on the cover in faded gold letters: *The Rayburn Encyclopaedia of Life.*

'Show me that bit, Da. About the mastery of life.'

Jennie was darning a sock by the fireside. She shook her head at Owen as he got out of his chair. 'What nonsense have you been telling her now? The girl has enough new things to pick up, without you packing her head with that stuff.'

Owen leaned down beside Megan. He opened the book and flicked through the pages until he came to a section headed 'Great Thoughts for Modern Living'. He ran his finger down the columns until he found the part he was looking for. 'There you are, Megan. In black and white.'

It was a quotation from the work of a foreigner with a name Megan couldn't pronounce. She read it once, then read it again, over and over, until she was sure she would never forget it.

Life is a gift. Cherish it always and learn to master its challenges. The mastery of life is the key to full living, when every true path will show itself and no gate shall ever be barred.

8

By the late spring of 1907, Mrs Pughe-Morgan had implemented all the changes she had promised the year before. The kitchen had been repaired and refurbished, the gardeners had their new toolshed, the heating for their outhouse quarters and a brand-new lawn cutter. Rather more slowly than anticipated, the indoor servants' quarters had been renovated, and now Mary, the senior maid, and Agnes, her junior, had larger fresh-painted rooms at the rear of the house; Mrs Edgar now had two small rooms which she had been waiting for since the time she was widowed, three years before.

Megan, although she had been offered a new room on the ground floor, elected to remain where she was. Mrs Pughe-Morgan understood. She provided Megan with a flowered carpet that covered the entire floor, a larger wardrobe and a framed picture of Cardigan Bay to hang above the dresser.

Other changes had occurred. Robert Pughe-Morgan had visited his Welsh home only five times during 1906, and on three occasions his wife had gone to join him in London. So far, the master had not visited the house this year at all, and his wife had made no trips to London. No one among the staff made any mention of the change in the mistress. She had become quieter, spending more time alone in the library with her books and her letters, taking solitary walks in the gardens and, occasionally, in the fields and hills beyond. She entertained less. In the evenings she retired early to her bedroom, although the lamps usually remained lit until well past midnight. She rarely looked in on Megan any more.

The transformation in Mrs Foskett, although it had set in more than a year before, was still a cautiously aired topic among the servants.

'There's not the fire in her any more,' Mary had observed. 'Still as sour and as strict, mind you, but not the shrew she was.'

'Something to do with her bowels,' the kitchen maid, Clara, stated flatly. 'When a furious big harpy like her goes broody, you can be sure the cause is in her bowels. My Gran was just the same.'

Mrs Edgar saw a simpler reason behind the change. 'Foskett's getting old. Can't be much under fifty-five. She gets blue round the mouth if she has to climb many stairs lately. Plain old age, that's what's ailing her.'

Megan Roberts voiced no opinion on the matter. She had other preoccupations, enough to fill her and keep her mind and her emotions steadily on the move.

Late in January 1907, three weeks after her fourteenth birthday she had begun to notice very odd feelings in herself. She would be dusting, or laying a table, or simply sitting in her room when she would experience an abrupt shift in her senses, a powerful awareness of herself and everything around her; the shift was sometimes upwards, so that Megan could take immediate, unreasoning pleasure in the smallest things, or it would be downward, bringing her to the verge of tears for no reason she could determine.

Odd things were happening to her body, too. She had grown thinner, yet her hips seemed to be widening. Her back, arms and legs ached some mornings and there were nights when she felt so tired she could scarcely wait to fall into bed.

Mrs Edgar, having noticed Megan's occasional lassitude and the darkening of the skin beneath her eyes, issued her own furtive hint. 'You're not going to be a child much longer, girl. Plenty of beef tea's what you need. That and regular hot baths.'

It was Mrs Pughe-Morgan, however, who applied some common sense to the girl's confusion. On a mild evening in late April, she invited Megan to join her for a stroll around the gardens.

The sun was low and slanting, putting finger shadows across the lawns and warming the scent from wild strawberry plants, flowering bramble, spindle tree and cowslip, all clustered on the borderland which, the mistress had decreed, should always remain uncultivated. They walked slowly, pausing every few

81

minutes as Mrs Pughe-Morgan identified a flower or a herb for Megan. When they reached the border of the wood they stopped, watching the sun burn gold over the tops of elms and silver birches.

'You're not feeling quite yourself these days, are you, Megan?'

The question came as a surprise; the talk, so far, had been directed away from themselves, aimed entirely at what surrounded them.

'I've been a bit up and down, ma'am,' Megan admitted. 'Nothing all that serious, though.'

Mrs Pughe-Morgan smiled, making Megan think how pretty she was, how delicate in feature and movement for someone so strong-minded. 'It's terribly serious, my dear. Not sombre-serious, mind you. But important-serious. Tell me honestly now, have you been worrying?'

'Yes, ma'am.'

'About how you're feeling?'

Megan looked at the ground for a moment. 'A bit, but I'm worried about my Da, too.'

'Oh.' Mrs Pughe-Morgan looked instantly concerned. 'Is something wrong with him?'

'I think he's very ill, ma'am.'

It boiled down to such a simple phrase, all the bad signs Megan had stored, the astute guesses she had made on her visits home. Owen went on claiming he was all right, but the look of him, the way he moved, the steady loss of vigour in his voice, told Megan otherwise.

'Something in his chest, it is. Every month I go over to Drynfor he's worse. He's been on my mind quite a lot.'

'Megan – I'm terribly sorry.' Mrs Pughe-Morgan put out her hand and touched the girl's hair. 'You should have told me.' She was silent for a moment, then she said, 'Does your father see Dr Watkins, at all?'

'Saw him once. Dr Watkins said there wasn't anything could be done.'

'I see.' There was another long pause, then Mrs Pughe-Morgan slapped her hands together softly. 'Let's not go thinking the worst, Megan. If you don't object to it, I'll have a word with the doctor. Maybe he can tell me more – more that'll help. I do want to help in any way I can.'

Megan smiled at her. 'Thank you, ma'am.'

'And in the meantime try not to worry. It won't help you and it won't do anything for your father, either.'

They began walking again, through the dappling shadows of the wood, watching late birds peck the ground and glide their way faultlessly between the trunks and branches. At a small clearing they came across a hedgehog, doing his best to scuttle as he moved to cover.

'Fine, gentle things,' Mrs Pughe-Morgan said softly, watching him. 'As you get older, Megan, you grow to value gentleness more and more.' She turned, her face troubled. 'I'm sorry if I've been rather distant lately . . .' She made a short, tremulous sigh, as if she might be on the verge of some revelation, then she checked herself. 'Sometimes I get very distracted by this and the other,' she murmured.

Megan nodded, remembering at once what she heard from behind the drawing-room door on the night Mr Pughe-Morgan last visited. There had been strong emotion, subdued and throaty, as the mistress had said, 'You've always made dark rooms in your heart, Robert'; a terrible pause as Megan passed the door, then, just audible, his guttural retort: 'And you keep making dizzy poetry out of my boredom.'

In silence they watched the hedgehog wriggle his way under a shrubby thicket. For almost a minute after he had disappeared, they could hear his small rustling sounds as he went deeper and deeper into the tangle of leaves and roots.

'Just then,' Mrs Pughe-Morgan said, turning to Megan, 'when I talked about your worries being important-serious, I didn't realize about your father. I was talking about something entirely different. About yourself, Megan. I've noticed you're a little off-colour these days – it occurred to me it might be troubling you.'

'It has, ma'am. A bit.'

'Well. I'm not the oldest or wisest person you'll ever encounter, but I'm old enough to know what's happening. Tell me, Megan, did your mother tell you anything about growing up? About what happens when you become a woman?'

Megan shook her head gravely.

'Well, it doesn't simply happen. You're not a child one day and suddenly grown up the next. There's a time of transition – do you know that word at all?'

'No, ma'am.'

'Transition means the passage from one state to another – in your case from being a girl into being a woman. It's the time between, Megan, and it can be very distressing. But, do believe me, it's natural and it isn't an illness. Far from it. Your body's *changing*, and it's such an important change that you're bound to feel as if you're at the centre of a storm, being tossed first one way, then the other.'

Megan nodded, finding the description apt. Like a storm. That was exactly it, it was the way she felt, like something being bobbed around without being able to decide its own direction.

'It can be terrible, quite terrible, but never let yourself believe there's anything wrong with you.' Warming to her topic, Mrs Pughe-Morgan started walking again, shaking her clasped hands in front of her as she made each point. 'It happens to every girl, Megan; it happened to me and it frightened me, because I lived in a very old-fashioned world where there was too much ignorance and superstition. There's still a great deal of that about, but I want you to be influenced by none of it. I'm going to make sure your transition is as easy and as *un*frightening as possible.'

The sky was turning dark when they returned to the house. In the short time she had been outdoors Megan had learned more, she suspected, than her mother – in spite of having borne five children – would ever know about the serious matter of being a woman.

In the library, Megan stood by the big table and watched as the mistress shuffled through piles of papers and pamphlets she had tipped from file boxes. The difference in the woman was astonishing. She had become sharp, decisive, animated. She was everything she hadn't been for months. And it had all happened down there in the wood, Megan reflected. Mrs Pughe-

Morgan's return to her old manner had occurred with the speed of a firm decision.

'Ah! Here we are.' The mistress held up a slim book bound in yellow cloth. 'Take this, Megan, read it and absorb every word. It's quite the best thing I've seen for girls of your age.'

Megan took the book and read the title on the cover: *Light on Dark Corners − a Young Woman's Guide to Growing Up.*

'Thank you, ma'am. I'll look after it.'

'Oh, don't worry about caring for it, Megan. Get it as scruffy as you like. So long as you *read* it, my dear, read it and learn from it.'

Later, sitting in her room and absorbing the book's simple wisdom and its comfort, Megan realized how alert she was to the sounds from the garden. Instinctively, she had been adding them to what she was learning. There was a marvellous unity there. The birds − an owl, some sparrows chirruping in their nests, the sharp cry of a starling − seemed to link with the natural facts Megan took in with such intense concentration.

She paused and looked up. It was dark outside. The window-glass reflected her face, a trifle gaunt, tired, but nevertheless alert. Megan closed the book and put it down on her lap. She smiled at her reflection, feeling calmer than she had for weeks.

'Hello, young Megan,' she murmured, giggling at her impersonation of Griffiths's voice.

She was turning into a woman − the book confirmed and explained what the mistress had said. The day-to-day chaos of her body and mind had a sound cause; she was reassured to know of it. Most of all, though, Megan was happy for Mrs Pughe-Morgan. Whatever shadows had been dimming that kind lady's days, whatever sadness had been following her, she was overcoming it all. Nothing was clearer.

'God', said Agnes, 'is always watching. There's no wickedness he doesn't see.' The observation was in the form of a rebuke to Mary, who had stayed out very late on her night off and now, in the light of morning, looked tired and drawn.

Both maids were in Mary's room. Agnes had brought a cup of

tea to Mary, providing herself with an excuse to be there and to pass on her moral message.

'He didn't see no wickedness if he was watching me last night,' Mary assured the younger woman. 'Just a lot of arguing.' She turned from the dresser mirror where she had been pinning up her red hair. 'Argue, argue. It's about all we do these days, me and Tom.'

'Can't see much enjoyment in that,' Agnes muttered. She was a plain girl with a dark, fine-haired moustache that she plucked at irregular intervals and not at all thoroughly; as a result, she usually looked as if someone had scribbled on her top lip. Agnes had a fierce virtue that stemmed from a total lack of temptation. She had embraced religion five years before, at the age of eighteen, in the absence of anything else to embrace. 'I mean,' she went on, 'where's the sense in getting yourself all done up just to have a row with somebody?'

'I don't start it, Agnes. Well, I don't *try* to.' Mary was twenty-nine, single, and terribly anxious to be a married woman before she was much older. 'Tom just don't look at things the way I do. He keeps saying he wants to wait, until he's set up, like.' She sighed and took a sip from the teacup. 'Three years ago it was, that's when he asked if I'd marry him. He didn't tell me it was going to be such a time before we got around to doing it.'

'He's just trifling with you,' Agnes said darkly. 'He'll go off with somebody else, once he's had what he wants.'

'Don't talk daft, Agnes,' Mary said wearily. 'You make Tom sound like he's got horns and a tail.'

'Satan resides behind many a kindly face,' Agnes warned, repeating a line from the latest Baptist tract she had been reading.

'Not behind my man's, he doesn't. If there's anything back of that face it's a big old donkey. Stubborn he is. Got to have everything just so before he'll move. Wants us to have a proper cottage, rugs, chairs, a table and a feather bed, all new and paid for. I told him my Mam wants us to stay with her, but he won't hear of it.'

'Men!' Agnes groaned.

There was a knock on the door. Mary crossed and opened it.

'Good morning, Mary.' Megan was standing there in her black dress and white apron, ready for work. 'Sorry to bother you, but I wasn't sure who was doing the upstairs this morning.'

'Tell you the truth, Megan, it was supposed to be me,' Mary said. 'But I'd take it kindly if you'd do it for me, just this once. I had a late night and a glass or two of sherry too much.' She tapped her forehead. 'I'm buzzing up here.'

'Right, then,' Megan said. 'Will I sweep the carpets while I'm at it?'

'Oh, you don't want to go wearing yourself out. Agnes can do that.' Mary turned. 'You'll give Megan a hand upstairs, won't you?'

Agnes nodded gravely. 'I was going to offer to do the carpets, anyway. You're in no state for it.' She came out into the passage beside Megan. 'Take it easy today,' she told Mary. 'And think on. Strong wine drives the strength from the soul.'

Suppressing a smile, Mary said she would finish her tea and do her best to catch up on things later. She made the shadow of a wink at Megan as she closed the door.

The gallery of the first floor was railed with mahogany that was polished every three days. While Agnes used the Grand Rapids sweeper on the carpet, Megan worked in the opposite direction with the beeswax. She used three dusters – one for putting on the polish, one for taking it off and one for the final shine. She worked steadily, waxing a yard at a time, taking her tempo from the back-and-forth rhythm of the carpet sweeper. When both maids drew level halfway along the gallery, Agnes stopped and watched Megan as her duster flashed along the dark-shining wood.

'You've a lot of strength for your size, you have.'

Megan paused, drawing the back of her hand across her forehead. 'The more you do this, the stronger you get,' she said.

Agnes nodded. 'Strength through endeavour.'

Religion again, Megan thought. Agnes never stopped. At first Megan had wondered if the girl was perhaps wrong in the head; now she knew that Agnes was simply obsessed, a person

87

clinging fiercely to values that appeared to answer all her questions and fill most of her needs.

'You'll not go far wrong in life if you stick by the right rules,' Agnes went on. 'I was only telling Mary the other day – '

'I think we'd better get on,' Megan interrupted. 'I can hear Mrs Foskett down in the hall. She'll be up in a minute.'

Agnes sighed. 'We can take a breather now and then. No law against it.' She stepped closer to Megan. 'I've been meaning to ask you – would you like to come along to one of our meetings?'

Megan had expected to be invited sooner or later. Agnes had asked everybody else in the house – apart from Mrs Foskett and the mistress – if they would care to join her at the weekly Baptist prayer meetings she attended on Tuesday nights. No one had accepted so far, and Megan had no intention of being the first.

'I have to work late, Agnes . . .'

'I'd ask the mistress to give you permission.'

'Well . . .' Megan trailed the duster thoughtfully along the rail. 'To tell the truth, I'm not much of a one for churches.'

Agnes looked startled. 'That's a terrible thing to say, Megan.'

'I'm not saying I'm an unbeliever,' Megan assured her. 'It's just that I can't let myself join in the way some folk do, just taking it all for granted. There's questions I want to ask, and church people don't seem to like that.'

'But you have to accept the Lord, you can't go questioning him.' Agnes wagged a finger. 'Doubters have no place in the congregation of souls. A person has to be strong in faith, Megan, or there's no salvation.'

'But how do you know that?'

Agnes's eyes widened. 'Because I was told it.'

Megan shrugged. 'When I'm told something, I have to find out if it's right. If I didn't do that, I'd go around believing any old thing.'

'Oh, you can't talk that way about scripture,' Agnes breathed. 'It's blasphemy to – '

A door clicked open softly behind them and Agnes spun

round. Mrs Pughe-Morgan was standing in her bedroom doorway. She beckoned to Megan as Agnes began pushing her sweeper again, eyes fixed on the carpet.

'Yes, ma'am?'

'Come in for a minute, Megan. I want to talk to you about something.'

Megan had never been in the room before. It was usually cleaned by Mary, who had often talked about the fine things in there. Now, standing on the soft woollen carpet and watching the mistress as she crossed to the window and opened it, Megan thought how wonderful it must be to lie down to sleep in such a place. Everything – from the pink-covered bed to the stools, dressing table and flower vases – seemed to harmonize perfectly, and the tall windows filled the room with light.

'I have to make a confession, first of all,' Mrs Pughe-Morgan said, coming back to the centre of the room. 'I was eavesdropping just now. I heard what you said to Agnes about those little doubts you have about religion.'

'Oh ...' Megan flushed. 'I wasn't being disrespectful, ma'am.'

'I'm sure you weren't. And I happen to agree with your point of view.' She pointed to a stool. 'Do sit down, Megan.' She waited until the girl was settled with her hands folded in her lap before she went on. 'I've noticed certain things, things that set me thinking.'

'Things about me, ma'am?'

'That's right, Megan. For instance, when you're dusting in the library, you quite often stand there for minutes at a time, reading the titles of the books ...'

'Sorry, ma'am,' Megan murmured, staring at the floor.

'Healthy curiosity's nothing to be sorry about,' Mrs Pughe-Morgan said, smiling. 'On other occasions, I've seen you crane your neck to read from newspapers lying on the floor or folded on the table – in fact, Megan, it seems to me that at every opportunity you're trying to soak up little bits of knowledge. Now am I right about that?'

Megan frowned, then she nodded at the mistress. 'I suppose so, ma'am. I do like reading and such. Always have.'

'Well, I'd halfway reached a decision about you, and when I heard you just now, defending your right to question things, I made up my mind.' Mrs Pughe-Morgan clasped her hands and leaned down towards Megan. 'You've not really had much schooling, have you?'

'Just the same as everybody else in Drynfor – although I left a year early, because of me having to go to work . . .'

Mrs Pughe-Morgan nodded slowly. 'What I'm going to suggest is entirely up to you, of course.' She paused, smiling gently. 'I believe you're a very bright person, Megan. Intelligent. And I believe you need to grow – inwardly, that is. You need to *expand*. So . . .' she leaned closer still. 'I think you should have an education.'

'Ma'am?'

'An education, Megan. The real kind, not the parish-school learning-by-heart business you've been subjected to so far, but a broader kind. Oh!' Mrs Pughe-Morgan clasped her hands tightly. 'You could do so much with yourself, *so* much.'

Megan felt confused and a little troubled. 'Would I have to go to a school or something, ma'am?'

'No. Not at all. You would do your learning right here, in this house. And I would help you, encourage you, get you the right books, set you on the right paths. What do you say, Megan? Do you like the idea?'

The proposition was too sudden and too unexpected for Megan to comprehend properly. There were a dozen questions forming at once. 'But there's my work, ma'am . . .'

'You would have time set aside for your studies,' Mrs Pughe-Morgan assured her. 'As much time as you needed. Just think of it – literature, art, the sciences, they're all there waiting for you. You only have to say yes.'

'It's very kind of you,' Megan said. She was beginning to realize the scale of the undertaking. To become what her mother called 'an educated person'; it was a grand thought, dizzying really, and she was being offered that opportunity. Freely. Megan's heart began to beat a little faster. 'I think I'd love to do it, ma'am.'

'Splendid!' Mrs Pughe-Morgan put a hand on Megan's

shoulder. 'You shall have the education you deserve, my girl, and you'll have it the very best way, by learning to educate yourself. Oh, Megan, it'll be a great adventure!'

Megan smiled, feeling the woman's excitement, feeling it start to build in herself. 'Yes, ma'am,' she said, 'I'm sure it will.'

9

It began early on Sunday. At eight, Griffiths knocked on the door of Megan's room and announced he had brought up the bookshelves Mrs Pughe-Morgan had instructed him to clean and repaint two days before.

'And there's a couple of parcels have been delivered for you,' he panted, as he dragged the long bookcase into the room and positioned it by the wall. 'The carter brought them. Big parcels, Megan. Heavy as bundles of housebricks, they are.'

Excitedly, Megan hurried downstairs. Under the glowering, silent gaze of Mrs Foskett, she slid the heavy parcels across the hall and with Mary's help began lugging them upstairs.

'What've you got there, then?' Mary whispered as they paused on the landing, adjusting their grip on the massive brown-paper bundles. 'Is it your birthday or something?'

'It's some books, I think,' Megan said. 'The mistress told me to expect them.'

'Books? What do you want with so many of them?'

'I've things to learn, Mary.' Megan grinned, struggling with her side of the load. 'I think I'll be growing some more muscles while I'm about it.'

Ten minutes later, the parcels were unpacked and the books stacked in neat piles across the floor of Megan's room. It was an impressive collection. Among them there was a five-volume encyclopaedia, illustrated with colour plates and line drawings, a thick copy of *Beeton's Household Management*, Thomas Carlyle's *The French Revolution*, a compendium of poetry, including the works of Blake, Campbell, Chatterton, Shelley and Words-worth, and a book that particularly caught Megan's attention – Finlayson's *Adventures in Science*.

Kneeling among them, Megan found herself becoming daunted by the sheer bulk. 'Such a lot of reading,' she murmured to Griffiths, who had helped her to unpack the books.

'It'll take you a couple of lifetimes to get through that lot, Megan.' Griffiths rubbed his chin. 'That one there would keep me going till my retirement.' He tapped a thick copy of *Brewer's Dictionary of Phrase and Fable.* 'Longer, in fact. You've got a right job on, lass. Can't say I'll be envying you.'

When Griffiths had gone Megan began transferring the books to the shelves. In spite of her attempts to stay cheerful about the new possessions, her spirits dropped lower with every armful. She began to wonder what terrible punishment she had agreed to.

'They're there for you to learn,' she told herself firmly. 'To get an education from.'

But she had only the one small head; how could all of that be crammed into it? Or even the half of all that? She remembered Miss Digby at school, telling her she had to work harder to remember things. She could remember, and easily, so long as she was remembering something that really interested her. How could she be interested in all those books? How could she ever be expected to absorb *so much*?

By the time Mrs Pughe-Morgan came to her room, Megan was beginning to feel tearful.

'I see the first lot's arrived then,' the mistress said brightly. She ran her finger slowly along the spines. 'The novels I picked out should be here in a day or two. Then there are the grammars, and the two-volume world history . . .' She paused, catching Megan's stricken expression. 'What's wrong, my dear?'

'So many,' Megan managed to say.

'Oh, there'll be three times as many as this. We'll have these shelves filled by the end of the month.' She frowned. 'What is it that's upsetting you?'

'If I've to learn all that . . .'

Mrs Pughe-Morgan suddenly understood. 'Megan, I'm sorry, in all the bustle to get these books ordered I didn't take time to explain, did I?' She patted Megan's arm consolingly. 'Did you think you were going to have to wade though all these, word by word, page by page? Is that what you thought?'

Megan nodded, chewing the corner of her lip.

'Listen to me. Education isn't a painful thing, Megan, it's not

93

a penance or a struggle. It's a challenge, certainly, but your own enthusiasm will soon overcome that. These . . .' She waved her hand at the bookshelves. 'These are your reference works, my dear. If you need to know something, you'll be able to find it by going to the shelves and looking it up. I told you, remember? It's not going to be like at the parish school. Not at all like that.'

In the hour that followed, Mrs Pughe-Morgan took pains to explain that Megan would be allowed to study at her own pace. There would be no hard supervision, merely guidance and help where it might be needed.

'And that's a process that's unending,' the mistress added. 'A process you'll enjoy, every day of your life.'

Plans were laid carefully and Megan, her enthusiasm restored, was encouraged to make notes in a pocket notebook as the mistress suggested various starting points. Megan would learn good English by reading good authors; as her reading progressed, she would be able to check the rules of structure, syntax and grammar from the appropriate reference works. Similarly, her appreciation of art and poetry would be stimulated, in the first instance, by pictures and poems; the underlying movements, trends and rules would be absorbed later when she was familiar with the subjects and had developed preferences of style and content.

Throughout their long talk together, Mrs Pughe-Morgan kept emphasizing the same point: education was an adventure, something exhilarating and enjoyable.

'Do remember, you'll be teaching yourself. If you ever need to know anything you can't find in your books, or something you can't quite reason out for yourself, come to me. I won't always be able to help, but I'll always try. Don't look on me as your teacher, though. That job's yours.'

Over the next two weeks the number of books on the shelves more than tripled. Mrs Pughe-Morgan, in an effort to make sure that Megan's choice of material was as broad as possible, finally made it necessary for another small bookcase to be installed alongside the first one. Swiftly, Megan began to understand the real value of a reference library. As the volumes mounted, so did her pleasure. She realized there could never be enough books.

Much that had been unformed in the girl began to take firm shape. Slowly, Megan began to realize she had a real passion for literature. The only stories she had read before had been childish fictions, designed to entertain infants and simpler-minded adults. Now she discovered the Brontës. *Jane Eyre* was difficult, there were many times when Megan had to stop in her reading and look up words in the big dictionary she had been given, but the power of that tale kept her spellbound late into the night.

Art and poetry began to fascinate her, too, but increasingly it was literature, history and science that held Megan's attention and fired her. By late summer she had finished *Jane Eyre* and started on *The Tenant of Wildfell Hall.* She had begun to understand that history was more than dates and dusty accounts of wars. The human body and its workings became less of a mystery. Megan felt herself expanding, just as Mrs Pughe-Morgan had said she would.

At the beginning of September she wrote to her father, who had encouraged her to send him periodic letters – 'just to tide me over between your visits'. After explaining how increasingly full her days were becoming, Megan added a short paragraph that she knew would please Owen.

I have written down the words you showed me in your big book, the words about getting a mastery of life. I keep them near me when I am reading and I never forget them. I think I truly know what they mean now, and I will always be glad you showed them to me.

What Megan didn't express, because she thought it might sound foolish, was the joy of anticipation she felt whenever she knew that, before long, she would be back with her books and the wide, wondrous universe they showed her. That pleasure was almost as intense as the pleasure she drew from learning.

Mrs Pughe-Morgan was immensely pleased with Megan's progress. She had watched the girl tiptoe into her studies, hesitant and occasionally unsure of herself; now, in a few months, Megan Roberts was becoming a confident, eager student who knew that to learn was to nourish herself.

There was one small concern which Megan's reassurances had not quite allayed. Mrs Pughe-Morgan wondered if perhaps her protégée was overtiring herself. She still worked long hours in the house, fulfilling her duties as well as she ever did; at the times set aside for her studying – and the extra time she took, her free time that was now consumed with reading and note-taking – Megan worked with total concentration, seeming never to allow herself time to relax.

The worry persisted until an answer presented itself to Mrs Pughe-Morgan: Botany.

'I wondered if you'd mind helping me out this weekend, my dear. I'm going up among the fields and hills to collect some plant specimens. They keep me going through the winter, if I can get enough of them. It would be a great help if you could bag some for me, and it'd do you good to get out for a while.' The mistress paused, then added casually, 'You never know, you might enjoy learning more about that sort of thing.'

It was a sound prophecy. The first trip, up on the moorland between the house and the deep slope of the valley, produced an enthusiasm in the girl that Mrs Pughe-Morgan could scarcely believe. Her talent for learning was superbly tuned. And being away from the house was, as the mistress had hoped, highly beneficial. Megan came back glowing.

On later trips it became clear that Megan had been studying in the meantime. She began to expound on species and their characteristics. Gradually she learned to identify native plants the instant she saw them. By the autumn she was starting to learn about special herbal properties – medicinal, aromatic, culinary.

'You're a small wonder, Megan Roberts,' the mistress told her one evening. They were in the kitchen, where they had just brought back twenty separate plant specimens for classification and cataloguing. 'In a matter of months you've learned things about my hobby that it took me years to find out.'

'The books have been a big help,' Megan told her.

'It's the way you use what you learn from the books. You apply it directly to the practical work.' Mrs Pughe-Morgan tipped her plants carefully on to the kitchen table. 'Tell me, have you had any thoughts about what you might do in the future?' When she looked up, Megan was staring at her. 'What is it?'

'I want to stay here, ma'am.'

'Well, I can't say I would be sorry if you did. But you could make a lot of yourself, I believe. More than a parlour maid, certainly.'

'I've not thought about it.' In truth Megan didn't want to think about it. She was happier in that house than she had ever been. The place, the staff, her mistress, they had become the centre of her world, just as once her little room had been. 'Perhaps when I'm a bit older . . .'

'Of course,' Mrs Pughe-Morgan said hastily. 'It was just curiosity on my part, Megan. You've years yet to think of things like that.'

Relieved, Megan began sorting through her plants, setting them out in species groups. Beside her Mrs Pughe-Morgan absently fingered her own specimens and smiled down tenderly at the bowed, busy little head.

'It's not right, so it isn't.'

Mary looked up from the washing basket. 'What's not, Agnes?'

Agnes pointed to the kitchen window, ten feet from the coach-house where they did the household laundry. 'In there with their plants and flowers again, while we're out here slaving.'

Mary watched for a moment as the mistress and Megan gathered up their bundled specimens and took them down to the pantry where they would be dried on sheets of paper. It was a pleasant evening, Mary thought, nice and warm, with the lovely scents of the garden wafting around them. And all Agnes could do was complain. It was Mary's firm opinion that Baptism was drying all the charity out of that girl.

'I don't see no harm in it, Agnes. Megan does her work, same as the rest of us. More than some of us, come to think of it. And it's up to the mistress what she does, anyway.'

'What do you mean, "More than some of us"?'

'Just what I say.' Mary pursed her lips and blew a strand of hair away from her forehead. 'She squeezes work in, that girl. Does as much now as she got done before, when she didn't have the extra time off to do her reading and such.'

'Still like to know what you mean by "More than some of us",' Agnes grumbled. She disappeared into the coach-house and came back with a bundle of freshly washed bedsheets. She dropped them into the big basket. 'It's all foolishness, anyway.'

'What is?'

Agnes waved her arm at the house. 'The learning Megan's doing. Where's the use of it? She's in service, like the rest of us. Her Da's a miner. Fancy learning isn't for the likes of her.'

'God, Agnes . . .'

'That's swearing, Mary.'

'She's a clever lass, isn't she?' Mary went on. 'Why not give her a chance? There's no saying what she might be able to do one day. Bright and willing, is Megan. That and a bit of learning might set her on her feet when she's up in years.'

'All that book learning's going to do', Agnes said, 'is put her nearer the edge of the pit.'

Mary froze with a clothes peg halfway to her mouth. 'How do you make that out?'

Agnes pulled a face that suggested she could smell brimstone. 'Them books. I've seen them. Not a Bible among them, for a start. She's getting no scripture at all. That's bad enough. But there's worse.'

Mary waited, but Agnes's mouth had closed in a tight rictus of virtue. She took a damp cloth from her apron pocket and began wiping it along the washing line, which stretched from the coach-house to an oak tree near the gardeners' quarters.

'Well, go on, then,' Mary said.

'What? Go on with what?'

'You said there's worse. What kind of worse?'

Agnes shook her head sharply. 'I wouldn't soil my lips with it.'

Mary took a sheet from the basket and started pegging it on the line. 'If it's something that bad,' she observed quietly, 'and you're keeping to yourself, then you're most likely soiling your mind with it, aren't you, Agnes?'

Anger crossed Agnes's eyes as she glared at Mary. 'I'll have you know I keep pure thoughts,' she hissed.

'Then why don't you spit out the impure one before it spoils all the rest?'

Agnes was silent for a moment, wiping furiously at the line. 'It's the kind of thing I ought to be reporting to Reverend Powell,' she finally said. 'Moral laxity's what it is. And me living under the same roof.'

'I wouldn't report anything that goes on in this house to old Powell if I was you, Agnes. The mistress would send him packing with a flea in his ear – and you too, I shouldn't wonder.' Mary finishing pegging the sheet and turned to Agnes. 'Come to think of it, he's got a touch of the moral laxity about him himself, from what I hear.'

'He's a man of God!'

Mary smiled. 'So was that preacher over by Wrexham we heard about. Remember him, Agnes? The one they caught with – '

'All right, then! I don't want to hear none of that!' Agnes stuffed the cloth back in her pocket. 'I'm just saying there's things in Megan's room as shouldn't be. They shouldn't be in the house at all, they should be burned.'

Exasperated, Mary stepped across to Agnes and stood facing her, hand on hips. 'Tell me, and tell me now.'

Agnes looked at the ground, moistening her lips with a small, flicking tongue. 'Books,' she mumbled. 'Wicked books. I saw them when I went in with her bedlinen.'

'You mean you fished about among Megan's things like you do Mrs Edgar's sometimes, and mine too for all I know.' Agnes's mouth opened in a big oval, ready to issue a denial, but Mary put up her hand. 'Don't go soiling your lips with any lies, Agnes. Now out with it, what's evil about these books of Megan's? I might as well tell you now, I don't believe any of it.'

'It's true!' Agnes fixed her eyes on the ground again. 'There's two, all gaudy-covered. Got pictures in them of – ' She broke off.

'Of what?'

'People. Men and women.'

'Lots of books have pictures of men and women. I've got one or two myself – '

'Evil pictures!' Agnes blurted. 'They don't have no clothes on.' She looked up slowly, her neck scarlet as the righteousness reasserted itself on her face.

'Big books they are,' a voice behind Agnes said, 'with blue leather covers.'

Startled, Agnes turned and saw Mrs Edgar, standing by the gardeners' quarters with her arms full of apples. 'You've seen them too, then.' She whirled back to Mary. 'You see? Cook's seen them too . . .'

'You're a wicked girl, Agnes,' Mrs Edgar said gravely. 'A wicked, jealous, spiteful girl. Stupid, too. Your head's full of prayers, jealousy and spite. There's nothing else in there at all.'

'You've no right to talk to me like that! It's not me that's wicked, it's that . . .' Agnes pointed at the house, her lips trembling with anger.

Mrs Edgar came forward. 'Them books she's on about, Mary,' she said, 'Megan's very proud of them. She showed them to me the day they came. They're all about biology and the like.' She shot Agnes a look. 'You'd need a terrible wicked mind to find anything evil in books like that.' She sniffed. 'Easier to find a bit of dirt in the Bible, I'd say.'

'That's blasphemy!'

'No, that's a fact, Agnes.'

Mrs Edgar stood watching as Agnes spun on her heel and went flouncing up the path to the house. Her heels dug the ground so hard that gravel flew up at every step.

'She could be a real troublemaker, that one.'

Mary shrugged. 'I think it's like you said. She's just stupid. And jealous.'

'That's all it takes,' Mrs Edgar observed.

'But she can't harm Megan,' Mary said, picking up another sheet. 'The kid's as good as gold.'

'Right enough.' Mrs Edgar tightened her arms around her bundle of apples, her eyes still on the retreating figure of Agnes. 'Woe betide the lass, though, if she ever gives that one cause or chance to hurt her.'

10

The nearest approach to bustle in Drynfor was achieved every Saturday night in the Lion. As many as twenty men at a time would jostle each other in the tiny bar and proceed to get as drunk as they could on the few pennies and shillings they kept back, or were given, from their wages.

It was a noisy process. In no other public place could the men of Drynfor express themselves so freely, and there was nothing better than Eddie Parry's beer for loosening their tongues. Well past midnight, the hardier drinkers could still be heard yelling and singing at each other in the dark, smoky, ten-foot by ten-foot bar. Dozens of Sunday-morning headaches and bilious attacks were regularly ascribed – by the sufferers and their scowling womenfolk alike – to a single cause: Parry's ale.

Eddie Parry brewed the stuff himself, in a malt-smelling, barley-strewn shed that the Baptists and Methodists called Satan's Kitchen. The formula for the brew was locked safely in Eddie's head and had not yet been passed on to his heir. Although there were plenty of theories about the secret of the beer's legendary power, there were only two prominent opinions of the substance: Parry's ale was either the best or the most vile drink in the region.

Both George Roberts and Idris King thought the stuff was marvellous. On the last Saturday in September they came into the bar at nine o'clock. It had become a weekly ritual, a half-hour spent among the men whose rights and future both George and Idris fretted over with such passionate intensity.

'No company so rewarding', Idris would often say, 'as that of the working man.' To which George had lately added, 'And there's no individual but the worker that's fit to call himself a man.'

Their view of themselves as workers' champions wasn't shared by many of the regulars in the Lion, who tended to mistrust anybody who was involved in politics, whatever the shade. George and his tall, stooping companion were usually left to themselves.

George went off to find a table in the far corner while Idris eased his way through the drinkers and stepped up to the bar. He nodded to Eddie Parry. 'A fine warm night out there,' he said.

Eddie returned the nod and reached for two pint mugs. 'Warm enough to keep the lads supping.' He had a broad, strong-featured face that smiled from habit. 'Been hard at it again, have you, Mr King?' he asked, skilfully pumping the frothy beer. 'Hammering out another one of your pamphlets?'

'I've been taking it a bit quieter lately,' Idris told him. 'Keeping an eye on developments, as they say.'

'Fair enough,' Eddie said noncommittally. He set two pints on the bar, slopping froth on his knuckles. 'That'll be fourpence.'

When Idris came over with the drinks he found George peering in the gloom at a crumpled sheet of notepaper.

'I think you can give that a rest for a while,' Idris murmured. He handed George his pint and sat down opposite. 'Let it soak in. It's more than words, you see. It's a scheme of things, try to let yourself see it that way.'

George folded the paper and put it in his pocket. 'I like to have the facts lined up in my head,' he said. 'It gets confusing sometimes, if I don't just check on what's what. You know what I mean?'

Idris nodded sympathetically. 'All the same,' he said, 'it's principles and action that have to concern us. It's very easy to turn into one of those theory men.'

'That won't happen to me,' George said firmly.

That evening they had been discussing the effects of the general election held the year before. It had been a landslide victory for the Liberals. The Labour Representation Committee, to which Idris and George belonged, had gained thirty seats, and their close relations with the Liberals had given them genuine parliamentary power. The LRC had now changed its name to the Labour Party, which had set up its own organization in the House of Commons, under the leadership of Keir Hardie. Hard policies were about to be implemented.

'Just as long as you bear in mind', Idris said now, 'that it's important how the party's put together, but it's what they do for people that's really vital.'

Although Idris had been talking all evening about strategies and possible consequences under the new arrangement, George had remained preoccupied with the structure of the party, the machinery of Labour's policies.

'I still need the facts,' George grunted, sipping his beer.

Idris sighed. 'That kind of understanding comes automatically when you study policy and strategy.'

For the first time, George decided to reveal the outline of his own strategy. 'I know our manifesto inside out. And I know I stand for everything it stands for.' He leaned closer. 'Some day I'm going to be more than just a supporter of the cause, Mr King. I'm going to be a leader in our movement.'

'A leader.' Idris stared at him. 'You're not old enough to vote yet, and you're talking about being a leader? Have you any idea the amount of work that would take?'

George tapped his chest. 'All it takes is the kind of fire I've got in here.'

Idris swirled his beer, thinking. There was no doubt George Roberts was a soul-deep socialist, young as he was. He had fire, just as he said; it had been smouldering in him since the time Idris took him under his wing three years ago. And he had just enough dedication to make his mark. But then Idris considered his own devotion to the cause, the years of it, the pains and doubts he had suffered as he forged his way against the opposition of colleagues, neighbours, the chapels. Even after all that, he'd never believed he was leader material.

'It does take fire, George,' he said, 'and a *very* special kind of person.' Idris saw the surly look deepen on the young man's face. 'I'm cautioning you against overreaching, that's all. Just think about what you're saying. Leadership. You're talking about working for parliamentary candidacy. That's an enormous ambition.'

'It's what I want,' George said bluntly.

'And how long have you been feeling this way?'

'Long enough to know it's not just a bit of fancy.' George took a deep gulp from his glass and wiped his mouth with his hand. 'I'd have thought you'd be pleased, after all you've taught me.'

Idris shook his head, his white hair glinting in the lamplight. 'What I've taught you hardly breaks the skin of it, George. To go for Parliament a man has to know, I mean really *know* his history, his economic theory –'

'His rights and what he stands for,' George interrupted. 'I told you, I know what it takes, Mr King.' He drained his glass and stood up. 'I'll get you another pint.'

The place was full. George had to lean on people, forcing gaps between them to get to the bar. As he put his elbow on the worn oak top a man shouted from the other end.

'Well, have a look at this, will you! It's Ramsay MacDonald himself!'

George turned his head sharply and saw Willie Paget, one of the neighbours from Conway Terrace. Paget was short and fat, a barrel of a man with a fleshy mouth that sneered a great deal, especially when he was drunk. George ignored him.

'Another two pints, please, Eddie.'

Eddie put up fresh glasses. 'Two pints it is, George.'

'Hoi!' It was Paget again, trying to shove himself closer to George. His belly bulged over the wood as he panted his way along, open-mouthed and glassy-eyed. He got jammed a yard away and settled for leaning down over the bar, staring along at George. 'What've you been doing for the workers today?' he demanded. 'Got us them better conditions you were on about?' Paget had been a prime critic since the time of the election, when George handed out pamphlets to the miners and had stood on street corners with a banner while Idris addressed the passers-by. 'The movement still on the move, uh? Got Jerusalem built yet, have you?'

'Shut your mouth, Willie,' George snapped.

'Oh!' Paget looked around him, comic outrage on his face. 'Listen to that! Told a fellow worker to shut his mouth – and him a man of the people!'

A few men near the bar laughed.

105

'Terrible, so it is,' Paget went on, encouraged now. 'First he's letting us know we're all equal, then he's denying a worker a bit of free speech.'

'You're no kind of worker,' George said.

'What was that?'

George moved in on Paget until he could smell the whisky on his breath. 'You're no worker, I said. You're the manager's monkey. Make his tea and fetch his paper, don't you? Bow and curtsey, yes sir, no sir.'

Paget's face changed. His cheeks reddened and his eyes bulged. 'I'm disabled, you cheeky young bugger! Everybody knows I am! Disabled!'

'In your head,' George said. He turned away and put fourpence on the bar. He was about to pick up the beer when his arm was grabbed.

'You'll take that back!' Paget roared.

'Steady now,' Eddie cautioned from behind the bar. 'I don't want no squabbling.'

'Then tell the fat one there,' George said, his own face going scarlet now. 'He started it.'

'Take it bloody back!' Paget was trying to drag George along the bar. His free hand was clenched, ready to land a punch. Men were moving away, edging into the throng by the fireplace.

'Get your paw off me, Willie,' George warned. 'I'll belt you if I have to. If I do, you'll be disabled for sure.'

For a moment Paget stood there, reading nothing but clear intent on George's face. Slowly his fingers slid away from the younger man's sleeve. 'You're not worth it, anyway,' he mumbled, turning back to his glass.

George collected the two beer glasses and started towards the corner with them. He froze as Paget's voice came at him again, loud on a renewed wave of malice.

'Don't see how the like of you can call yourself a Labour man, anyhow.'

George turned. Paget's face was livid. He had the look men get when they decide, suddenly, to reclaim themselves from humiliation.

'What's that supposed to mean?'

106

'It means your so-called worker's principles are a load of rot,' Paget said, his teeth barely parting. 'You're looking to do a bit of climbing, boyo. Your crowd aren't above sucking up to the toffs now, are they? Why don't you do some campaigning in that quarter, if your feelings are so strong?' The sneer crept back along Paget's mouth. 'Little Megan's quite the lady these days, isn't she? All fine with the hat and gloves.' He spat. 'Getting her set up in life, eh? Bloody hypocrite!'

George's hands were round Paget's throat a second after the beer glasses smashed on the floor. He jerked the man away from the bar and slammed him hard against the wall, knocking the breath from him.

'Foul-mouthed tub of lard!' George flexed his arms and threw Paget against the wall again, banging his head on the bricks.

'Leave him be, for God's sake!' Idris King shouted. He was behind George, pulling him away from Paget. 'Stop it, George! The man's not worth it!'

Other, stronger hands were grasping George now, dragging him to the door. He saw Paget recede, blue-faced, as his own heels scraped the stone flags. He was tilted back suddenly, realized he was being carried, rough-handled out to the street. There was a motionless instant as the hands left his arms, then he felt himself drop. The pain tore along his back as he hit the cobbles. He lay groaning for what seemed minutes, eyes clenched shut, wondering if anything was broken.

'Come on, George. Up.'

George opened his eyes. Idris King was beside him, pulling him by the elbow.

'You're all right, just a bit of a bump.'

'Feels like my back's broke.'

'I can promise you it isn't. Come on.'

'Not too fast, then. It hurts bad.'

When George was finally on his feet and dusted off, Idris suggested they go back to his place for a cup of tea. George, hands in pockets, taciturn, agreed with a shrug. They walked along in silence, their feet on the cobbles making the only sounds.

Eventually, after they had been walking for ten minutes, Idris spoke. 'That was a damned silly thing you did,' he said. 'I know you expected me to say that, but it needed saying.'

'That fat swine goaded me.'

'Yes.' Idris paused and looked up at the stars. 'I'll make a point in that respect, if you'll permit me. It's a mark of leadership, George, that you don't give in to the goading. Any goading.'

'But what bothered me . . .' George sighed and rubbed his back. 'What bothered me, Mr King, was that he was part right.'

'About what?'

'About my sister.'

'We've been into that before,' Idris said. He began walking again with George a step behind him. 'Your sister's in service. She's a working girl.'

'She's in the service of outdated traditions. What she's doing is keeping the class structure intact.' George saw a stone shining dully in the gutter. He kicked it. 'They're the masters, we're the servants. It's an obscenity and my sister's one of the people who perpetuate it.'

'Oh, George . . .'

'It's true. And I'll tell you another thing. She's having every trace of her own class washed out of her. That lump Willie Paget got it right. The real la-di-da lady, that's what Megan's turning into.' He stopped and rubbed his back again. 'Think of what it does to me, people knowing about her. A grand socialist it makes me look, eh? My sister living among the gentry, doing their bidding and picking up their habits.'

They fell silent again as they walked slowly on. Idris King had no wish to pursue a topic on which his companion had a closed mind. George, for his part, was brooding over what had happened in the pub.

As they were passing the bottom of Conway Terrace George stopped and craned his neck, peering along towards his own house. After a minute he turned to Idris and said, 'I think I'll just go straight home, after all.'

'Right, then.' Idris slapped his arm. 'Get a good rest, you'll have a stiff back to contend with in the morning.'

'I'll get over it.'

'And, George, do think carefully about what you were saying. About your ambitions in the movement, that is. Maybe better to aim a shade lower and be sure of attainment. There are some disappointments that leave bad marks on people.'

George shook his head. 'I've thought about it, Mr King. Done all the thinking that's needed. Action's the thing from here on.'

They said good night and moved off their separate ways. Trudging slowly along Conway Terrace, George kept his eye fixed on his house. When he drew close he stopped and sighed. It was just as he had thought. His parents' bedroom lamp was lit. That meant his father had suffered another one of his attacks. Jennie would probably have to sit with him all night, holding his head up while he coughed and choked and tried to pull in enough air to keep himself alive.

As George stood in the road staring at the dim-lit window, a sudden wave of anger surged through him. It was directed at every injustice that burned him daily – his family's poverty, the illness of his father and mother, his brother's crippled leg that only money, if anything, would help. Most fiercely of all, George felt anger at his own helplessness.

'Some day,' he said, breathing the words against the night air.

Some day there would be a change. He had sworn it to himself. When the time came there would be savage reversals, whether Idris King believed it or not. George Roberts would wield a righteous axe and he would use it to do some long-awaited levelling.

He walked across to the house, hearing his father's gurgling cough. At the door a stab of pain in his back revived a sudden image of Willie Paget's sneering face. An instant later he saw his sister, clear in his mind as daylight, toffed up and full of herself.

'Bloody Megan,' George hissed, feeling something close to hatred.

11

The yellows and dark golds of autumn faded subtly into the first grey, crisp days of winter. Frost at night and morning resisted the faint heat of the sun. The November mists came and the daylight hours dwindled to half the length of a summer day. At the Pughe-Morgan house fires were lit early, hot thick soups were added to the mealtime fare and Griffiths the gardener began using embrocation for what he called his year's-end aches.

One month before Christmas, on a dark cold morning with a hint of snow in the wind, Mrs Foskett rose later than usual and realized she wasn't quite herself. Slowly, she dressed in her small bedroom and sat for a few minutes by her living-room fire, trying to decide what was wrong.

It could have been indigestion. There was a vague uneasiness in her stomach, not precisely a pain or even a discomfort, more a coldness that seemed to shift from side to side. On the other hand, it could be a colic. Mrs Foskett understood about colics, how they stealthily invaded the soft inner parts and grew suddenly to shoot griping pains along the nerves. Yet again, what she had might be the start of a cold, for there was a definite feverishness about her.

She stood up and went to her medicine box, noticing as she walked to the sideboard that her legs were unsteady. She opened the lid of the teak container and ran her eyes over the remedies stacked in packets, boxes and bottles. Foxglove, elder bark, dill, horehound – Mrs Foskett's finger moved along the containers and hovered over a box labelled 'Feverfew'.

'Just the thing,' she muttered.

She took the box back with her to the fireside and opened it, tipping the dried herb leaves into a small pan. She half filled the pan from the kettle and set it on the coals to boil.

As she sat and waited, she rummaged her memory for the

ailments that would be banished by an infusion of feverfew. Colds, for a start, and flatulence. It would also tackle worms, hysterics and kidney pains. She did recollect, too, that the leaves could be used as a poultice.

The water in the pan started to bubble and darken. Mrs Foskett got up to fetch a cup. She took two steps and staggered, hanging on to the edge of the table for support.

'In the name of God . . .'

She was panting softly and there was a clammy sweat on her skin. Her head was reeling and the coldness in her stomach had spread, enclosing her entire middle. She leaned down on the table with stiffened arms, fearful her legs would give way.

'Salts,' she grunted, and began moving arm-over-arm along the table edge until she could reach out to the medicine box, still lying open on the sideboard. She fumbled with one hand, keeping the other on the table, until she felt the smelling-salts bottle. Snatching it out of the box she turned, resting her legs against the table. With trembling fingers she unscrewed the cap and put the neck of the bottle to her nose, inhaling deeply.

'Aah! Lord . . .' She gasped as the fumes filled her head and swept down into her throat. Coughing violently, she dropped the bottle and hung on to the table again, waiting for the spasm to subside. The salts were strong, the strongest she had ever made. Ammonia crystals and oil of garlic, guaranteed to revive.

The coughing passed. So had the dizziness, she realized. And the cold, clammy feeling inside her. Cautiously she eased herself away from the table and stood still, unsupported, testing the strength in her legs.

'Better,' she said, still tasting the garlic on her tongue and throat. 'Much better.' She lifted a cup from the table and took a long, deep breath before she turned to the fireplace. She would be right as rain now, she told herself. The salts would do the trick. The salts and the restorative power of feverfew. Whatever ailment had attacked her, it didn't stand an earthly chance against medicine as strong as that.

By eleven o'clock the sky had brightened a little, but there was still an icy wind and the metal-grey warning of snow in the clouds. In the morning room, Mrs Pughe-Morgan sat poring

111

over her newspaper, reading an article about a new invention called Bakelite.

Megan came in with the tea tray.

'Ah! Just what I need. Set it down here, my dear.' Mrs Pughe-Morgan cleared the scattered letters from the middle of the table. 'And how are things in the household this morning?'

'Much the same as ever, ma'am.' Megan put down the tray and began pouring the mistress's tea. 'Cook's having a time of it with the stock pot – it keeps boiling over. Clara's cut her thumb. Mary can't find her clean aprons and Agnes is in a huff about something. Oh, yes, and Mrs Foskett's been giving the carter a telling-off, because he dropped one of the boxes of laundry soap and broke it.'

Mrs Pughe-Morgan nodded. 'Much the same as ever, as you say. I'm sure it's the strife that keeps us all going.'

Megan set the cup and saucer in front of her mistress and moved away from the table, smiling. Mrs Pughe-Morgan watched her as she turned to leave. It was less than a month to the girl's fifteenth birthday, but already her body had filled out and there was a marked gracefulness in her movements.

'Any problems of your own, Megan?'

Megan paused by the door. 'Nothing special I can think of, ma'am.'

'Are you making any headway with Dickens?' Megan had recently used some of her savings to buy a set of the novels. 'It's years since I read anything of his.'

'I'm enjoying *Nicholas Nickleby*,' Megan said. 'Makes me weep a bit in places, though. That poor Smike.'

'Oh yes, I remember.'

It was interesting to Mrs Pughe-Morgan that Megan always sympathized, sometimes fiercely, with the underdogs of history and fiction. One evening they had spent an hour talking about Van Gogh; Megan hadn't been too impressed by the paintings, but she had been moved to indignation at the injustices the man had suffered. Her keen interest in healing, the mistress believed, was another mark of Megan's concern for life's unfortunates.

'Which one will you read next, do you think?'

112

'*Dombey and Son*,' Megan said.

'Mm. You might find yourself shedding a tear or two over that one as well.'

Megan began to say something when suddenly the door was rapped loudly and swung open before Mrs Pughe-Morgan could respond.

'Ma'am, quick!' It was Mary. She looked frightened. 'It's Mrs Foskett!'

'What?'

'In the hall, ma'am. Oh, do come quick!' Mary dashed out again with the mistress and Megan behind her.

'Good Lord!' Mrs Pughe-Morgan stared across at the bizarre sight of the housekeeper, half lying behind the front door. Her head was lolling on one side, tongue protruding, lips and cheeks blue. She was grunting feebly as she tried desperately to raise herself.

'Oh, ma'am . . .' Mary had her fingers pressed to her mouth. 'What is it? What's up with her?'

Megan pushed Mary's arm sharply. 'Bring a coat from the stand!' she snapped, running across to Mrs Foskett. 'Quickly, Mary!'

Shaken, Mrs Pughe-Morgan turned back to the morning room. 'I'll call the doctor,' she cried over her shoulder.

Megan dropped to her knees beside the gurgling housekeeper and took her firmly by the shoulders. 'Lie down now, Mrs Foskett. Lie down on your back.'

The woman resisted, trying to pull herself up against the door.

'Please.' Megan pushed down hard on her shoulders. 'You've got to lie. You have to.' Gradually the woman began to sink and Megan got behind her, drawing her out full length as she rolled on to her back. 'Now just stay there. Don't try to move.' Megan put a hand on either side of Mrs Foskett's head and turned it sideways, then she pushed a finger into the panting mouth and pressed the tongue flat. 'Hurry with that coat, Mary!'

When Mary brought the mistress's tweed cape Megan told her to roll it into a bundle. 'That's it. Now put it under her feet.'

'Oh, my, she looks bad,' Mary whispered, raising Mrs Foskett's legs and resting them on the bundle. 'Why've you got your finger down her throat, Megan?'

'I'm making sure she can breathe.'

'So what's wrong with her?'

Megan made a tight frown and nodded at the housekeeper, indicating that she could hear what was being said.

Mary stood back. 'What'll I do now?' She was shifting from foot to foot, grimacing at the trickle of saliva running out over Megan's hand.

'Just wait for the doctor. He'll tell us what he wants done.'

Dr Watkins took fifteen minutes to get there. When he arrived he stood in the hall for a moment, looking down at the figure on the floor. Mrs Foskett was barely conscious now and very pale. Megan still knelt by her, holding open her jaw with one hand and pressing on her tongue with the other.

'Whose idea was it for her to do that?' Watkins murmured to Mrs Pughe-Morgan.

'Her own, doctor.'

Watkins raised one bushy eyebrow. 'Bright girl,' he said, snapping open his bag and kneeling down stiffly by his patient. 'I'll take over now,' he told Megan. 'And thank you.'

By half-past twelve Mrs Foskett was in her bed, dosed with digitalis and sleeping soundly, watched over by Megan, who had volunteered to stay with her.

In the dining room Dr Watkins and Mrs Pughe-Morgan sat down to a hastily prepared meal of steamed cod and boiled potatoes, covered in Mrs Edgar's special cheese sauce. The doctor, a bachelor who usually cooked for himself, ate rapidly and in silence. When he had finished he set down his knife and fork and nodded at the empty plate.

'Superb,' he said. 'Your cook's a talented woman.'

'Especially in a crisis.'

Mrs Pughe-Morgan rang the small silver bell beside her water glass. A moment later Agnes came in, throwing furtive glances at the doctor as she cleared away the dishes. As she left the room, Mary brought in the coffee. The mistress waited until the cups had been filled and Mary had left before she raised the worrying topic of Mrs Foskett's health.

'What exactly happened to her, doctor?'

'It's her heart. It's softening.' Watkins spooned sugar into his cup and poured on the cream. 'Myocarditis, to give the condition its proper name. Tonics will help – iron, bitters, nutritious animal foods and good clean air. But they won't cure the condition, they'll only slow down the rate of decline.'

'Does that mean she'll have to stop working?'

Watkins shrugged. 'A housekeeper's tasks can be performed without undue physical exertion. It's her authority that gets things done, isn't it?' He drank from his cup, his eyebrows coming together thoughtfully. 'The attack she had was serious enough,' he said slowly, 'but I'd be inclined to view it as an advance warning. She should rest a great deal more, but I would say she can carry on in her work.'

'I really thought she was going to die, when I first saw her.' Mrs Pughe-Morgan shuddered. 'She looked ghastly.'

'If she'd died, it would have been because she suffocated. Your little parlour maid saw to it that no such thing happened.'

'Megan's an extraordinary girl,' Mrs Pughe-Morgan said, with a distinct light of pride in her eyes.

Watkins stared at her. 'Megan? Megan Roberts?'

She nodded. 'That's right. I spoke to you about her father, remember?'

'Oh, I know the family well enough. But Megan – I didn't recognize her. My goodness, she's changed rather a lot.'

'In a number of ways, doctor.' Mrs Pughe-Morgan revolved her cup on its saucer, gazing at it pensively for a second. 'Tell me, is there absolutely *nothing* that can be done for Mr Roberts? Megan worries over him so.'

Watkins sat back in his chair, shaking his head. 'There's no help for it. Pneumoconiosis is a miners' disease and like most of them it's degenerative. It makes changes that can't be reversed. The lung goes very fibrous, there's sometimes complication from tuberculosis and other infections – oh . . .' He put up his hands. 'A man can go on for years and years with it, if it doesn't

115

turn complicated. In Roberts's case it's a nuisance, a bad one at times, but it isn't threatening his life.'

'Yet,' Mrs Pughe-Morgan murmured.

'Did you say anything to the girl, after you'd spoken to me?'

'Yes. I told her what you've just said. His illness is a terrible burden, but it's one he can live with. That didn't seem to give her much comfort.'

'No, I can appreciate that.' The doctor drank some more of his coffee, then took out his pocket watch and scowled at it. 'The enemy's moving on, Mrs Pughe-Morgan. I have to be getting back to Drynfor.' He thanked her profusely for the meal, then stood up. 'I'll call in to see Mrs Foskett in a couple of days. She'll be fine for now with the tablets I've left. But remember, she must stay in bed.'

They walked out together to the hall. At the door Dr Watkins repeated his instructions about the housekeeper remaining in bed, then he patted Mrs Pughe-Morgan's arm gently and said, 'She's got a competent little nurse over there with her. Don't fret.'

'If I do any fretting, doctor, it'll be over Megan. Mrs Foskett's grumpy enough when she's in good health. Lord knows what she'll be like when she wakes up and has nobody to growl at but that poor girl.'

Camphor oil, lavender and coal smoke. Those were the three odours Megan could detect strongly in Mrs Foskett's cottage. Separately they were fine, but in combination they added to the locked-in feeling the small rooms gave her.

For the first hour that the housekeeper slept, Megan had stayed at her bedside, watching the small changes in her colour and listening to the strengthening rhythm of her breathing. After an hour, growing restless from sitting so long, Megan stood up and wandered through into the living room. It was a place she had often wondered about: what does a woman like Mrs Foskett surround herself with in private?

It was dark, with only two small windows. The combined odours of the room seemed strongest in the corners, where the housekeeper had chosen to pile most of her bric-à-brac. There were plaster statuettes, ornamental brass pots with place names engraved on them, faded postcard pictures propped in grooved wooden stands, even a stuffed crow. The table that took up most of the floor space was varnished a dull brown and had a square mat of embroidered sateen in the centre. The same material had been used for antimacassars on the two armchairs by the fireplace.

Inevitably, it was the row of books on the back of the sideboard that took Megan's attention. There was a big family Bible and a three-part work entitled *The Lore of the Ancients*. Beside them, laid on their sides to keep the other books from falling over, there were three slim volumes: *Moral Tales, Sketches of Virtue* and, surprisingly, Megan thought, *The Child's Bedtime Companion*.

In total, the dwelling disappointed Megan. She stood by the table and looked around her, realizing that she had expected something richer and certainly more forbidding. The place was just terribly ordinary. It didn't seem to reflect Mrs Foskett at all.

Megan heard a soft moan and hurried back into the bedroom. Mrs Foskett's legs were shifting under the bedclothes and she was moving her head slowly from side to side. As Megan stood by the bed, watching, the movements ceased suddenly and the housekeeper became terribly still.

'Mrs Foskett?' Megan whispered, concern leaping up in her.

The stillness was complete. The woman could have been as inert as the bed she lay on. The skin of her face looked taut; the familiar lines at the eyes and mouth were fewer. Mrs Foskett looked dead.

And then her eyes opened. Glassy, distant, they gazed up at the ceiling for a minute, then turned slowly to Megan.

Relieved, Megan bent down over the bed. 'How are you feeling?' she asked softly.

The tip of Mrs Foskett's tongue appeared and moved heavily from one side of her mouth to the other. Her eyes remained fixed on Megan.

'Would you like something to drink?'

117

One large hand moved on the coverlet, plucking weakly at the material. Mrs Foskett's lips drew back from her teeth. 'Tea,' she croaked.

Megan had made sure to keep the kettle close to the boil. She had the tea ready in minutes, strong the way the housekeeper liked it, with plenty of sugar. She took the cup back to the bedroom and set it on the night table. With an effort she raised Mrs Foskett's shoulders and put another pillow behind her, then sat down and put the teacup to the dry, bluish lips.

'Careful, now, it's hot.'

As the woman drank in small sips her eyes stayed on Megan's face. The girl found it unnerving but she persevered, taking the cup away after each swallow, waiting until the mouth opened before she tilted it gently forward again. When the cup was half empty Mrs Foskett raised her fingers on the coverlet, letting Megan know she had taken enough.

Megan put the cup down and sat back, folding her hands. 'You've just got to rest, the doctor says. You're going to be fine.'

The tea had restored the woman. There was colour on her face now and her eyes, still watching Megan, were more alert. She cleared her throat. 'My heart, was it?'

Megan nodded. 'You overtired it, I expect.'

'I thought it was my heart. There was a bad pain.' The voice was gaining in strength, but it sounded thin and reedy, compared to Mrs Foskett's usual booming enunciation. She closed her eyes for a moment, then opened them again. This time she wasn't looking at Megan. She appeared to be studying the door, or something beyond it.

'Is there anything else you'd like?' Megan asked her. 'Can I get you another pillow or –'

'Megan Roberts,' Mrs Foskett said, interrupting. 'You're a good girl.' Slowly, her face expressionless, she returned her gaze to the girl's face. 'I know what you did. I was choking, girl. I'd have choked for sure if you hadn't done that.'

Megan felt her cheeks colouring. 'I was only –'

'Shh. Let me talk while I've a mind to.' Mrs Foskett's tongue moved leadenly across her lips again before she continued. 'I

118

want to say I'm sorry. Truth is, I've been sorry for a while now.' She sighed. 'You've had a hard time from me and you never deserved any of it. This morning, you could have let me perish if you'd wanted to. Instead of that you helped me. You saved me. You're good and kind and I'm very, very sorry for all . . .' She broke off, swallowing hard.

'There, there, now.' Megan saw the tears in the corners of Mrs Foskett's eyes and watched the growing agitation on her face. She reached forward, touching one cool hand. 'You mustn't go upsetting yourself,' she said. 'You have a rest. Rest and more rest, that's what the doctor said.'

'Rest is for the dead, Megan. I'm not dead yet, though I'm likely not far off it.' She nodded towards the night table. 'I think I could tackle the rest of that tea, now.'

When she had drained the cup, taking the tea down in gulps this time and obviously relishing it, she let her head sink back against the big soft pillow.

'You're looking very much better,' Megan observed.

'I feel better. Just weak, that's all.' The housekeeper smacked her lips softly and made the trace of a smile. 'You brew a fine cup of tea, girl.'

'I used to make it all the time for my Da.'

Mrs Foskett nodded. 'It was my father taught me to make tea. And to boil an egg and fry bacon the proper crispy way.' Her eyes became troubled again. For a minute she remained silent, then she said, 'Megan, I want to tell you something. It's important. No one's been told it before – not by me, at any rate.'

Again, Megan saw the agitation, she watched it creasing Mrs Foskett's brow and tightening her lips. Megan wanted to urge her to relax, to say nothing and rest, but she decided not to. She could see the woman needed to voice whatever troubled her so badly.

'My father', Mrs Foskett said, 'was a very strong man. Big, a collier, worked all his days at the face. He was big in his spirit, too, and in knowledge. Clever, he was, and hard on me. Firm. Is your father like that, Megan? Hard on you, is he?'

'No. He's very gentle.' Megan almost said what she privately thought about Owen Roberts, and sometimes whispered to the dark: a quiet man, right through to his heart.

'Well,' Mrs Foskett said, 'until not long ago, I believed my father's way with children was the only way. Now I'm not sure what I think.' She pursed her lips for a second, then shook her head. 'A child has to be broken, that's what he used to say. Like breaking a horse, Megan. It can't be no good to itself nor anybody until it's broken. I've no children, but I've always followed that way with staff. Break them first. Make them understand duty.'

Make them cry, Megan thought.

'When I was a girl, eighteen or so, I went very wrong, Megan.' Mrs Foskett's voice was low now, almost penitential. 'I met a lad, a seaman, and I think I must have lost my head. I ran away with him. We went to Cardiff. I suppose I was happy at first, but then he went back to sea for a spell and I was left alone and I didn't like it. So I found myself another young man. And another one after that. I got so I was drinking and carrying on . . . Oh, I wound up getting myself a bad reputation – very bad.'

Megan could scarcely believe it. Mrs Foskett was the incarnation of frowning morality, a termagant. To imagine her as a girl was hard enough; to picture her as a girl given to running around with men, laughing, *drinking* – that was near to impossible.

'In the end, when it got so nobody would give me work and not many wanted to know me, except the worst kind, I went back home. But my father wouldn't have me. Sent me packing, he did. Before I left, he told me he'd made a bad mistake with me. Hadn't broken me right, that's what he said.'

Megan was nodding. 'And what happened?' she asked. 'After you left, I mean.'

'I went back to Cardiff and sank a bit lower, lower than before. Then when I was nearly twenty and working for a laundry I met Harry Foskett. He was a butler to a family of builders in Cardiff.'

'And you married him?'

Mrs Foskett nodded. 'That man changed me. He was hard, as hard as my father, but he let me have the second chance my father didn't give me. He taught me standards, Megan, brought back my pride, taught me how to apply myself.' She smiled. 'Just like the mistress has been doing with you.'

Megan was intrigued. 'Did you go into service along with Mr Foskett?'

'I did. And by the time he died, twelve years after we married, I was housekeeper to the same family he'd served.' Her voice was growing weary again. 'There were people down there that knew me, though. People with long memories. That's why I came up here.' She fell silent again, staring at her clasped fingers.

'Thank you for telling me,' Megan said at length.

'I wanted to. Maybe it's my penance for treating you so bad.' Mrs Foskett sighed. 'You never needed breaking, far as I can see. I'm heart-sorry that I tried so hard.'

'It's all right,' Megan assured her.

Minutes passed and it began to look as if Mrs Foskett would sleep, but she suddenly rallied, holding up an unsteady finger.

'One other thing I'll tell you,' she said. 'It might come in useful. Don't ever take the trouble to run away from anything bad in your life. It'll follow you, whatever.' She made a wry, tired little smile. 'All this way I came, right up into the wilds, and what happens?'

'What?'

'That gardener, Jenkin. He knows all about me and my early days.'

'How?' Megan asked, surprised. 'How could he?'

'He found out through his brother,' Mrs Foskett said. 'His brother who just happened to be a special constable in Cardiff. He was up here on a visit once, about ten years ago. Recognized me and had a bit of a gossip to the gardeners. Since then, Jenkin's been in quite a position to crow.'

'I'm sure he wouldn't,' Megan said.

'I'm pretty sure, too. But he handed out a threat of sorts, a while back, just to keep me on my toes.'

'Even so,' Megan said, 'he's not a man to do you a real hurt.'

'No, I suppose not.' Mrs Foskett closed her eyes. 'I think I'll sleep for a while, Megan.'

'You do that, Mrs Foskett.' Megan hesitated, then patted the woman's hand. She stood up and went to the door. 'I'll go across and tell the mistress how you are,' she said softly, 'then I'll be back.'

Mrs Foskett nodded slowly, almost asleep already.

Going out through the living room, Megan paused for a minute and looked around her again. Then she smiled: that little cottage did reflect Mrs Foskett, after all.

12

Events during the early months of 1910 provided Mrs Pughe-Morgan with an opportunity to streamline her household. Although she had wanted to do it for over a year, there was enough foreseeable upset in the process to make her delay.

Then, at the beginning of March, Mary announced she would soon be getting married. During the same month Dr Watkins warned that the housekeeper was still working rather too hard and would need to take more rest. Megan, without being instructed to, began doing more of Mrs Foskett's work. The changes were occurring almost automatically; it only remained for Mrs Pughe-Morgan to add a few of her own and put them all on an official footing.

She waited until the third week in April, when a terse paragraph on the back page of *The Times* gave notice of the formal separation of Robert Pughe-Morgan and his wife Gwendolyn.

The mistress gathered the staff together in the library and explained the position to them clearly and without emotion; she was to be entirely responsible for the running of the house and its lands, which were now her property.

'And I believe', she told them, 'that, since this is such a turning point in my life, it's time to make a few domestic revisions.'

'What's that mean?' Agnes whispered darkly, and got a sharp nudge from Mrs Edgar.

'We'll be losing Mary soon,' Mrs Pughe-Morgan went on, 'and I've decided I won't be replacing her. Megan, who has lately been trained by Mrs Foskett in the mysteries of house management, will become our assistant housekeeper, as it's necessary for Mrs Foskett to take things rather more easily in future.'

Mrs Foskett, older-looking now and stooping a little, nodded silently at the floor. A few feet behind her, Agnes was scowling.

'Double the work for me,' she mumbled, 'and her ladyship gets made up to housekeeper.'

Mrs Edgar issued another swift bump with her elbow and glared a bright-eyed warning at the parlour maid.

'I would like the kitchen to be run as before,' the mistress continued, 'in the capable hands of Mrs Edgar and Clara. As for the gardens and grounds, I'll be taking on a lad to help, since the work there seems to be getting heavier every year.'

'Praise be,' Griffiths said.

'Amen,' grunted Jenkin.

'The revised arrangements will leave us with only one parlour maid. Accordingly, since I believe I only need one nowadays, I'll be putting the heavier house-cleaning duties in the care of a lady from Drynfor, a Mrs Bryant, who will come in three days a week. Agnes will find that her duties will be practically the same as before.'

'See?' Mrs Edgar murmured to Agnes. 'Always jumping to conclusions, you are.'

'All the same,' Agnes whispered huffily, 'I'm older than Megan. Been here longer, too. Should have been me as was made up.'

Mrs Edgar stared at her. 'You're about the daftest girl I've met, Agnes. That's without a word of a lie.'

'And so', Mrs Pughe-Morgan concluded, 'I hope the arrangements will suit everyone concerned. As for myself, I would like all of you to know that I'm suffering no great distress over the revisions in my own life.' Her face was calm, almost serene. 'It's inevitable that such events become the subject of gossip, even scandal. I'm sure I can rely on none of it originating in this household.'

'You can certainly rely on that, ma'am,' Mrs Foskett said firmly.

'Thank you. So it only remains for me to say how pleased I am, as I know you all must be, that Mary and her Tom are to be married. Warmest congratulations, Mary, and my very best wishes for the future.'

'Very kind, ma'am,' Mary said in a small voice, her cheeks flushing. 'Thank you very much.'

When the others had gone, Mrs Pughe-Morgan and Megan sat down with the monthly household accounts, which Megan had now taken on as her responsibility. She worked within a strict budget, taking weekly lists of requirements from Mrs Edgar, the gardeners and the mistress, making inventories of household sundries and maintaining supplies, in addition to regular ordering from tradesmen.

As was customary, they went over the outstanding accounts, the recurring expenses, and added up the total. Megan then showed the mistress the previous month's receipts, each one attached to the relevant account. When they had been checked and verified, Megan made appropriate entries in the household books.

'We saved two pounds on last month's bills,' she said, handing over the domestic ledger. 'This month and from now on, what with the extra fruit and vegetables we're getting from the gardens, I think we'll save more than that.'

The mistress scanned the entries, nodding and smiling. 'Smart work,' she said. 'Even though I did say it's not imperative that we cut down.' She looked at Megan. 'In many ways I'm better off now, you know.'

'It doesn't hurt to save, though,' Megan said.

'No, indeed.' The mistress returned her attention to the ledger, reminding herself that thrift was as indelible a feature in a miner's daughter as the colour of her eyes. When she had checked the figures and approved them with a flourish of her pen, she looked up and realized Megan was staring at her. 'Is something wrong?' Mrs Pughe-Morgan asked.

'I was wondering . . .' Megan looked down, shuffling bills. 'Sorry, ma'am,' she muttered.

'Go on, tell me. I don't bite, Megan, you should know that by now.'

'I was wondering how you're feeling. About what's happened . . .'

'I'm feeling remarkably fine, my dear. I wasn't pretending when I told you all that I'm suffering no distress. If this had happened two or three years ago – well, it might have been a different story. But I've had time to accept the inevitable, time to prepare myself for change.' She tapped the side of her head. 'The change is all in here, anyway.'

'So long as you're all right,' Megan said, moving her pieces of paper around again. 'I didn't mean to pry.'

The concern for the mistress remained with Megan, however. That evening, sitting in her room with *The Essays of Elia* open on her knees, she found her attention drifting. She looked up from the book and let her gaze rest on the paperweight by the window.

As she had grown older – she was well past her seventeenth birthday now – she had begun to notice the curious power of events to alter the pattern of life. Now, her own life and Mrs Pughe-Morgan's were so much different from the way they might have been; it was all because of events, large and small, triggering new events and diverting others.

It had been over two years since Mrs Foskett's heart attack. It had been almost the same length of time since Mrs Pughe-Morgan had seen her husband. He had come to the house a week after the housekeeper was taken ill, and he had stayed for only three hours. It had been Mrs Foskett's condition, Megan was sure, that had influenced the events of that evening, and perhaps the entire future course of the mistress's life.

Megan had heard it all. She was not an eavesdropper by nature, but it had been impossible for her not to hear. She had served at table that evening, and Mrs Pughe-Morgan's temper had run so high that she had abandoned her usual caution in front of the servants.

'I don't like living in London,' the mistress had told her husband. 'I fail to see how anyone can. Why should I abandon the beauty and the peace of this place? You're asking me to exchange the home I love for a smoky town-house and the society of bores and lechers, people to whom money and excess are the natural goals of every underhanded endeavour they make.'

Robert Pughe-Morgan, immaculate in a dark evening coat and rich purple French tie, had sat staring through his wine glass as his wife spoke, holding it up and frowning like a pharmacist judging the quality of a preparation.

'I'd forgotten,' he said quietly.

'Forgotten what?'

'That I'd be tearing you away from the social delights of this region.' He shook his head and tut-tutted softly. 'The scintillating conversations you must have. The witty cultural exchanges. The place is brimming with the fruits of civilization, isn't it? Foolish of me to have forgotten.'

'We can do without your sarcasm,' Mrs Pughe-Morgan snapped.

'And we can dispense with your slanders against my friends, too.' Mr Pughe-Morgan slammed down his wine glass, spilling burgundy on the white tablecloth. 'The people in my circle were good enough for you before.'

'They changed. You changed.'

'And you didn't, I suppose? Swapping a good place in society for your grubby committees and your good causes.'

At that point Megan had left the dining room. She hadn't wanted to go back, but eventually the mistress rang the bell. As Megan went in to pour the coffee, the couple were glaring at each other along the length of the table.

'It's an ultimatum, frankly,' Mr Pughe-Morgan was saying.

'Then I'm rejecting it.'

Megan had never seen the mistress look like that before. She was trembling. Her face was chalk white and her hands were clenched in fists on the table. The anger in her eyes was fierce, a warning and a challenge as she confronted her husband.

'Everything I care for is here, Robert. You'd have me shut the place up, discharge people who've given devoted service . . .'

'You're sentimental, Gwendolyn. That's your whole problem in a nutshell. Solace and succour to every lame dog within sight. That housekeeper, for a start. Useless now, isn't she?'

'She is nothing of the sort – '

'Be practical, woman,' Mr Pughe-Morgan cut in. 'What right-minded employer keeps on staff who've come to the end of their useful years – years for which they've been well paid, fed and sheltered. Yet you're talking about keeping her on . . .'

'I *am* keeping her on!' The mistress was almost shouting. 'If

127

she were blind and paralysed I'd keep her on! I owe it to her!'

'Indeed?' Robert Pughe-Morgan's voice had dropped suddenly to a growl. 'We're forgetting who's master, aren't we?'

His wife narrowed her eyes. 'What do you mean by that?'

'I mean that I expect to see this house run properly. On sensible and economical lines. You may well have preferred it otherwise, but let me remind you I'm not a charity.' He leaned forward, rapping his knuckles on the table with a crack. 'She is going, Gwendolyn.'

'That's spite! Sheerest spite!'

'I'll be informing her myself. First thing tomorrow.'

Mrs Pughe-Morgan was trembling violently. She pushed back her chair and jerked to her feet. 'If you so much as try . . .'

Megan was on her way out of the room again. The last words she heard from her mistress still rang clear in her memory, over two years later.

'You won't do this, Robert,' she hissed, her voice barely recognizable. 'You've shown how despicable you can be, so I'll give you a taste of how I can defend myself and my own. By word, deed and carefully placed document, Robert, that's how I'll do it. I can damage you terribly, and I will, if you insist on this . . . this viciousness.'

Whatever power the mistress's threat held, it had clearly been effective. She might never have taken such severe action at all, Megan reflected, nor have found her life so changed, if Mrs Foskett's heart hadn't succumbed to the natural ravages when it did.

A more pleasant event, occurring a year later, had brought about an important and unforeseen change for Megan herself. Mrs Pughe-Morgan had asked if she would like to go with her to Trillyn, a town nearly twenty miles away, where there was to be a national conference on educational reform.

'It's ages since you've been away anywhere,' the mistress pointed out. 'Trillyn's no holiday resort, but it's different, Megan, and variety's important in anyone's life.'

They took a train from Drynfor and travelled first class. That experience alone had thrilled Megan. Dressed up in her new

128

mustard coat and matching skirt, with a high-necked white blouse and white linen gloves, she looked and certainly felt like a lady. Men on the train tipped their hats to Mrs Pughe-Morgan and inclined their heads with similar respect towards Megan. The ticket collector even called her 'ma'am'.

The conference was held in a large public building, a tile-floored Victorian edifice full of echoing corridors and imposing arched doorways. The people attending – perhaps a hundred of them, Megan guessed – were mainly school administrators and district councillors. A few, like Mrs Pughe-Morgan, were landowning gentry, people who sympathized with the new moves in education, men and women whose patronage was valuable.

It was a friendly gathering, Megan was relieved to discover. The word 'conference' had conjured a picture of serious-faced individuals banging lecterns and sternly demanding reforms. Instead, there were groups of people standing around the main hall chatting and laughing, waving to each other. Megan began to understand that it was possible to be serious and concerned without being solemn.

'I intend to introduce you as my companion,' the mistress told her as they moved towards a group by the platform. 'On this occasion that's precisely what you are.' She squeezed Megan's arm reassuringly. 'Don't be nervous, my dear. They're all friends.'

In the space of twenty minutes Megan met and exchanged words with over a dozen people. There was a headmaster from Portmadoc, an animated little man who kept referring to Megan as 'missy'. She was introduced to an elegant, white-haired lady who had been in correspondence with Mrs Pughe-Morgan for over ten years, and another whose pioneering work in the teaching of mathematics had earned her a medal. Megan found it exhilarating to encounter so many new faces, such a variety of personalities. The talk was light and inconsequential, but, as Megan deduced, it served its purpose. They were establishing their unity, and by the time the speeches began Megan felt that she was one of them, not merely a visitor.

There were four principal speakers. When the third one had

129

said his piece and sat down, Megan was delighted to learn that the final address would be delivered by Mrs Pughe-Morgan herself.

She sat entranced, listening to her mistress talk about the fundamental rights of schoolchildren, of the need for human dignity to be taken into account in the planning of educational programmes. With immense feeling she related some grim statistics of poverty, overcrowding and squalor in the Welsh country districts as well as in the towns, and she concluded by arguing, convincingly, that progressive educational policies lay at the very heart of broad-scale social reform.

Afterwards, as they took afternoon tea in the large, green-draped dining room, a woman came forward, bearing her cup and saucer in one trembling hand, and asked if she might sit down with Mrs Pughe-Morgan and Megan.

'Of course,' the mistress said, pulling back a chair. 'It's Mrs Lawton, isn't it?'

'That's right.' The woman had dark-brown hair scraped back into a severe little bun at the nape of her neck. Her eyes were restless, jumping from Mrs Pughe-Morgan to Megan as she sat down and set her tea shakily before her. 'I wanted to tell you how impressed I was with your speech.'

'Thank you, that's very kind,' Mrs Pughe-Morgan said. 'Oh, let me introduce you. This is my companion, Megan Roberts. Megan, Mrs Lawton is a senior inspector of schools from Flintshire. One of the very few women doing that kind of job, I might add. We've been seeing each other at these affairs for quite a few years now.'

'How do you do,' Megan said, watching the eyes dance over her face, as if Mrs Lawton were memorizing her a fraction at a time.

'Delighted to meet you, Miss Roberts.' Mrs Lawton extended a limp, tremorous hand and touched Megan's fingers briefly. 'Is this your first conference, then?'

'Yes,' Megan said. 'I'm finding it very interesting.'

'Oh, I get excited by them. It drives out the staleness from my job, somehow, just to hear the delegates reaffirming their principles and putting forward new ideas.'

'I sometimes wonder, though,' Mrs Pughe-Morgan said, 'if we achieve much. Things are still in a sorry state.'

'But you hammer at complacency, Mrs Pughe-Morgan.' The woman emulated a hammer-head, gavelling the tablecloth softly with her small fist. 'That's what's important. The dents are piling up; it won't be long before the cracks start to show.'

For five minutes more Mrs Lawton went on in the same vein, sending metaphor hurtling after metaphor as she praised the pioneering work of delegates and committee members. Megan found the woman intriguing. She was as thin as a bird, a wispy little creature who nevertheless exuded the energy of a person twice her size.

When Mrs Pughe-Morgan mentioned Megan's own programme of self-education, though, Mrs Lawton really began to sparkle. She listened, lips parted, as Megan reeled off the subjects she had been studying, the new ventures she planned and the breadth of cultural topics she now comprehended, in fair depth, after only two years.

'That is *wonderful*!' Mrs Lawton cried. 'Quite, quite wonderful! If people could only realize . . .' She spread her fingers and held them, claw-like, in front of her forehead. 'That's a cathedral in there. Every normal human head is a gigantic building with acres of space for adornment. Art. Music. Literature. I've no need to tell you that, Miss Roberts, I'm quite sure you're aware – but, oh, if we could make *more* people aware of it.' She paused, almost panting, and smiled at Megan. 'Education has been my life,' she said, her voice softer now. 'I'm a worshipper of education, a fanatic in many respects. What you have done makes me very glad.' She turned to Mrs Pughe-Morgan. 'I've no doubt you had a hand in it, of course.'

'I provided a spark or two to the kindling,' the mistress said modestly.

'And what a fire was lit!' Mrs Lawton's face was radiant. 'This has been a grand day,' she said, 'perfectly grand. And to think, I almost couldn't come to the conference, I've been so busy.'

Now, over a year later, sitting in her room, Megan remembered those words and smiled. A grand day it certainly had been; a milestone day, as it turned out to be. Before they had parted company with Mrs Lawton, she confessed that she had approached Mrs Pughe-Morgan, in the first place, with a view to asking a favour.

'Although I did want to congratulate you, too, of course,' she added, with a self-mocking smile.

There was a young man in Drynfor, she explained, a twenty-year-old miner who was intent on getting himself some night-school qualifications. He had written to the authorities in Flintshire, where a number of classes had been organized, asking if he could attend, or take some form of postal tuition.

'I was impressed by his letter,' Mrs Lawton said. 'He's had very little education but he expresses himself well. And he does so want to get on. I was wondering, Mrs Pughe-Morgan, if you would have a word with him.'

Mrs Pughe-Morgan nodded, although she was frowning a little. 'If you think I can help . . . What precisely . . .'

'Oh, I wanted you to convey a message, if you would. So much better than writing, I think. I want the lad to know that I'm personally trying to set up a system of postal courses for him, and that he should hear something from me in about a month.'

'Why, that's splendid,' Mrs Pughe-Morgan said. 'I'll be happy to go and see him.'

'There's nothing formal in that direction yet,' Mrs Lawton explained, 'but we can surely make an effort to help those who want to help themselves. And I know it would be encouraging for him to be told by you.' Mrs Lawton smiled impishly. 'Presumption's one of my bad streaks, I'm afraid. Are you sure you don't mind?'

'Not in the least. If you'll let me have his name and address, I'll see to it before the end of the week.'

In fact, Mrs Pughe-Morgan had seen to it that same evening. They had arrived back at Drynfor railway station shortly after seven o'clock. Griffiths was waiting with the carriage, chatting idly to the old horse as Mrs Pughe-Morgan and Megan came down the steps.

As she settled into her seat, the mistress had a sudden idea. 'Griffiths,' she said, 'how far are we from Trevor Road?'

'Trevor Road . . .' Griffiths thought for a moment. 'Other side of the town, ma'am. Not more than a mile out of your way.'

Mrs Pughe-Morgan turned to Megan. 'You don't mind waiting an extra half-hour for dinner, do you?'

'Not at all, ma'am.'

'Fine.' The mistress opened her bag and took out the piece of paper Mrs Lawton had given her. 'Take us to number eight, Trevor Road, then, Griffiths.'

It was a little two-rowed huddle of single-storey terraced houses, each fronted by a low brick wall that enclosed a piece of garden no more than five feet across. When Mrs Pughe-Morgan stepped out on to the pavement she stood staring at the chipped and time-pitted front of number eight.

'So tiny,' she said, half to herself. She walked up the short path and rapped the door with its black iron knocker.

After a minute the door opened a crack, showing half of a woman's pale, suspicious-eyed face.

'Good evening,' the mistress said brightly. 'I'm Mrs Pughe-Morgan. I wondered if I might have a word with Alun Rees – this is where he lives, isn't it?'

The woman nodded. 'He's my lad.' She opened the door a fraction wider. 'What was it you wanted to see him about?'

'It's just a little private matter, Mrs Rees.'

'Private.' The woman's face clouded. 'Some kind of trouble, is there?'

Mrs Pughe-Morgan assured her there was no trouble. 'I won't keep him more than a minute or so.'

'I'll get him, then.' With obvious reluctance the woman turned away, pushing the door almost shut. From the carriage, Megan saw the curtain at the small front window move, then a moment later the door opened wide.

More than a year had passed, but Megan still remembered the jolt that had passed through her at the sight of Alun Rees, standing in the doorway of that little house with his shirt sleeves rolled back, his face wary. Just seeing a person had never affected Megan like that before, especially seeing them for the first time. Alun was tall, with regular features that were

133

pleasant enough; he had thick dark hair that was rather too long, and the typical broad, chap-knuckled hands of a miner. He was ordinary looking. Yet his immediate effect on Megan had been startling.

In the ensuing days, she had tried to define what had happened, but the increase in her powers of description seemed to offer no help. Tentatively, she began to think she had experienced what a poet somewhere had called an epiphany.

That notion was soon rejected, though. What she had felt, Megan next decided, was a surge of something like kinship, as strong as she felt for her father, but decidedly different. In the end, knowing it was damaging to examine an idea or emotion too closely, Megan settled on one simple phrase to remind her how she felt the first time she saw Alun Rees:

He put a sharp sigh across my heart.

Megan had seen Alun and spoken to him several times since that evening on Trevor Road. Characteristically, the mistress had added her own measure to the encouragement of the young man; she had invited him to call at the house and make use of the library whenever he wished. He had accepted the invitation. It happened that his chosen subjects, English and history, were particular passions of Megan's. Consequently, at the suggestion of Mrs Pughe-Morgan, Alun borrowed as many books from Megan as he did from the library.

There were long gaps between Alun's visits, so Megan and he were still shy with each other, being still not properly acquainted. Nevertheless there was a strong, unspoken link between them; Megan was certain of that.

Now she yawned and closed the book on her lap. Her mind was still held by events and their power to change life without warning. If she hadn't gone to that conference in Trillyn, or if Mrs Lawton had been too busy to attend, then Megan Roberts wouldn't have found herself in the condition she hesitated to call love.

'*Love,*' she said, getting out of her chair and smiling at the mock passion in her voice.

Megan believed that the love between man and woman was something she still lacked the capacity to feel. But she did have a bystander's understanding of it, and she could feel that her detachment grew less every day.

As she prepared herself for bed, Megan thought again about the mistress, of how much pain that strong woman could withstand, and how much of it she could conceal. Life was different now, changes were taking place all around. Perhaps there was a measure of happiness in store for Mrs Pughe-Morgan; perhaps, by standing at a different angle to life, she would see hopes and opportunities that had been concealed before.

That night, Megan went to bed with the strong feeling that something important was beginning. She wasn't sure if it was an omen, or the result of simple, unconscious deduction. She couldn't be sure, either, if it boded good or ill. All she knew was that her sense of its importance was strong. And reliable.

13

On a hot, sun-soaked day in late July, a day when barefoot children had to keep to the grass and the dusty backyards to avoid burning themselves on the pavements, Owen Roberts was sent home from work four hours early.

He stopped at the top of Conway Terrace, dabbing his brow with his sweat rag and trying to think up a story that would placate Jennie. He had been trying to think of one for twenty minutes now, knowing she would be clutched with fright the instant she saw him walk through the door.

'God, it's a broiler of a day,' he grunted, resting his back against the hot iron of a lamppost. There was a high singing in his head, a steady whine that got louder whenever he exerted himself. His chest ached, it was like a pressure on the inside, trying to widen the spaces between his ribs. Owen knew that if he coughed the pain would flare and double him over. That had happened up at the quarry less than an hour before. He had coughed once and a sudden knifing pain had sliced across his chest, putting him on his knees, leaving him weak and dizzy and aching. The manager, Mr Hesketh, had insisted that Owen go home straight away.

'And get yourself to the doctor,' Hesketh had added sternly. 'That chest of yours needs looking at. You can't just go on letting it pull you down the way it does.'

Lately it had been impossible for Owen to make Jennie believe that he wasn't as ill as he looked, or that he was capable of doing his job, even. She watched him with fear in her eyes, she shook her head whenever he dropped his guard and allowed himself to wince when the occasional sharp pain caught him. And the worry of it was making Jennie's own illness a shade or two worse, Owen believed.

He pushed himself away from the lamppost and started to walk down the terrace. He would take it as it came, he decided.

He would smile at her. He would give her the truth and let her rant a bit, then he'd make some promise or other that would keep her from the edge of hysteria.

'Hey, Da!'

Owen looked round and saw young Tom hobbling down the road behind him. The boy was thirteen now; as the doctor had warned years ago, his left leg grew much more slowly nowadays than the right one did.

'You're home early, then.'

Owen nodded, waiting for the boy to catch up to him. Tom walked with a stick, an old blackthorn his father had cut down to size. He was grinning as he came up alongside Owen, drawing his shirt sleeve across his shiny forehead.

'You shouldn't be out tiring yourself in this heat, lad.' Owen ruffled the boy's thick hair. 'That's why I'm back early, see. Too nice a day to spoil it with working.'

'I've been over at the Beacon with Gareth and Billy,' Tom explained. 'But I can't keep up with them.' There was no trace of pity for himself. He was simply stating a fact. 'Thought I'd come back home and give Mam a hand.'

'We can both of us give her a hand, then.' Owen took Tom's hand and they walked slowly down the road. Keeping up, Owen reflected, was a problem he too was beginning to suffer from. His son's limping pace was as much as he could match today. His whole body felt heavy, heavy as lead, even though he had been losing weight steadily for weeks.

Jennie was in the lobby as they went in. She stood staring at Owen, rejecting the reassurance of his smile.

'What's happened?'

'Nothing's happened.' Owen took off his jacket and hung it on the peg by the door. 'Nothing at all's happened.' He looked down at Tom. 'How about you going out in the yard and cool yourself? Splash some water on your hands and your arms and sit down in the shade of the fence. I'll come out and sit with you in a bit.'

'I thought we was going to help Mam . . .'

'Go outside like your Da tells you.' Jennie hadn't looked at the boy. She was still watching Owen. When Tom had gone she

137

stepped closer, touching Owen's arm. 'Tell me. What are you doing home at this hour?'

'Oh . . .' Owen tapped his chest. 'I had a bit of a spasm, that's all. Mr Hesketh thought it was best I called it a day.'

'A spasm? You mean you've had them pains again, don't you? It must have been bad if the manager noticed. Real bad, I'd say, if he sent you home.'

'Now don't go getting yourself in one of your states . . .'

Jennie's eyes were wide, hiding none of her apprehension. 'They'll stop the time out of your pay, won't they? Your packet'll be docked at the end of the week.'

'Not much,' Owen protested. 'A few coppers. I'll find a way of making it up.'

'And you'll kill yourself doing it!'

'Ssh, now.' Owen put his hand on Jennie's shoulder. 'You're making too much of this, lass.' He could see already that it was no ordinary flare-up. Maybe he had come in at a time when Jennie was feeling especially low; perhaps she had been dwelling on the dark side a bit more intensely than usual. Whatever the case, Jennie was starting to shake, seeing herself on a downward spiral with no hope of stopping. Owen tightened his fingers. 'Look at me, now,' he said soothingly. 'I'm here, on my feet, and I'm all right. I'll be back at work in the morning.'

Jennie clung to him suddenly, twisting her fingers in the front of his shirt. 'You're *not* all right!' she cried. 'You've not been all right for near enough two years! Just the sight of you takes the heart out of me, you're that thin and weak. Oh, God, Owen . . .' She pressed her head against his chest and began crying softly. 'You have to see the doctor. *See* him, get him to help you.'

Owen looked down at her, feeling that one strong hope put bitter strength in her sobbing. 'All right, then,' he heard himself say. 'I'll go and see Dr Watkins.'

Her head jerked back. She was gazing at him warily through her tears. 'You promise me that, now?'

'Promise.'

Jennie stepped smartly away from him and went into the living room. She picked up her shawl from the chair by the fireside. 'Today, then,' she said. 'We'll get the appointment made today. I'll go down and make it for you, that way I'll know it's done proper. With any luck you'll get to see the doctor tonight.'

'There's no need to rush it . . .'

'There's all the need in the world,' Jennie said, wrapping the shawl around her shoulders. 'You just have a wash and take it easy. There's tea in the pot. I'll not be more than ten minutes.'

Owen stood in the living room when she had gone. To see the change in her had been like witnessing a cure. He could easily tell how she felt. At long last, she would be thinking, he's decided to put himself in the hands of a real doctor. She would be entertaining all manner of bright dreams as she went hurrying down the road, picturing his recovery, seeing a way out of all her gnawing anxiety.

'Jennie, Jennie,' Owen murmured, shaking his head at her empty chair. He felt guilty, though perhaps he had done the only thing he could; maybe it had been time to fulfil Jennie's hope before it fled her completely. But what could he put in its place, once she discovered there was no help forthcoming from old Watkins?

'You coming out, Da?' Tom called through the open window. 'Nice and cool back here, it is.'

'In a minute, son. Just going to pour myself a drop of tea.' Owen smiled at the boy and went to the hob. As he bent to lift the teapot a pain jarred across his chest. He stood motionless, waiting for it to pass, noticing that the sensation of heaviness in his body had increased markedly.

'A damnable life it can be at times,' he sighed, and for one self-sorrowing moment he felt a trace of the fear that had dominated Jennie for such a long time.

Thunder was building as George Roberts made his way across the square by the Methodist chapel and climbed the twelve steps to Dr Watkins's front door. He turned at the door and looked out across the centre of the town, sniffing the hot, still air, watching the clouds get darker and lower. For a moment he

139

tested his mood, wondering if his foreboding had been real, or just anxiety at being asked to come here. George hated visiting posh houses. They always offered their owners an advantage; such people were fortified by the adornments of their power.

George was still in his work-clothes, which made him feel even more at a disadvantage. However, the message he had been given through Mr Hesketh had been brief and pointed: go to Dr Watkins's house immediately after work; do *not* go home first.

George raised the brass knocker and tapped twice. He waited, moistening his lips, listening for a sound behind the door. He heard nothing and almost jumped when it opened suddenly and a small, tight-smiling woman cocked her head at him.

'I'm George Roberts,' he said.

The woman nodded, waiting for more.

'I had a message. At work. Dr Watkins wanted me to come here straight away.'

'I see.' The woman pulled the door wide and ushered George into the small, sombre hallway. 'If you'll wait,' she murmured, indicating a bentwood chair by the fireplace. 'The doctor's with a patient in the surgery. He shouldn't be many minutes.' She closed the front door and went off down a passageway by the stairs.

George sat for five minutes gazing at the marks of the doctor's success. Framed certificates hung on every wall, surmounting walnut occasional tables, a pair of button-backed cabriole easy chairs and a massive black sideboard with carved trusses and brass-inlaid drawers. The rug was Persian or Indian, George couldn't decide which, and there was a similarly eastern look about the painting above the fireplace.

A desire to be observed, considered and esteemed; vanity is the keenest disposition in the heart of man.

Idris King had shown George the words and he had found himself in strong agreement, memorizing them on the spot. The vanities of rank, the value some people placed on material things – they were thorns to George's view of decent human values. Feeling his apprehension grow as the waiting minutes passed, he called to mind another little proverb with which he could shield himself:

Fools take to themselves the respect that is given to their office.

A door he hadn't noticed before, set deep in a shadowy archway, opened slowly and shed dim evening light across the carpet. George stood up.

'Ah, good evening.' Dr Watkins emerged, dark-suited, a coiled stethoscope dangling from one hand. The light behind him touched his white hair, giving him the look of a patriarch. 'I'm glad you could get here. Do come in and take a seat.'

For the first few seconds George's anxiety threatened to swamp him. There he was, grey-faced with slate dust, his clothes patched and soiled, sitting in an elegant study being confronted by an elderly gentleman in authority. The natural timidity of the downtrodden, as Idris King put it, was invading George by rapid inches. He sat beside the desk, hands clenched tightly on his knees and his heart beating too fast, watching as the old man carefully opened a set of folded papers that lay in front of him.

'You're aware that your father visited me last week, aren't you, George?'

'Yes, I am,' George said, stopping himself before he added 'sir'.

'He told me that no other member of the family, apart from your sister Megan, knew that he'd seen me once before about his chest complaint. On that first occasion, I explained there was nothing medicine can do for the condition.'

George was immediately indignant. His timidity withdrew far enough to let him speak. 'Unless the patient's got a bit of money about him,' he said.

Watkins frowned. 'I beg your pardon?'

'The slate made my father's chest bad,' George said firmly. 'Working the slate keeps a man poor. So there's no help for him.'

Watkins looked startled. 'You really believe that? You think that if he'd had money it would have made a difference?'

'It makes a difference all round.'

'Well.' Watkins drummed his fingers for a moment. 'I don't think this is the time to discuss the social inequities, George. I'll grant you that cash can open a lot of doors that poverty can't budge, including medical doors. But not in this case.' He looked George straight in the eye. 'Most certainly not in this case. Pneumoconiosis – that's what your father suffers from – resists every treatment we know of, so far. No amount of money would help.'

'A certain amount', George said stubbornly, 'would make sure he'd do his suffering in a bit more comfort.'

Watkins shook his head impatiently. 'George. Please understand this. I know about the improvements that could be made for the working people of this town, and most other towns in the region. I'm aware that conditions are bad and I know the men's pay is inadequate. But that's not what we're here to talk about. I want to discuss your father's health with you, how it will affect your family's future.' He lowered his eyes to the papers in front of him. 'Just try to put your bitter feelings aside for a moment. This is a report I received earlier today. It concerns your father and it's my reason for asking you to come here –'

'My family's future?' George was leaning forward, looking openly anxious. 'What about my family's future? What do you mean?'

Dr Watkins looked up. 'How old are you now, George?'

'Twenty-one.'

'In every respect a man, then.' Watkins folded his hands on the papers. 'I sent for you this evening because, like it or not, you'll have to assume the responsibilities of a man from now on.'

Earlier, when Hesketh gave him the message, George had felt a terrible foreboding. He had fought it, he had kept it down and refused to let himself scan it. Now it rose up in him again, tightening his throat. 'That report,' he said, pointing. 'What's it about?'

'It's an analysis of a sputum sample from your father. He's very ill, George –'

'That's been plain enough,' George rasped. 'But nothing was done about it. Not one damned thing –'

'George. Listen to me. When I first examined your father for the chest complaint, I told him there was no treatment. But I also advised him to come to me if it ever seemed to get worse. I wanted to keep an eye on him. He didn't come near me again until five days ago. This condition, this new condition, must have set in a while before that.'

'And can you do something for him now?'

Watkins shook his head. 'I can make sure he doesn't suffer unduly. The pain's all I can attack, though. There's no cure at all for the disease.'

George remained silent for a minute, staring at the papers on the desk, aware now that the foreboding had been real. He did not want to ask, nor to be told. Finally he looked at Watkins. 'What is it he's got?'

'He has a cancer,' Watkins said quietly. 'It's in his right lung. There are signs that it may have begun to spread to the left lung as well.'

The word numbed George. Cancer. People hardly ever mentioned it above a whisper. It held every dark, unspeakable implication. It was the surest sentence of a terrible death. And it had entered his family.

'How long will it –'

'Just sit quietly and hear me out, George.' Watkins opened a drawer and took out a flask. He poured a measure of brandy into the silver cup and passed it across the desk. 'Drink that. It'll help.' He watched George pick up the cup and sip from it. 'Let me tell you why I sent for you – though perhaps you can guess, anyway.'

George nodded, swallowing more from the cup.

'In cases like this it's always difficult to know who should be told, if anybody,' Dr Watkins went on. 'In the case of your father, I think it would be cruel to tell your mother the truth. She isn't strong enough, she hasn't the strength of body or will, in my opinion, to withstand such knowledge. But someone has to be prepared in advance, George. It had to be either you or your sister, or both of you.'

George looked up, his eyes moist from the sting of the brandy. 'Megan isn't one of our family any more.'

143

Watkins was surprised at the sharpness of the retort. 'She's a strong, capable young woman,' he said. 'I have good cause never to forget that. When the time comes, your mother will need all the support she can get.'

'I can give her all she needs.'

Watkins shrugged. 'Just as you wish. But I think your sister ought to know . . .'

'That's up to you, doctor.' George put the empty cup back on the desk. 'But she'll be having no say in what happens in our house.'

'Very well.' Watkins closed the folder and put it in the desk drawer. 'Now, about your father. To be blunt with you, I don't know how long he'll have. A couple of months, perhaps. But he must stop work at once. He should have stopped a year ago.' Watkins hesitated, seeing the hardness on George's face get harder still. 'Money. I know. But he *can't* go on working, it would be an act of savagery to let him . . .'

'I understand, doctor.' George stood up. 'What'll my mother be told?'

'The same thing I'll tell your father. He has to rest, because the pneumoconiosis has weakened his lungs.' He got up and came around the desk. 'I won't use any doom words, George. And I'll call regularly to make sure his pain's not too severe.'

Watkins saw George to the front door. They stood together watching the first spots of rain darken the dusty pavement.

'My poor Mam,' George murmured.

'Yes. She's the one to think of.' Watkins patted George's shoulder lightly. 'I'm truly sorry. Nobody deserves this. Do your best to see she keeps hoping, won't you? Your father tells me she's always got to have a hope to hang on to.'

George looked at him. 'I'll see she's always got one.' He wiped his hand on his jacket and held it out. 'Thank you, and I'm sorry if I –'

Watkins squeezed his hand. 'Nothing to apologize for.'

George was about to move off, then he stopped. 'Dr Watkins – about Megan.'

'Yes?'

George frowned, closing his eyes for a second, then his face cleared and he said, 'Maybe it's best you let her know. Her and my father's a bit close, like. She'll be better off knowing.' He turned quickly and hurried off down the steps.

14

In September Mrs Pughe-Morgan had a letter from Mrs Lawton, telling her that Alun Rees was doing well in his studies. His English grammar had improved and his written answers to questions showed a strong flair for language, as well as an unflagging enthusiasm for his subjects. Mrs Lawton said she hoped Alun would continue to do well, and added that she was sure Mrs Pughe-Morgan's encouragement had been important to the young man's progress.

That same afternoon Mrs Pughe-Morgan called Megan to the library and showed her the letter. 'When Alun calls tonight, we must tell him what Mrs Lawton thinks about his progress,' the mistress said. 'I think a lot of the credit's due to you, too. Alun's becoming quite the historian under your tutorship.'

Megan took greater pride in that remark than she showed. It had become one of her special pleasures to guide Alun Rees, and to keep learning more so that her own studies were always a few paces ahead of his. She no longer simply loaned Alun books; they often sat in the library and discussed his work, losing all sense of time as they worked out problems and exchanged points of view.

'I've discovered something,' Megan told Mrs Pughe-Morgan. 'The only way for people to do any real learning is to keep talking to one another.'

'You mean teachers really are necessary?' Mrs Pughe-Morgan had never doubted it, but she delighted in hearing Megan make her own deductions. 'Books and practical experience aren't enough, is that what you're saying?'

'It's the talking that gives real quality to an education,' Megan said. Increasingly, she made her observations without hesitation or uncertainty. 'I can learn all about, oh, let's say the Crusades. And so can you. But what I learn gets changed, it gets *broadened* by my own opinions and my instincts. The same happens with you. So when we voice our knowledge it's got . . . I'm not sure how to put it . . .'

'An extra dimension?'

'Yes, that's it, an extra dimension, so we're passing on a bit more than we took in, and we're getting some of that expanded kind of knowledge in return . . .'

'Which we then add to what we know . . .' Mrs Pughe-Morgan began laughing. 'It's comical when you think of knowledge flying back and forth like that,' she said, 'getting altered, expanded, absorbed again and altered some more – but it's what happens, I suppose.'

'Enrichment,' Megan said, relishing the word. 'People enrich knowledge and they're enriched by it. But to properly know anything, they have to talk to each other.'

'Hear, hear.' Mrs Pughe-Morgan put a confident, motherly arm around Megan's shoulder. 'I'll tell you something else,' she said confidentially. 'It's something you notice when you have to air your views as often as I do. People are never aware of how much they really know until they start talking.'

Megan was thoughtful for a moment, then she nodded firmly. 'That's true,' she said. 'That's absolutely true. Sometimes, when I'm talking to you or to Alun about books and such, I come out with opinions I never knew I had.' Her smile faded. 'It happens when I talk to my father, too.'

Much later that day, Megan had cause to recall what she'd said about talk and the exchanging of knowledge.

When Dr Watkins had told her in July that her father was dying, she cried for almost an entire day. The day after that, she was so preoccupied that she could scarcely do her work. On the third day, her practical nature prevailed. Megan reminded herself that grieving achieved nothing. Her father had only a short time left; it was her duty to do what she could to make that time peaceful and happy. The sorrow stayed with her, eating steadily at her heart, but it was kept firmly under control.

Megan now visited her father every evening. She stayed only an hour each time, sitting by his bedside talking quietly to him. She showed none of her distress at his obvious pain, or at the way he had shrunk almost to a skeleton.

This evening the change in him was heartbreaking. In the space of a day Owen's skin had taken on the colour of old ivory. His lips seemed unable to close properly over his teeth and his eyes had sunk alarmingly deep into their sockets. When he turned his head to look at Megan, the fleshless tendons in his neck moved like criss-crossing bowstrings.

'And how are you feeling tonight, Da?' Megan sat down by the bed and took one of his hands in hers. It felt dry and lifeless.

'Better for seeing you, my love.' His voice was only a croak now, bereft of its old strength. 'I seem awful sleepy all the while, now. There's times I can hardly keep my eyes open.' He smiled and his teeth appeared to push forward from his mouth. 'Promise I won't drop off while you're here, though.'

It was then, looking at Owen, that Megan perceived a flaw in what she had said earlier about talking. She had told Mrs Pughe-Morgan that talk was necessary to learning. But, when it came to expressing love, talking was a barrier. Talk could never teach Owen Roberts the depth of his daughter's feelings for him; words either coarsened or diluted the emotions she tried to express. Aching now with love for her father, Megan wished she could speak to him in feelings, not words.

For ten minutes they discussed the weather, as Owen enjoyed doing, and the changes Megan had noticed in the gardens and in the wood and around the lake at the Pughe-Morgan estate. She talked about the beautiful shiny green-and-yellow celandine clumps she had discovered, the late poppies that had appeared among the trees, and her rarest find of all that year, a blue pimpernel. She began to tell Owen about the blackface ram that had wandered into the orchard that morning, then she noticed he was no longer looking at her. His head had sunk deeper into the pillow and he was staring at the mottled ceiling.

'Da? Are you all right?'

'Looking at the pictures,' he murmured.

'Pictures?'

'The ones you're painting for me.' He closed his eyes. 'I'd part with a lot just to see all that, Megan. Trees, gardens, the flowers. Just to take your hand and walk among it, that would be champion.'

'We will, one day. We'll go for walks just like before.'

Owen lowered his chin slowly and opened his eyes. 'No need to pretend for me any more, my lamb.'

The look chilled Megan. Her father's face was like a skull, staring at her from the very edge of life. Impulsively she snatched up both his hands and kissed them. Then, too late, she realized she had let go her rein on herself; she was crying.

'Don't fret,' Owen said gently. 'I'm ready enough, my love. There's been time lately to –'

'I don't want you to say that, Da, please . . .'

Owen drew one hand free of Megan's and touched her tear-streaked face. 'You've been very good,' he said, his voice frail and dry. 'It must have been hard, putting on your bright face every night, sitting there and cheering me up.'

Megan couldn't control herself. She was doubled forward, her tears dropping on the bedsheet, her shoulders jerking with the force of her sorrow.

'Ssh, now. We don't want your Mam hearing.'

Megan sat up in her chair and pulled out a handkerchief. She wiped her eyes and took a few deep breaths, calming herself. 'I'm sorry,' she said.

'And so am I.'

'You've nothing to be sorry for, Da. It's you that's done the suffering . . .'

'And caused a lot because of it,' he said. 'I can console myself, though, Megan. About all of it. There's consolation for everything.' He smiled at her. 'It's all down to balance, you see. Everything balances out.' He stopped sharply, wincing.

'Da? What is it?' Megan leaned over him anxiously. 'Got a pain, have you?'

Owen nodded, touching his chest. 'Feels at times as if I'm tearing apart, like dry old paper.'

Megan picked up the bottle from the bedside and undid the cap. 'Where's the spoon?' she asked.

'Don't use it no more. Straight from the bottle nowadays.' Owen let Megan raise him and put the bottle to his lips. He took one long swallow and lay back, smacking his lips. 'It's grand stuff, whatever it is.' He let out a long sigh. 'Something that powerful can't be doing me no good, but I'm terrible glad of it.' He closed his eyes and sighed again. 'Can feel it working already,' he murmured.

In silence Megan watched him glide off to sleep. The laudanum compound had meant the difference between controllable pain and protracted agony. Owen now got through a bottle every five days. Dr Watkins never hesitated to bring along more when it was needed. Megan wondered what her father would have said if he had known he was drinking tincture of opium; Watkins had told him it was a tonic that induced healthy sleep.

Owen was fast asleep in five minutes. Megan stood up, kissed his cheek and tiptoed downstairs. Her mother was in her chair by the fire, her shawl drawn tight around her shoulders.

'He's sleeping, Mam. I thought it was best to leave him.'

'He looks terrible today,' Jennie said. The old apprehension was in her voice again. 'Skin the colour of caked mud . . .'

'You know what the doctor said about you fretting,' Megan warned her.

'But he's wasting, Megan,' Jennie insisted. 'He's not coughing as much these days and he sleeps better, but to look at him . . .'

'That's the way it is with some illnesses, Mam.'

Worry had deepened the lines on Jennie's face. She gazed up at Megan, her eyes begging more reassurance than anyone could give her. 'The doctor never says much. Just leaves the medicine, he does, and tells me your Da's got to have plenty more rest.'

'Just do what he tells you,' Megan said softly. 'The rest and the medicine are what Da needs. And get more rest yourself.' Megan looked out into the yard, then went to the lobby door and listened. 'The boys out again, are they?'

'Playing up the road somewhere,' Jennie said listlessly. 'George is at a meeting with Idris King.'

Megan nodded. 'They're always out when I come, these days.'

'That's true,' Jennie said, adding nothing.

'I'd best be getting back, then.' Megan buttoned her coat, feeling inadequate, unwilling to linger in case her mother started on about Owen again. 'I'll come over tomorrow night, as usual,' she said. 'I'll have some vegetables for you, and a cake from Mrs Edgar.' She looked at her mother. 'No more fretting, mind. My Da's sleeping sound. He's fine.'

Jennie went to the front door with Megan. 'All this walking you do,' she said as Megan stepped outside. 'Four miles a night, here and back. You must get terrible tired by bedtime.'

'I like walking, Mam. And I can have a ride over if I want. It's just that I don't like putting Mr Griffiths out.' She leaned forward and kissed her mother on the cheek, making her frown as usual. 'Night night, Mam. Get to bed early.'

Later, walking over the high-curving road at the south of the town, Megan wondered how her mother was going to cope with the future. She had wondered before, but now it seemed urgent that plans be made. Inevitably, because she could think of nothing that would console her mother over the coming months, Megan's mind wandered back to Owen and his own consolation.

'Balance,' she murmured to herself. Perhaps like her, at the back of his mind and almost hidden by the pain, Owen Roberts still carried the bright, incandescent hope of the confident child.

To think of Owen as a child almost made her cry again. It was over for him, he'd had his arc of childhood, manhood, health and decline. Now it was ending on a rickety bed in a bleak little room, with Owen patiently imagining pictures on the ceiling as his body devoured itself inch by inch. Miraculously, he could see no injustice. He even managed to detect balance in what had been done to him.

God has a grim sense of balance, Megan thought, wiping away one small tear from the corner of her eye.

That evening Alun Rees came to the house at half-past eight, punctual as usual and blushing, as he always did, when Mrs Foskett showed him into the library.

'Well now, Alun.' Mrs Pughe-Morgan greeted him cheerfully from behind her writing table. She had taken to wearing spectacles when she worked and she pushed them to the end of her nose as she stood up and took the bundle of books Alun had brought back. 'Still making headway?' She hefted the bundle. 'Your reading gets heavier by the week.'

'My appetite for it's improving all the time,' Alun said. He spoke slowly, and always inclined his head as if he were saying something he had thought over carefully. Mrs Pughe-Morgan had told Megan that it might be true, for Alun rarely wasted a word.

'And how about Gibbon, Alun? I see you've survived volume two. D'you think you'll make it all the way through to number six?'

'Dusty-dry a lot of it, ma'am. But it's a fine work, all the same. I'll get through the lot of it – with your permission.'

'Granted, my dear, granted.' Mrs Pughe-Morgan rummaged among the papers on her table and held up Mrs Lawton's letter. 'I've a small tribute to your talents here. It arrived this morning.' Mrs Pughe-Morgan pushed up her spectacles again and read Alun the relevant passage.

'It's very kind of Mrs Lawton to say that,' Alan mumbled. 'She doesn't mention my shortcomings, though.'

Mrs Pughe-Morgan looked amused. 'You know what they are, do you?'

Alun nodded gravely. 'Every one, ma'am. Knowing them's one thing, mending them's another.'

'But knowing them's the start of mending, Alun.' She looked at him, taking in the broad set of his shoulders, the large hands slow-moving across each other, restless with their own energy. 'You're going to do very well,' she said on an impulse. 'It's right to entertain doubts about yourself, but don't overdo that. Success is your element, given enough judicious prodding along the way.'

Later, as he sat alone with Megan at the big table in the middle of the library, Alun received the sharpest educational prod so far.

'Your trouble', Megan told him, 'is you try to memorize the way a thing's written, as well as the message it's carrying.'

'So? That's wrong, is it?' For fifteen minutes Alun had been

152

noticing how abrupt and touchy she was. 'There's a lot to be got from a writer's style, isn't there?' he said.

'There's nothing to be got from reciting it like a parrot,' Megan snapped. 'You should develop your own way of expressing things.'

Alun thought about it. 'Is that how I sound? Like a parrot?'

'Sometimes.' Megan riffled to a passage in a book they had both read and had discussed at three consecutive meetings. 'See. The author says, "That man remains truly a child who remains in ignorance of his race's history." And what did you say not two minutes ago? I'll tell you what you said. You said you thought a person *remained truly a child* if he didn't know about the history of his own race.' Megan sat back and folded her arms. 'That's parrot work.'

'But I didn't say it exactly the way he does . . .'

'You used some of his words. "Remains truly a child" – that's not the way you really speak, Alun. It sounds downright daft coming from you. And you didn't really absorb the notion, you just stored it for being smart with whenever you got the chance.'

Alun had never known her to be so outspoken. It hurt, both to hear her snap at him, and to know she was right. He did save up some remarks and ideas purely for repeating. He watched Megan's mouth tighten as she slapped the book shut and pushed it away from her.

'You're quite right, Megan.' Confession had a bitter taste for Alun, but he knew it would be even worse to blurt out some makeshift defence of himself. 'I'll try to get rid of that habit.'

Megan said nothing. She sat staring at the closed book, her lips still obdurately tight, her eyes stubbornly avoiding Alun's. He felt he should leave; there was a rawness between them that would only be soothed by separation. After a minute he stood up and buttoned his jacket.

'I'll be going, then,' he said. He picked up the books he had borrowed and went to the door. 'Thank Mrs Pughe-Morgan for me, will you? And thanks again for –'

'Alun.' Megan was on her feet, her face pained and uneasy. 'I didn't mean all that.'

153

'But you were right.'

'Being right doesn't excuse rudeness. I'm not feeling so cheerful just now. I was taking it out on you . . .'

Alun smiled at her, without knowing how that could affect Megan. 'I know,' he said. 'Your father, is it?'

'Yes.' Megan came towards him uncertainly. 'He's worse, a lot worse. It's been weighing on my mind.'

'It's understandable.' Alun squared his shoulders. 'Megan, I was wondering . . .'

She saw him falter and immediately prompted him to go on, knowing it was important.

'Well, I wondered if, you know, when you walk over to Drynfor like you do, I wondered if some time I might walk back with you.' Alun's face was crimson, but he kept his eyes steadily on Megan's. 'If you wouldn't mind, that is. Just for a bit of company . . .'

'That would be nice.' Megan believed she was blushing too. 'Very nice. Next time you're coming over, maybe.'

'I was thinking of coming tomorrow. There's one or two things I need your help with. We could talk about them on the way across. No need for me to stop . . .'

A big lump swelled in Megan's throat. She took three steps forward and reached out, touching his arm for the first time. Tears welled and brimmed, coursing freely down her cheeks. 'Oh, Alun, I'm so sorry . . . Do forgive me.'

'I told you,' he said gently. 'You were right. Don't cry. Your father wouldn't want you to.' His hand touched hers tentatively, then he moved away and opened the door. 'Tomorrow, then. I'll wait for you at the foot of Conway Terrace.'

Megan nodded, bewildered at the cascade of feelings in her. For several minutes after Alun had gone, she could still feel the touch of his fingers on the back of her hand.

15

Owen Roberts died in the second week of October. Before it killed him, the cancer reduced Owen to a child-thin, pain-racked ghost of himself. He was incontinent, ulcerated with bedsores and delirious on laudanum for an entire week, before one massive haemorrhage gave him the peace he had finally begged for.

Leaf smoke hung in the air at Drynfor cemetery on the day of the funeral. A cold wind fluttered the black and dark-grey garments of the mourners as they stood around the open grave, listening to the minister's emotionless recital of the burial service.

'Man that is born of a woman hath but a short time to live, and is full of misery. He cometh up, and is cut down, like a flower; he fleeth as it were a shadow, and never continueth in one stay. . . .'

At the head of the coffin, George Roberts glowered steadily across at Mrs Pughe-Morgan, who was standing apart from the others, her head bowed. On either side of George, Gareth and Billy stood ready to take a cord each. The undertaker's men were on hand to take the remaining cords, since there were no other male relatives apart from Tom, who was too unsteady on his feet to help lower a coffin.

'In the midst of life we are in death: of whom may we seek for succour, but of thee, oh Lord, who for our sins art justly displeased? . . .'

Megan, Tom and Mr Hesketh from the quarry were gathered in a protective huddle around Jennie, who was weeping into her handkerchief. Beyond them, in clusters of three and four, acquaintances of Owen stood with their wives and families; at the very back Idris King hovered in the shadow of a drooping willow, keeping himself separate from the Christian ritual.

155

'Thou knowest, Lord, the secrets of our hearts; shut not thy merciful ears to our prayer; but spare us, Lord most holy, oh God most mighty, oh holy and merciful Saviour, thou most worthy Judge eternal . . .'

Megan held firmly to her mother as the coffin was raised and the supports removed. Jennie was mumbling something into her handkerchief, chanting it over and over, her eyes wide as the coffin slowly disappeared below the edge of the grave.

'Don't leave me, Owen!' she cried out suddenly. 'Don't leave me here! What am I going to do?' Her mouth gaped as she howled and tried to pull herself away from Megan's restraint. 'Owen! Owen!'

'Mam! Shush, now!' Megan tightened her arm on Jennie's shoulder and drew her close, muffling her cries. 'Settle, now! Take hold of yourself!'

'I don't want him gone! It's not right!' Jennie sagged suddenly and Mr Hesketh grabbed her before she landed on her knees. For one wild moment she struggled, trying to get to the graveside, then she collapsed against Megan and buried her face in her collar, sobbing wildly.

The minister frowned for a moment, then continued with his chant. Throughout the rest of the burial Jennie wailed on, crying herself hoarse and earning the embarrassed pity of everyone but the minister.

After the service Megan went back to the house with her mother and brothers. There was no foregathering with sherry and sandwiches, no traditional congregation of neighbours and friends to offer final condolences; George had forbidden it.

'And I might as well tell you', George said to Megan as they stepped into the tiny living room, 'that you're not welcome in this house any more.'

Megan stared at him. 'What are you talking about?' She looked from George to her mother and back again. 'I'm one of the family,' she said. 'I'm Owen Roberts's daughter and that's my mother over there, your mother and the mother of all of us. I was born here, George. What right do you think you've got to talk to me like that?'

'The right of any betrayed individual to reject his betrayer!'

'Oh, don't be so fatuous, George! You sound like one of your stupid pamphlets!'

George's breath smelled strongly of whisky. He stared at Megan for a moment, then put his face close to hers, showing her the full flush of his loathing. 'That was a martyr we buried up there today, in case you hadn't noticed. A man who got ground to dust under the capitalist boot, the selfsame boot you kiss and polish every breathing second of your life!'

Megan felt her own anger spark. 'How dare you!' she snapped. 'I honoured my father above any other person in this world. He was the finest man I ever knew. Don't stand there pretending you bore him anything like the love I did, or my Mam and the boys did. He's been nothing but a symbol to you for years, something to point at while you're spouting your cheap prejudice against people you know nothing about!'

'Don't, now,' Jennie protested, standing close to the fire, regarding them both with wide, fearful eyes. The three boys had withdrawn to the lobby, muttering nervously to each other as they watched through the open door.

'I saw the grand lady today,' George snarled, ignoring his mother. 'Standing at a proper distance in her black finery. Seeing another one safely under the ground –'

'George!' Jennie shrieked. 'That's enough!'

'That's a foul thing to say!' Megan shouted. 'Mrs Pughe-Morgan was at the cemetery out of respect. *Respect.* It's not a word you understand, though, is it? You respect nothing.' She swallowed hard, feeling a tremor of righteous rage thrumming in her breast. 'I'll tell you something else while I'm at it, George Roberts. You go on so much about the rights of the workers, but you're determined you'll not remain one of them for much longer.'

George's eyes narrowed. 'Just what do you mean by that?' he demanded.

'You fancy yourself as a workers' champion,' Megan told him. 'A politician. One of an elite. That's a terribly capitalist ambition, George.'

His flattened hand swung up and cracked on Megan's

157

cheek. The force of the blow knocked her backwards. She tripped on the rug and fell heavily on the floor.

'My God!' Jennie screeched. 'Stop it, George! Stop this minute!'

As Megan got to her knees George crossed and stood over her. 'Now you listen,' he hissed. 'Get yourself away from here. We don't want you back shaming us, ever. I only let you come these last months because of my Da. Now he's not here. So you stay away. I'm head of this house now and I'm ordering you. Set one foot inside that door after today and I'll throw you out.' He leaned closer. 'Just stick with your own kind.' He straightened and turned, striding out into the lobby. 'Be out of here by the time I get back!' he shouted over his shoulder. A moment later the door slammed shut behind him.

Jennie came across and helped Megan to her feet. 'Mad, he is,' she mumbled, dusting Megan's coat with her hands. 'Got a stupid, terrible temper.' She looked at Megan's face. 'Lord, you can't go back looking like that! He's put a great weal on you.'

'Don't worry about it.' Megan shook back her hair and began poking loose strands into place. 'Go and sit down, Mam. I'll make you some tea.' She glanced at her young brothers, staring sheepishly at her from the lobby. 'Come on, you three, you can lend a hand. One of you get Mam's old slippers, the comfy ones. Gareth, you can go and –'

'No, Megan,' Jennie interrupted. She was looking at the table, not meeting Megan's eyes. 'Best do as George says. Just tidy yourself up and go.'

'Mam . . .' Megan stared at Jennie incredulously. 'You don't mean that. He can't stop me coming here. You're letting him play the bully. Just sit down. You need a rest and a good strong cup of tea.'

'No, I mean it,' Jennie said. 'He's the man here now and he's got to have his say. There might be a lot that's wrong-headed about George, but time'll take care of that. It's his place to say what's what.'

'But that's ridiculous! Do you realize what you're saying?

You're ill, you've had a terrible day – just look at the state you got yourself into at the cemetery . . .'

'I'm over that now.'

'You're not! You need a lot of attention. And there's the boys to think of. You can't be running after them all the time. Mrs Pughe-Morgan's told me I can have extra time off to help look after them. You'll need some more help with the money now, too. The insurance won't hold out for ever . . .'

'I said no, Megan.' Jennie's voice was firm. 'George talked it over with me. All of it. We're going to cope, no need for you to concern yourself on that score.'

Megan glanced across at the lobby. The boys had gone into their room and shut the door. She looked back at her mother. 'You're telling me I can't visit my own family? Ever?'

Jennie sighed. 'It's right what George says. You've changed a lot. It's not like you're really one of us in the old way . . .'

'Mam!'

'You even talk different from before, when you were little. It's your ways that make it uncomfortable when you're here –'

'Uncomfortable?' Megan couldn't believe what she was hearing. 'Who's ever been uncomfortable?'

'Megan. It's the truth. Even the boys feel it, they feel it as much as anybody. You went into a different kind of life. You're part of it now.' Jennie made a helpless gesture with her hand. 'You coming here – it doesn't help us any.' She turned away and stood staring at the fire.

'I see,' Megan said, not seeing at all, not understanding such complete, unconditional rejection. She turned towards the scullery door. 'I'll just wash my hands, then, and I'll be off.'

That evening, as she stood in the garden with Mrs Pughe-Morgan and watched Griffiths and Jenkin building their bonfire, Megan explained what had happened. She had intended to say nothing, but the mistress insisted on knowing how the bruise came to be on her face, and that explanation had opened the floodgate.

159

'It's almost unthinkable, Megan. But the world's full of harsh paradoxes.'

'It'll torment me,' Megan said. 'I know it will. To think that, all this time, it was my father that kept me from knowing what was happening. He always treated me the same. I was always his little girl, right up to the end.' She sighed. 'I never felt that terrible coldness, not until today.'

'Well, you've certainly changed,' Mrs Pughe-Morgan said. 'But I can't see that it's grounds for your family turning away from you.' She squeezed Megan's hand. 'I've only one small piece of advice to offer. Put the past gently to rest. There's the future waiting. Don't miss any of it by constantly looking over your shoulder. And do remember, my dear, you're where you most surely belong.'

In the next hour, as she performed the small duties that rounded off her day, Megan began to badger herself, the way she had learned to badger Alun when periodically he doubted his own ability.

She took stock of herself. She was virtually manager of an environment that had shaped and supported her. She was fed and sheltered, and she was begrudged nothing. There were friends, good and loving, and a mistress who treated her like a daughter. She had her studies with Alun Rees, and her own burgeoning affection for him.

She was, Megan decided, a very fortunate young woman.

At nine o'clock she felt it was time to go to bed. She went to the front hall as usual to make sure the door was locked. She found Mrs Foskett there, peering out of the narrow window, watching the last faint traces of light on the trees.

'I thought you'd turned in,' Megan said.

'I nearly did.' Mrs Foskett came away from the window with a tired little smile on her face. 'Then I decided I'd see the day off first.' She peered at Megan. 'Whatever happened to you, girl?'

'Oh, a bad end to things at home,' Megan sighed, touching her cheek.

Mrs Foskett grunted. 'This is your home nowadays, Megan.' She pointed at the bruise. 'Even if you did pick up one of them here, too.' She stepped close and patted Megan's shoulder. 'It must have been a terrible day for you, all round.' She began moving off slowly along the hall. 'Sleep well, Megan. And remember this, you've got to put it all behind you. Hang on to the good bits of what's past. The rest's not worth having.'

Lying in bed, Megan marvelled at the small coincidence, both the Mistress and the housekeeper giving her identical advice. She decided it hadn't been such a terrible day after all. Her father was gone, but in the end that had been a mercy. There would still be the sense of loss, the shocked realization, over and over, that Owen Roberts was no longer in the world. But there would be his memory, too, a golden ray from the past to add to the pleasures of present and future.

She would miss the family terribly; there was no way of softening that prospect. Megan could do no more than keep warm her love for them, and hope the pain of loss would be sufferable for as long as it endured. While her mother and her young brothers lived their lives apart from her, Megan would still count herself a part of their unity. No one could deprive her of that.

'A mastery of life,' she whispered softly. She would honour that hope of her father's. She felt she had the closeness of another good man to help her fulfil it. She didn't know how long it would last, and nothing at all was planned, but for the moment the determination was enough.

Minutes later, Megan fell asleep hearing Owen's voice. He was telling her she was his angel, his jewel, his flawless diadem.

Part Two

Part Two

16

On a bright Saturday in June 1913 a picnic was held on the broad lawn behind the Pughe-Morgan house. The mistress had decided that, although Alun Rees was perhaps too old for birthday parties, some kind of celebration was in order. On that date Alun turned twenty-four; it was also the day, after nearly four years of study, that he was officially awarded the Higher-Grade Certificate of Proficiency in English Language and History by the Flintshire Education Board.

'Now you're not to be embarrassed,' Megan told Alun as she led him across the kitchen and out through the back door. 'You know everybody here and they know you. You're among friends.'

Alun shrugged awkwardly. 'I'm just not used to gatherings.' He eased his fingertip around the edge of his shirt collar. 'I'm not all that accustomed to dressing up, either.'

They paused at the corner of the house, out of sight of the others who were already on the lawn. Megan stood back, appraising Alun's appearance. 'You look very smart,' she assured him.

'My sister told me I look like a store dummy,' Alun said balefully.

'She was only teasing you.' Alun was wearing the dark-blue blazer Megan had bought him for his last birthday. Although she had told him it wouldn't be necessary to wear a tie, he had one on anyway. 'Just relax and let the mistress make a fuss. She's every bit as proud of you as I am.' Grasping Alun's lapels, Megan stood on tiptoe and put a kiss on his cheek. 'Come on, then, Mr Brainy, everybody's waiting to slap your back.'

Hazy sun warmed the slope of lawn where the food had been set out on two large white tablecloths. The staff, with the exception of Mrs Foskett, sat around on the grass, chatting and laughing.

'It's just like having a day away,' Mrs Foskett remarked to the mistress. 'I never knew it could be so nice, sitting out here.' The old housekeeper was in a wicker chair, shaded by a big parasol that Griffiths had driven into the ground. Mrs Pughe-Morgan was beside her, looking cool and serene in a beige cotton summer dress.

'I don't know why we haven't done this before, Mrs Foskett. A household picnic seems a splendidly civilized event.' Mrs Pughe-Morgan pointed to the top of the path. 'Look. Here comes our guest of honour.'

Griffiths led the rippling applause as Megan and Alun approached. Jenkin added a couple of cheers and Mrs Edgar, resplendent in her red-and-yellow floral frock, waved her napkin like a flag. Alun, blushing and grinning, acknowledged it all with nods to left and right. Megan went forward to a table that had been set up under a tree and began pouring glasses of cold cider from a tall jug.

'Happy birthday, Alun!' Mrs Pughe-Morgan cried. 'And congratulations!' She came across and handed him a small box wrapped in shiny blue paper. 'A little gift,' she said. 'Something to show my gratitude to you.'

'Gratitude, ma'am?'

'For living up to my expectations, and Megan's.'

Alun undid the wrapping and turned the black leatherette box in his hands for a moment before he opened it. There was a pocket watch inside, a sterling-silver-cased hunter on a heavy silver chain. Alun lifted it out of the box and wrapped his fingers around the heavy case.

'It's . . . it's marvellous, Mrs Pughe-Morgan.' He looked at her. 'I never had a watch before. Always wanted one, since as far back as I can remember.'

'Megan told me. Carry it in health, Alun.' To his astonishment Mrs Pughe-Morgan leaned forward and gave him his second kiss of the afternoon.

A simultaneous cheer went up from the gardeners, their lad Dick, Clara the kitchen maid and Mrs Edgar. The parlour maid Agnes, sitting alone and sourly plucking at the grass, turned her head away sharply.

166

'Shameless behaviour,' she muttered, throwing loose grass into the breeze.

Agnes had come to the celebration because it would have been discourteous not to, but she had no wish to be here. Agnes didn't hold with frivolity and she didn't like Alun Rees. She didn't like the way he was allowed to come and go as he did, either. Most of all, she disapproved of Alun being alone for such long periods with Megan. Anybody with any sense could tell what they'd be getting up to behind closed doors and on their long walks together.

'Here's yours, Agnes.' Megan was bending down, offering a glass from the tray she was carrying.

Agnes glared at the golden liquid. 'What is it?'

'Cider.'

'What?' Exaggerated dismay seized Agnes's face. 'I'm not letting any of that past my lips, thank you very much.'

'It's only made from apples, Agnes,' Megan pointed out. 'It's Mr Griffiths's own recipe. The devil didn't have any hand in it.'

'Make a joke of it if you like,' Agnes snapped. 'That's a fermented drink and I'll not soil myself with it.'

'Very well,' Megan sighed. 'I'll get you some lemonade in a minute.' She crossed the lawn to Mrs Foskett and handed her a glass. 'I'd be careful with it if I were you,' she murmured. 'It didn't pass the purity test with Agnes.'

Mrs Foskett sipped from the glass and glanced across at Agnes. 'Vinegar's her tipple, I fancy. It might do that one a bit of good to get roaring drunk now and again.'

After Mrs Pughe-Morgan had proposed a toast to Alun and congratulated him again, they all set to filling their plates and devouring the food Mrs Edgar and Sarah had prepared. Griffiths and Jenkin, with their carrot-haired lad Dick beside them, lay stretched at the top of the slope, each propped on an elbow, munching contentedly and watching the others.

'Big changes there've been round here,' Jenkin murmured. 'Wouldn't have believed this, ten years back.'

Griffiths nodded. 'A picnic. Not a soul in the place doing a stroke of work.'

167

'Didn't you have no picnics before, then?' Dick asked through a mouthful of cold chicken.

Jenkin studied the boy for a minute before answering. 'No picnics, no nothing,' he said. 'It was a tight-run ship, as they say. We had a master with firm notions about staff. Work, work and more work, with time off for sleep. Then for a while we had a lot of broodiness about the place. And then, praise the Lord, things changed for the better.'

Dick took another lump of chicken and pushed it into his mouth. 'What made it all change, then?' Dick had been Mrs Pughe-Morgan's employee for two months, the third garden lad in three years. He was duller than the previous two, but he was a better worker. For that reason alone, Griffiths and Jenkin tolerated his primitive manners and his endless questions.

'Megan came,' Griffiths said.

Dick frowned at him. 'She changed the place?'

'The place, the staff, the mistress, even.'

Dick was having trouble coping with the notion. 'How could she. . . ?'

'Just take my word for it,' Griffiths said flatly. 'You see old Mrs Foskett over there? Time was when she wouldn't tolerate the servants having the kind of grub you're sitting there trying to strangle yourself with. Look at her now. All roses and light, most of the time. She's been like that since she was taken bad, five years ago. It was Megan that nursed her and some way or other worked the change. Bit of a magician, our Megan.'

'Good-looking, too,' Dick said with some feeling.

Jenkin leaned towards him. 'Best keep your admiration to yourself,' he warned. 'That's if you don't want big Alun Rees pulling your ears off.'

'I didn't mean nothing by it,' Dick said hastily, reaching for a slice of boiled ham.

'I'm sure you didn't.' Jenkin lowered his voice. 'If you're after fancying a bit of backstairs nonsense, now, I'd recommend that Agnes.'

Dick stared across at the parlour maid, who was picking sullenly at her plate. 'Her?'

'Her,' Griffiths confirmed, serious-faced and nodding slowly.

'You wouldn't think she'd let anybody near her,' Dick said. 'Got a real old scowl on her, most of the time. And Mrs Edgar says she's terrible religious.'

'That's all show,' Jenkin grunted. 'She can't go round letting all and sundry see how she feels, can she, now? That girl's got enough carnal passion locked up in her to blister you.' He winked. 'Don't go asking me how I know, neither.'

Dick sat staring at Agnes, thoughtfully chewing his ham. 'Well I never,' he murmured.

Later, when Megan had helped Clara and Mrs Edgar to clear away the dishes, she joined Mrs Pughe-Morgan and Alun by the little white summerhouse.

'Alun's been telling me about his plans for the next three years,' the mistress said. 'I must say I'm impressed.'

Megan nodded proudly. 'He took some pushing, mind you. I think for a while he didn't know what he wanted to do, until I told him.'

'Right enough,' Alun said. 'Maybe I was scared at the notion and just buried it. Teachers' college is a heady goal for a lad from Drynfor. But the more I think about it, the more I know it's what I want.' The cider had made Alun more voluble than usual; he was even prepared to let Mrs Pughe-Morgan see some emotion. 'I'd never have got beyond dreaming distance of a real education if it hadn't been for your help, ma'am. You and Megan between you . . . well, you've made something of me.'

'I think your correspondence classes should get some credit, too,' Mrs Pughe-Morgan observed. 'But if I've truly been a help to you then I'm gratified to know it.' She turned and looked out across the lawn. 'Mrs Foskett's on her own. Will you excuse me? I think I should go and chat to her for a while.'

When Mrs Pughe-Morgan had gone, Megan turned to Alun and cocked her head at him. 'Well?'

'Well what?'

'How do you think the day's turned out? Has it been a birthday to remember?'

'For the rest of my life, I should think. We've never

celebrated a birthday in our family, you know. Couldn't ever afford to, mind you, but I must say it's a pleasant thing to do.' He nodded at the retreating figure of Mrs Pughe-Morgan. 'She's a marvel, isn't she? I mean, doing all this for me . . .'

'It gives her a lot of pleasure, Alun. There's a few years' misery to make up for.'

Alun took the watch from his pocket and looked at it again. 'I'll never part with this. Not if I'm starving . . .'

Megan laughed softly. 'You won't starve. You haven't the credentials any more.'

They decided to walk in the wood for a while. Alun had been there with Megan once before and he had been charmed by the place. It had been on the afternoon, two years before, when he had finally managed to tell Megan that he loved her. She had received a letter from him two days later, an impassioned little testament to the strength of his feelings. He had used a phrase towards the end that touched Megan as deeply as anything she had ever read: 'the slow growth of our love is the mark of its permanence, for no lasting thing ever matured in haste.'

Tenderness and sound mutual respect had produced a bond that hardened steadily with the passage of time. Megan's restraint had kept their relationship within the bounds of so-called purity, although there had been times when Alun's healthy ardour had almost overwhelmed her. She had no disapproval of physical love; her informed understanding of human nature had killed off any traces of prudery long ago. Nevertheless, the act was still special to Megan. It represented nothing less than a celebration, as much spiritual as bodily. She had the strength of will, she believed, to wait until she and Alun were married.

Now the subject of marriage was raised by Alun as they strolled among the trees, watching the birds and listening to the wind-sounds through the branches.

'How long will it be, do you think?' he asked Megan.

'A few more years, I suppose.' She stopped and turned to him. 'Don't look so morose. We still have each other while we're waiting. All marriage will do is consolidate that.'

'You sound like you're tutoring me again,' Alun murmured.

'That's just me sounding practical. When you've had your teacher training you'll have a job and a bit of security. In the meantime I'm saving hard and so are you. I don't want us ever being poor, Alun. Not rich, either,' she added hastily. 'That can have its agonies. I just want us to be secure.'

'You're right, you're right.' Alun put his broad hands on her shoulders and solemnly kissed her on the mouth. When he drew back his head he was smiling. 'What did I ever do to deserve you, Megan Roberts?'

'You got a hunger for learning.'

They began walking again, their feet rustling on twigs and fallen leaves. 'They're calling me the professor at work now,' Alun said. 'It's all good-natured, though. I think some of the lads are actually proud of me.'

'So they should be. You've got ambition. It's something to be admired.'

'What about you, Megan? The way you apply yourself, the energy you put into whatever you do – I'd have thought you'd want to go for something more than being a married woman.'

Megan started to say something, then closed her mouth again tightly.

'What is it?' Alun looked at her. 'Did I say something wrong?'

'No. It's just that my own ambition's something I'm not clear about. I've deliberately never gone for any qualifications, even though I know I could get them. It's as if . . .' She paused and closed her eyes, summoning words that would come close to describing her dilemma. 'Oh,' she said at length, 'I don't know. I get torn between my restlessness to get on and the enjoyment I get working here. But don't go thinking I'd ever want to end my days in service. Even though there was a time when it seemed like a perfect idea.'

'But getting qualifications wouldn't hurt in the meantime,' Alun pointed out, bringing her back to the point.

'I've avoided qualifications because I don't ever want to stop learning. I don't want some final stamp on my education.' Megan turned and stared at Alun. 'Do you know something? This is the first time I've realized that!' An instant later she

171

recalled Mrs Pughe-Morgan's words: 'People are never aware of how much they really know until they start talking.' She continued, 'I suppose that's the truth of it, Alun. My real ambition's to go on learning and understanding more . . .' She took his hand and held it. 'And to help you, always.'

Alun tightened his fingers on hers. 'There's something I want to ask you. What you said just now, it makes it easier for me . . .'

Megan narrowed her eyes, looking mock-suspicious. 'You want to ask me something? Here? In the woods? Am I going to have to make a run for it?'

'I came here today wondering if I'd have the courage to ask you . . .'

'And has the cider done the trick?'

'Megan, I'm serious.' He took her other hand. 'I want us to get engaged.'

For a moment Megan appeared not to have heard. Then, slowly, her mischievous look faded. 'Engaged? You and me, an engaged couple?'

'What's so odd about that?'

She shrugged. 'I'm not sure. It just strikes me as an odd thought. Engaged couples are always so . . . well, staid. Correct. *Musty*. Why do you want to get engaged, anyway? You know I'll marry you.'

'I can't be sure why. Don't laugh, but I think it's because of me being steeped in all that history for so long. Betrothal, the age-old symbol and seal of a solemn promise . . .'

'That's sentimental, Alun.'

'What if it is? I'm a sentimental person.' He kept hold of her hands. 'Will you consider it, at least?'

Megan shook her head. 'No. Engagement's . . . it's like abandoning choice. And it's like being mistrusted. You have my word I'll marry you. I'll never want *not* to. Surely that's enough.'

'It's not to do with trusting you or not trusting you, Megan.' He stared intently at her for a moment. 'Engagement is an honourable estate, just like marriage.'

Megan suddenly understood. Alun was talking about honour and dignity. They had been prime obsessions in all his essays on cultural history. He was a man to whom the civilizing traditions meant everything.

'I'm only twenty, Alun . . .'

'You'll be twenty-one by the end of the year. If we left it till then . . .'

'Well . . .' Megan was moved suddenly by the intensity in him. 'Ask me again, on my birthday.'

'Oh, I will. Rely on it.' He kissed her, his mouth moving slowly and lingeringly on hers, then abruptly he stepped back. 'Damn!' He fumbled the watch from his pocket and looked at it. 'I promised my uncle I'd help him mend the yard door.'

Megan grinned. 'A momentous event,' she said.

'To my uncle it is.' Alun stuffed the watch back in his pocket and looked anxiously towards the house. 'The picnic's all over, isn't it? I didn't think it would run on so long.'

'It's over,' Megan assured him. 'And it's Saturday. I think you'll find Mr Griffiths and Mr Jenkin are going over to Drynfor for their weekly visit to the pub. I'm sure they'll take you with them in the cart.'

Back at the house they found Mrs Pughe-Morgan surveying the vegetable garden with Mrs Edgar. Alun thanked the mistress again and explained he had to be back at Drynfor.

'I thought maybe the gardeners would give Alun a ride,' Megan said. 'It's about their time for leaving.'

'They're harnessed up and ready,' Mrs Pughe-Morgan said. 'Take Alun through the quick way, Megan. You should catch them before they go.'

As Megan and Alun trotted through the kitchen they heard a bump against the pantry door, a scuffling and then a sharp, outraged whimper. Agnes appeared, stumbling, her face twisted with disgust. She was panting and spluttering as she ran for the back door. She collided with Mrs Edgar, who had come up the path behind Megan and Alun.

'Whatever's the matter, girl?' the cook demanded. 'You're half out of yourself.'

'That one . . .' Agnes pointed at the pantry. 'That *filthy* garden lad . . .'

As they all watched, Dick came hurrying out of the pantry,

173

head ducked low, and scuttled off past the parlour maid and the cook.

'Never in my *life*,' Agnes gasped, her eyes swinging wildly around her, 'not ever have I been treated in such a . . . such a . . .'

'There, there,' Mrs Edgar said, patting her shoulder. 'It can come as a shock if you're not expecting something like that.' She turned her head for an instant and flashed a grin at Megan. 'And I'm sure you weren't expecting it at all, Agnes. It's like you're always saying. Men are vessels of sin. They're a cross we have to bear.'

Megan and Alun hurried away across the hall, smothering their laughter until they were out of earshot.

On the Monday morning after the picnic, Mrs Foskett opened the front door to a tall, lean-shanked man in a coal-black suit and clerical collar. He was bald, with a fringe of straggly grey hair at the back of his head. His face, with its hooked nose and lined cheeks, gave the impression that displeasure was his only mood.

'I wish to speak to your mistress,' he announced. The corners of his mouth turned down when he spoke. 'If you will tell her it's Reverend Powell.'

Mrs Foskett already knew who he was. 'Do you have an appointment?' she asked curtly.

'I need no appointment. Just tell your mistress I'm here.' He made to move past her into the hall.

'Wait there,' Mrs Foskett said, pointing at the doorstep. 'I'll find out if Mrs Pughe-Morgan will see you.' She was pleased to see a small flash of outrage as she pushed the door to.

In the morning room the mistress was trying to compose a letter of encouragement to Mrs Pankhurst, who had been sentenced to prison earlier that year for inciting people to put explosives outside David Lloyd-George's house.

'It's old Powell, ma'am,' Mrs Foskett said. 'You know, the Baptist.'

Mrs Pughe-Morgan groaned. 'What can he want? He's bound to know by now I'm not one of his flock.'

'Will I send him away?' There was more than a trace of eagerness in the housekeeper's voice.

'No, no, I'll see him. And send along some tea, will you?'

'Certainly, ma'am.' Mrs Foskett went out. She came back a minute later. 'Reverend Powell, ma'am.'

Mrs Pughe-Morgan came forward and extended her hand. 'I don't believe we've met before . . .'

'No.' Powell shook her hand and watched Mrs Foskett leave. 'You have a very surly housekeeper there,' he said.

'Her abruptness isn't intentional,' Mrs Pughe-Morgan said lightly. 'Do take a seat, Mr Powell.'

'I prefer to stand.'

'As you wish.' She crossed to the window and sat down on a high-backed chair. 'What did you wish to see me about, exactly?'

The preacher glanced at the floor for a second, then furled a hand at his mouth and issued a short, peremptory cough. 'I regret I have to call on you about matters that I find distressing, Mrs Pughe-Morgan.' He sighed with theatrical sadness. 'Duty obliges me to do many things which, as a man, I would prefer not to do. In this instance, I have searched my heart before coming here, searched it long and hard, I may say, before deciding that the only course open to me was to bring myself to this house and speak directly to you. It's no easy task for a servant of the Lord to – '

'I'm rather busy this morning, Mr Powell. If you could perhaps get to the point . . .'

He glared at her. 'The point, madam, to make no bones about it, is that I am disturbed, as a man of conscience, to know of the low esteem in which Christian ethics are held in this household.'

'Indeed.' Mrs Pughe-Morgan folded her hands carefully in her lap. 'Tell me, Mr Powell, even if I were to run a bordello on these premises, what business would it be of yours?'

His lips pursed cautiously. 'A what?'

'A bordello. It's a place where women let men use their bodies in exchange for money.' She calmly watched the bluster building on his face. 'What I'm telling you is that you're exercising presumption, not duty.'

The preacher gulped audibly. 'My duty is defined by Holy Writ. It is not to be questioned by mortal man or woman.'

'You're entitled to your opinion. Now, before you go any further, would you care to explain what you're here for? So far, you've only made some vague reference to Christian ethics being held in low esteem in my household. Whatever does that mean?'

Powell's eyes were starting to bulge. 'I am not a man to be talked down to!'

'Nor am I a woman to be bullied by old gentlemen of spurious authority.' Mrs Pughe-Morgan stood up. 'Kindly say what you have to say. I've told you already, I'm very busy.'

'Very well.' Powell's hands worked at his sides as he swallowed back his indignation. 'I have learned that sinfulness goes unpunished in this house. I have learned that church and scripture are disdained.'

'I beg your pardon?'

'Is it not true that none of your servants is obliged to attend Sunday services?'

'It's quite true,' Mrs Pughe-Morgan snapped. 'Again I'd remind you it's no business of yours. For your enlightenment, though, let me tell you I believe that enforced faith is no faith at all.'

'There is such a thing as guidance! Sheep stray if they are not properly tended!'

'That's a very faulty metaphor, Mr Powell. And kindly don't shout – it's a rule I do enforce.'

There was a knock on the door. It opened and Megan came in, carrying the tea tray. 'Excuse me, ma'am.'

'Come along in, Megan. Put the tray on the table and stay. I believe this concerns you.'

Powell looked thunderstruck. 'My business is with you alone – '

'Nonsense. You've been issuing allegations about this household. Megan is a prominent member of the household. She's entitled to know what you have to say – and she's entitled to refute any of it if she sees cause.'

'So,' Powell grunted, 'she's Megan, is she? Hmph!'

Megan put down the tray and stood by the table, eyeing the visitor cautiously.

'To dispose of the matter of my staff and their religious torpor,' the mistress said briskly, 'they are free to do as they wish, in that direction. I merely accede to the freedom that was granted by God when he gave man choice.' She put up her hand, silencing Powell as he started to contradict her. 'Now, what's this other nonsense about sin going unpunished?'

Powell's self-assurance rallied suddenly. He stepped to the

177

middle of the floor as if he were mounting a pulpit. 'Can you deny that a young woman in your service was carnally assaulted, not two days ago, by another of your servants?' He paused to let the thunder of his accusation set in. 'And can you deny that you let the culprit go scot-free? A person could be forgiven, Mrs Pughe-Morgan, for thinking you *condoned* the fiend's action.'

For a moment the mistress simply stared at Powell, then a laugh broke shrill in her throat. She clasped her hands and leaned forward, shaking with mirth.

'I see no grounds for amusement, madam . . .'

'Oh, I do,' Mrs Pughe-Morgan gasped, still laughing. 'You're priceless, Mr Powell, absolutely priceless.' She recovered herself while Powell stood trying to glare, his confidence visibly slipping again. 'Really, you've got no grasp on reality, man. Oh, dear.' She shook her head in disbelief. 'Culprit, you say? *Fiend*? You're talking about Dick, aren't you? Dick and his misguided attempt to extract some warmth from that poor stick Agnes.'

'She is a good girl,' Powell intoned. 'Pure and unsullied.' His eyes switched suddenly to Megan. 'Not like some, who fill their heads with lewd teachings and go off with men in secret . . .'

Mrs Pughe-Morgan's anger was sudden and startling. The muscles of her face tautened in a scowl as one hand came up and pointed a steady, daunting finger at Powell's chest. 'Are you impugning Megan's virtue?' she demanded.

Powell had taken a step back. His lips moved uncertainly.

'Answer me!'

'What do you mean?' Powell asked huskily.

'To impugn', Megan said, her clear voice startling him, 'means to call into question, to challenge as false. It's a word I picked up from all that lewd teaching.'

Realizing he was now confronting two very annoyed women, Powell took another step back and bumped into a table. 'I know what I know,' he began, desperate to keep some firmness in his tone. 'The truth will out –'

'You believe the spiteful tittle-tattle of a stupid girl with

God-mania, and you use it as an excuse to come into my house and foul the air with your hysterical cant!'

Powell was shaking his head as if something were caught in his hair. 'My duty brought me here –'

'Duty!' Mrs Pughe-Morgan spat. 'You're a disgrace to the notion of duty.' She strode to the door and jerked it open. 'Get out. Don't presume, ever again, to set foot in these grounds. And take this with you as a parting thought. If you slander anyone in my service again, I'll invoke the law to silence you and extract damages.' She pulled the door wider. 'Good day, Mr Powell.'

The preacher was shaking with impotent rage as he strode out of the room. He crossed the hall and found Mrs Foskett holding the front door open for him. Her look, if anything, was sterner than Mrs Pughe-Morgan's. Powell averted his eyes and hurried past her. She shut the door with a bang before his heels had cleared the top step.

'Do come in, Mrs Foskett,' the mistress called from the morning room. 'Have a cup of tea. I'm sure we all need one.'

For a couple of minutes the women just sipped their tea and looked at one another, crystallizing their separate reactions to what had happened. Finally Mrs Pughe-Morgan said, 'That was simply extraordinary.'

'Typical of him, though,' Mrs Foskett grunted. 'He's a madman, that Powell.'

'I take it you got the gist of what he was saying?'

Mrs Foskett nodded. 'I was listening at the door, ma'am. So I could come in and turf him out, if need be. But you managed nicely on your own.'

Mrs Pughe-Morgan was looking bewildered. 'Whatever possesses people to get that way? He should be locked up for his own good.'

'He should be locked up for murder,' Mrs Foskett said. 'They say he drove his wife to kill herself, what with his eternal lecturing about sin and purity and the rest of it. Flung herself under a train in the end. According to him, she was harbouring an unclean spirit – that's what he told the others in his herd.'

179

Megan rose and put her cup and saucer on the table. 'What exactly happened between Dick and Agnes, anyway?' she asked the mistress. 'I saw her come flying out of the pantry and him running off down the garden. To tell the truth, it was one of the funniest things I've seen.'

'All he did', Mrs Pughe-Morgan said, 'was put his arm round her waist and try to kiss her on the cheek. It took me five minutes to get that out of her, after she'd come babbling to me with her wild tale about being molested. To Agnes, apparently, what he did was the prelude to some act of towering lust.' She smiled. 'I told her to forget it, it was ordinary mischief.'

'And not the vicious kind Agnes specializes in herself,' Megan observed.

'I sent for Dick and told him he mustn't bring his urges to work with him,' the mistress said. 'The poor lad was scared out of his wits. He won't go anywhere near Agnes again, that's for certain.'

Mrs Foskett nodded. 'And old Powell won't come back near here, if he knows what's good for him.' She stood up and shuffled to the table with her cup. 'What's to be done about Agnes, ma'am? She needs curbing.'

'I'm still mulling that over, Mrs Foskett. I don't want to make any hard decision until the memory of this morning's encounter is a shade cooler.'

'Very good, ma'am. But if you'll pardon me saying this, she's got poisoned with all that twisted religion she's swallowed. There's harm in her and her lot. I've not seen anything but bad come out of their do-gooding. Agnes takes it as her bounden duty to cause trouble.'

'You mean I should dismiss her?'

'It's for you to say, ma'am.' Mrs Foskett walked slowly to the door. 'If you'll excuse me, there's things I should be doing.'

When the housekeeper had left, Megan began piling the tea things on the tray.

'What do you think, Megan?' the mistress asked her. 'Should I get rid of Agnes? These past couple of years her holy fervour's been difficult to cope with. And now this little outrage.'

Megan shrugged. 'I feel the way Mrs Foskett does. Agnes is

harmful. I'd go so far as to say she's malignant. But to think of her not having a job . . .'

Mrs Pughe-Morgan went to the window, sighing. 'Look at it, Megan. Just come here and take it in.'

Side by side, they gazed out at the sunlit front lawns, the trees and the flowers.

'Now *that's* God, as far as I'm concerned,' the mistress said. 'Lush summer. The leaf-and-flower-laden abundance, as somebody called it. It's like a visible cry of joy, isn't it? When I was a girl, I used to weep over it – the ecstasy of the plants at just being there, for however short a time.' She turned to Megan. 'Some people can't see that. Their Lord's a glowering old monster whipping everybody into line and burning them if they put a foot wrong. There's Powell's merciful Creator for you.'

Megan nodded, remembering her own agonizing over the concept of the Almighty. She had thought about it a great deal at the time when her father was dying. The God of love was also the God of rickets, consumption and cancer. There was only an idiot's consolation in believing that agony was the devil's work. God was either omnipotent or he was good; all the evidence pointed to the fact that he couldn't be both.

'Nature, love and enlightenment,' Megan murmured. 'That's religion enough. There has to be a God in that trinity.'

Mrs Pughe-Morgan turned away from the window. 'I'd better get on. I've letters by the basketful to write.' She watched as Megan picked up the tray and went to the door with it. 'So,' she said, 'you think perhaps Agnes should be given a fierce warning and another chance?'

Megan nodded. 'It's the charitable way. Though we might all regret it, of course.'

'Very well.' The mistress sat down at the table and drew her writing case towards her. 'In an hour or so, tell Agnes I want to see her, will you, Megan? I'll have her in here and give her a reading from the gospel according to Gwendolyn Pughe-Morgan.'

181

18

Early on the morning of her twenty-first birthday, Megan crept out of the house to spend time alone in the garden. She wore a thick coat and a scarf over her head to shield her from the frosty wind that sliced across the estate from the edge of the Pantmynach valley. The sharp cold air was exhilarating, bringing Megan fully awake, alert, the skin of her face and hands tingling.

Frozen grass crunched softly underfoot as she walked to the far edge of the central lawn and stopped by her favourite tree, an elm Jenkin had estimated to be roughly the age of herself. Megan touched the bark, feeling the glaze of ice. An owl cried down in the wood and she took the melancholy sound as a greeting. After a long, troubled night, she felt at peace with the world.

She had gone to sleep thinking of other birthdays. The dreams that followed had been vivid, disturbing. As often happened she saw her father, a man she still missed every day of her life. She saw him ruddy-faced on a summer hillside, lifting her high and swinging her round so that sky and trees flew past her eyes in a blur. She heard her own laughter, a child's sound, and when her father set her down she came no higher than his knee.

Times had overlapped. Turning from her father she saw her young brothers, just as they had been the last time she set eyes on them, transformed into shy, foot-shuffling strangers, unwilling to take one particle of the love she bore them. When Megan moved towards them they turned away and hurried off across the grass, Tom at the rear, hobbling desperately to evade her touch.

Her father had come to her side and now she was taller, as high as his shoulder. He was thin, pale, his skin like dusty parchment.

Everything after that was a jumble. Her brother George was

pushing her, shoving her out of her father's presence and bullying her off the hillside. Megan saw Alun run towards her. It was dark now and he couldn't see her, he ran past and vanished into the blackness. Her mother, lamplit, stood frowning nearby as Megan howled after Alun. She stopped suddenly, realizing that her father had gone away. Megan stood motionless, stunned. She seemed to stay like that for a very long time.

Moments before she woke, aware that she was in her bed and that she was still sleeping, she heard Owen Roberts's voice, clear and strong; he spoke words that he had never spoken to her when he was alive, yet they were typical of him, they had precisely his stamp.

'I'll tell you this, Megan. You'll master anything you set your heart on. Setting your mind isn't enough. The mind follows the heart; it's a servant of your wanting.'

When she woke she felt wonderfully rested, in spite of the dreams. As she dressed, she knew she would go into the garden, simply because it was the one thing she wanted to do.

Now, standing by the silent elm, seeing the sky begin to lighten, Megan felt convinced her father had really come to her in those minutes before she woke up. It made nonsense of everything she believed about death and the afterlife, but it was a solid conviction all the same. She would keep it to herself and she would never question it or submit it to the tests of reason. It was too precious for that.

'Who's this trespassing in our gardens, then?'

Megan turned, startled, and saw Griffiths, bundled in his winter work-coat with its belt of string. He was wide-eyed and grinning, as if he had been up for hours.

'Good morning,' Megan said. 'I was just having a look at the dawn.'

Griffiths glanced at the sky. 'Cloudy old article it's going to be, by the colour of it. But it's still the best time of day.'

'Are you always up at this time?'

'Every day,' Griffiths said, and then, unwittingly, he gave Megan her own reason for being there. 'It's a good time to be grateful for what's past, before you get on with some more living.' He smiled warmly. 'It's especially nice to do it on your

183

birthday.' Tentatively, he leaned forward and put a stubbly kiss on Megan's cheek. 'Many happy returns, pet.'

At noon Mrs Pughe-Morgan called everyone to the dining room. There was some uneasy speculation among the staff. After announcing that they would wait for Mrs Edgar and Clara, the mistress stood at one end of the long table, saying nothing, while Megan, Mrs Foskett, Agnes and the gardeners stood at the other.

A minute later the door was opened by Agnes. She stood aside as Mrs Edgar came in, carrying a large, pink-and-white iced birthday cake.

'Happy birthday, Megan!' Mrs Pughe-Morgan cried. The others applauded as Mrs Edgar set the cake on the centre of the table.

When the small commotion had settled the mistress stepped forward, leaning both hands on the table as she beamed at the assembly. 'Today, as I'm sure you all know, Megan comes of age. I must say, though, I believe she's been a grown woman in every real sense for a long time now. Nevertheless I'm happy to observe an old tradition and congratulate Megan on having attained her majority.'

There was more applause as Megan, flushed and delighted, accepted handshakes, pats on the shoulder and a kiss from Mrs Foskett. The mistress put up a hand for order. 'It's at Megan's own request that we don't turn today into a festival. Instead we will spend an hour celebrating here with her. There's plenty of cake for everyone and a punch that's not too powerful to keep us from our work during the rest of the day.' With a fleeting glance at Agnes, the mistress added, 'For those who would rather have something less potent, there's another punch that's had the warming ingredient left out.'

'I don't suppose, ma'am,' Griffiths said, 'you've got some warming ingredient with the punch left out?'

'On New Year's Eve, perhaps,' Mrs Pughe-Morgan laughed. 'For the moment, Griffiths, you may bow in the direction of temperance, without actually embracing it.'

184

When the candles were lit everyone crowded round as Megan made her silent wish – nothing she could ever put into words, a bright, shimmering hope for the future, with Alun at its centre. She blew out the candles to loud applause.

'Presents, now,' Mrs Edgar said. She handed Megan a small oblong packet. 'There you are. It's from Clara and me.'

Megan unwrapped the paper and found an elegant crocodile leather purse with a silver lock. 'Oh, Mrs Edgar, Clara . . .'

'There's sixpence inside,' Clara said. 'For luck.'

'It's terribly good of you.'

Megan kissed them both, then turned to find Jenkin standing behind her with a packet in his hand and his lips puckered ready.

'Another one!' Megan said delightedly. 'Really, this is marvellous . . .' She kissed Jenkin, who immediately relinquished his grip on the packet. There was almost a yard of paper around the box. Megan finally got it open and gasped as the lid flipped back. There was a Swan fountain pen inside, shiny black with gold bands. She took it out and slowly unscrewed the cap. 'This is beautiful . . .'

'Really like it, do you?' Griffiths asked.

'You shouldn't have spent so much on me,' Megan chided. 'But yes, I like it. I adore it.'

'Good,' Jenkin said. 'Young Dick here chipped in his bit, too.' He nudged Dick, whose ears had turned pink. 'Didn't take much persuading, neither. His bruises should be gone by the end of the week.'

Megan was genuinely embarrassed. It was hard for these people to save anything, that had been clear enough in the eight years she had been with the household. They had responsibilities and commitments that used up most of their earnings, yet both the purse and the pen, she knew, must have cost more than ten shillings apiece. She was still trying to convey her gratitude properly when Mrs Foskett took her own gift from her apron pocket and laid it on the table.

'I hope they suit,' she said gruffly, not wishing to appear sentimental in front of the others.

'Thank you, Mrs Foskett.' Megan opened the carefully folded square packet and took out a dozen hand-stitched French

185

cambric handkerchiefs, each one embroidered with her initials. Not a month before, she had remarked to Mrs Foskett that she would like to get herself some good-quality handkerchiefs, as soon as she could afford them. 'Oh, dear . . .' A wave of emotion flooded over Megan.

'They're for blow, mind, not show,' Mrs Foskett said. She noticed Megan was having difficulty and promptly turned to Mrs Pughe-Morgan. 'Shall we start cutting the cake then, ma'am?'

'A good idea.' The mistress took up the knife and set to cutting eight generous slices, which Clara distributed on little white plates. Mrs Edgar, meanwhile, went to the kitchen and brought back the punch in two steaming jugs. Goblets were filled and handed around; as Agnes was given hers she was assured, pointedly, that it was perfectly harmless.

'Miserable little Baptist witch,' Clara whispered to Mrs Edgar as they moved to a corner with their own pieces of cake. 'Never gave Megan nothing. Not so much as a good wish.' When she had been asked if she would care to contribute a few pennies to the price of the purse, Agnes had refused bluntly. 'Not a bit ashamed of herself,' Clara went on. 'Standing there wearing her holier-than-the-rest-of-us face.'

'It's her way of showing what she really thinks of Megan,' Mrs Edgar murmured. 'Rotten through with jealousy, she is. Mind you, she's turned into a good parlour maid. She's been working like a Trojan ever since the mistress gave her that tongue-lashing.'

'I'd have give her a backside-lashing and heaved her out,' Clara observed with some feeling.

The hour passed quickly. When it was time for everyone to go back to work, Mrs Pughe-Morgan took Megan on one side.

'My gift comes later,' she said. 'Alun is going to be over this evening, isn't he?'

'Oh yes, ma'am. About seven, he said.'

'I was banking on that.' The mistress made a cryptic little smile. 'Don't work past six tonight. I want you to take plenty of time to look your best for him.'

It was half-past seven when Alun arrived. Megan greeted him in the hall wearing her best dress, dark-green pleated cotton with green silk facings and a short white ruffed collar. Her hair was tied back in a green bow, making her face seem younger and rounder.

'You look lovely,' he told her.

'And you look very smart.' Alun had on a dark-grey suit with a faint pinstripe, a retailored gift from Mrs Pughe-Morgan, who had bought it years before for her husband, but had never given it to him. 'You look like a lawyer,' Megan observed. 'But not too much like one.'

They went straight to the library, as was customary when Alun called. As soon as the door closed behind them Alun laid down the bundle of books he had brought back, put his arms around Megan and kissed her. 'Happy coming of age,' he murmured. 'I'm glad I waited for you to grow up properly.'

'It'll be nice when you do, too.' Megan ruffled his hair. 'So where are you taking me tonight? The theatre? Ballet? I've heard there's a nice opera on at the Miners' Welfare Hall . . .'

'Very witty.' Alun stepped away from her and looked slowly around the room, as if he were seeing it for the first time. 'I thought we could talk, but somewhere less spacious. More intimate.' He grinned awkwardly. 'It's a bit of a job, trying to play the suitor in here. I feel dwarfed, sometimes.'

'We can always borrow Mr Griffiths's shed,' Megan suggested, 'or there's the pantry . . .'

There was a tap on the door and Mrs Pughe-Morgan came in.

'Good evening, both of you,' she said. She stood in the doorway, hands clasped, smiling at them like a proud aunt. 'My, but you make a handsome couple.' Instead of closing the door as they had expected, the mistress opened it wider. 'Would you like to come with me? It's time I delivered my birthday present.'

Bewildered, Megan and Alun followed her across the hall. Outside the dining room Mrs Pughe-Morgan stopped, performed a small bow and threw open the door. 'A table for two, sir and madam. Please be seated. The soup is on its way.'

Speechless, Megan stepped into the dining room with Alun behind her. The large table had been moved against one wall and in its place, in the centre of the carpet, a small table had been laid with two settings of the mistress's best silver. As a centrepiece three candles burned in an ornate silver-gilt candelabra. By one of the chairs a bottle of Chablis was chilling in a bucket; on the table there was a carafe of rosé.

'Mrs Pughe-Morgan . . .' Megan began, wide-eyed.

'Come along, now,' the mistress said briskly. 'Sit down. You're having dinner in private this evening – which is, I might tell you, one of the most pleasingly civilized things to do on special occasions.'

'Aren't you joining us?' Alun asked her.

'Heavens, no. This evening is yours to share.' She smiled. 'It's my very great pleasure to make it possible for you – you'll understand now, Megan, why Mrs Edgar told you dinner would be rather late this evening.' She went to the door. 'Now, I want you to relax and let yourselves be waited upon. Enjoy it; I can't promise it'll happen too often.'

When they had sat down Mrs Pughe-Morgan left them. Alun and Megan stared at each other across the table.

'She's amazing,' Alun breathed.

'Absolutely,' Megan agreed. She was trembling with purest pleasure; the day had been perfect, and there was still so much to anticipate.

They ate splendidly. After the French onion soup they had skate cooked in butter, followed by stuffed veal escalopes with sauté potatoes and spinach. Finally they had a cold raspberry soufflé. Mrs Edgar served every dish herself and insisted she would not disturb the couple until the bell was rung. Throughout the meal Alun made light, superficial conversation, obviously enjoying himself and clearly content to save his big question until later.

When the meal was over and they sat drinking coffee, Alun shook his head at the two empty wine bottles. 'Decadent,' he said. 'If that brother of yours knew how we'd sat here and gorged ourselves, he'd assign our names to the scrolls of the hopelessly lost proletariat.'

'I'm on that list already, as far as George is concerned,' Megan said, making a face. 'Let's not talk about him, Alun. I might get indigestion, and that'd be a pity.'

'He's getting hard to ignore,' Alun sighed. 'Pamphlets through the door, little inspirational talks at work, jibes . . .'

'Jibes? At you, personally?'

Alun nodded. 'They're always *addressed* to somebody else, though. Issued just loud enough for me to hear.'

'I'm surprised he doesn't insult you right to your face. George has the courage of his own narrow-minded convictions.'

Alun smiled easily, his usual tension softened by the food and drink. 'He did bark at me directly. Once.'

Megan frowned. 'When was that?'

'Oh, a fair while ago. At about the time people were beginning to know that you and me were walking out together. George came up to me and asked how it felt to be learning class betrayal from an expert.'

'No!' Megan was shocked. 'What did you say?'

'I answered him with another question. I asked him how he'd like to try eating with no teeth in his head.'

Megan thought about it and decided it was a laughing matter. She was still laughing when Mrs Pughe-Morgan came in, carrying a small silver tray with three brandy glasses on it.

'I decided to interfere, after all,' she said. 'But only for a moment.' She put a glass in front of each of them and took the third one herself.

Alun got up, pushing back his chair hastily. 'Please, do sit down, Mrs Pughe-Morgan.'

'Not at all. Let me stand, it enhances the motherly role I'm adopting for the evening.' When Alun sat down again she raised her glass. 'Here's to you both. Health, happiness, *endeavour*.' She took a sip of brandy and closed her eyes, miming supreme ecstasy. 'Much too good for my Welsh palate, I'm sure.'

Alun pushed himself to his feet, wielding his own glass. 'To you, Mrs Pughe-Morgan, for reasons too numerous to count or retell.' Blushing suddenly at the untypically florid remark, he gulped from the glass, inhaled sharply, then said, 'We really are most grateful to you, ma'am. It's been a lovely evening.'

'Yes, lovely,' Megan echoed him.

There was an instant of perfect accord. The room seemed to hold them in a vortex of warmth, three people with an understanding that was unique for its time and its place.

'You're most kind.' The mistress inclined her head at the couple, then began moving to the door again. 'I only wanted this small moment with you. The evening is yours, as I said. Stay here as long as you wish.'

They were silent for a long time after she had gone. So often, each of them had tried using words to encompass the changes and the colour Mrs Pughe-Morgan had brought into their lives. Now their silence was immaculate testimony to their gratitude.

Eventually Alun looked up and said, 'Can we walk somewhere?'

'It'll be cold . . .'

'You can wrap up against it. I don't feel the cold.'

'The garden, then?' Megan smiled. 'I love the garden.'

It was colder than either of them had imagined. The wind raked across harsh from the east, churning the trees and hurling icy raindrops against their faces as they moved cautiously down through the orchard.

'Are you sure this is what you want to do?' Megan called out over the howl of the wind. 'You'll catch a chill without a coat on.'

'What's that?' Alun asked her, pointing to a small square building showing dull white through the fruit trees.

'It's where we keep our plants and botanical specimens. We store some, pot some and dry the others.'

'Can we get in?'

Megan's shawled head nodded. 'There's even a lamp.'

'Let's get out of this lot for a while, then.'

They reached the building and after some fumbling Megan managed to find the handle and push the old door open. They hurried inside and pushed the door shut. The sound of the wind died at once, smothered by the thick stone walls. The place was pitch dark.

'Don't move,' Megan said. 'You'll fall over something if you do. I'll get the matches.'

In the darkness, standing with his back to the door, Alun tried to separate the aromas that were crowding around his head. Sage, mint, a trace of lavender, garlic . . .

A match flared in the far corner. Megan touched the flame to the wick of a big brass paraffin lamp and the box-shaped room was bathed in soft light. She put back the glass chimney and turned to Alun. 'There. It's quite a cosy little place, isn't it?'

Alun nodded, seeing baskets, sacks, wire trays and string-bundled plants stacked like fortifications around the walls. In the middle of the floor there was a thick pile of empty sacks. He went forward and eased himself down on them, patting the space beside him. When Megan sat down he put his arm around her shoulder.

'Maybe we should have stayed in the house,' he said.

'Why?'

'I'd imagined myself standing in a light breeze, with just a touch of moonlight. This outhouse doesn't quite seem right.'

'We can go back out in the gale, if you like,' Megan murmured. She giggled and pecked Alun's cheek. 'If it's a bit of wild Welsh drama you want, boyo, we could go down to the edge of the lake.' She was deliberately mimicking his strong accent. 'Or there's a bit of a hill, like, over on the far side of the wood . . .'

'Chuck it, you.' He nuzzled her neck, making her giggle harder, then sat back, his eyes intense in the lamplight. When Megan stopped laughing he said, 'I'm asking you again, then. On your birthday, just like you told me to.' He frowned anxiously at her. Megan adopted a frown of her own.

'It really is very important to you, isn't it, Alun?'

'Yes, it is.'

'All right. We'll be engaged. As of this minute.'

Alun looked staggered. 'I expected an argument.'

'I've had time to think over all the arguments,' Megan said, 'and I still have a different view of the matter from yours – but I believe yours should have precedence.'

'I don't want you being half-hearted about this, now . . .'

'If I was half-hearted I wouldn't agree to it. I'm saying yes,

191

Alun. Now do you want to accept that, or would you rather just argue me out of it?'

He touched her cheek lightly with his fingertips. 'You're a love, so you are.' He reached into his pocket and brought out a ring box. Easing up the lid, he extended it towards Megan. 'I had to borrow one of your other rings to get the size.'

'Alun ...' Megan's voice was a whisper. She took out the ring, a thin gold band mounted with three small diamonds and a ruby, sparkling in the yellow light. 'You're supposed to be saving your money ...'

'Can't go being practical all the time,' he murmured. 'Here, let me do it properly.' He took the ring and slipped it on the third finger of Megan's left hand. 'There now. You're an engaged lady.'

Megan stared at her hand. 'It's beautiful, Alun.' In spite of what she'd thought she would feel, she believed she was overwhelmed. She looked up at Alun. 'What would you have done if I'd said no?'

He thought for a moment. 'I'd have sold the ring and bought you a set of Shakespeare.'

They embraced suddenly, hugging each other, rolling sideways on the soft hessian. Alun's mouth closed on Megan's and he groaned, prising her lips softly apart. Among the surge of feelings in her, Megan felt a moment's giddiness; *the wine*, she thought, and remembered that Alun had taken much more than she had.

'Oh, you're my precious,' he whispered. His mouth moved close to her ear and his lips traced the soft line of her jaw and her chin, then pressed firmly on her mouth again.

Megan recognized the current of this embrace, the passion within it, the very ardour she had damped a hundred times before. Now she found herself submitting, abandoning reason on the sharp swell of her own desire. The myriad happy moments of the day re-echoed in her and intensified, firing her body as Alun's hands became urgent on her. His touch was gentle but determined, drawing from her a response that she did not will, but simply allowed to grow.

'Alun, Alun ...' Moving with an instinct she hadn't known

she possessed, Megan rolled over on the sacking and spread herself to his cool probing fingers. She felt nerves tingle eagerly as Alun readied himself, and when he sank down on her she let out one sharp cry of pain that was cut off, abruptly, in a gasp of amazed pleasure.

It was over in a minute, a breathless, feverish joining of their bodies that brought them to the verge of something like madness. A churning need to be within each other ended in an electrifying jolt that abandoned them, swiftly, to soft-panting separateness, warm against each other and dazed.

'My God,' Alun breathed at length. 'I never even meant to – '

'Ssh.' Megan shifted her leg lazily against his. 'There are some things you don't discuss and write essays about.'

Alun drew back his head and peered at her face. 'You're not mad at me?'

'It wasn't entirely your doing.' She put her lips to his and gave him a long, moist kiss. 'I'm glad it's happened.'

'Truly?'

'Yes. Now don't talk. Just hold me.'

It was strange, Megan thought. She had been primed by literature, religion and hearsay to expect so much more. The act hadn't disappointed her, though she was sure it would be better next time; what she found lacking was the crushing remorse, the sense of hovering doom. In truth she felt no loss of regard for herself, no shame. Beyond a sensation of physical and mental calm, there was no strong emotion at all. The notion of saving herself until marriage, she reflected, seemed very trivial now.

'Ah, my love, my little love,' Alun moaned against her cheek.

Megan tightened her arms around him, feeling a soft, distant flicker of renewed desire. She moved her body closer to Alun's; as she did, she reflected that her coming of age was certainly complete. On top of that, her education had leapt forward quite a distance.

19

On 28 June 1914 the Archduke Franz Ferdinand of Austria and his wife were assassinated at Sarajevo, in Serbia. That single, sudden act of violence began a chain of events that would soon engulf the entire continent of Europe in war.

It was also in June that Alun's preoccupation with the European powder-keg began to trouble Megan seriously. When they were together he spoke of practically nothing else. It was as if he were mesmerized by the relentless move of events towards catastrophe.

'You've more important things to concern yourself with,' Megan reminded him. She had watched Alun's interest in other things – in his own appearance, even – gradually falling off. She had also noticed that his correspondence essay work, while it was well set-out, had begun to lose the incisive quality that had once been its hallmark. 'Stick to your own subjects,' she urged him. 'Leave the politics to politicians.'

'History's one of my main concerns,' Alun replied. 'This is history in the making.'

By July, Austria had declared war on Serbia; as Alun had predicted, Germany requested Russia to cease its own mobilization.

'We'll be involved any time now,' Alun told Megan. 'There's no way of avoiding it.'

Megan read the signs differently. Britain could declare herself neutral, just like the Italians and the Americans would. 'We're an island, Alun. We can afford to let the Europeans fight it out. They've been spoiling for a fight for years; they want to grab land off each other. We don't want their land and they don't want ours. We're no part of that conflict.'

But Alun's predictions continued to be accurate. And the more he concentrated on what was happening across the Channel, the less attention he paid to his studies. He had less than two years' work to do towards teachers' college entrance in Cardiff, Megan warned him; it was a time when he must intensify his efforts, not slacken off. In late July Alun received a curt note from one of his postal tutors in Flintshire:

Your recent work shows a looseness of structure that could be called careless. Simple lapses in grammar are compounded, in almost every paragraph, by factual errors. There are clear signs that you lack interest in your present assignments. There must be rapid and substantial improvement if you are to achieve crucial passes in the November examinations.

Megan was furious. 'Do you realize what you're doing to yourself?' she demanded. 'You're throwing away years of hard work! Years of achievement! And you're destroying your chances for the future – you'll be splitting slate for the rest of your days if you don't knuckle down, right now, and get some decent work done!'

'I *am* working hard,' Alun complained. 'I study every night – '

'And half the time you're studying German and Austro-Hungarian history,' Megan snapped, 'drawing parallels, making your neatly measured forecasts about how Serbia and Montenegro are going to move, or how long it'll be before Brussells is occupied – '

'Don't shout at me, Megan.'

'You need shouting at! You need banging over the head until you get back your sense of proportion!'

Germany went to war against Russia on the first of August. Three days later, Britain declared war on Germany. An hour after Mrs Pughe-Morgan heard the news, she called Megan to the morning room.

'I'm co-ordinating with a group in Cardiff and another two in London,' she explained. 'I'll need your help, Megan. We must make a two-pronged effort – first, to get it across to the people how futile this war is, and second to send what help we can to the young men who'll be shipped over there in boatloads.' She stopped herself suddenly. 'You *do* agree with me that the war's unnecessary, I take it?'

Megan assured her she did. 'I'll be what help I can, naturally, ma'am. But I'm not sure I'm so well organized as you are at this kind of thing.'

'Don't worry about that, my dear. We'll both be following leaders, in effect. All that's needed is your enthusiasm.'

Megan's enthusiasm would have been stronger if she hadn't been so distracted by Alun's scholastic decline. It alarmed her. One afternoon, a week after the declaration of war, as she and Mrs Pughe-Morgan were in the linen store packing spare bedsheets, Megan voiced her fears.

'I'm worried sick about what's happening. He just doesn't seem to care any more.'

'You should have told me sooner,' Mrs Pughe-Morgan said. 'Since you and Alun have been engaged I've been less inclined to monitor his work.'

'I kept hoping he'd shake himself out of it. But he's obsessed with the war. All the energy he had for his work is getting poured into his study of the campaigns, the strategies and tactics. If he had to sit his finals with the European conflict as the only subject, they'd award him a degree on the spot.'

The mistress paused and gazed absently around the shelves at the snowy abundance of linen. 'I suspect what's happened is that Alun's found his speciality. His true focus of interest. Do you remember how he tackled the Peloponnesian War? That essay he wrote?'

Megan nodded. 'He took six pages to discuss the Athenian successes at Pylos and Sphacteria and another five dissecting the defeat of Lysander.' She smiled faintly. 'I've kept a copy of that. It's a brilliant piece of work.'

'And a clear enough pointer to his persuasions,' the mistress said. 'With some people its gambling, with others it's drink or women – for Alun it's warfare.'

'The difference in this instance', Megan said gloomily, 'is that he's taking it personally. He sees himself as being involved. This war's *happening*, he's living through it.'

'I'm sure his sense of balance will prevail, Megan.' Mrs Pughe-Morgan sounded sincere, but not at all convincing. 'Have you given him a good talking-to?'

'Half a dozen good talkings-to. But I can't crack the shell he's put round him. I'm sure he does try to work, but the distraction gets stronger all the time. Do you know, he spent ten minutes the other night trying to interest me in the reconstruction of the French Cabinet. I could have screamed.' Megan slapped the final sheet on top of the box she was packing, remembering her exasperation and how near she had come to hitting Alun.

'What about his family? Can't someone there make him see the harm he's doing himself?'

Megan shook her head. 'They'd prefer him to go on being a miner. They don't really hold with Alun having an education. They don't hold with me much, come to that. I've only spoken to his mother once and a couple of times to his sister. They're a bit like my own family where I'm concerned. You know, wary, uncomfortable.'

As with so much in her life that had been painful, Megan reflected, her brother George was a key ingredient in the Rees family's coolness towards her.

Alun had explained it to her. His mother's built-in class resentment had been fuelled by a few of George Roberts's pamphlets. From his speeches, too, she had picked up more bigotry and a clear notion of just how much distaste, bordering on hatred, George felt towards women of Mrs Pughe-Morgan's station. And towards his own kind who served the gentry.

'It's only good plain sense he's making,' Alun's mother had told him. 'You want to listen to some of it and think on. Stop getting ideas above your station.'

Alun had asked his mother what that meant.

'My meaning's clear enough,' she'd said. 'You going over to that house, letting Mrs Big-Bug fill you up with her notions. You're not her kind. Sucking up to her won't make it no different.'

Later, when Mrs Rees had found out that a close relationship had developed between Alun and Megan, her warnings became shriller and more frequent.

'Of all the girls you could take up with, why's it have to be that one? Her brother's got her mapped right, and you'll be the next one catching it from him.'

197

'George Roberts,' Alun had told his mother calmly, 'is a thick-skulled, loud-mouthed bully-boy.'

'Oh? And what's his sister, then? Cotton parading as silk. All airs and graces.'

The war over Alun's visits to the Pughe-Morgan house and his emotional involvement with the maid hurt Alun a good deal less than Megan.

'It's nothing,' he had insisted. 'My Ma's never had a right-headed notion about anything, as far as I can remember.'

'She seems to be in agreement with a lot of people when it comes to my airs and graces,' Megan had sighed.

'I made up my own mind about that,' Alun told her. 'They're just picking things up the wrong way, that's all.'

'What do you mean?'

'It's not airs and graces you've got, Megan. It's an air of grace.'

Mrs Pughe-Morgan patted Megan's hand, snapping her out of her reverie. 'I'm sorry, Megan, I really am.' She paused for a moment then said, 'The best thing – the only thing, I fancy, is to keep on at Alun. Remember what water does to a stone.'

'Yes, ma'am,' Megan sighed. 'And I can remember how long it takes, too.'

Throughout September the bulletins from Europe grew more numerous and harrowing. Everyone talked about the war; it displaced health and the weather as a primary topic of conversation. General Kitchener's appeal, first published in the newspapers, was soon pasted on notice boards and the walls of public buildings and houses in Drynfor:

YOUR KING AND COUNTRY NEED YOU
A CALL TO ARMS
An addition of 100,000 men to
His Majesty's Regular Army is immediately
necessary in the present Grave
Emergency

Mrs Pughe-Morgan was energetic in putting across her own point of view. Pamphlets printed in London and Cardiff were distributed in Drynfor and to several of the outlying villages and farms. They discredited the conflict as a barbaric game of territory-grabbing, and reviled Kitchener and Sir John French as warmongers with no regard for the lives in their charge. A personal message from Mrs Pughe-Morgan was attached to each pamphlet, reminding the local people that the flower of young Welsh manhood was being snatched away to bloody battlefields by false promises and cheap emotional appeals to patriotism.

Megan, in the meantime, with the enthusiastic support of Mrs Foskett, Mrs Edgar and Clara, was organizing soldiers' parcels and bulk supplies of food and warm clothing. Appeals to other landowners for donations met with a good response; by doing no more than giving what they could easily afford, they were encouraged by Megan and the mistress to feel they were making a positive contribution to the welfare of the troops.

A visitor to the house in late September brought about a significant change in Megan's view of the war. Violet Rawlings, a cousin of Mrs Pughe-Morgan, was a senior nursing sister with the VADs, the Voluntary Aid Detachments, who were groups of nurses formed by the Red Cross to staff the field hospitals in Europe. Violet was thirty, and she had been trained in nursing at St Bartholomew's Hospital in London. She had come to the house during a spell of leave to help with the organizing of supplies, which she was authorized to send abroad through the services of the Joint War Committee, formed by the Red Cross and the Order of St John of Jerusalem.

Violet was soft-voiced and pale, with large brown eyes that looked distant and alert by turns. On the day of her arrival she sat in the morning room and talked to Mrs Pughe-Morgan and Megan about her experiences in France.

'The conditions are primitive,' she told them. 'I've seen newspaper reports back here in Britain that talk about well-organized, well-equipped hospitals. I've even seen letters praising the efficiency and morale of the nurses.' She shook her head sadly. 'It's all lies. Propaganda. It's been chaos right from the start. There's no overall control of the hospitals, there aren't enough of them, and half the women wearing nurses' uniforms have no right to wear them at all.'

Mrs Pughe-Morgan was surprised. 'I'd heard there were eighty thousand volunteer nurses from this country already overseas . . .'

'There are,' Violet said. 'The hospitals are flooded with them. Some have good training, but most haven't. The VAD apron with its comforting red cross covers a multitude of shortcomings. The majority of VADs come from the upper and middle-classes. They haven't all had my training or experience.'

'Violet is something of a freak,' the mistress explained to Megan. 'At the time when other girls of her age and background were attending society balls and spending their weekends at house parties in Esher, she'd already opted to get herself a training. She's the only woman in our entire family who ever did.'

'Don't the VADs have any training, then?' Megan asked.

'Of a sort,' Violet said. 'It's called an express nursing course. About three months long, in most cases. A properly trained nurse spends a minimum of three years studying and working in the wards – and most of *them* are from working-class and lower-middle-class families. They know about hardship and hard work. But in the field hospitals the girls from the upper reaches of society expect to take automatic precedence over the trained nurses.'

'And are they allowed to?' Mrs Pughe-Morgan asked.

'Far too often. It would be a bad enough state of affairs in an ordinary hospital. In a battlefield a nurse needs a strong stomach, strong nerves and tons of experience. We have the ludicrous situation of so-called senior nurses fainting, panicking, having hysterical fits, while their juniors have to buckle down and get on with the job.'

Megan was intrigued. She was listening to a professional woman, a person with a breadth of experience she could only guess at. 'The injuries you have to deal with,' she said, 'are they very bad?'

'They're appalling, most of the time. Blast wounds, gangrene, chests and bellies riddled with machine-gun bullets. Three weeks ago I saw a twenty-year-old boy who'd had both his legs torn off when a shell exploded in his trench. He was too deeply in shock to be given ether.'

'My God,' Mrs Pughe-Morgan said. 'What did you do?'

'Three of us had to hold him down while the surgeon sawed off the ragged ends of thigh bone and stitched the flesh around the stumps. It took an hour, and the soldier was awake and in agony the whole time.'

'Horrible,' Mrs Pughe-Morgan groaned. 'Simply ghastly.'

'Are there many like that?' Megan asked.

'Dozens,' Violet assured her, 'hundreds. No two are the same. Boys, a lot of them are, children who lied about their age just so they could fight for king and country. This land of ours is going to be littered with cripples and amputees for decades after the war's over.' Megan noticed that as Violet put down her teacup there was a steady tremor in her hand. 'We work for twelve hours at a time when there's been a heavy raid, and the incoming stream of wounded is as thick when we go off duty as it was when we came on.'

'It's butchery,' Mrs Pughe-Morgan sighed. 'And it's all for nothing.'

During the remaining two days of Violet's visit, Megan learned a good deal more about a nurse's life at the front, and about the savagery and squalor that typified a soldier's day. The men in the trenches were all infested with lice, Violet said, and they were often bitten by rats while they were asleep. Field dressings for wounds were sometimes so badly contaminated with filth from the trenches that they caused serious – occasionally fatal – infections. Soldiers blinded by mustard gas were led back to the hospitals strung together with ropes, their burned eyes bound in filthy rags.

'There's no vestige of comfort or hygiene available to anyone on a battlefield, unless he happens to be an officer,' Violet said bitterly. She told Megan about special underground quarters fitted with oil heaters and beds for the officers, while a few hundred yards away common soldiers lived in muddy, freezing dugouts where severed limbs were sometimes used to prop the entrances. There were separate arrangements in the hospitals too. Officers had priority when medical supplies were scarce, and whereas an ordinary soldier would be bedded down in any available corner, usually without a mattress, officers had individual rooms or tents with real beds and clean linen.

On the evening Violet left, Megan and Mrs Pughe-Morgan stood with her by the carriage while Griffiths loaded her bags and the three large boxes of supplies she was taking back to London.

'You will be careful, now,' the mistress said. 'The papers say the fighting's getting worse. I hate to think of you out in the thick of it.'

'I'm not going to be alone, Gwendolyn. And I'm getting to be quite an old hand at saving my own skin.' She kissed Mrs Pughe-Morgan's cheek. 'Just you keep the boxes and parcels rolling over to the railway station. They're badly needed.' She turned to Megan. 'It's been a pleasure meeting you,' she said. 'I hope I haven't given you nightmares with all my grisly reminiscences.'

'Not at all.' Megan shook Violet's hand. 'It's been a privilege to share this time with you.'

A privilege and an education, Megan thought later when she was alone in her room. Two striking things had happened because of her meeting with Violet Rawlings. She had sensed the powerful dedication in a person who was truly exceptional, and she had been given a shockingly revised view of war.

Violet was an inspiration, Megan decided. She was a woman who had set aside the comforts of her background to give direct aid to the helpless and suffering. Megan had occasionally felt the prodding of that same impulse. There was a part of her that wanted to help people who were sorely in need; she had known it strongly when Mrs Foskett had been taken ill, and again when her father was dying. Megan felt honoured to have been near a woman who had actually seized that impulse and had seen it through to fruition.

As for war, Megan now felt a total revulsion. Before, although she had seen no sense in it, she had pictured men going gallantly into battle, brave souls armoured in their valour and bearing their colours with pride. Now she knew that was all wrong. They were sad, deluded, frightened souls, shamefully exploited and living like the rats which fed off them. They were mercilessly bludgeoned, maimed and mutilated in a conflict that robbed them of their pride and their dignity. War reduced men to beasts, Megan realized now. It was an obscenity.

Two evenings later, Alun came into the library and found Megan wearing her extra-determined look, the one she saved for times when she would not be diverted from her decided course.

'Sit down, Alun.' She watched him do as he was told, his eyes troubled, hands nervous on the table. 'There's less than two months left,' she told him. 'Two months, then you'll have to face the examination board. I've decided I'm going to work with you every night until you're up to standard. Instead of bleaching your brains with the degrading muck of war and politics, you'll get your mind back where it belongs. I've some holiday time due to me, and the mistress has agreed we can –'

'Megan, listen –'

'No, you listen. You can say I'm domineering, you can call me a tyrant and even a bitch if you like, but I'm going to get you through those exams, Alun. Your future is *my* future, too.' She pointed to two piles of books on the table. 'Starting tonight, we're going to put you back on the rails and get up a head of steam.'

'I'm not going to take the exams, Megan.'

She blinked at him and felt her heart jolt. 'What? What are you talking about, for heaven's sake? Of course you're taking them, it's what you've worked for, driven yourself for –'

'I can take them later.'

'Later? Of course you can't!' Megan's eyes glinted with sudden anger. 'There isn't the time, you have to get your exam passes *now*!'

'They'll make allowances,' Alun said quietly. 'There's more important things I have to do.'

'Oh?' Megan glared at him. 'Such as?'

'I'm joining the army.'

The words struck Megan like a hammer blow.

Alun's face was calm. 'I've made up my mind, Megan. There's no way you can make me change it.'

203

20

After nights of frightening dreams and bouts of wakefulness when she could do no more than stare at the window, Megan found there was no change in herself. She still couldn't accept the idea of Alun leaving her. She had listened to his reasoned arguments, she had even agreed with a lot that he said, but still she was gripped with fear and a terrible sense of abandonment.

I am still the man you first knew.

His words repeated themselves to her every day as she went about her work. Alun hadn't simply said that, he had proved it. He had spent an hour patiently reminding Megan about the bonds that still held them, and about the sense of order that they shared. Megan had first loved him, among other things, for his principles and his integrity. It was those same principles, Alun told her, the same belief in dignity and honour, that had brought him to decide he must join in the war.

'The Germans have forced this, Megan,' he told her. 'We can't just stand with our hands at our sides.'

'War is filth, Alun!'

In something close to breathless anger Megan had put forward her pacifist views to him. She repeated the tales Violet Rawlings had told her, the harrowing catalogue of meaningless atrocities that underlined the waste and shamefulness of war.

'I see it differently,' Alun told her. 'We're being assaulted. Bullied. We're having our political and historical heritage torn to pieces. We have to defend ourselves.'

'You're talking about going out and killing people. That's plain barbarity.'

'No, Megan, I'm talking about a lot more than that. I have beliefs. They're being challenged with force. We've got a fight on our hands. I couldn't live with myself if I didn't cross that Channel and stand up for what I believe in.'

Megan's earlier fears seemed trivial now. She had been worried about his wandering attention, his preoccupation, never realizing that Alun was being drawn towards a decision that would physically involve him in armed conflict. He had considered it all very carefully. His reasons were sound.

Megan's own argument, by comparison, had seemed feeble. She had finally accused him of not loving her. 'How can you just walk away from me and all you've worked for? Am I that unimportant to you? Is your education suddenly worthless? You say you love me as much as you ever did, but you prefer to turn your back on everything we've both cared for and go marching off to a filthy battlefield somewhere . . .'

Alun's answer had silenced her, although the bitterness still raged inside. 'Our love isn't threatened,' he said. 'It's solid as a rock. But other things I love *are* threatened. And I'll defend them, Megan, as hard as I'd defend you if you were ever in danger.'

Mrs Pughe-Morgan gave Megan as much support as she could. While she agreed with none of Alun's reasons for joining the army, she could understand his idealism. She tried to convince Megan that he was taking an honourable stand.

'His principles are much bigger than he is, my dear. Alun has a fierce intelligence and sometimes, I think, it blinds him to the other issues. But he's determined and we must accept that. I can understand how raw you feel – but try to remember that he's abandoning nothing. As Alun sees it, he's upholding everything that matters.'

Five days after he had broken the news, Alun walked with Megan across the stretch of moorland between the estate and the north-western slope of the Pantmynach valley. They walked over a mile, talking almost shyly about every trivial topic they could muster, cautiously avoiding the subject of Alun's departure. Finally, as they stood on a hillside above a wood and watched the blaze of the sunset on russet and yellow leaves, Alun put his arm around Megan's shoulder and drew her close.

'I'll be gone in two days,' he said.

Megan stiffened. 'I'd thought it would be longer.' She kept

her eyes stubbornly averted, as if nothing mattered more to her than the trees and the flurrying birds.

'They're getting them in fast, Megan. Half a million recruited already, and they're starting the recruitment of another half-million soon.'

'Cannon fodder.'

'Megan, don't –'

'It's what I think.' She tried to move away, but Alun kept his arm firmly around her. 'Your life will be nothing over there,' she murmured bitterly. 'Pride and principles have nothing to do with what's going on. If you'd open your eyes you'd see that.'

Alun bowed his head and kissed her hair. 'I don't want us to argue, Megan . . .'

'Nor do I. But you're making it hard for me, Alun. You've hurt me and I can't help letting you know it. I've dreamed about so much for you, *prayed* for it, and you go and do this.' She looked up at him. 'I know all about your reasons, there's no need to tell me them again. What I don't understand is how you can walk away from everything so . . . so easily.'

'But it hurts, Megan.'

'Does it? I wouldn't say you look like a man in any kind of pain. As far as I can tell, you're fidgeting to get on that boat and go chasing your dreams of glory.'

'That's not fair.'

'It's accurate.'

He tried to kiss her but she pulled away and began running down the hillside. Alun watched for a moment, then ran after her.

'Megan, stop! Megan!'

She reached the trees and ran through a shadowed hollow to the dark centre of the wood, her feet churning up leaves and dried earth, her eyes blurred by tears. The impulse to run was wild and senseless – she knew that and she didn't care. The new hurt in Megan had resurrected all the old ones, making her frightened, angry.

'Megan! Please!' The dense trees muffled Alun's voice as he raced along the twisting paths, seeing Megan one moment and losing sight of her the next. He heard a sudden crunch and

Megan's sharp cry. Breathless, he stopped and tried to make out where she was. 'Megan? What's happened?' There was a shrouding silence, with only the faint rustle of wind in the treetops. Then Alun heard Megan groaning, somewhere off to his right. 'Stay where you are!' he called out. 'I'm coming!'

He found her sitting at the foot of a tree with her hands cupped around her face.

'My God, what's happened?' Alun knelt by her, holding her in his arms. 'What is it?'

Megan took her hands away and looked at him. Her cheek was smudged with leaf mould, but apart from that she seemed unharmed. 'I ran into a branch,' she said in a small voice. 'Winded myself.'

'Oh, Megan, Megan . . .'

She began crying against Alun's shoulder, holding onto him as tightly as he held her. 'I'm feeling terribly ashamed of myself,' she said.

'You've no cause to be.' Alun kissed her brow, her cheek, rocking back and forth with her. 'It's me that's causing all the trouble.'

'And I'm the one who's full of self-pity.' Megan sat back, wiping her cheek with her sleeve. 'I've been building a sorry picture of myself, Alun.' She nodded at the low-slung branch that had felled her. 'I think I collided with that just in time. There's nothing like a shock for knocking some sense into you.'

After a time, when Megan was in control of herself again, they stood up and brushed the twigs from their clothes. 'Let's go back to the hill,' Megan said. 'I want to see the sun go right down over the horizon.'

For ten wordless minutes they watched the banks of cloud turn from misty blue to yellow, then to a rich copper colour, as the sun's disc dipped below the hills to the west.

'If I watch it go down at night, will you, too?' Megan asked.

'When I'm over the water, you mean?'

'Yes.'

'Of course I will,' Alun said. 'Every chance I get. We'll share it.'

Suddenly Megan held him fiercely, her eyes glinting in the

last orange of the sunset. 'I'm going to miss you so terribly. I feel the pain of it already. Promise you'll keep yourself safe, as safe as ever you can.'

'I promise.'

'And you'll write? Every day?'

Alun smiled. 'If that's possible, yes . . .'

'Oh God, Alun.' Megan threw her arms around his neck and kissed him, keeping her mouth clamped to his until they were both out of breath.

'You're not angry with me any more, then?' Alun asked softly against her cheek.

'I'm mad at you,' she said. 'Blazing mad. But that's neither here nor there, is it?'

Alun's hands slid along her back as he leaned forward, lowering her urgently to the ground. Hungrily Megan's lips closed on his as he pushed back her skirt and readied himself between her thighs. Megan groaned deep in her throat and thrust her hips at him.

'Megan, Megan.' Alun's sigh mirrored the rhythm of his body. In one blinding, perfect instant of union they soared beyond reality. The surging need drew a long cry from Megan; Alun buried his face in her hair and submitted to the sudden, devastating spasm that gripped them both. When it passed they lay breathless, wondering at the fierceness of their love.

They rose as the last light was draining from the hill and began walking back to the house. When they reached the foot of the main drive they stopped and kissed tenderly.

'I'll see you tomorrow,' Alun said. 'And then, the day after – '

'Alun, I won't be seeing you off.'

He peered at her in the darkness. 'Why not?'

'Because I'm entitled to just a little bit of self-delusion. I'm going to pretend there was no parting. I don't ever want to be parted from you. There'll be just a widening of distance, for a while.'

Alun nodded. 'If that's what you want, my darling.' He kissed her again and felt a warm tear on her cheek.

21

On the fourth anniversary of Owen Roberts's death, a cold Sunday morning in October, Megan decided to walk across to Drynfor and visit his grave. She had been to the small cemetery a number of times since Owen had died, but 1914 had been a busier year than most and Megan hadn't tended the plot as often as she would have liked. She took along a canvas bag packed with flowering shrubs Griffiths had cultivated for her; on top of the bag was a trowel and a pair of stout gardening gloves.

The cemetery was deserted. Megan walked slowly along the sunlit rows of graves, reading the inscriptions on the rough tombstones. Occasionally she noticed – each time with a little shock – the names of people she remembered from childhood, men and women she had never realized were dead. She saw, too, the grave of Barry Meredith, a boy from Conway Terrace who had been killed by a fall of slate thirteen years before, when he had been playing with friends up at the workings. Megan stared at the tiny grave, thinking how strange it was. All these years later Barry was still only nine. He would always be nine.

As she approached her father's grave she noticed the difference at once. Where there had once been an oblong of turned earth, now there was a flattened rectangle covered with green marble chips; in place of the stone flower vase there was a large headstone, black marble with gilded lettering.

ERECTED TO THE MEMORY
OF
OWEN GEORGE ROBERTS
1856–1910
'He Sleeps in the Peace of Eternal Love,
Far from the Woes of Drear Life'

Megan could scarcely believe the vulgarity of the thing. Its shiny, curlicued corners flanked the carved effigy of a sullen angel with downcast eyes. To complete the mawkish effect there were two trumpet-shaped flower-holders, one on either side, both empty.

Only George, Megan thought bitterly, could have put up such a hideous memorial to their father. It was a mark of her brother's poor grasp of taste, and his complete misunderstanding of the kind of man Owen Roberts had been. In life, Owen would have laughed himself silly at a monstrosity like that.

Megan had heard of George's rise in the world, partly from Alun and partly from a brief note in *The Socialist Newsletter*, which Mrs Pughe-Morgan had delivered to the house with all the other political journals she could lay her hands on. The report said that George had been appointed secretary to the Slate Miners' Union in Abergele. According to Alun, he had left the slate workings on a blistering note of warning to the management; the day of the worker was coming, he had told them, so the handmaidens of oppression should watch out.

There were consolations, Megan thought, as she stood shaking her head at the tombstone. George's new job brought with it a house and a good salary. He had moved the family with him, Alun told her, and he had found good jobs for Gareth and Billy. Megan was pleased about that, and she didn't doubt for a minute that her mother was being well cared for. But God, she thought, that stone . . .

'It's rather . . . uh . . . imposing, wouldn't you say?'

Megan turned and saw Dr Watkins standing a few feet away. There was no mistaking the irony in his voice, or in his smile.

'Overwhelming, doctor.' She moved to where he was standing and shook his hand. 'I thought I had the place to myself,' she said, then hastily she added, 'in a manner of speaking, of course.'

'I'm here most Sundays.' Watkins pointed to a grave at the end of the row with a bunch of fresh flowers on it. 'My sister's buried there. There's a curious kind of companionship, just standing by the grave for a while.'

'I know,' Megan said. 'I'm going to find it harder to feel that in future, mind you.'

'I'm sure a bit of weathering will work wonders,' Watkins

said. 'I never yet saw the gaudy edifice that didn't turn quite respectable after a few North Welsh winters.'

Megan looked down at her bag. 'I was going to plant some shrubs,' she said. 'I'm not sure it's such a good idea any more.'

'Of course it is. They enhance anything. Come on, I'll give you a hand.'

They spent twenty minutes digging in the plants around the base of the stone. When they had finished, Dr Watkins winked at Megan and told her that, given a good spring, the shrubs would probably grow tall enough to soften the garish effect of the memorial.

'And now', he said, 'I'd like to suggest a short constitutional around the town, followed by some of my housekeeper's excellent coffee. What do you say?'

It was such a simple thing the doctor had suggested, a pleasant hour's diversion that Megan agreed to at once, yet the effect of that hour was profound and disturbing. For the first time since she had left home, over eight years ago, Megan became aware of just how much she had changed.

'I'd never have believed this,' she said as they came to the bottom of Conway Terrace. 'I was born here. I hardly ever spent a day away from Drynfor until I turned thirteen. But it's all strange to me now.'

'I get the same feeling in Swansea,' Watkins said. 'I grew up there, but there's no sense of familiarity when I go back.'

'It's uncanny.' Megan looked along the row of little houses, remembering who lived in each one, recalling what some of them were like inside. She had nostalgia for this place, but now it felt as if her fond remembrance was for a town that didn't exist any more. 'It's only today that I've noticed it – how separate I am from the place.'

'And the people?'

Megan shrugged. 'A lot of them have died or moved on. The rest have either forgotten me or turned strangers for reasons of their own.'

There was a hollow, desolate feeling growing in Megan as they walked along Conway Terrace and stopped outside her family's old house. It was empty now, the door partly open, dust and debris lying in drifts along the walls of the lobby.

'Do you want to go in?' Watkins asked her.

'No. I don't want to see it like this.' Memories tumbled, echoes of her father's voice and the boys' racket in the yard beyond. Unaccountably, Megan wanted to run, she longed suddenly to be away from the mean little dwelling and the narrow terrace. 'Lord,' she said, 'it's all too depressing.'

They walked back slowly through the centre of the town and crossed the square towards Dr Watkins's house. On the way they passed a few people who watched Megan guardedly, averting their eyes when she looked directly at them.

'It was never the friendliest of communities,' the doctor observed as he led the way up the steps to his front door. 'It may seem a harsh thing to say, but I believe you're best out of it.'

As they sat in the drawing room sipping their coffee, Dr Watkins broached the topic of Alun's military service. 'How's he enjoying it, now he's got the reality to contend with?'

'Well, it's been a month now, and so far I've only had three letters. But, from what I can gather, he's seeing plenty of action.'

Megan had memorized every line, she had pored over the closely written pages and tried to detect the truth hidden under Alun's bland, almost stiff cataloguing of the daily events at the front. She was sure he was disillusioned already; there hadn't been one word about the rights or wrongs of the war, no hint of the idealism that had driven him into uniform.

'You must miss him badly,' Watkins said sympathetically. 'You have strong ties.'

The remark put sudden fear into Megan. The word 'ties' had been in her mind since they came away from Conway Terrace. She had believed her ties with Drynfor were strong and permanent, yet in just one hour she had discovered they were gone, totally. What if Alun, for all the binding strength of his love, should find himself an emotional stranger to her when he came back? Time and distance seemed to cancel ties. Time, distance and a change of viewpoint.

'Is there something the matter?' Watkins was leaning

212

forward in his chair, staring at Megan. 'You've gone pale, my dear.'

'Just a passing thought, doctor.' She forced a smile. 'Some thoughts do that to me.'

'Probably because your physical resistance to them is low.' He raised a professional finger. 'It's my opinion you need a tonic. The stresses and strains of separation can debilitate a person, you know. Before you leave, I'll give you a bottle of something I've sworn by for years. Take it regularly, together with a restorative piece of advice – stop worrying.'

'My worrying shows, does it?'

'Indeed it does. And it's destructive. I've had enough opportunity to study that scourge. There's always been a lot of it trotting through my surgery, disguised as headaches, lassitude, insomnia and general collywobbles. Since this war's been on and so many young men have gone overseas, worry has flourished, Megan.'

She sighed. 'It's hard not to be worried.'

'But it's worthwhile fighting it. In your case, I'd say the best thing is to divert yourself. You've an active, inquisitive mind. Drive it, get your nose buried in some more books. The idle mind is worry's playground.'

'Studying makes me restless, sometimes,' Megan said.

'Restless?'

'Yes. I gain some knowledge and I can't use it. It's not always like that, but some of the time – well, medicine's an example. I'm fascinated by it. But I somehow want to do more than just *know* about it. It's frustrating to understand illnesses and not be able to do anything about them.'

'But knowledge is never wasted,' Watkins insisted gently. 'Pursue it, and who knows where it will lead. Do as I say, drive yourself.'

For a week afterwards Megan took Dr Watkins's advice and scarcely allowed herself a vacant moment. Her duties at the house kept her occupied during the day and in the evenings she revived her studies. She set herself nightly targets. On Monday, tired as she was, she wouldn't allow herself to go to bed until she had read all about Bright's disease – the cause, the method of discovering it, the symptoms and the treatment. Tuesday was set aside for a special study of dropsy. On Wednesday she made cautious inroads on the mysteries of infantile paralysis, and by Friday she was struggling with all her available literature on typhoid fever.

The programme worked. Megan was so tired by the end of every day that she fell asleep minutes after the light was turned out. She was less preoccupied during the day, she noticed. Her capacity for worry had been reduced. She stopped brooding so much about Alun; instead she went about her work with no more than a proper concern for him. She never allowed herself to speculate in areas where there were no available answers.

In the final week of October, however, Megan began to wonder if perhaps she was working a little too hard. Her outlook remained balanced and bright, but by early evening she felt desperately tired. She began doubling her doses of the tonic and went to bed an hour earlier. Even so, the tiredness persisted.

'What you need', Mrs Foskett told her one morning, 'is an infusion of Culver's Root.' They were sitting at the table in the housekeeper's cottage, going over the lists of supplies to be ordered for Christmas. Twice in ten minutes Mrs Foskett had remarked on Megan's poor colour. Now, having prescribed a remedy, she got up and started rummaging in her herb cabinet.

'I've already got a tonic,' Megan told her. 'Dr Watkins gave it to me.'

'Chemical rubbish.' Mrs Foskett had her head halfway inside the box, peering at the labels. 'Nature has an answer to every ill, Megan. And the best of them are in here.'

'What will Culver's Root do for me? I don't think I've come across it before.'

'It goes to work on the liver. That's where half a human being's troubles lie, right in the liver.' Mrs Foskett found the packet she was looking for. She handed it to Megan. 'A sprinkle in a cup of hot water, first thing in the morning. There's enough in there to last you a week – and a week should do it.'

Megan slipped the little envelope into her dress pocket. 'I'll give it a try, then.'

'See that you do. You don't look right at all.' Mrs Foskett sat down again. 'Peaky. It's always an early sign of trouble, looking peaky.'

'I'm just so blessed tired. I can't look at food before noon, either.'

'Definitely a job for Culver's Root,' the housekeeper said with finality. 'Now let's get on with these orders and accounts, before the mistress comes chasing them up.'

It was two days later that Megan began to make her own tentative diagnosis. She had derived nothing but a severe stomach cramp from Mrs Foskett's remedy. Her tiredness persisted, but now it came in waves. Between times she had as much energy as ever. She observed a developing pattern, day by day, and explained to no one why she was becoming quiet again and withdrawn.

In mid-November a letter came from Alun. Megan took it to her room and tore open the envelope eagerly. She found only one sheet of paper inside. The short note, dated three weeks earlier, confirmed what she had already suspected.

My Dearest Megan,

We have been in the trenches from Thursday until Monday, doing no more than sheltering from the endless rain and the hail of shells from the Kaiser's lads. Last night Alec Bruce, our corporal, got killed when he lost his way coming back from the supply truck to our trench. He was only twenty.

I have to confess to you, Megan, that I'm heart-sick. There is no campaign here, no hint of strategy. We're simply two lots of badly fed soldiers shooting at each other for some of the time and lying low for the rest of it. The brisk, well-devised movement we were led to expect doesn't exist. There are 400-odd miles of trenches stretching from Belgium right across Europe, and they're full of disheartened souls without decent leadership or even a believable goal.

How I'm longing to get back to you. I dream of nothing else. I know now that you were right, I can do nothing special in this shambles. My place is beside you, and I'll never doubt that again.

All my love,
Alun

Megan folded the letter carefully and put it in the drawer with the others. She went to her window and looked down at the garden, seeing Griffiths and Jenkin rolling fruit nets on the lawn and stacking them against the wall. The pain of Alun's absence suddenly soared in Megan. She put a hand to her mouth, holding back the small moan, willing herself to bear up. She wasn't sure if she had been particularly brave up to the present; she was very sure she would have to be from now on.

She went downstairs and tapped on the drawing-room door.

'Come in.'

Mrs Pughe-Morgan turned from a table stacked with transit boxes as Megan entered. 'Such a confusion,' she said. 'Seventeen separate destination addresses, Megan. I'm sure I'll get it wrong and the Germans will end up with half this stuff.'

'I wondered if I might have a word, ma'am.'

'Of course you can.' The mistress wiped her hands on a handkerchief. 'Sit down if you like. You look rather pale.'

'It's about my health I want to talk to you.'

Mrs Pughe-Morgan looked instantly concerned. 'Whatever's wrong?'

'I've been off-colour for a long time,' Megan said. 'Dr Watkins gave me a tonic, so did Mrs Foskett. I've been getting to bed earlier and I've been sleeping well. But my symptoms haven't gone. They've changed, but I still have them.'

'My dear, if you're asking me if you can have time off – a little holiday, perhaps, somewhere quiet. You've been under a lot of strain since Alun went . . .'

Megan shook her head. 'I've come to you because you're the only person I can talk to about it, and it's your right to know.'

'To know what?'

Megan clasped her hands tightly in front of her. 'I've been pretty sure for a week or two now, ma'am,' she said shakily. 'Now I'm absolutely certain. I'm afraid I'm going to have a baby.'

22

The rumours began spreading as soon as Megan's pregnancy started to show. Word travelled first in whispers among the staff. Mrs Edgar openly consoled Megan and made every effort to treat the matter as something to be glad of. Clara tried to do the same, but what she truly felt for Megan was sadness; she couldn't keep that from showing. Agnes displayed a degree of shock that suggested she might have discovered plague lurking in the house.

'Terrible, isn't it?' she said to Clara, creeping up on her in the pantry and nearly making her drop the jelly pan she was easing on to a shelf.

'What is?' Clara demanded, glaring.

'Megan. What she's gone and done.'

'She hasn't done anything terrible.'

Agnes made a sour mouth. 'Must have, to get herself like that.'

'You've got a terrible dirty little mind, Agnes.'

'It's not me that's the dirty one . . .'

Clara moved very close to Agnes. 'Listen. You've had a telling-off before about your muck-spreading. Just you mind that bucket of a mouth you've got there, or it'll land you out of a job.'

Agnes sniffed. 'I'm not so sure I'll be wanting to work in this house now. It isn't decent what's going on –'

'Agnes! I'm warning you! I'll crown you with that ladle if you don't shut your teeth!'

Agnes scurried away, taking her outrage with her.

Within a few days most of Drynfor knew about Megan. Alun Rees's mother, feeling it necessary to defend her son, was heard to declare publicly that she'd warned him no good would ever come of the relationship. 'I could see it in her, the looseness. Showed in her eyes, it did. I always said the poor lad would pay the price for going around with that stuck-up bitch - but women like that can tempt saints even, can't they?'

Urged on by Mrs Pughe-Morgan, who hadn't offered her one word of censure, Megan carried out her duties as usual. Her moods varied wildly, from moments of elation at the thought of carrying Alun's baby, to hours of lonely despair, agonizing about the news from France, about how she would ever tell Alun she was pregnant, and about the whole uncertain future.

In March, after waiting more than a month for word from Alun, Megan decided to write and tell him. It took four attempts before she finally had it down on paper.

We're going to have a child, Alun. All being well, he or she should be born in June. Although we never planned it to happen, I'm not too sorry it has. As the baby grows day by day so does my love for both of you. Be cheerful over my news, darling, for in spite of the obvious difficulties, our child can only increase our happiness.

Another week passed before Megan had the courage to send the letter. On the same day Mrs Pughe-Morgan sent for her. They were served tea in the library by the dark-frowning Agnes; as soon as she had left them the mistress came directly to the point.

'We have to decide about your future, Megan. I thought it best not to raise the matter too soon, until we'd both had time to think things out and accustom ourselves to what's happened.'

'I've been thinking about it, certainly,' Megan said. 'My mind keeps shying away from plan-making, but I've half decided that, if I could work on as long as I'm able, I would be in a position to rent a place for myself and the baby, then when Alun comes back – '

'What?' The mistress was shocked. 'In heaven's name, I wasn't expecting you to leave here.'

'But I can't stay on, can I?'

'I was hoping you would.'

Puzzled, Megan stared at Mrs Pughe-Morgan for a moment. 'How can I? It's not right. And it wouldn't be fair or practical, would it? I can't burden other people with my problems, certainly not to that extent . . .'

'Megan,' the mistress said, 'you are no burden. On the contrary, I have spent a number of years thanking providence you ever walked in through that front door. Now I've no wish to embarrass you with cloying compliments, but you've contributed something immeasurable to my life, and I'd go to fair lengths to make sure you remain with me for as long as possible.'

'That's very kind, ma'am. But I do have a sense of duty and I think –'

'Not another word!' the mistress snapped. 'Duty, indeed! Megan, you've been my maid, deputy housekeeper, protégée and companion, you've *dutifully* fulfilled those roles for years and it's high time we shone the light on my duty towards you.' She put down her teacup and clasped her hands decisively. 'I did say we should discuss this, but, since I don't care for the direction your plans seem to have taken, discussion can be set aside. Instead, I want you to listen.'

Megan listened for five minutes. The mistress began by pointing out that there was no need for her to give up work. After the birth of the baby, when she felt well enough, Megan could resume her duties and still – with the help of the cook, kitchen maid, Mrs Foskett and Mrs Pughe-Morgan herself – look after the child.

'I'm aware, of course, that the arrangement wouldn't be ideal – but on the other hand it's extremely practical, and I believe it would be rather fun.'

Then there was the matter of marriage. Mrs Pughe-Morgan was well aware that Megan would want to marry Alun as soon as he came home, and naturally they would set up house together.

'But that might not be for a year or two yet, Megan. We have to face facts, this damnable war is going to drag on. So, until you're reunited with Alun, I would like you to have new quarters here – those two nice sunny rooms on the first floor. Just the atmosphere for a baby to begin its days in, plenty of light and air. And when you do settle into your own place you might, if I could persuade you, carry on working for me until Alun's passed all his exams and got himself a job in teaching.' Mrs

Pughe-Morgan sat back, appraising Megan's slightly bewildered look. 'So. What do you think of all that?'

'I don't know what to say.'

'Say you accept.'

'Well, yes, I do. It's just so kind of you . . .'

'Fine, then.' The mistress stood up briskly and took Megan's empty cup from her. 'I suggest you get back to what you were doing, now, before you're tempted to lavish thanks on me. As I told you, it's nothing more than my duty, and the arrangements *would* work as much to my advantage as yours.'

As Megan was on the point of leaving, the mistress detained her for a moment. 'How are you feeling, now that I remember to ask?'

'I'm still sick first thing, but otherwise I'm fine,' Megan told her.

'Good. Keep taking the horrid little pills Dr Watkins gave you and don't let yourself get too tired.'

As Megan closed the door behind her, she reflected that no one could have had a better mother than Mrs Pughe-Morgan.

'Of all the rocks set by the devil to trip unwary humankind, there is none more treacherous, none more cunningly fashioned to bring down man in his frailty, than the woman of easy virtue.'

Reverend Powell's bald head shone pale in the sun as he jerked his eyes from listener to listener and twisted his black Bible between his hands. It was the first Sunday in April, and by tradition the Baptists were having an open-air day of worship. Powell stood on a portable platform in the square at Drynfor. He was surrounded by his followers, two dozen nodding, grim-faced men and women with a scattering of muted children among them. On the perimeter a dozen other people, Sunday-bored, were giving Powell their attention for want of anything better to do. A little way beyond, at the open window of his sitting room, Dr Watkins stood watching and listening, his face as stern as the Baptists', though for very different reasons.

'There is no limit to their evil,' Powell went on, his voice rising with dire warning. 'In every quarter they lurk, ready to twist the straight and sully the pure.' One thin hand detached itself from the Bible and jabbed a finger towards the south. 'Near this very spot there is an unholy dwelling where moral turpitude thrives and spreads its sweet poison. A house, a place of grandeur and vain display, owned by a person who mocks her own sacred vows of marriage and nurtures a harlot bent on the vilest corruption. I will name no names, but I will loudly affirm God's condemnation of those who wallow in the sins of the flesh.'

At other times Dr Watkins would have found Powell's harangue amusing. But lately he had known there were rumours flying – inflated, distorted tales that the Baptists and others had leeched on to, drawing nourishment for their spite. As he watched Reverend Powell, the doctor entertained an unprofessional desire to do lasting and painful harm to the scrawny old preacher's throat.

'I am talking of the strumpet at her worst,' Powell ranted, 'of rank evil clothed in a shell of demure virtue. We must never forget, brethren, that those acquainted with the indulgences of the flesh have the cunning to show the world a face of honest industry, a mask of compliance with God's moral law.' Powell leaned closer to the congregation, the Bible clutched to his heart. 'The simpering, smiling, pure-faced harlot,' he growled, 'is the perfection of Satan's craft.'

Dr Watkins craned his neck as the preacher pointed to a girl standing near the platform. For a moment her face was obscured, then she turned and Watkins saw it was Agnes, Mrs Pughe-Morgan's parlour maid.

'A sister has borne witness, she has laid pained eyes on the wickedness in that cauldron of vice. Her vigilance is our warning – we must reject fleshly sin, totally, and its standard-bearers must be shunned, lest their cause find a foothold in honest Christian hearts.' Powell raised a solemn hand towards heaven. 'These people, these most wicked of women, have no place amongst us. Let our scorn be visible, brethren, and let it be steadfast.'

Watkins shut his window with a bang. He crossed to the telephone and dialled a number from memory, then waited.

221

'Hello? Ah, Mrs Pughe-Morgan. Good morning, it's Dr Watkins. Look, I realize you're busy and Lord knows you don't need any more problems than you've already got. All the same, I thought I'd better let you know what the witch-hunters are getting up to over here.'

He took two minutes to give her a rapid summary of Powell's sermon, remembering to mention Agnes's involvement. 'It's standard, old-time bigotry, and I get the impression Powell's only warming up. There'll doubtless be more of the same – more and wilder.'

'I suppose it was only to be expected,' Mrs Pughe-Morgan said. 'Having an illegitimate child in these parts is still considered a stoning offence among the faithful.' She sighed. 'I'll take the appropriate steps with Agnes. The really important thing, I suppose, is to keep Megan from knowing. Thank you for calling me, Dr Watkins. Goodbye.'

But Megan did find out, the very next morning. She heard it all from Mrs Bryant, the faded wife of an ailing miner who came to the house three times a week to do the heavy cleaning.

Megan listened in shocked silence as the little woman recited the patches she had remembered from Powell's oration. Her voice was hushed, almost frightened. 'He's a terrible man, that Powell,' she said. 'Whipping up the folk like that, saying all them bad things about you and Mrs Pughe-Morgan.'

Mrs Bryant meant well. She had a high regard for Megan and thought it was only right that she should pass on what she'd heard. It didn't occur to her that she was causing Megan terrible distress.

'Thank you for telling me,' Megan said when the woman had finished. 'Don't go upsetting yourself over it, whatever you do. It's sticks and stones that hurt. Name-calling's just hot air.'

Later, alone in her room, Megan gave in to the pain and fell on her bed, sobbing. The whole world outside, it seemed, was aligned against her. Loneliness, daily sickness and her fluctuating fears for Alun had worn her down, but she had withstood it. Ostracism, condemnation and hate were too much to bear. It burned Megan's heart to know there were people wishing her so much ill, people who had inflicted on her the image of a whore and who would use it as an excuse to heap on more agony.

'Alun,' she moaned, wishing in every fibre that she could reach out to him and find him, so that she could protect herself with his warmth.

She gasped suddenly and touched the gentle mound of her belly. The baby had moved; she had felt one firm kick. Megan sat up. An image crystallized, more crushing than she could have imagined. She saw people's hate, she felt it, and it was being directed as much at her precious child as it was towards her. Megan let out a long, deep cry of despair and fell back on the pillow, crying helplessly.

After a while, she had no idea how long, she was aware of a knocking at the door. She was about to sit up again as the door opened and Mrs Foskett came in. Without preamble or enquiry the old woman shuffled across to the bed and sat down on the stool beside it.

'I know what you've heard,' she said, 'and I know what you must be feeling. Now just you settle. Don't stop your crying on my account, the hurt's got to get out somehow.' She put forward her hand and stroked Megan's brow. 'It'll pass, girl, I promise you that. You'll not forget, but in time there won't be the sorrow.'

Megan tried to say something, but choking sobs had control of her voice.

'Ssh, now, and let me tell you something.' Mrs Foskett leaned close, talking quietly, like a fond grandmother soothing a child. 'When I was younger than you are now, the holy rabble came after me. It was down in Cardiff, at the time I told you about. They were a crowd calling themselves the Brothers of the Tabernacle. They had a mission in life, see, they made it their business to hunt out wickedness.' She shook her head slowly, remembering. 'I was a bad girl, I'd not deny it, but my badness wasn't deep in the bones, like theirs. They took sticks to me, Megan. Cut open my head and both my hands when I tried to cover myself. Three of them, big heavy men, picked me up and threw me in the river.'

Megan snuffled back her tears. 'That's horrible,' she said. 'You could have died.'

'Almost did,' Mrs Foskett grunted. 'First I near to drowned, then the cuts on me went septic from the dirt I picked up in the water. I was in the charity ward three weeks.' She patted Megan's arm. 'There's a reason I'm telling you this. Folk like that, the badness eats them away. And before it does that it blinds them, so they can't see what's real. Do you follow that, now?'

Megan nodded.

'Their hate and their spite and their cruel ways, none of that's important, because it's all wrong-headed. What should concern you is how the other sort of people think about you. They're all that matters.'

'Yes,' Megan said after a moment, 'you're right, it makes sense. But it just feels so terrible . . .'

'I know,' Mrs Foskett said. 'But remember this while you're feeling so bad – the other kind of folk think the world of you.'

Agnes returned on Tuesday morning after spending two days in Drynfor with her family. She had been in the house less than ten minutes when the mistress called her to the library.

'Stand there,' Mrs Pughe-Morgan said, pointing to the mat in front of the writing table where she sat. She was wearing her spectacles, which reinforced the sternness of her appearance. She watched as Agnes did as she'd been told, cow-eyed, trying to make her mouth firm. 'Right. What have you got to say for yourself?'

'Ma'am?'

'You heard me. Don't try to look innocent, it doesn't suit you.'

'I don't know what you mean, ma'am.'

'So you're a liar as well as a spite-ridden little bigot.'

Agnes flushed. 'You've no right to go calling me that.' Her voice was husky and she was starting to tremble. 'I don't tell lies . . .'

'Yes you do,' the mistress snapped. 'I'm not going to argue the point with you.' She pushed an envelope towards Agnes. 'Take that. It's your severance pay.'

'My what?' Agnes gaped dully at the envelope.

'It's the money you're given when you leave a job. Severance means cutting off. I'm cutting you off, Agnes. It's an act of pruning I should have performed a long time ago.'

'D'you mean I'm sacked?'

Mrs Pughe-Morgan nodded. 'Sacked. Ejected. Severed. It must come as a great relief to you. I can't think why a person of your virtue would want to remain in this seething cauldron of vice any longer than you could help. I want you packed and out within the hour.'

Agnes looked deeply troubled. 'I wasn't thinking of leaving...'

'What you were thinking of doing is no concern of mine. After the mischief you've caused I don't want you anywhere near the place.'

'I didn't cause no mischief...'

The mistress stood up. 'Agnes, I can scarcely keep myself from hitting you. I'd suggest you pick up that envelope and get out of here.'

Agnes snatched up the money. 'I ... Do I get a reference?'

'What?' the mistress shrieked. 'A *reference*? The only reference you'll get from me is a testimonial to your viciousness, your jealousy, your general malice and your stupidity. Now get out of my sight, you odious lump!'

Agnes went. Mrs Pughe-Morgan sat down again, staring at the closed door. When her breathing had settled she looked down at a letter lying folded on the desk. It had been delivered an hour before and she had read it three times already. She opened it now and scanned it again. It was from her estranged husband, a flowery, wheedling plea for a reconciliation. He used words of endearment and spoke of his terrible emptiness without her. He said he loved her.

Meticulously, Mrs Pughe-Morgan tore the letter into strips, doubled them and tore them again. There were days, she reflected, when nothing pleasant seemed to happen. She threw the pieces of paper into the basket and stared at them. 'Go to hell, Robert,' she said quietly. She stood up and went out into the hall. 'Megan,' she called.

After a moment the door to the kitchen opened and Megan appeared. 'Yes, ma'am?'

'I've made one of my instant decisions,' the mistress said as Megan crossed to her. 'I'm going away for the rest of the week and you're coming with me. We both need a change, if only a small one.'

'Away?' Megan blinked. 'You and me?'

'Of course. We've earned some respite, my dear.'

'Where are we going?'

Mrs Pughe-Morgan shrugged. 'Prestatyn, perhaps. I haven't decided yet. Does the idea appeal to you?'

Megan smiled. 'It certainly does.'

'Well, off you go and pack a bag. Right this minute. *Don't* carry it down the stairs yourself – Clara can bring it down with mine.'

Still smiling, Megan turned to the staircase; as she did, the doorbell rang.

'You carry on,' the mistress said. 'I'll get it. Can't remember when I last answered my own door.'

As Megan reached the landing she glanced down into the hall and stopped. There was a girl standing by the open door, talking to the mistress. For a moment Megan didn't recognize her, then she realized the girl's hair was different from the last time they had met, more than a year ago. It was Alun's sister. Megan was back down the stairs and crossing the hall before the mistress turned, her face perfectly blank as she ushered the young woman in.

'You're Grace, aren't you?' Megan said, puzzled.

'Mam said I wasn't to come,' the girl said. 'But it wouldn't have been right ...' She was holding out a piece of yellow paper.

Megan's eyes darted from the paper to Mrs Pughe-Morgan's face. She still looked blank, almost dazed. 'Grace, what's up?' Megan's heart began to thud. She took the paper, staring as the words danced before her eyes. Then she could read them, stark and clear.

It is my painful duty ...

Megan looked up. 'Grace? What is this? Grace! Tell me!' Grace began to cry. Megan looked back at the paper, terrified.

a report has this day been received from the War Office notifying the death of No L/98073 Private Alun Rees . . .

A far-off sound rang in Megan's head, high-pitched and shrilling. Her fingers slackened, letting the paper fall, then she saw the floor spin sideways and rush to meet her. An instant before darkness closed round her, she knew the sound was her own scream.

23

For two months the other members of the household watched,
unable to help or console, as Megan's spirit was consumed with
despair. She moved about the house with the distracted, half-
absent look of a permanent invalid. Loss was like a blunt, slow-
moving knife across her heart, an agony that was as persistent as
it was cruel.

'It would be better if she would give in to hysteria,' Mrs
Pughe-Morgan told Dr Watkins on one of his visits. 'She's
bottled up her grief and it's poisoning her.'

'Possibly,' the doctor replied. 'On the other hand, I can't see
Megan having much time for hysterics. Whatever's going on
inside her, it's her own special reaction. You can only keep an
eye on the girl and put your affection at her disposal. She'll need
it sooner or later.'

The summer came early that year. Through the first warm
weeks Megan continued to suffer beyond the scope of the
others' sympathy. She saw no point in trying to convey what she
felt; even if they understood, it would be no help. The mistress
tried to persuade her that it was even more important now that
they should go away for a time, but Megan declined quietly,
drawing her grief about her like a dark shawl.

The baby was born on the last day of June. The delivery was
long and difficult. As the small body was brought out into the
light, Megan suffered the last tearing pain of separation and
passed into a sudden delirium that gradually gave way to a deep
sleep.

'She's exhausted,' Watkins told the mistress. 'Her body hung
on to the child as if she didn't want it to leave her. Stay nearby.
She's well enough in her body, but I can't speak for the rest of
her.'

Mrs Pughe-Morgan and Mrs Foskett sat with Megan and
watched as dreams troubled her sleep and made her whimper.

After an hour she woke with a start and lay staring up at them, her eyes anxious and enquiring.

'The baby,' she said through dry lips. 'Is it –'

'Your baby's fine,' Mrs Pughe-Morgan said. She smoothed Megan's hair and smiled at her. 'Pretty hungry by now, though.' She watched as Mrs Foskett brought the little bundle from the cot by the window. 'What are you going to call her?'

For the first time in months Megan began to look alert. She pushed herself up in the bed and the mistress propped pillows behind her as she took the baby in her arms.

'A girl,' Megan breathed. She moved the shawl away from the tiny head. The baby immediately began to make suckling sounds with its lips. 'She's so little.'

'Four and a half pounds,' Mrs Foskett said. 'Sound in wind and limb. Go ahead then, girl, feed her before she starts howling the place down.'

Awkwardly Megan put the child to her breast. She watched in wonderment as it took her milk, sucking eagerly and making gurgling sounds in its throat. After a moment Megan looked at Mrs Pughe-Morgan and said, 'I'll call her Bronwen. It would have been Alun if it had been a boy – Bronwen was his favourite girl's name.'

After five minutes of energetic feeding, the child fell asleep. Megan rocked her gently in her arms, staring intently at the miniature features, almost sombre in repose. Without looking up she said, 'Thank you both, thank you very much. It must have been terrible for you, these past weeks . . .'

'And hell for you,' the mistress said softly. 'But what's past is past.' She gazed at Megan's tired face, looking for traces of the old strength. All she saw was fatigue. 'I think you should rest again, my dear.'

'Just a few more minutes,' Megan said. Her eyes remained fixed on the baby. 'I'm still taking it in.'

What had begun to happen in that moment grew clearer as Bronwen's first weeks passed. Megan came to know, with a certainty that began somewhere beyond thought, that she was changing; the baby was both the cause of the process and its reason. Megan had been through the darkest time of her life, a time when no one could reach her with the help they longed to give. Now, with the miracle of her baby beside her and long hours of rest when she could dwell on ends and beginnings, Megan realized that one life could contain many small, separate existences. She was entering a new one, and she could almost dare to believe it would be happy.

Some of her wounds healed faster than others. All of them left scars. At certain times of the day when Bronwen slept and Megan could stand watching her, the longing for Alun became almost unbearable. But, even in those moments, Megan detected a change in herself. The sorrowing was deep, but it carried acceptance. Alun was dead. She no longer tried to reject that certainty.

A lesser pain, but a pain nevertheless, was caused by the peculiar clarity of Megan's memory. She could see Alun and hear his voice whenever she wanted to. The resonance of his words came to her many times a day; at night, she would lie awake hearing the baby's breathing and the parallel softness of its father's voice, whispering endearments. Megan began to develop a special patience; she waited for the time when the memories would no longer bruise her.

Towards the end of September she decided to start working again. Bronwen no longer needed her mother's constant attention, and Megan's increasing energy was making her restless. She announced her decision to the mistress as they walked in the gardens, wheeling Bronwen in her new white pram.

'Well, if you feel you're up to it, my dear. Your help's been sorely missed these past three months.' Mrs Pughe-Morgan shook her head, smiling. 'Three months, and just look at her.' Bronwen was holding on to one side of the pram, squealing delightedly as Griffiths and Jenkins waved to her. 'I'm looking forward to playing aunt more often, too.'

When they reached the summerhouse Megan lifted Bronwen out of the pram and set her on the grass by the wooden steps.

'There's a proposition I want to put to you,' the mistress said, watching the child as she made energetic efforts to crawl towards the bird-bath. 'I've been holding on to it until you felt ready to take up the reins again.' She peered at Megan. 'Now you're sure you *are* ready?'

'I'm positive. The sooner the better.'

'Very well. I'll put you in the picture, first of all. Mrs Foskett, I'm afraid, will have to give up work entirely. Dr Watkins keeps telling me that and I keep putting off the decision to retire her. But it's got to be done.'

Megan was nodding. 'She looks terribly tired lately. But I don't think she'll take very kindly to the idea of retirement.'

'I know,' Mrs Pughe-Morgan said. 'But I intend to let her stay on in her little cottage, give her a pension and allow her to interfere as much as she likes in the household affairs – as long as she doesn't do any actual work. That way she won't feel rejected in any way, or so I hope. Now, I presume you've guessed what my proposition is?'

'Well . . .'

'I want you to take over as my housekeeper, Megan. You know the work, you've been doing the major part of it for a long time. What you'd do, additionally, would be to train and supervise a new parlour maid and take over the jobs Mrs Foskett's doing at present. What do you say?'

'If you think I'm competent to do it, ma'am . . .'

'Of course I do.'

'In that case I accept. And thank you.'

The breeze blew a large dock leaf across the grass. Bronwen reached out for it and rolled over on her back. Megan rushed to her and picked her up, cooing softly in her ear, soothing her small fright.

'Do remember,' the mistress said, 'that being a mother can be hard work, in spite of all the help you'll have. If you feel at any time that running the house is too much of an added strain, don't hesitate to tell me.'

'Oh, I'm up to it,' Megan assured her. 'I think I'm a stronger person since I've had Bronwen. I've got more resilience, too.'

'That may be so, but be careful not to assume too much about your strength, Megan. It's a bad mistake I've made a few times.'

Three days later, Megan discovered that she had made the mistake too. Sorting through the morning's mail, she came upon an envelope which jolted her and made her drop the others. It was a letter from Alun.

Breathless, she ripped open the envelope and took out the single sheet of paper. Her mind was racing, speculating. *What if he's . . .* With shaking fingers she unfolded the letter and stared at it, snatching pieces of it at random, unable to find the calm to read it through.

It was much as before. He talked about the loneliness, the boredom, how much he missed her and longed to be home. Megan couldn't comprehend. She turned the sheet over, read the last line and turned it back again. Then her eye fell on the date: 2 March. The letter was seven months old.

Megan felt her strength disintegrate. With trembling legs she climbed the stairs and went into her new bedroom. She sat down on the edge of the bed and stared across at Bronwen, asleep in her cot. The stillness matched the sudden chasm within her, a yawning hollow in her spirit. She looked at the letter, crushed to a ball in her hand. Smoothing it, she saw the last line again.

Until we're together, my love . . .

With an effort that left her sweating, Megan fought down the chilling despair that had seized her again. She pushed herself to her feet and strode to the cot.

This was the reality of her life, she told herself sternly; this child and the life she would make for both of them. Alun was gone; there was no earthly way to reverse that.

'Alun is dead,' she whispered fiercely. 'He's dead!'

Grief threatened to swamp her again as she bent close to Bronwen and touched one tiny hand curled on the blanket. The baby made a sound and turned her head on the pillow. Megan felt one sob build in her throat and swallowed it back.

'Bronwen is the future,' she hissed. Saying it did something; the encroaching loneliness fled her. She touched the baby's hand again and stood back, grasping control of herself. It was working, she realized. Her resources of will had weakened but she was prevailing. For ten minutes she stood there. She didn't move until she was certain she was whole again.

That evening as she bathed Bronwen, Megan reminded herself over and over that she must become harder. She was still vulnerable; she had to toughen the weak spots in her spirit where she could be so badly wounded. Acceptance was the key. Acceptance of the past, acceptance of the future, symbolized by the child splashing happily in the water.

Megan paused with the towel in her hand, caught by another thought. There would have to be acceptance of her own lost ambitions. In the past months she hadn't thought of them; she had been smothered with her grief. But now she did think about them. A marriage, a home, a strong involvement in her husband's career – there had even been a faint notion of a separate career of her own. That horizon had been cancelled.

Instead, she now realized, she must accept the idea of being a housekeeper and of possibly remaining in service until she was as old as Mrs Foskett. It was not a prospect that particularly pleased Megan.

'But I do have to accept it,' she murmured as she lifted Bronwen from the water and laid her on the towel across her knees.

24

By the summer of 1916 the Pughe-Morgan house had acquired a new air of bustle. As the mistress involved herself with more anti-war societies and soldiers'-aid committees, visitors came and went steadily. The evenings became active again; when influential guests weren't being entertained, there were frequent lecture sessions at which Mrs Pughe-Morgan explained the aims and strategies of the Women's Social and Political Union, of which she was now the most prominent Welsh supporter.

From Monday to Friday, Megan rose at seven and worked until six o'clock, taking time off when it was necessary to attend to Bronwen's needs. As the child grew and began to walk spread-footed around the house, everyone took it upon themselves to look after her and to contribute something to her upbringing.

'It's a good job Megan isn't a jealous mother,' Mrs Foskett had observed to the mistress. 'We've all taken ourselves a share of that little one.'

Mrs Edgar and Clara often had the baby with them in the kitchen; it was no rare occurrence, either, to see Griffiths or Jenkin wheeling the delighted child around the garden in a high-sided cart fashioned from old pram wheels, a crate and sacking padded with chunks of tow. By the time she was fifteen months old Bronwen could call everyone in the household by name. She was the child of them all, 'a dark-haired, bright-eyed angel with irrepressible spirit', as one gushing visitor felt compelled to describe her.

On one of the quieter Sunday afternoons, as Megan and the child were in the garden kicking up the multi-coloured leaves and chasing a ball, a young man called at the house and asked to see Miss Roberts. Edith, the new parlour maid, came to the garden to tell Megan.

'Did he give his name?'

Edith coloured. 'Sorry, Miss Roberts. I forgot to ask.'

'Never mind.' Megan stooped and picked up Bronwen, brushing the leaf dust from her coat. 'Tell the gentleman I'll be right along.'

'Where shall I have him wait, miss?'

Megan thought about it. 'I'm not sure,' she said. The only person who had ever called on her before had been Alun. 'Leave him in the hall until I find out who he is and what he wants.' As Edith hurried back to the house, Megan damped her handkerchief and began wiping the smudges from Bronwen's face. 'Fancy that, now,' she said. 'We've got a visitor. Can't have you meeting him with a dirty face, can we?'

As she walked up the path with the child in her arms, Megan wondered idly who the caller might be. Most likely a salesman, she half decided. There had been quite a few coming to the door in recent months, and one or two of them knew her name. None of them had ever called on a Sunday, though.

Megan went in by the kitchen door and through into the hall. Her visitor had his back to her and at first he appeared to be a stranger. When he turned, however, Megan recognized him at once.

'Tom!' The face was older, older than she would have imagined, but it was unmistakably her young brother, grinning at her the way he always had. 'What a surprise!'

'Grand to see you, Megan,' he said, limping towards her, leaning heavily on his stick as he extended his free hand. 'Really grand.'

Megan ignored the hand. Instead she wrapped her arm around Tom's waist and kissed him on the cheek. 'You're the last person I expected to see.' She stepped back, admiring the fine suit he wore and the shiny black leather boots. 'Quite the toff now, too.' Megan pointed to him and said to Bronwen, 'This is your Uncle Tom.'

'Unca Tom,' Bronwen echoed her.

'Tom, this is your niece Bronwen.'

Blushing a little, Tom leaned forward and kissed Bronwen's cheek. 'Nice to meet you, young lady.'

Megan led the way into the morning room. 'Mrs Pughe-Morgan's away,' she explained over her shoulder. 'I'm sure she won't mind us using her favourite room for a while.' She indicated a chair near the window. 'Sit down, Tom. I'll get Edith to bring us some tea.'

Tom eased himself into the chair with obvious difficulty. When he was settled, the deformed leg jutted out stiffly in front of him. Megan sat down opposite, letting Bronwen scamper off to the corner to play with the magazine rack.

'Now tell me all about yourself,' Megan said excitedly, unbuttoning her coat with one hand and ringing the little bell with the other. 'How old are you now? Nineteen it'll be, is that right?'

Tom nodded. 'Nineteen just past.' He looked like a much older man, nearer thirty. 'And you're what? Twenty-three?'

'Twenty-four soon.'

Tom shook his head. 'It's hard to take in. You being twenty-four. You've been up here for ages.' He pointed at the bell she was putting back on the table. 'Well settled in, too, I notice.'

Megan laughed. 'I'm the housekeeper now. I've been nearly eleven years with Mrs Pughe-Morgan.'

'Dear, oh Lord.' Tom sat back and folded his hands. He waited until Megan had asked Edith to bring in tea, then he said, 'I've been thinking about coming to see you for a long time. For years, in fact. Then not long ago I heard about Alun Rees, how he'd been killed over in France, like . . .' He stopped and looked at Megan awkwardly. 'Sorry, maybe it was daft talking about it . . .'

'No, it's all right. I'm mostly over it.'

'Well, as I say, I'd been thinking about looking you up, and at long last I stopped thinking and got down to doing it.'

'And it's marvellous to see you.' Megan leaned forward, clasping her hands around her knees. 'Give me all your news.'

It took Tom twenty minutes and two cups of tea to bring Megan up to date on the family. Her mother was in reasonable health, although she still suffered bouts of anxiety and had been in hospital for the past month being treated for some complication of her rheumatism. Gareth, twenty-two now and

Billy, who was twenty-one, were in Cardiff doing munitions work.

'They reckon they're going to stay on down there, when the war's over. Billy wants to do engineering and Gareth's got a notion he'd like to be a steelworker. Better than the slate, either way.'

George was still with the union, a rung or two further up now and still climbing. His political ambitions had been suspended after a couple of salutary scrapes with riot-breakers in London and Birmingham, followed by a reprimand from party headquarters.

'And the drink's got a bit on top of him lately. Since Mam went into hospital he's really been banging it back. It don't seem to have harmed him in his job, though.' Tom paused, choosing his words carefully. 'He's not a real happy bloke, if you know what I mean. Never could laugh much and nowadays he never does at all.'

'Does he still feel the same way about me?' Megan asked.

'Never mentioned your name, after the move to Abergele.' Tom shrugged. 'He's talked a fair bit of guff in his time, has George. And it's cost him. Maybe he's altering his views about you – he's done that in a lot of quarters.'

Tom went on with his news. Aunt Peg, who had been in a charity home since long before Megan's father died, had passed away in 1914. She had stopped recognizing anyone for the last three years of her life.

'As for me,' Tom said with a modest little smile, 'I'm not doing too badly.'

Megan had been astonished at how affluent he looked. Of all her family, she had imagined Tom would have fared least well.

'Go on, then,' she urged him, 'tell me what's been happening to you.'

'Until I was sixteen, nothing very nice.' He tapped his leg. 'This got a lot worse. I had to have an operation to cut away the thickening round the knee joint. All they did was make the thing stiffer. I could hardly get about, and finding work was out of the question. I'd a notion of myself peddling matches and bootlaces on a windy corner somewhere.' He sighed. 'Then when I was fifteen, the pain started.'

'Your leg?'

'No, my back. It was the leg that brought it on, so I was told. It was worse than anything I could've dreamed of. Pure agony, day and night. It had me acting like a baby – and not one as chirpy as young Bronwen there, neither. I was a real cripple, howling with the pain half the time. George got in two different doctors and they both said the same thing – I might as well get used to the idea of being like that for the rest of my life.'

Megan was shocked, but her curiosity deepened. She resisted the urge to hurry Tom along, however. She remained quiet and let him tell her at his own pace.

'It's an odd thing, pain. If it's bad enough and if it's with you all the time, it'll either break you or make you fight. For a while, I got so I was lying on my bed day in and day out wondering when I'd go off my head. Then something happened. It was my sixteenth birthday. I woke up earlier than usual. The pain woke me; it was getting worse. I decided I'd fight.'

Tom's eyes became distant as he described how he had felt. It was like a rush of anger in him, he said. There he was, sixteen years old, ready for the scrap heap. The thought was unbearable. He had forced himself out of bed, a sock clenched between his teeth to keep him from screaming with the slicing pain in his spine. For minutes he had leaned against the wall, feeling the anger rise to match the pain.

'All my life I'd been used to being damaged, used to being the slow one. It was just the way I was. But now I didn't want to give in to that. It was too unfair.'

He told Megan how it took him half an hour to get into his clothes that morning, sweating and nearly passing out at times with the pain. Then he had taken his stick and a spare one from the cupboard. Leaning on both he had crab-walked out of the house before the others were up. He began walking along the deserted street, teeth gritted, whimpering.

'Lord, Megan, it was a nightmare. I must have looked a fright, held up on the sticks and moving slow as a snail. A constable saw me and told me to hang on, he'd get me some help.

I told him no, I *had* to get along to the end of that road and back. I convinced him, the anger in me did. So he walked with me, crawling at my pace, and he came all the way back with me.'

Tom had arrived in the house feeling half dead. But in spite of his mother's pleas and George's commands, he refused to go back to bed. In the afternoon, feverish and with the pain still seething in him, he got on the sticks and went out again.

'I did that every day for a week. I fought the pain and the stiffness and it was like fighting a bull. Once I fell over and, d'you know, that made me angrier. I battled my way to my feet, covered in dirt, and when I started moving again I was going faster. I'll never forget how that felt. I was in agony but there was pure joy in me, too. I went clumping down that road thinking I was galloping.'

That had been the turning point. By agonizing degrees Tom had made himself walk again; that determination and success strengthened his entire will. He decided he would make his own way in the world, just as his brothers were doing.

Megan couldn't contain her curiosity any longer. 'What is it you do, then?'

'Feed,' he said.

'Feed?'

'Animal feed. Specialized products for economical yield – that's a bit of the patter I was taught to use. It works, too, both the patter and the feed. I go round North Wales, talking to farmers and explaining how our products can up their incomes and halve their bills. I get a wage and commission on what I sell.' He brushed his smooth lapel with a comic, self-important gesture. 'Doing all right on it, too.'

Megan was delighted. 'However did you manage it?'

'The anger again, I think. Just knowing I wouldn't be considered for most jobs because of the disability, that got me riled enough. I put in for a few vacancies and sure enough I got turned down. So before I went for the interview with this firm I studied up the products, got books out of the library on the subject. By the time the manager spoke to me, I knew as much about the business as he did – or at least I made it sound that way.' He paused, choosing his words again. 'Megan, it's possible to *will* people, if you've enough driving you. And I didn't cheat them, I'm good at my job. I've been doing it less than a year and they're talking about giving me a bigger territory.'

'Tom, I'm so pleased for you. So proud.' Impulsively Megan got out of her chair and crossed to him, clutching his hand between hers. 'And are you a happy person now? Content with the world?'

'No,' he said. 'I'm a man with a bad leg and I still get terrible pain with my back. I get awful lonely travelling round on my own all the time. And I've a lot to prove that other folk don't have to. Every day's a fight, but I've got a little saying I don't forget: happy folk have no stories to tell.'

Tom stayed for another hour. He quizzed Megan about her work, about Bronwen and the plans for the future. He confessed to having missed his sister terribly. His brothers were cooler in their regard for her; his mother seemed almost to have forgotten she had a daughter at all. But Tom had always remembered the childhood days when Megan had played with him and tended his leg and told him stories she made up on the spur of the moment. He relived those times often, he said, and he drew warmth from them.

When it was time for him to go, Tom was close to sad-happy tears. So was Megan.

'Promise you'll come and see us again,' Megan said as they stood on the front steps.

'Try stopping me.' Tom kissed her cheek and smiled down at Bronwen in her arms. 'She's your image, Megan.' He kissed the baby. 'Cheerio, then, Bronwen pet.'

'Unca Tom.' Bronwen beamed back at him.

Megan stood and watched as Tom made his way across to his little black motor car. When he was inside – a slow, painful process that left him gasping – he started the engine, waved once and drove off. ''Bye, Tom,' Megan whispered, then hugged the baby to comfort herself.

Later, as she settled Bronwen in her cot for the night, Megan felt a small tremor of pleasure when she thought again about Tom. Seeing him had been a tonic for her; talking to him had given her a keen reminder of a truth she tried hard to observe nowadays: despair had to be opposed; it never died without mutilating its victims. Tom's disability and Megan's bereavement had a great deal in common, and they could be overcome by the identical means, so long as you could muster the spirit for a long, hard fight. Tom was a fighter and so was his sister. They were both making a go of life because their pain had offered them no alternative.

25

The following spring Megan and Bronwen went to Rhyl with Mrs Pughe-Morgan to visit Violet Rawlings, the mistress's cousin. Violet had been invalided out of the VAD the previous October, after being caught in a shell attack on a field surgical unit at Verdun.

Megan was shocked at the change in the woman. She was still in her early thirties, but her dark hair had turned yellowy-grey at the ends and her skin appeared to have lost its sheen. The bright, alert eyes had become dull. Violet's spirits, nevertheless, were as high as ever.

'It's splendid of you to come and see me,' she said as they all sat down in her room at the convalescent home. 'This is a nice place, in fact it's paradise compared to what I'd been used to, but it does get rather dull.'

'You'll be glad of the dullness by the time we've gone,' Mrs Pughe-Morgan told her. 'We've taken rooms at the Orion. We intend staying a week and we'll be visiting you every day.' She nodded towards Bronwen, who was dismantling the flower arrangement on a table by the veranda door. 'No chance of a dull moment with that young woman around.' She smiled at Violet, but her eyes were wrinkled with concern. 'How are you now? Apparently you were in a sorry state for a few months. They wouldn't let anyone visit.'

'I'm mended, Gwendolyn. Well, repaired, since I'm technically an invalid from now on. I had a lot of injuries in my back and my chest. They joined forces to produce pneumonia and a number of other complications. But that's all over.' She looked at her folded hands, pale against the dark plum of her dress. 'My active career in nursing's over too. That's the real sadness.'

'But you've landed an administrative position with somebody or other . . .'

'The College of Nursing. Yes, it's all very grand and I'm flattered.' She looked at Megan. 'I don't know if you've heard of the College at all . . .'

'No. I've been out of touch, I'm afraid,' Megan told her.

'The College of Nursing was set up last April. It's founded on the lines of the Royal College of Physicians and Surgeons. They hope to provide a uniform standard of training – and that's long overdue – plus facilities for postgraduate study and so forth. Laudable, Megan, I have to say that; it's a dream come true. But the College is definitely a place for old ladies with a penchant for paperwork. Not my cup of tea at all. Still,' she sighed, 'it's better than being out of the profession.'

As before, Megan found herself being held by what Violet said. She expressed nursing in terms that sounded precise and unambiguous, as if she saw a clear, exhilarating shape to the profession and conducted her life in accordance with it. 'I'd love to know more about the College,' Megan said. 'Nursing interests me.'

'And I'll be happy to tell you. Perhaps Gwendolyn will take Bronwen down on the beach one morning while we have a tête-à-tête.'

'Of course I will,' Mrs Pughe-Morgan said. 'Now tell me, what kind of social life do they let you have here? I can't imagine you spending each and every day in this little room, staring at the walls.'

'Oh, it's very wild at times,' Violet said, laughing. 'Every afternoon around two, to be accurate. I have a gentleman caller.'

Mrs Pughe-Morgan mimed dismay. 'They permit *that*? Heavens. Convalescent homes have certainly changed.'

'His name's John Sykes. A nice man really, a solicitor from Newcastle. He's an inmate here, getting over a bad motoring accident. Every day he comes in and we play two-handed bridge until four o'clock.'

'You see, Megan?' the mistress said. 'I told you before, it's a much more assenting society, once you get away from the dire shadow of Drynfor.' She returned her attention to Violet. 'Do I detect a romantic attachment in the budding?'

243

Violet shook her head. 'John Sykes is younger than I am, Gwendolyn. I also suspect he's not what's called my type, nor am I his. But we're comparatively mobile, so we make good company for each other.'

There was a crash as Bronwen finally brought down the flower vase. Mrs Pughe-Morgan leapt up and snatched her away from the broken glass as Megan hastily gathered up the pieces.

'I'm terribly sorry,' Megan said, dropping the pieces into a bin. 'She's so lively . . .'

'So lively it warms my heart,' Violet assured her. 'She's a lovely child. You look after her very well.'

'That's Megan's great talent,' Mrs Pughe-Morgan murmured as she bounced Bronwen gently on her knee. 'Looking after people. Hence her interest in nursing.'

That remark, Megan believed, carried a hint of conspiracy. Two days earlier, the mistress had spent a long time on the telephone with Violet. Later, she had sat with Megan over afternoon tea and talked exclusively about nursing. She had said Megan would enjoy nattering to Violet about the profession again, as she had done before; she had also remarked that it would do no harm for Megan to widen her understanding of the training procedures.

As they were leaving the convalescent home that day, Violet asked Megan if she would like to drop by the following morning. 'We could have a little chat,' she said, 'if Gwendolyn doesn't mind having the baby for a while.' Again, Megan thought, the whiff of conspiracy.

That evening, when Bronwen had been put to bed, Megan and Mrs Pughe-Morgan sat in the broad sun-lounge of the Orion, looking out across the sea to the purpling north-western sky. The expanse of silver water soothed Megan. She became mesmerized by its shifting highlights and the vast, rhythmic, eternal sighing. As she watched she began to fall asleep.

'You're very quiet,' Mrs Pughe-Morgan remarked, making Megan jump. 'Oh, my dear, I'm sorry, I didn't realize you were cat-napping.'

'It's all right.' Megan rubbed her eyes and sat up in the chair.

'If I sleep now I might not be able to later. All this inactivity's leaving me with energy to burn.'

'Nonsense. The sea air is relaxing you. Otherwise you wouldn't have started to nod off just then.'

Megan looked along the row of other reclining visitors and shook her head. 'I feel guilty, you know.' Megan said.

'What about?'

'Leaving Mrs Edgar, Clara and Edith to keep an eye on things. They've enough to do.'

'When we're not there, they don't have anything to do, apart from look after themselves. Mrs Foskett's about the place, remember. If there are any emergencies she'll see them coming and take appropriate measures. Besides, they've got a telephone number for us. Just relax, Megan. You needed this break.'

'Is that really why I'm here?'

Mrs Pughe-Morgan glanced sidelong at her. 'What do you mean?'

'I was wondering, that's all.'

In fact Megan had stopped wondering, almost as soon as they got back from visiting Violet Rawlings. In the foyer the mistress had remarked, rather too idly, that she had detected a strong similarity of interest between Megan and her cousin. 'Like minds, I'd say,' she added. 'It probably denotes like interests. Like talents.' That had been several hours ago, and Megan's certainty of a conspiracy hadn't wavered in the interim.

After a minute, the mistress leaned across to Megan. 'Did you say you were wondering?'

'Yes.'

'Wondering what, my dear?'

'If I was perhaps being guided rather elaborately in a certain direction,' Megan replied, smiling.

Mrs Pughe-Morgan sighed. 'Have I been that clumsy?'

'Maybe I've just known you long enough to understand your methods, ma'am.'

'There's no need to call me ma'am away from the house.' The mistress sighed again. 'Oh, very well, but my deviousness is benign, you must understand that. I've been having thoughts about your future again, that's all. Frankly, I think it's a terrible waste of talent and energy for you to spend the next God-knows-how-many years in domestic service.' She leaned closer, lowering her voice. 'Frankly, I've let my own selfishness muffle my sense of fairness. Even when I pointed out that I was doing myself a favour by keeping you on, I wasn't admitting how little I was truly doing to help you.'

'Now you're being unfair to yourself,' Megan said. 'I have a child to bring up and fend for, and I'm in the ideal position. You made it possible.'

Mrs Pughe-Morgan sniffed impatiently. 'Megan, can you put your hand on your heart and tell me you're happy with the prospect of a life spent answering doors and ordering staff about?'

'Oh, there's a lot more to it than that . . .'

'Can you?'

Megan stared out at the darkening sea for a moment. 'Well, no,' she said. 'But I've made myself accept it. It's easy to do that because I might have ended up in a real predicament, without your support. In the circumstances, I'm very fortunate.'

'You should have a career,' Mrs Pughe-Morgan said flatly. 'A real career.'

'Nursing?'

'Of course. It's an honourable calling for a woman, and with your intelligence and energy you could go far. As far as you wanted.'

'I'm twenty-four years old . . .'

'It's no age at all.'

'I've a baby who's not quite two, yet.'

'That's a difficulty, I'll grant you. But it's far from insurmountable.' Mrs Pughe-Morgan fell silent for a minute. 'A child shouldn't be a millstone,' she murmured eventually. 'I'm suggesting to you, Megan, that when Bronwen is five we start her in school. Three years from now. Think of it. You'll still be three years short of thirty. Plenty of women go into nursing after thirty. And many of them do well. I've talked it over with Violet. She agrees with me . . .'

'What happens when school's over?'

The mistress frowned. 'I don't think I follow.'

'Every day, at half-past three . . .'

'No, no, *no*,' Mrs Pughe-Morgan hissed. She glanced around, realizing she was attracting attention. 'I mean school in the real sense, Megan. A school where she can learn as you eventually did, by developing her individual talents, under caring supervision. A place of light and freedom, where Bronwen can be a happy child among other happy children. A boarding school, the very one I went to – and adored, I might say.'

Megan was stunned. She would do that for my Bronwen, she thought. The proposition was overwhelming. She needed time to stand back from it and see it all, see how it would change every assumption she had made about her future and Bronwen's. For the moment, Megan couldn't even tell whether she liked the notion.

'Don't say anything now,' Mrs Pughe-Morgan advised, wisely catching Megan's dilemma. 'Don't even try to come to a conclusion until you've talked with Violet tomorrow.' Lowering her voice again, she said, 'I'll confess to you just how devious I've been. Do you remember you once wrote an essay on nursing? You called it 'The Craft of Caring'. It was among some work you showed me when you were seventeen. I hung on to it all these years. Well, I sent that to Violet weeks ago and she read it.'

'What did she think?' Megan asked, still rather shaken.

'She was impressed. In fact she said that, if there were such a thing as a test for enthusiasm and a clear-thinking approach to the subject, your essay would get you into any nursing school in the country.'

The following morning Megan's mind was much clearer. She had literally slept on the proposition, and she could at least see it in perspective. Nevertheless, it was a daunting perspective.

'Gwendolyn called me a few minutes ago,' Violet told her as they sat down in her room to take coffee. 'I understand it's time to put cards on the table and own up.' She smiled. 'My cousin means very well, you know. She was afraid you'd resist her plans if you weren't eased into them, so to speak.'

'I understand,' Megan said. 'And I promise that my mind's as wide open as I can get it.'

As Violet proceeded to talk about the profession of nursing, about the role of the nurse in medicine and society, Megan listened intently and heard sentiments that exactly mirrored her own. She learned facts which made her aware that her half-formed notions were often, if not always, on the right track. Minute by minute the certainty hardened. Given the opportunity, she would certainly love to become a trained nurse.

'But I still have doubts about my own ability,' she admitted to Violet. 'For one thing, I'm sure it must be harder than I'm imagining. I see it as a clear, logical path of achievement and service – as I remember writing in my little essay – and perhaps that means I've not properly got the grasp of what's entailed.'

'It can be murderously hard,' Violet said. 'Heartbreaking, too. But what you *have* grasped thoroughly are the principles of nursing. With those to sustain you, you'll find that the training, the harsh discipline and the million humiliations you suffer along the way can be withstood much more easily. Megan, you have a vocation. All Gwendolyn has done is unearth it from the signs you've given her.'

Megan considered that for a moment. 'I must say I've had the feeling, now and then, that it would be a marvellous thing to do.'

Violet nodded vigorously. 'You have plenty of time to consider it – and, if you decide within the coming months that you want to go ahead and train, then you'll have ample time to prepare yourself on the theory side. You seem to be pretty well ahead in that direction already, from what Gwendolyn tells me.'

They were interrupted by a hesitant tapping on the door.

'I'd know that knock anywhere,' Violet murmured, looking at her watch. 'I've never heard it this early, though.' In a louder voice she called, 'Do come in.'

The door opened and a man stepped into the room. He was tall, perhaps thirty, with a handsome, delicate-featured face. Megan noticed his eyes at once. They were pale blue and almost innocently wide. His look of apology deepened when he saw Violet had a visitor.

'I'm terribly sorry, I didn't realize . . .'

'That's quite all right,' Violet assured him. 'Do join us for coffee. Megan, this is John Sykes, my bridge-playing companion. John, meet Megan Roberts, a friend of mine.'

'Miss Roberts.' His handshake was unexpectedly firm. 'I only stopped by to say I won't be able to play this afternoon,' he said to Violet. 'My mother's going to be visiting me. She just called to say she'd be here at one o'clock.'

'Oh, that's sad. I'll miss having my game.' Violet stood up and fetched the coffee pot and a third cup and saucer. 'But never mind. We can have an extra long game tomorrow.' She sat down and began pouring.

'Indeed we can.' John Sykes looked at Megan. 'Are you from these parts, Miss Roberts?'

'Further south,' Megan said. 'A town called Drynfor.' She knew she was blushing. Blushing for shame. In the instant he turned his eyes to her and spoke, a torrent of sensations had started, all of them familiar and all of them taboo. She had felt things in that instant she thought had died long ago.

'Drynfor?' John Sykes said politely. 'I don't believe I'm familiar with it.'

So deep, his voice. And those eyes, signalling a familiarity with silence. Megan thought it without wanting to. She was making comparisons, seeing parallels. It was disgraceful, she told herself sharply. She had never compared any man to Alun. They didn't even look alike. What was worse, this man hadn't been in the room two minutes. Then there came the blinding memory of that first time she saw Alun, standing on his mother's doorstep.

He put a sharp sigh across my heart.

'I'm . . . I'm sorry,' Megan stammered. She realized she'd been expected to respond to what John Sykes had said.

'I was wondering just where Drynfor lay.'

'It's near the Pantmynach valley . . .' Her voice was drying. 'It's not a spot many people have heard of . . .'

She had to get away from there. Her responses, vocal and

emotional, were out of control. There was an agonizing familiarity in the man that was splitting her. Megan shot to her feet.

'I'm afraid I have to be off.'

'So soon?' Violet said. 'Why not have another cup with us?'

'No, no, it's something I forgot. Foolish of me.'

'Oh, well, in that case . . .' Violet stood up. 'You'll come tomorrow, will you? There are a lot of pamphlets somewhere in my belongings and I'd like you to have them.'

'Of course, yes.' Megan shot John Sykes a glance. 'Nice to have met you,' she murmured. Trying not to hurry, she crossed to the door and opened it. As she turned, she saw they were both eyeing her curiously. 'Do forgive the rush. I'll be over tomorrow.' She stepped through the doorway, almost tripping on the mat. 'Goodbye.'

She deliberately took the long way back to the hotel, walking along the wide sweep of the beach road. The turmoil in her mind settled slowly, but not before she'd had time to burn on the sense of shameless betrayal that had gripped her heart.

'Alun, Alun, forgive me.' The wind carried her words towards the sea.

It would have seemed impossible before that day; every ounce of that special feeling had been put to rest with Alun's death. Men were just other figures in the landscape, to be responded to socially, without emotion. Yet John Sykes touched the same fine nerve in her that Alun had, and he induced the same curious helplessness.

'It was a familiarity,' she murmured, 'just a few shades of likeness.' Calmer by now, she knew that was true. What still shocked her, though, was that one short encounter with someone, however familiar in movement or nature, could resurrect so much. So much that was Alun's.

Seeing the hotel ahead, Megan forced a decision on herself. Her idea of the future had been eradicated entirely; that was what made her vulnerable to renegade emotions. The new vistas – nursing, a fine education for Bronwen, the whole panorama opening to show wider and wider possibilities – it had caused a tilting in her emotions for a brief, disturbing time. That was all.

As she went through the hotel door and saw Mrs Pughe-Morgan and Bronwen, standing by the staircase waving to her, she suspected that her analysis wasn't too convincing. For the time being, however, and for her peace of mind, it would have to do.

26

'It's the purity of infant life that I adore,' Violet said. 'They're so glad of the world. They get amazed by everyday things and they're overjoyed at the simplest of surprises.'

She and Megan were at the beach, sitting on a rug and watching Bronwen tackle a bucket and spade. The small hands had trouble co-ordinating the movements necessary to fill the bucket, but Bronwen was determined. Cascades of damp sand flew to right and left as she furiously dug a furrow into her own patch of beach and aimed the loaded spade, with varying accuracy, at the gaudy tin pail.

'Did you ever nurse children?' Megan asked Violet.

'Yes, I did a year's fever nursing and after that I spent six months in a children's sanatorium. But I was never very good at that kind of work. I was very young at the time and it distressed me to see children suffering.'

'I can imagine that.'

'What about you, Megan? Do you think you could cope with nursing youngsters?'

'I'm not sure. The notion of helping them appeals to me, but maybe I'd be like you, especially having a child of my own.'

It was the third morning of the holiday. For an hour they had sat and talked about nursing, Megan being as eager to ask questions as Violet was to answer them. They had discussed surgery, obstetrics, orthopaedics and the special nursing care given to the elderly. Now Bronwen's antics with the spade had brought them around to paediatrics.

'I think you'd get an idea of how you'd feel', Violet said, 'if you were to visit a few children's hospitals in advance. Some people take to the work at once. Others, like I did, soon get to a point where they wish they'd never gone near that branch of the profession.'

Megan recalled how protective she had felt towards Tom

when he had been a child. There had been days when she wouldn't let him out of her sight because he looked so vulnerable among all the sturdier children. 'I suppose', she said, 'there's a danger of exhausting yourself, just by trying to spread your concern among so many little patients.'

Violet nodded. 'It's the case with patients of any age, Megan. But with children it's a special danger. You can't explain to babies why they're ill. You can't offer excuses or cool their apprehension. They lie in their cots wondering why they feel so awful, why they hurt, while all you can do is attend them and hope they don't think it's your fault.'

Bronwen came stumbling across the sand, bringing a small conch shell with her. 'Look,' she said excitedly, holding it up for her mother to see. 'Pretty, Mummy.'

Megan took the shell and held it to Bronwen's ear. 'That's the sea you can hear.'

The child listened for a moment, then turned and pointed to the shore. 'That's nicer,' she said, making Megan and Violet laugh.

'She's a treasure, Megan.' Violet watched Bronwen go back to her patch of sand. 'The sea air appears to agree with her. She's been on the move all morning.'

'And she'll be off to the Punch and Judy show with Mrs Pughe-Morgan later. She doesn't seem to want to sleep during the day since we've been here.' Megan smiled fondly at the little figure in her striped bathing dress. 'I'm glad she's having this holiday.'

'Are you glad you're having it, too?' Violet asked her.

'Oh, yes.'

'In spite of it being planned as an indoctrination course?'

'That was only part of it,' Megan said, 'and I don't resent it anyway. You know that. Mrs Pughe-Morgan is a great one for killing as many birds as she can with one stone.'

'Indeed she is.' Violet lay back on the blanket, easing the strain on her back.

Megan grinned. 'I'm pleased it didn't take a whole week of soul-searching before I made up my mind. That could have taken the edge off the holiday.'

'And you really have made your mind up?'

'I have. Those training pamphlets of yours finally convinced me. I want to be a nurse.'

'I'm so pleased,' Violet murmured. 'I love making converts – especially the kind who have the talent to master the profession.'

Megan smiled to herself, remembering with sublime clarity the words her father had spoken to her in a dream, years before. 'You'll master anything you set your heart on. Setting your mind isn't enough. The mind follows the heart; it's a servant of your wanting.' A mastery of life, a mastery of her calling – they could be the same thing. And Megan was sure that both her heart and mind were set on being a nurse.

Violet, her eyes closed against the brightness of the sky, said, 'Bronwen's going to have quite a future, too.'

'When I was able to think about it calmly, I realized just what was being offered her,' Megan said. 'It's wonderful.' As she lay in bed the night before, she had pictured Bronwen grown up, her future a palace of opportunity: ornate, embellished, gleaming. 'I can't find the words to convey what's being done for both of us. Mrs Pughe-Morgan is simply the kindest, most loving – '

'Good morning, ladies.'

Megan looked up and felt her heartbeat trip. John Sykes was standing two yards away, looking smart and cool in a blazer and flannels.

'Why, hello.' Violet pushed herself up on her elbows. 'Another brave soul venturing out from the temple of convalescence, eh? How are the legs holding up, John?'

'It's my first day on the beach,' he said, making an uncertain face. 'I might not be as stable as I thought.' He pointed to the vacant centre of the big rug. 'Would you mind if I sat with you for a while?'

'Please do.'

As John Sykes came forward and lowered himself cautiously, Megan felt her cheeks grow warm again. This time, however, she was sure there would be no runaway emotions. She was simply uncomfortable to be sitting so close to the man.

'Such a lovely day,' he murmured.

'And such lovely company you've found.' Violet laughed. Megan tried to continue looking relaxed.

For ten minutes the three of them made weightless conversation, touching on the weather, the zestfulness of sea air, the pleasant lack of crowds at that time of year and the curious way sand had of getting into the shoes, even when a person walked carefully. Megan contributed what she could, while her mind ran a separate course from her voice.

She could face it now, she decided after a time, she could tell precisely why she felt so stricken the first time she saw John Sykes. It was all to do with similarity, as she had already guessed. He did have mannerisms that were like Alun's. Even the rhythms of his speech had a similarity. The way he used his eyes, looking away in mid-sentence and occasionally staring at the palm of one hand – that was Alun, too. It was still faintly disturbing, but Megan no longer felt any shame in acknowledging the likeness.

'Mummy! Look!' Bronwen came ploughing through the sand with another shell, almost identical to the first one. As Megan held out her arms she caught a small frown on John Sykes's face.

'It's *beautiful*, darling.' Megan caught Bronwen in a hug and swung her on to her lap. 'What shall we do with this one, then?'

Bronwen thought for a moment, then sat the shell squarely on top of her head. 'A hat.'

John Sykes laughed dutifully. 'She's a fine-looking little girl,' he said to Megan. 'I have to apologize, but yesterday I gathered you were *Miss* Roberts.'

Megan nodded calmly. There had been plenty of time to harden herself against ostracism and disdain. 'That's right. I'm not married.' In a perverse way, she suddenly hoped the information would shock him.

But he simply smiled. 'Thank goodness,' he said. 'I thought for a minute my ears had gone faulty, as well as my legs.'

The remark was calculatedly diplomatic, Megan knew, but it was disarming nevertheless. She found herself returning John Sykes's smile.

*

On three successive mornings, John Sykes joined Megan and Bronwen on the beach. By gentle stages he made himself their escort and companion. The excuse was provided by Violet, who had become overtired and had to rest in the mornings, and Mrs Pughe-Morgan, who had located a soldiers'-aid post in the town and now spent the hours from nine until noon helping them to streamline their methods of collection.

On the first morning Megan learned a great deal about John. He was thirty-one and shared a solicitor's practice with his father in Newcastle. He had come to North Wales to recuperate after running his motor car through a dry-stone wall on a moor near his home. John had almost died from his injuries. It had taken six months of surgery and a further three months in Rhyl to bring him to his present condition. It would probably be another month, he believed, before he would be fully recovered. Megan learned, in addition, that he was a keen angler, a lover of Beethoven and a fanatical bridge-player.

But none of the important things Megan learned about John was actually told to her by him. They emerged from observation and what Mrs Pughe-Morgan called listening between the lines.

For a start, the young solicitor was very lonely. He was also shy, romantic, intensely kind and compassionate. Megan would swear, furthermore, that he had never been emotionally close to any woman but his mother who, although John loved her, emerged as a domineering and fiercely possessive old woman.

Three long, eventful mornings saw the acquaintanceship firmly established. John had played games with Bronwen, he had carried on animated conversations with Megan and simultaneously built sandcastles; most pleasing of all, he had offered his friendship and his respect, without patronizing Megan or intruding on areas of her nature that she chose to keep dormant.

On the day before they were due to go back home, as she wheeled Bronwen back to the hotel for lunch, she was forced to confront her own feelings towards John Sykes. By now, there was no doubt about his growing feelings for her.

She liked him, she couldn't deny that. She enjoyed his

companionship. In John she found a response to her ideas and her humour that had been missing from her life since Alun had gone. He was good for her and he had cancelled some of her own loneliness. But she could never love him.

After all her early shame at responding to him as she did, Megan knew now there was no need for guilt or self-reproach. Companionship was no threat to the sanctity of Alun's memory. Neither was friendship. She would be honoured to give John both and to accept the same from him. But nothing more.

As Megan strode up the hotel drive she realized she would have to make that clear to John. He would need to be warned that he was coming dangerously near to loving a woman whose own love rested, and always would rest, with Alun Rees.

The following morning, John was waiting to see them off at the station, as he had promised. He carried the heavy bags along the platform, even though Megan begged him not to try it for fear of harming himself, and loaded them on to the luggage truck at the rear of the train. Mrs Pughe-Morgan had swiftly sensed that the young man was anxious to talk privately with Megan. She thanked John profusely for his help, said goodbye, then took Bronwen with her into the carriage.

'Well, then,' John said diffidently, 'it's been a lovely few days . . .'

'Lovely,' Megan said. 'I've enjoyed myself enormously. You've been very kind to us.'

'Not at all.' He glanced nervously along the train, seeing the guard approach, unfurling his flag as he banged the doors shut. 'Megan, I'd like to say something.' The wide blue eyes were brimming with his intent, but his mouth was moving uncertainly. 'I know it's only been a week – less, in fact, but – '

'John, listen.' Her own voice sounded calm. She also wanted it to sound sincere. 'I'll write to you as I said, and I'll look forward to your letters. I'd like to see you again, too. Often.' She saw the glint of hope in his eyes and realized she was misleading him. The guard blew a shrill warning on his whistle. Hastily, Megan went on, 'John, what I'm saying is that I value you as a friend. Truly. Can you accept me as only that? A friend?'

For a fleeting moment his whole face rejected the idea. But then he was smiling; his lawyer's diplomacy was there to rescue the moment. 'That would please me very much,' he said. He put out a hand and helped her into the carriage. 'Thank you again, Megan. For brightening things this week. And for being a friend.'

The guard closed the door and blew his whistle again. A moment later the train began to move. Megan leaned out of the window and waved. John waved back, a broad smile on his face, his eyes full of inexpressible sadness.

27

Following Violet Rawlings's advice, Megan began to study the craft of nursing in earnest. She bought *Cassell's Text Book for Nurses*, which had been a standard work since 1909, and two more recent texts, *Hull's Anatomy for the Nursing Student* and *Skills of the Sick Room*. These, together with the knowledge she had already absorbed, began to give her a solid picture of a nurse's duties and the scope of her training.

There had been goals in Megan's life before, but none so determinedly sought as this one. In the evenings as she put Bronwen to bed, she would talk to the child, telling her over and over about the exciting, fulfilling future they would both have.

'While you're at your school with all your new friends, I'll be in my school with mine, and we'll have lots to tell each other in the holidays. When I'm a nurse we'll have a little house somewhere. At the times when you're not staying with Aunt Gwendolyn you'll stay with me, and you can bring friends to stay, too.'

Apart from her confident predictions about the new career, Megan's picture of her future with Bronwen was hazy, a fantasy made up of a few certainties and a lot of hopes. Mrs Pughe-Morgan, on the other hand, saw it all very clearly. In a letter to Violet, thanking her for the way she had encouraged Megan, she wrote:

'It will be the finest kind of relationship between a mother and daughter. Bronwen will have a parent who is not simply a figure of tradition tending the home and being denied the world, but a trained professional person to be respected and to be allowed her own separate life. No apron strings, Violet, no tribal notions of duty and obedience. They will be two fulfilled, modern women, people with choice. I am delighted, as you must surely be, to have taken a hand in the foundation of such an enviable state of affairs.'

Two evenings a week, from nine until she could keep her eyes open no longer, Megan sat in her small sitting room with her books, following the course of study recommended by Violet Rawlings. It would not be wise, Violet warned, for Megan to turn up in a hospital in three years' time prepared simply to go through the motions of learning, believing that she knew all there was to know. The work in the wards was demanding and tiring. Megan couldn't prepare for that in advance. But, if she learned as much theory as she could beforehand, then her book study during training would demand much less of her; she could conserve her energies for the heavy work of practical nursing.

Late one night, as Megan sat at her table memorizing the group names of the spinal bones, she heard Bronwen moan in her sleep. She went to the open sitting-room door and listened.

A dream, she decided after a minute. The child was having one of the sleep-time adventures she tried to tell Megan about some mornings while she was being dressed.

As Megan turned back to the table, Bronwen moaned again. Megan crossed to the bedroom door and opened it slowly. She put her head into the room and listened again. Bronwen's breathing sounded disturbed.

Megan tiptoed across the room and switched on the lamp beside her bed. By the cot, she leaned close and put her fingers on Bronwen's cheek. It was hot. Too hot.

The child woke suddenly and cried out, then she began coughing. Alarmed, Megan lifted her out of the cot and laid her against her shoulder, patting her back gently. Bronwen's chest made a congested, rattling sound as she drew in air between coughs.

'There, there, my pet.' She sat on the bed with her, feeling the clammy fingers of concern. When the coughing spasm subsided she sat the child on her knee and looked at her face. It was blotchy red and her curls were plastered flat to her forehead. Her eyes looked glassy and distant.

'Oh, Bronwen, my love. Whatever's happened?' It'll be a cold, she thought, or perhaps even croup. As Megan put out her hand to touch the hot little cheek again, Bronwen gulped sharply and vomited.

In a full-scale panic Megan swung the child face down and let her choke up the thick mucus and half-digested food. Oblivious to the mess on the carpet and on her clothes she cradled Bronwen and made for the bathroom with her. In the passage she met Mrs Pughe-Morgan hurrying from her bedroom, one arm in her dressing gown.

'What is it, Megan? I heard her coughing . . .'

'I don't know.'

Megan swept on to the bathroom with the mistress behind her. At the wash-basin she sponged Bronwen's face with cold water. The child still looked dazed.

'She's terribly red,' Mrs Pughe-Morgan said anxiously, grasping Bronwen's hand and squeezing it. 'My God, she's boiling.'

'Definitely got a temperature.' Megan flattened her hand on Bronwen's cheek and felt the dry heat where she'd wiped away the sweat. 'Before bedtime she said her head was sore. But she's said that before. I thought it was just tiredness.'

'Perhaps we should –'

Bronwen coughed again, four rasping jerks of her throat and chest that left her blue and breathless. For a second it looked as if she wouldn't inhale. When she did it was with a short howl, as if she had been struck.

'Oh, Bronwen, Bronwen.' Megan was distraught. She held the child close to her. Beneath her fright she felt anger. She had been fancying herself as a nurse in the making, yet she hadn't the instinct to know what to do when her own child was taken ill. 'I think we should get the doctor.'

'I was about to suggest that. Just hold on to her, Megan.' Mrs Pughe-Morgan hurried out of the bathroom as Bronwen began to cough again.

It was after midnight when Dr Watkins arrived. By then Bronwen had vomited again, twice, and the bouts of coughing had become more severe, leaving her groaning weakly against her mother's shoulder.

Watkins's examination took less than two minutes. Megan held Bronwen as he ran the stethoscope over her back and chest, then peered at her reddening eyes.

'Pertussis,' he grunted, stepping back. He saw the incomprehension on Mrs Pughe-Morgan's face and said, 'Whooping cough, I'm afraid.'

Megan's heart sank. 'But that's dangerous . . .'

'Potentially dangerous,' Watkins corrected her. 'All childhood lung infections usually are.'

'The poor lamb looks so weak,' the mistress agonized. 'What's the treatment, doctor?'

'It's a long disease, with regular bouts of sickness,' Watkins said, 'so the main aim is to keep the child nourished. She'll need plenty of fresh air, too, because when she goes blue at the mouth it means she's short of oxygen. The only other ingredient is patience.'

Mrs Pughe-Morgan glared at him. 'Are you saying there's no medicine for this hideous condition?'

'None at all,' Watkins said simply.

'That's disgraceful.'

'I agree.' He put his stethoscope in his bag and snapped it shut. 'However, that little girl has a lot more to fight the disease with than most children in these parts. She's the best-fed, rosiest-cheeked toddler for miles. She has reserves, Mrs Pughe-Morgan. Plenty of protein in her and clean open country around. Most cases of pertussis I see are in children who don't have the resources to fight a sore throat.'

Bronwen, moaning softly, began to drowse in Megan's arms. Then with a sudden lurch she stiffened her back and emitted a rasping cough that doubled her over, wheezing for air. Wide-eyed with fear, Megan put her finger into the child's mouth and pulled free a thick blob of mucus.

'Oh, my God . . .' Mrs Pughe-Morgan turned away, her face as distressed as Megan's.

'Watch for that, the first day or two,' Watkins told Megan. 'And don't let her sleep on her back – when she sleeps at all.' He picked up his bag and moved to the door. 'Give her as much simple food as she can get down. Soup, milk, that kind of thing. I'll call back tomorrow.' In the doorway he paused and smiled wanly. 'If either of you can, try to get some rest. This'll be a long job.'

When Mrs Pughe-Morgan had seen Dr Watkins to the door she came straight back to the bedroom. Megan was still standing where she had left her, staring anxiously at Bronwen. The infant was slumped against her breast.

'Give her to me,' the mistress said, gently easing the child into her own arms. 'Now, you go and get the mess cleaned off yourself. After that I'll go to bed for a couple of hours. After *that*, you can get some sleep.'

'No, no,' Megan said, 'I'll sit with her, it's perfectly all right.'

'And what if you nod off with exhaustion just when she needs your help?'

'I won't.' Megan was still looking at the half-sleeping child. Her fever seemed to be worse. As she laboured for breath her chest heaved pathetically under her nightgown. 'I'm too worried to sleep.'

'Megan, we have to tend to Bronwen between us. Nobody can stay awake all day and all night and still function adequately. We owe it to her to be alert.' She pointed to the door. 'Now off to the bathroom with you.'

Megan obeyed. She stayed in the bathroom for five minutes, sponging the stains from her dress and apron, wondering faintly why there had to be so much misery in human lives. Especially in small, blameless lives.

As she turned from the basin she saw her face in the mirror. She looked haggard. It was a familiar look; once she'd had it for months on end. She knew, then, that there was a great deal in what Mrs Pughe-Morgan said about resting and sharing the vigil. That look, those hollow eyes and drawn cheeks, were the clear sign that Megan's rehabilitation wasn't complete. She was like the children over in Drynfor that Dr Watkins had mentioned – she didn't have too much in the way of reserves.

When she got back to the bedroom the mistress was lowering Bronwen gently into the cot.

'She's asleep,' she whispered, tucking the blanket around the child's shoulders. 'Get yourself a stool and sit by her. A basin would be a good idea, too. We might as well be prepared.'

When Megan was settled by the cot Mrs Pughe-Morgan

patted her shoulder. 'I won't say, don't worry. But don't worry more than you have to.'

Worry, Megan thought as the mistress left. She'd done more of that in her life than anything else, or so it seemed.

She put her hand on the side of the cot and rested her chin on it. Bronwen looked peaceful, but her breathing was irregular and the fever had bloated her face. Megan felt her heart clench. 'My poor little lamb,' she whispered, then sat back sharply, knowing she mustn't get over-emotional. She had to be like a good nurse, concerned but not so involved that she made silly mistakes. She had to be objective.

It wouldn't be easy to do that. Megan glanced uneasily at the cot, wondering how to distract herself for two hours, how to keep from falling apart over the heartbreaking condition of the child.

She decided to think about the future again. The fantasy was familiar now – herself a little older, Bronwen fifteen or sixteen, both with a sound love and understanding of each other. That seemed a fine unity, the very finest. It was a sunny consummation of hope and effort. Megan sat motionless with the bright picture in her head. She remained like that until Bronwen groaned and began coughing again.

On the third day Mrs Foskett came to the morning room and offered the mistress a suggestion.

'Willow bark, ma'am.' She nodded at Mrs Pughe-Morgan's uncomprehending face. 'It's worked wonders before now. Chewing it helps rheumatics, boiling up an infusion's good for chest ills. It wouldn't hurt, and I'm sure it'd do a power of good.'

'Bronwen has a virus, Mrs Foskett. It's only time and constant attention that'll do any good.'

Mrs Foskett looked grave. 'She's got terrible thin, though. And the coughing's no better. Nor the vomiting. Fair churns my insides to hear it. I thought it might be an idea to try something before she gets weaker or loses much more flesh off her.'

'For the time being,' Mrs Pughe-Morgan said, keeping her

tone even and kindly, 'we'd just better do what Dr Watkins says. Bronwen's taking a little soup each day, and she's had quite a few drinks of milk this morning already. Nourishment's all we're supposed to give her. No medicine.'

Mrs Foskett went worrying off to the kitchen. Alone again, Mrs Pughe-Morgan removed the folded newspaper from the book she had been reading before the old woman came in. It was one of Megan's medical volumes. She put on her spectacles and read the small type carefully, sighing softly as she did.

PERTUSSIS: An illness of children caused by the virus *Bordetella pertussis*. The symptoms are of varying severity, among them fever, fits, nosebleeds, a discharge of mucus and always a severe cough. Complications in the more serious cases are pneumonia, collapse of the lung and injury to the child's brain.

She slapped the book shut, deciding to read no further. Given a grain less common sense, she might have been tempted to try Mrs Foskett's witch-woman remedy. Never in all her recollection of illness in children had the mistress seen a condition so distressing as Bronwen's. And even though Dr Watkins had warned that it would be a long time before they saw any improvement, it seemed barbarously unnatural that the child should have suffered as long as she already had.

The mistress went to the writing table and picked up her address book. She thumbed through it until she had the name she wanted, then snatched up the telephone and dialled the operator.

'Hello? Ah, this is Mrs Pughe-Morgan, Betsy. I have a London number I'd like you to get me, if you'd be so kind.' She gave the operator the number, then waited, tapping her foot until a distant voice answered. 'Good morning,' she said, 'is that the consulting rooms of Sir Bernard Clopton? My name is Pughe-Morgan, Gwendolyn Pughe-Morgan. Could I possibly have a word with Sir Bernard? I'm an old friend.'

There was more waiting while the physician was brought to the phone.

'Hello? Bernard? How are you? Yes, yes, I'm fine, never better. And Katherine, how is she? Super, do give her my love –

we must meet one day when I'm in town and have lunch or something. Look, Bernard, I'll come to the point. I'm not a person who normally favours one medico over another, since I think you're all charlatans, but I'm after a second opinion here, off the record, of course.'

She explained about Bronwen. She went into detail about the number of times she had thought the child was going to choke, about the vomiting, the nose-bleeds and the terrible pain. Breathlessly she recounted the two terrible, endless nights when Bronwen moaned for rest and couldn't have it, because her inflamed lungs insisted on purging their mucus in coughs as harsh as a miner's and twice as damaging. She told him how the child had become so weak she could scarcely hold her head up to be sick.

When she had finished, Sir Bernard told her exactly what Dr Watkins had told her.

'Bernard,' she said, exasperated, 'this is supposed to be an age of medical enlightenment. Clinical wizardry. Are you seriously telling me that nothing can be done with a disease they've had countless years to study and millions of cases to experiment with? Is that what you're telling me?'

That was precisely right, Sir Bernard said. Then before she could say any more he excused himself; he had a patient waiting.

Mrs Pughe-Morgan put down the telephone and stared at the wall. She had never felt so powerless. 'Damn bloody doctors to bloody hell!' she hissed, not meaning it at all.

When she felt calmer she went upstairs and softly opened Megan's bedroom door. Megan had her back to her, bending over the cot.

'How is she?' The droop of Megan's shoulders told her there was no improvement. The mistress crossed to her side and put an arm round her. Bronwen was lying on her side, mouth wide open, gasping. Her cheeks and mouth were blue. 'Another spasm?'

'The longest yet,' Megan said. She turned dark-rimmed eyes to the mistress. 'There's no end to it, is there?'

'Go downstairs and have some coffee, Megan. Chat to Mrs Edgar, distract yourself for a while. I'll stay with Bronwen.'

'You stayed with her most of last night.'

'Because you were worn out.'

Megan sat down on the stool. 'I'll stay. I want to. If I'm away from her ten minutes I get in a panic.' She looked up at Mrs Pughe-Morgan and smiled faintly. 'It's getting to be like a dream. Night, day, night, day. Endless, no real sense of time.'

'Until she gets to the turn in the road,' the mistress said. 'Then we'll feel time move. Hold that thought in your head, my dear. Bronwen's moving towards recovery, and we're with her however long it takes.'

At four o'clock that afternoon, Bronwen suffered a coughing fit and a bout of vomiting simultaneously. As Megan held the thin body extended between her arms, face down over a bowl, the child began to shudder as the collison of events cut off all air and her brain threw the body into a fit.

'Ma'am!' Megan screamed. 'Ma'am!' She struggled to get Bronwen under one arm and unblock her throat with her fingers. The child gurgled and her eyes bulged. '*Ma'am!* Quick! Oh God, quick!' Bronwen's head snapped back and her teeth closed on Megan's fingers. 'Help me with her! Please!'

The door flew open. Mrs Pughe-Morgan took one disbelieving look, then rushed across the room, arms outstretched. She held Bronwen, struggling to keep from dropping her as the fit worked its course. Megan, sobbing wildly, cleared the blocked mouth and squeezed the tiny ribs to encourage the lungs to breathe.

The attack passed abruptly. The fit left Bronwen and let her body sag. The coughing stopped, the stomach had no more to offer up. The child became calm, her breathing shallow and rasping like the wrinkling of coarse paper. Mrs Pughe-Morgan put her carefully in the cot, then turned and strode to the door.

'That damned doctor's coming and he's going to do *something*,' she hissed as she went out.

Megan stood by the cot, exhausted, watching Bronwen's eyes close in sleep. It was hard to be glad the attack was over, when she knew there were bound to be others, and others. She wiped her eyes with her sleeve, then knelt on the floor, watching the panting infant through the spars and trying to hum a lullaby to her. 'Bronwen, my dearest lamb,' she whispered.

Weariness drew her to the stool. Megan eased herself up on to it. She felt a flicker of gladness that the child could at least sleep for a time. She leaned close to the cot and tilted her head; she was probably imagining it, she thought, but Bronwen's breathing seemed a little easier now. Megan kept watching, trying to determine if she were right. After a minute her own eyes began to close, gradually, as sleep overtook her.

Mrs Pughe-Morgan waited for the doctor in the hall. She paced from the door of the morning room to the hatstand and back again, arms stiff behind her back, head down. He had argued on the telephone, he had as much as told her she was wasting his time. Mrs Pughe-Morgan had been obliged to draw on her reserves of persuasion. She had warned Watkins that if he didn't come right away she would send her gardeners and have him brought, struggling if need be. Watkins said he would be along as soon as he could manage.

She opened the front door at the first knock. Dr Watkins stood frowning at her.

'Well,' he said stiffly, 'I'm here.'

'The time it took you, I imagined you'd decided to walk.'

'Now, Mrs Pughe-Morgan –'

She put up a hand. 'Doctor, I am distraught. I may have said things to you that I will regret in time, but please don't encourage me to say any more of them.'

'Let's have a look at the child, then,' Watkins said huffily. 'Though I'm warning you, there's nothing in this bag or in my head that can be of much help. The disease has a course to run, and –'

'Something will have to be done.'

The voice was imperious enough to silence him. Watkins followed Mrs Pughe-Morgan as she marched briskly up the stairs.

Megan woke with a start as the door opened. She saw the mistress and behind her the doctor.

'I must have dropped off.' She looked in the cot as they approached, then jumped to her feet. She couldn't believe it. Bronwen wasn't labouring to breathe any more. She was lying

268

halfway on her back, her little hands calm and her face dreamily serene. Even the terrible redness had left her face. 'Bronwen, my darling!' Megan reached down into the cot but the doctor restrained her.

'Don't, Megan,' he said sharply, leaning over the cot and touching Bronwen's face.

Megan didn't understand. She looked again. Such peace, such a miraculous change. The turning in the road, just as Mrs Pughe-Morgan had said. She looked at the mistress, standing apprehensively behind the doctor. 'Look, ma'am,' she breathed. 'Look at her.'

Dr Watkins turned from the cot and looked levelly at Megan. She returned his look, reading pain in his eyes.

'I'm afraid she's passed away,' Watkins said. 'I'm terribly sorry, my dear.'

28

'None of us is going to be much good to her, moping about the place like this. That lass needs a bit of cheer about her. She wants gingering up.'

Griffiths was leaning in through the door from the garden, watching Mrs Edgar chopping vegetables on the kitchen table. She moved slowly, like someone who had worked too long without sleep. Behind her Clara was stirring a sauce with an identical lack of energy, sullenly watching the whorls her spoon made in the creamy liquid.

'It's been a week,' Griffiths went on, 'eight days in fact, and you're all still going on like doomers. The mistress too. That's no way to buck Megan up.'

Mrs Edgar put down her knife and looked at Griffiths. 'And I suppose you're jaunting round spilling sunshine all day long,' she said flatly.

'I'm not in the house all the time, near her, like. If I was, I'd make an effort.'

'We're all making an effort,' the cook snapped. 'But it's Megan herself that's the worry – you can't be whistling and singing when somebody's like that.'

In truth the weight on Mrs Edgar, and on the others in the household, was twofold. None of them could forget the sight of Bronwen lying pale and beautiful in the small white coffin. That would haunt them for years; it would intrude and sadden every memory of the little girl they had loved. Just as agonizing was the recollection of Megan, standing beside her dead child, her eyes hollowed with grief and bewilderment. Since the day of the funeral, Megan hadn't spoken a word to anyone. When she moved in the house her misery and her suffering moved with her, like an impenetrable shroud.

'If there's to be a Judgement Day, like they reckon there is,' Mrs Edgar said, 'I'll be asking the Almighty a hard question or two.' She began chopping the vegetables again. 'There's not a bad bone in that girl's body, and Bronwen was as good and fine a child as anyone could want.' She paused and waved her knife at the window. 'There's herds of them out there as needs flaying, they're that steeped in badness, yet they're walking the world in health and good fortune . . .'

'It was always the way,' Griffiths sighed. 'Still, I think somebody should try to pull Megan out of herself a bit.'

Clara turned her head and stared at him. 'If you can think of a way, just be letting us know.'

Mrs Pughe-Morgan came into the kitchen. She still wore black. At her throat there was a slender silver chain with a tiny ornate silver locket. Inside it, though she had told no one, was a single lock of Bronwen's hair.

'Mrs Edgar, I've decided to cancel dinner this evening. I've called the guests and told them. I should have warned you earlier, but I only decided a few minutes ago.'

'That'll be all right, ma'am,' Mrs Edgar assured her. 'We wasn't all that far ahead with it, any roads.'

'Good.' The mistress went out again.

Mrs Edgar looked at Clara. 'That's every appointment she's cancelled, so far. I thought she was perking up a bit.'

'She's trying to, bless her.' Clara sighed glumly at the sauce. 'I suppose I'll have to chuck this lot away now. Seems I've done nothing but throw stuff out lately.'

'We'll all get back to normal soon enough, Clara.'

'We better had,' Griffiths grunted. He turned from the door and walked off slowly down the path. When he got to the shed Jenkin was dragging out his wheelbarrow, cursing softly as the wheel caught on the lip of the door-frame.

'Will we be going over to Drynfor tonight and getting ourselves disgraceful drunk?' Griffiths asked him.

Jenkin hauled the barrow free of the door and set it down on the path. He straightened, rubbing his back. 'There's times when you read my mind, boyo. Nothing like a gutful of Parry's balm to soften the cares, eh?'

'I'm going to try for two gutfuls tonight, I fancy,' Griffiths told him solemnly. 'It'll take that much to put some cheer in me.'

Jenkin nodded sagely. 'I'll do my best to keep up with you.' He gripped the shafts of the wheelbarrow and started off towards the vegetable garden. 'It's a damn good job that horse knows his way home,' he mumbled.

Upstairs in her bedroom, Megan was standing by the window, seeing the old gardener make his way slowly down the path with his barrow. Nothing of what she saw registered. It was a bright day and there were flowers in abundance. The bushes and trees were rich with the foliage that Megan called their livery, but none of the beauty could penetrate. Nor any of the peace.

She turned and looked around the room. It was so cold without Bronwen. Her eyes fell on the cot. The mistress had wanted to have it removed but Megan insisted it be left where it was. Now she realized it only made the emptiness worse.

Impulsively, knowing she shouldn't do it, Megan went to the small chest of drawers by her wardrobe and pulled open the top drawer. Bronwen's clothes lay in neat laundered piles, pressed and folded. Again her absence was like something solid, a wounding presence. 'She is elsewhere,' the minister had intoned, 'gone to a place of everlasting peace...'

Megan touched a woollen jacket, a nightdress, the bundle of cotton stockings so small they could have been made for a doll. By now she was beyond tears. She lived her days in a darkness of misery that had steadily removed her love of life, and her need for it.

Megan spun suddenly, sure she had heard a sound in the cot, a movement. It stood mute and empty in the sunlight. She looked down and saw she was holding a small woollen glove, pale pink with blue flowers embroidered on the back. Staring at it, she had a vision of her life stretched out behind her, a long road shadowed and without meaning. There was nothing ahead.

Mrs Pughe-Morgan heard the long despairing howl as she crossed the hall on her way to the study. She began running, hurtling up the stairs and across the landing. There was a scream an instant before she burst into Megan's bedroom.

'Oh, sweet Jesus...'

Megan was on her knees on the floor, her face twisted in a

paroxysm of anguish. Blood trickled down her forehead. In her hand she clutched a chunk of her own hair, ripped out by the roots.

'Megan, for God's sake . . .' Mrs Pughe-Morgan struggled with her as she put up both hands and tore out more. It was a terrible sound, like grass being uprooted. The pain made Megan scream again. Now there were three raw patches oozing blood and she tried to pull out more chunks, bigger.

'Megan!' The mistress roared in her ear and slapped her violently on the side of the head. Megan toppled, still clinging to her hair with both hands. Her feet kicked wildly as the mistress grasped her under the arms and dragged her across the floor to the side of the bed. With a violent jerk Megan was put on her knees, then pushed over on to the counterpane.

Without breaking pace, the mistress set one knee on the bed and grabbed Megan's wrists. She leaned down hard and forced her elbows on to the bed. Struggling, she put her face close to Megan's. 'Control yourself!' she shouted. 'Stop this! You're injuring yourself, stop it!' She felt Megan's resistance sag. 'Now be calm. Be calm.' When she felt it was safe, she released her grip. 'Just settle. Don't do yourself any more harm.'

For minutes Mrs Pughe-Morgan sat watching as the hysteria deserted Megan. She became calmer, but the look of derangement didn't leave her face. Blood had matted the front of her hair and was smudged across her forehead. She looked like a madwoman who had been in a fight.

'This does no good,' the mistress said softly. 'You must never turn your anger against yourself. It only causes more pain, more suffering . . .'

'I don't want to live,' Megan groaned. Her head moved restlessly. 'Life's all pain, I want out of it, away . . .'

'Don't talk like that.'

'It's true.' The derangement, the mistress realized, was really the far border of endurance, etching itself on Megan's face. 'There's nothing left. It's all been taken. I don't want the rest of my life.'

'Megan . . .'

'Everything I've loved, even the baby I grew inside me . . .'

273

Mrs Pughe-Morgan felt her throat tighten. For days she had wondered and fretted, seeking some way to get through to Megan and soothe the hurt. She hadn't known the girl was drifting away from reality, abandoning it a piece at a time. Now she was gazing down at ultimate despair. Her Megan could see no reason at all to go on living. Worse, Mrs Pughe-Morgan could think of no reason that she wouldn't reject.

'Lie still, Megan. I'll get water and antiseptic and bathe your head.' She went to the door. 'Promise you won't do anything more. Promise you won't injure yourself.'

Megan turned her head, showing a face of total abjection. The mistress read it and understood. Megan wouldn't hurt herself any more. But it was just as clear she had no intention of hanging on to life. She had discovered that awful territory of the mind where it is possible to let life drift away, unwanted. Mrs Pughe-Morgan slipped out of the room, fighting back her tears.

By the time the raw patches on Megan's scalp had been bathed and the mistress had dabbed on some stinging iodine, an argument of sorts had formed itself in her mind. It relied heavily on Megan's innate common sense.

'We live because we have to,' Mrs Pughe-Morgan said. She sat on the side of the bed, holding one of Megan's hands. It was limp, insensitive. 'No one has more talent than you for acknowledging that. Your loss has been terrible and I'm sure no one could imagine your pain – but you're alive, Megan, you have all the attributes of a whole and special person. You've got gifts that'll shine in you again. Time will prove that – and the time will be shorter if you'll accept life, unpleasant as it is for the present.' She leaned close. 'Life is a precious gift, my dear.'

'It's a gift I reject.' Megan's voice was cold, unnervingly assured.

'Don't say that . . .'

Megan moistened her lips. 'All I've learned from my life', she said, 'is that it attracts misery. I've tried hard to make it fulfilling and bright, ever since you showed me how. I think I've always made an effort to get the most from my existence. But my life's not the kind that anything works for . . .'

'That isn't true . . .'

274

'It is,' Megan insisted. 'I lost my father, that was the first black sign. Then, even when I tried to help my family, I lost them.'

'You're looking at it the wrong way . . .'

'I gave every particle of my love and support to Alun. I lost him, too. I thought I could never feel as bad as I did then. Even so, I learned to accept that loss. It tore me, but in time I managed to see some hope. A lot of it. I mustered a faith in the future and put all my love with my little Bronwen.' Megan stared at the ceiling. 'I'll tell you something. The prospect of death doesn't distress me at all. It's something cold, it promises no pain, and I can accept it. But I can't bear the notion of going on living.'

'Megan, Megan . . .'

'It's true.'

'But there have been good things in your life, good things you still have . . .'

Megan shook her head. 'None of them eases the pain of what I've lost.'

There was a soft knock at the door.

'It'll be the doctor,' Mrs Pughe-Morgan said. 'When I went down for the antiseptic I called him. He'll give you something, most likely. Something to help.' She watched the despondency darken Megan's face and realized her words were trite, empty. 'Excuse me, my dear.'

She went to the door and stepped out into the passage. Watkins looked at her warily.

'How is she?'

'Bad. Very bad.'

'Specifically?'

'She's lost her interest in living.'

Watkins looked at the bedroom door and sighed. 'She's suffering from compound tragedy,' he muttered. 'It can be hard curing a person of that.' He tapped his bag. 'I can give her something to delay matters and make her rest. But it'll be no cure. I suspect that lies entirely in your hands.'

'I'm not too hopeful I can manage it, doctor.' For once Mrs Pughe-Morgan had a despairing look of her own.

'Any particular reason why you feel that way?'

She nodded. 'Megan's arguments are a lot sounder than mine.'

The Lion was crammed tight with drinkers, elbowing and jostling, breathing their beer on each other and trying to make their voices heard. The air was thick with tobacco smoke and the wafting odours of snuff. An old man by the fireplace was singing to the assembly in loud, strident Welsh, while beside him his son did his best to harmonize, snigger and drink, all at the same time. If one sound occasionally predominated it was laughter. Even those who weren't enjoying themselves were trying.

'Regular foxhole, this pub,' Griffiths said to Jenkin. They were at the end of the bar near the door, squeezed into a corner. 'Just the place to come when you're dodging the guns of reality.'

Jenkin grinned over the rim of his mug. 'You don't half get poetic when you're part-way stewed, mate.'

'The beer seems to concentrate my thinking.' Griffiths said it straight-faced, as if Jenkin's observation were to be taken seriously. 'If things had been different, I fancy I'd be one of them bards by now, getting up on the platform at the Eisteddfod and spouting with the best of them.'

'And you could always trim the grass in the intervals,' Jenkin grunted.

They had been in the pub for two hours. True to his threat, Griffiths had consumed twice as much beer as he usually did, swilling down the first four pints in less than twenty minutes. Now his pace was leisurely and his movements had become fluid. He smiled at everyone who was thrust against him in the crush. Jenkin was less intoxicated, but he was numb enough to enjoy himself.

'It's true, though,' Griffiths said. 'When I was a lad I had a talent for versifying. Used to make up new words to old songs, and I could put rhymes together for different occasions.' He shook his head wistfully at his pint. 'My old man hated it. He used to belt me round the ear and tell me he didn't want no pansy poets round his house. He wanted me to be hard, like him.

Tough, see. Indestructible.' He sniffed. 'By the time he was the age I am now, he'd been dead five years.'

There was a commotion at the other end of the bar as a large fat man slipped on a puddle of beer and went down, taking two lighter men with him. Jenkin watched, beguiled by the entertainment. The fat man stood up, swayed, then slipped again and landed on his backside in front of the bar. He looked up at Parry, the landlord, and solemnly asked if he could have another pint, since he'd smashed the one he'd been holding.

Jenkin turned away, laughing. 'It's a fair old bit of fun, a Saturday night.'

'You look the better for it,' Griffiths told him. 'How're you feeling, anyway?' Jenkin's sciatica had been troubling him lately. 'The medicine working, is it?'

Jenkin rubbed his back and nodded. 'I can honestly say I'm feeling grand. I'm only in half the pain I was this morning.'

Another commotion was attracting the men standing by the door. It was outside, a clamouring of male and female voices. Through the etched glass of the windows torches were visible, waving and flickering.

'Don't tell me the Germans is dropping flares on us,' Griffiths mumbled, peering through a crack in the window frame.

The noise in the pub gradually subsided as more and more customers drifted to the door to see what was happening. The sound from outside became clearer. The people on the street were singing.

'Bloody hell,' Parry groaned. He pushed his way to the door and stepped outside. He came back in after a minute, his face rigid with loathing. 'Powell and his bunch again,' he told Griffiths as he passed. 'Peddling the good word while decent folk are trying to get drunk.'

Griffiths looked intrigued. He laid his hand on Jenkin's shoulder. 'Let's have a look,' he said. 'Bring your drink with you.'

The scene outside was like a confrontation before some comic battle. Gathered around the door of the pub and along the pavement were about twenty of Parry's customer's, most of them still clutching their beer mugs. Opposite them, flanked by

277

their gaunt-faced torchbearers, were the group of Baptists who called themselves the Night Sentinels, with Reverend Powell to the fore. They were giving a lusty rendering of 'See the Sinner at the Brink'. In the torchlight their holy zeal looked cave-eyed and daunting.

Griffiths and Jenkin came and stood near the edge of the road, gulping thoughtfully from their glasses. 'Look,' Griffiths said, nudging Jenkin. 'There's that flaming Agnes.'

On Powell's right, straining her jaw on the wrathful syllables, Agnes stood wide-eyed with conviction, clutching a Bible tightly to her bosom.

'That moustache of hers don't get any better,' Jenkin observed.

Griffiths shrugged. 'I'm not so sure. It's got thicker since I saw her last.'

Jenkin began to laugh. He had an infectious chortle and soon it began to spread. Men behind him and on either side started to giggle, each one finding his own source of hilarity in the Baptist congregation. Then Griffiths's baritone chuckle set in and within seconds every onlooker from the Lion was laughing without restraint. The noise of it brought out others. They caught the mood with the speed that only drinkers can. Their racket drowned the hymn.

Powell waved his followers to silence. He stood glaring at the rubber-kneed revellers, his lips drawn back from clenched teeth, his eyes laying a condemnation on every face.

'Vermin of the alehouse!' he cried.

Agnes stepped forward and whispered something to him. Powell's vulture head turned to Griffiths, who was laughing so hard he had to grip his glass with both hands.

'You mock men and women who are about the Lord's work!' Powell roared. He was shaking with anger, stepping forward into the road and waving his Bible as if it were a sword. 'You are intent on your own destruction!'

'Never saw nothing like it,' one of Parry's regulars told the man next to him. 'They used to just stand there and let him rant. They never *laughed* at him before.'

'You are lusting after eternal damnation!'

Suddenly the laughter began to fade. The sight of a man half crazed with anger was too bizarre to be laughable for long.

Powell's voice seemed to gain in strength as the noise died down. 'Braying jackals! You are enfeebled by your own corruption! Your spirits are withered by drink and licentious talk! The Lord does not hold you guiltless!' He took another firm stride forward. 'He knows your names. Your sins are indelible in his book of justice!'

Then his eyes fixed on Griffiths, who was grinning amiably at the roadside, nursing his drink.

'We are in the presence of some whose sin, whose complicity in vice have already consigned them to the flames!'

There was a moment of complete silence. The only movement came from the torch flames. As Powell continued to stare, the smile faded from Griffiths's face.

'There are some', Powell hissed, 'who should know that the Lord's wrath is awesome and relentless.'

Griffiths bent down slowly and set his glass on the ground. As he stood up his eyes were developing a wrathful glint of their own. 'Would you like to say what you mean, Reverend?'

Powell looked surprised. They had never dared laugh before; now they were talking back. 'My meaning is clear enough,' he said.

'Who's supposed to know about the relentless wrath you're on about?' Griffiths stepped into the road, confronting the preacher. His voice was menacingly quiet.

'You,' Powell said. The firm assurance had left his face. He glanced over his shoulder for an instant, as if to make sure his followers were still there. 'You and your cohort there.'

'And tell me', Griffiths said, 'how we should know better than anybody about this terrible wrath?'

Powell had not come out on the streets to conduct a dialogue. He was not conditioned to discussion or argument. Glaring at Griffiths, he retreated to his normal territory of bellowing rhetoric. 'It is known to all! I will not soil my mouth with the retelling . . .'

'You'll tell me, right in front of everybody,' Griffiths said, 'or you won't be going home tonight.'

Powell considered the impasse. The silence and anticipation were pressing on him. Suddenly he wasn't God's emissary. He was one man being confronted by another. He took a long, deep breath and trusted to his authority and the righteous command in his voice.

'A vile sinner has been punished,' he said, 'and the fruit of her sin has been carried off to eternal – '

He didn't finish. Griffiths took three steps forward, grabbed Powell by the neck and dragged him across to the pub. He slammed the wriggling body against the wall and put his face close.

'How old are you, Powell?'

'Let me go! Take your hands off me!'

Griffiths kept him pinned there with one hand on the stringy neck. No one made a move. The Baptists and the drinkers were like startled effigies.

'Tell me your age, Powell.'

The preacher gulped. 'I'm fifty-seven.'

Griffiths nodded, just once, and stepped back. His hand came away from Powell's throat. 'That's good,' he murmured. 'I don't want to go belting an older man.' His right arm shot out with startling speed. The bunched knuckles cracked on Powell's mouth and his head banged the wall. Griffiths stood and watched as the preacher slid slowly to the ground, then he turned and walked across to the huddle of torchlit Baptists.

'When he's fit to hear you,' he said, 'tell him I'll be ready to martyr him for his cause any time he likes.' He paused to let that sink in. 'And tell him this, too. He might be scared of God's wrath, but it's mine he's really got to worry about.'

In a silence that was now reverential, Griffiths picked up his glass, drank from it and walked back into the pub.

Everyone watched as Powell slowly got to his feet and staggered his way across to his followers. Agnes alone ran forward and put out a supporting arm, but Powell shoved her away.

In the pub, Griffiths was receiving his free pint and a brimming glass of whisky from Parry when the cheer broke outside. Seconds later the customers came pouring back in,

Jenkin at their head. They clustered around, slapping Griffiths's shoulders, tousling his hair and deafening him with congratulations and praise.

'He won't be back here in a hurry,' Parry said to Griffiths when the noise began to settle to the customary hubbub. 'You did us proud, boy.' He glanced to either side, making sure no one else was listening. 'Reckon you showed one or two of us up, too. Me included.'

'Don't go making me a hero,' Griffiths complained.

Parry shook his head. 'Folk like Powell, they come along and tell us what's what, and we don't say nothing, except to each other.' He considered the phenomenon. 'You know what? I reckon it's because him and the ones like him, they've got a flag, haven't they? We haven't, so we don't feel like we're an army, even if we look it. We're all who we are, each and every man. Powell's lot, they're all the same, toeing the very same line. It's like one bloke with twenty or thirty faces. We get overpowered, like.'

Griffiths downed his whisky in one. He stood gasping for a minute, clearly enjoying the effect, then he leaned both elbows on the bar. 'Powell's a bad bugger of a man,' he said. 'It wouldn't matter what flag he had. Bad is bad.'

Jenkin, who had been standing by in admiring silence, put an arm around Griffiths's shoulder. 'You're going to sleep sound tonight,' he said. 'I reckon you did yourself a hell of a favour out there. You're taking nothing home to ache over.'

'Maybe,' Griffiths said. He looked at his old companion. 'I didn't do it for me, though. That was for our Megan. Not that it'll make much change in her, I don't suppose.' He sighed heavily and set to attacking his pint.

29

For a week Mrs Pughe-Morgan watched Megan closely. She had no clear idea what she was watching for. Dr Watkins said that Megan had entered a phase of melancholia which could get better or worse at any time. 'Just watch her. Never let her out of your sight for too long.'

The watching produced a trace of encouragement for the mistress. As Megan resumed her duties as housekeeper, it became clear that she had pulled back from the edge of the blackness that threatened to devour her a few days before. Mrs Pughe-Morgan chose to believe that the crisis point had passed.

Megan wasn't at all cheerful, however. She conducted herself in frowning silence from morning to night, speaking only when she had to; but there was no sign of anguish. Instead, her spirit appeared to have anchored her in a territory midway between contentment and despair. She was accepting again, but this time she had accepted colourless monotony. Megan was putting up with life.

A month after Bronwen died, a letter came from John Sykes, addressed to Mrs Pughe-Morgan. In it, he explained that Violet Rawlings had told him the terrible news. He asked if it would be wise of him to write to Megan at present, offering his condolences, or if a discreet silence would be better for the time being.

In her reply the mistress told John that she was frankly in a quandary. On the one hand, it would seem better to wait until Megan put some distance between herself and the tragedy; on the other hand, she was obviously in need of distraction. Mrs Pughe-Morgan closed by telling John that the wisest course was probably to delay for a few weeks, then to write her a letter that was aimed at cheering, rather than consoling her.

John waited until August. Instead of writing he turned up at the house in person. The visit had been arranged in advance with

Mrs Pughe-Morgan, who warned John that Megan was still not communicating with people. Nevertheless, she said, it was well worth trying to distract her for a while.

John had been prepared for a change in Megan. What he found was a transformation. The bright girl he had known in Rhyl with her inquisitive eyes and mobile expression had been supplanted by a distant, pale creature who refused to meet his gaze for more than a second at a time.

There had been a moment's surprise when she saw John, but Megan quickly returned to her withdrawn state as they strolled across the broad lawn behind the house.

'I hope you don't mind me dropping in like this, all unannounced and so on.'

Megan shook her head. 'It was kind of you to take the trouble.' She paused, then added, 'Of course, I'll have to get back to the house soon. So much to do.'

They walked slowly. John still had a slight limp and had to wear a temporary hip brace which curtailed his movement. He told Megan that he was really quite fit now; he was back at home and had started handling cases at the practice.

'You came all the way here from Newcastle?'

'Oh, no. I've been in London for a few days, representing a client.' He stopped and looked across at the summerhouse. 'Megan, I don't want to disturb any wounds, but I want you to know how sad I was to hear . . .'

'Yes.' Megan stood with her hands folded, staring at the grass. 'Thank you.'

John cleared his throat. 'Are you feeling well enough, within yourself?'

'Well enough.' Megan showed him her eyes for an instant. They looked lifeless. 'I'm getting on with my work. There's plenty to keep me occupied.'

'I was wondering if perhaps a holiday might be the thing. We have a nice roomy place on the outskirts of town. It would be a pleasure to have you with us for a few days.'

Megan was staring at the ground again. 'I'm best on my own, John,' she said. 'I'm no company, I can't get along with people lately. But it's kind of you to suggest it, all the same.'

They walked as far as the summerhouse and stood by the wooden steps, looking back across the sweep of emerald grass towards the house. 'It's very peaceful here, Megan,' John said. 'I suppose this is really the ideal place for you to build up your spirits again . . .'

'I've been here twelve years,' Megan said dully, as if the fact depressed her. 'I was a little girl when I came. The place did raise my spirits back then, it did for years. I only had to come out in the garden, or go down to the wood or the lake and, no matter how bad I felt, the loveliness of this spot lifted me.' She looked at him. 'It's different now, John. I live here and I work here. It's a place to be, that's all.' She sounded almost bitter.

'You'll feel differently, I'm sure.'

She began to reply, but didn't.

'It's a bit like I was,' John went on, 'lying all those months in hospital, then in the convalescent home. I began to feel that was how it would always be. Pain, incapacity, just a grey life stretching ahead. Then one morning I felt the healing really begin. It was like a miracle.'

Megan suddenly appeared impatient. 'John, it was truly kind of you to come and see me, and I do genuinely appreciate that you're trying to encourage me. But I have to tell you I'm not the person you knew, and in spite of what you say I won't ever be.'

'Are you telling me you're not my friend any longer?'

'I'm not capable of being anyone's friend.'

John was silent for a minute, then he said, 'Megan, that doesn't alter how I feel towards you. It's strange, I hardly understand it myself, but I know I'll go on being your friend, even if I don't ever see you again.'

'Then you're being cruel to yourself.'

He frowned at her. 'Why do you say that?'

'Because you're giving your goodwill and your concern to somebody who . . .' She closed her eyes for a moment. 'To somebody who isn't a part of your life, or anybody else's.'

'You talk as if you'd moved away from the world,' John said. 'It's too soon to believe that, Megan. Time can –'

'I've heard all about time,' she told him. 'It'll do nothing but carry me along. I won't change. Friendship's wasted on me.'

284

They walked back to the house in silence. In the hall Megan excused herself. 'I'm sorry, John, but there's work to do. I know you've gone out of your way to come here – if you'd telephoned first I could have saved you the journey.'

John wanted to say more, but Megan had erected a daunting barrier around herself. 'I'll write,' he said. 'It's been wonderful seeing you again. I hope that soon you'll – '

'Goodbye, John.' Megan's mouth made the shape of a smile, then she turned and walked off across the hall.

As Edith was showing John out, Mrs Pughe-Morgan came to the door of the morning room. 'Ah, Mr Sykes. I was hoping to catch you. Can you stay a little longer?'

'Why, of course.'

'Good. Edith tell Mrs Edgar we will be two for lunch.'

The mistress indulged in nothing but pleasantries until they were seated in the dining room. There, she tackled John directly about Megan.

'Tell me frankly what you think, Mr Sykes. I've been close to her for so long that I fear I'm not objective any more. Is Megan going to pull herself out of this, in your opinion?'

He shrugged. 'I gather she's done it before.'

'But then she had the baby to sustain her. Now there's nothing, and this was one tragedy piled right on top of another, remember.'

'Well,' John said, 'I've seen people go like that before. You see them often in the courts. Poor, bewildered, despondent souls, hammered flat by circumstance. Usually they're older than Megan, and maybe that's something to be thankful for – her age. Time does heal, whatever she may think to the contrary, and she still has the greater part of her life ahead of her.'

'If she ever finds the heart to go through with living it.'

John looked shocked. 'Then you don't think she'll change?'

'I keep hoping someone will convince me otherwise,' Mrs Pughe-Morgan said. 'But she's declared herself, and the signs aren't contradicting her. Mr Sykes, I've known Megan since she was a child. There have been a few constant factors in her nature that never left her, even at her lowest. Not until now. Her spirit or soul or whatever's at her core seems to have dimmed. I know I may be wrong, another year might make all the difference, but something tells me that a vital nerve, or some important link with life, has been killed in her.'

John sat staring at his plate for a long time before he spoke. 'I'm afraid I feel helpless. I want to do what I can, of course...'

'You love her, don't you?'

He looked up, his cheeks reddening. 'Yes,' he said. 'Very much.'

'Then can you sustain that? For Megan's sake, even though she doesn't respond?'

'I don't have any choice, Mrs Pughe-Morgan.'

She smiled. 'Well, that's encouraging. I believe if anything will bring her back among us, it's sustained affection, from as many people as possible.'

'I certainly hope it happens,' John said with feeling. 'She's a fine person. A wonderful person.'

Mrs Pughe-Morgan looked at the wide, intense blue eyes. 'If I have one other dear wish,' she said, 'apart from wanting to see Megan restored, I think it might be to see her return what you feel for her. I haven't known you long, Mr Sykes, but I have a sound instinct for these things. You would be terribly good for each other.'

Eighteen months passed, a period when life in the Pughe-Morgan household underwent small changes, while the whole world outside changed profoundly.

The war was over. The young men from Drynfor who had survived returned home, some of them to find they had lost fathers, mothers, brothers or sisters in the epidemic of influenza that had raged across Britain from March to October of 1918.

It was a time of vast international flux. There had been a revolt of the communists in Berlin, followed shortly after by the formation in Germany of the National Socialist Party. The monarchy was declared in Portugal. In Dublin the Sinn Fein Conference adopted a declaration of independence and in Russia the Bolsheviks took Kiev. Science and technology

286

marched forward; 1919 saw the first successful flight of a machine called a helicopter.

Deprived of her war work, Mrs Pughe-Morgan found she had time on her hands. She spent much of that time applying her mind to the problem of Megan.

'To help her,' she told Dr Watkins in the study one day, 'I'll have to hurt myself. Badly.'

Neither the doctor nor the mistress had detected any encouraging change in Megan. Time had merely consolidated her glum detachment. She enacted a counterfeit of sociability with the other members of the staff and remained firmly on the other side of her barrier. Mrs Pughe-Morgan had even heard a tradesman describe her as sour.

'Do you honestly think you can help?' Watkins asked. 'I think your early diagnosis was correct. Some part of Megan's spirit died. Resurrection in any form seems a pretty long hope.'

'Any hope's worth pursuing.'

'What about the young man you told me about – the solicitor? Did he ever get any flicker of response from her?'

Mrs Pughe-Morgan shook her head. 'None. To this day he's trying, mind you. He's written to her twice a month for over a year. Megan hasn't answered one letter.'

'It's hard to imagine her the way she was,' Watkins said wistfully. 'She brightened people, just by exchanging a few words or casting a smile at them.'

'It's her talent, doctor, her finest one. A capacity for cheering people.'

'Well,' Watkins said doubtfully, 'it *was* . . .'

'I choose to believe that talent is still there, along with all the others. If it is, then I'll unearth it.'

'And how do you propose to do that?'

'Oh, there are ways. For a while I tried cajoling her, and I've used up a fair amount of logic and sympathy on her, too. Now I think it's time for bullying.'

'She's fragile,' Watkins warned. 'Hence the carefully constructed wall around her. I wouldn't like to think you'd do her some harm . . .'

Mrs Pughe-Morgan glared at him indignantly. 'I'd be the last person even to risk that. As I said, I'll be the one who's hurt if my plan works.'

'And are you going to tell me what the plan is?'

'No. I don't want you pointing out weaknesses in it and undermining my confidence. If it works, I'll let you know. If it doesn't – well, you'll know anyway.'

The following morning Mrs Pughe-Morgan sent for Megan to join her in the library. When Megan went in she found the mistress behind the long table by the window. Spread out before her were the loose pages of their botany file. Dozens of plant specimens were gummed to the pages, each one labelled and indexed.

'I was just going through this lot again, Megan. Remember the hours we spent, collecting them, cataloguing?'

'Yes, ma'am.'

'And I was just thinking, Megan, how once you'd have been straight across the floor rummaging through the specimens with me, the instant you set eyes on them. I wouldn't have been able to stop you.'

Megan made no response to that. She stood looking at the pages, waiting like any servant.

Mrs Pughe-Morgan came round the table. 'Sit down. I have to talk to you.'

There was a trace of impatience in Megan as she seated herself in the high-backed chair by the table. The mistress came and stood squarely in front of her.

'I dare say you're expecting another of my inspirational lectures. Well, that's not what I've brought you here for.' She paused. 'Megan,' she said sharply, 'look at me when I speak to you.'

Megan looked up, faintly startled.

'Listen to every word I say.' The mistress folded her arms. 'It has gone on long enough. I've watched you drift round this house like a ghost for the better part of two years. I have tried to help, everyone has tried to help, but you've steadfastly resisted or ignored every concerned gesture that's been made towards you. So, instead of coaxing you back to reality, back to who you are, I've decided to force you back.'

288

'Ma'am, I don't want to interrupt –'

'Then don't.' Mrs Pughe-Morgan's eyes were as resolute as her voice. 'Megan, I'm ordering you out of this house.'

Megan blinked with the shock. 'What?'

'I don't want you in my service any longer.'

Colour rose on Megan's face. 'But what have I done?'

'Oh, there are a number of offences with your name against them. Wilful neglect is one. Disrespect . . .'

'But ma'am –'

'All committed against yourself and your capabilities. You've buried your talents, Megan. I won't have you staying here letting them moulder.'

Now there was clear distress on Megan's face. 'But where will I go? I've only ever been here. This is where I learned my job. I don't think I could work for anyone else.'

'This is where you learned more than your job,' the mistress reminded her sharply. 'This is where you were educated, it's where you learned to enquire, probe, enrich your mind and your personality. You flowered here. You won't be here to wither.' The mistress leaned back on the table, supporting herself on rigid arms. 'As to where you'll go – well, Violet Rawlings could organize that.'

'Violet . . .' Megan frowned 'What are you saying?'

'I'm saying you're to take up nursing. You're going out into the world and you're going to get yourself a training.'

'Oh, no, I can't do that, not now.' Megan was beginning to sound tearful, making it harder for Mrs Pughe-Morgan to keep up her stern front. 'Once I wanted to, I was impatient to do it. But it's not in me now.'

'Of course it's in you. And you'll have to do it. The alternative is finding yourself another post in service somewhere.'

'Mrs Pughe-Morgan, why are you doing this to me?' There was pleading in Megan's voice, the first sign of emotion the mistress had heard from her in a long time.

'I told you long ago, Megan, that I didn't want to see you waste your life as a housekeeper. I told you this wasn't the life for you.' She pushed herself away from the table. 'That's even more true now. This place is turning into your spiritual mausoleum.'

'I . . . I have to think it over . . .'

'That should be easy enough. The alternative courses are few and clear.'

Megan stood up. 'May I go?'

'So long as you've completely understood what I've said to you. And Megan – I mean it. I won't keep you on here.'

Megan walked slowly to the door and went out. For a long time the mistress stood gazing down at the specimens scattered on the table. Eventually, as her breath caught, a single tear welled and ran shimmering down her cheek.

That night Megan suffered a fever. As she lay in her bed, shivering and bathed in sweat, the entire buried payload of memories and emotions washed over her, cancelling two years of withdrawal. She wept until there were no tears remaining.

As the fever diminished by slow stages, she became fearful, then despairing, then, towards daylight, strangely calm.

She rose at six. When she had bathed and dressed she took a chair to the window, where she sat and watched the sun rise over the estate. Silently she acknowledged that a miracle had taken place; a long night of the spirit was over and she was prepared, albeit timidly, to face the daylight.

It would never have happened, she knew, if the mistress hadn't delivered her ultimatum. She was aware, too, that Mrs Pughe-Morgan probably never expected it to happen this way; she would have been banking on the world outside bringing Megan back to reality. But the imminence of leaving, the certainty of it, had been enough.

Everything that went through her head during that strange, feverish night had played its part in dismantling her wall of numbness. Her father's voice had come to her again, so had Alun's, Bronwen's too. She saw now they were safe in her heart and for ever bright in memory. But what brought the odd calm had been the memory of her brother, Tom. Not a happy man, but a man nevertheless who fought his crippling and defeated it.

'It was like a rush of anger in me, Megan.'

Her own rush of anger was brought on by the impasse; she couldn't stay at the house any longer, yet she couldn't face the prospect of not being there. Her back was against her own crumbling wall. In her surge of desperation Megan found there was anger in her after all – dim, all but extinguished, but enough of it to make her knock down the remaining bricks and accept what was outside. And acceptance of that brought the calm.

When she got up from her chair she found she was trembling. Her legs felt weak. It was the way anyone would have felt after a long illness. She stood before the mirror and combed her hair, then pinned it into place. For the first time in ages she was conscious of her face, of how it looked.

She crossed to the wardrobe and took out a fresh apron, noticing that every second there was new awareness in her; smells, the colour of the light on the carpet, the growing sounds from the garden.

'I'm not sure if I believe it,' she whispered. But there was no way to disbelieve it. Against all the odds, Mrs Pughe-Morgan had pulled her through again.

At nine Megan knocked on the dining-room door and went in. The mistress was at the table, reading her morning paper. She looked at Megan over the rims of her glasses. Her face was studiedly severe.

'Well, then, Megan. Have you come to tell me when it'll be convenient for you to leave?'

'Yes, ma'am.'

Mrs Pughe-Morgan tightened her lips momentarily. 'And when will that be?'

'Whenever Violet Rawlings can get me placed in nursing school, ma'am.'

The mistress had to smother her pleasure. 'I'll telephone her this morning,' she said. 'I'm sure she'll be able to arrange something very soon.'

'Thank you, ma'am.'

'When Megan had gone the mistress all but ran to the

291

morning room and snatched up the telephone. She called Dr Watkins's number.

'Hello? Dr Watkins? It's Gwendolyn Pughe-Morgan.' She took a deep breath. 'Doctor, I've done it. God help me, I'll be a sorrier and lonelier soul for it, but I've actually done it. Megan's over her depression or melancholia or whatever it was. It's gone. What? No, of course she doesn't look well. She looks terrible. But she looks alive. *Alive*, doctor. Lord, if you could have seen her. In fact, do that, stop by and see for yourself. It's like a tonic.'

After promising Dr Watkins she would tell him later how the cure was effected, she put down the phone and stood smiling out at the morning. The pain would come soon enough, she knew. For the moment, though, it was simply a joy to stand there and relish what had happened.

'Hallelujah,' she whispered, wrapping her arms around herself. '*Hallelujah!*'

Later that morning, Megan took time off from the household accounts to write a letter. It was to John Sykes, apologizing for her long silence and for the way she had behaved towards him when they last met. She told him that she was much better now; she was on a slow road to full recovery, as he had been.

As she explained her plans to leave Mrs Pughe-Morgan's service and go into nursing, Megan felt a tremor of fear. *Fight*, she reminded herself, then sat still until it had passed. Taking up her pen again, she ended the letter by telling John she looked forward to the future with pleasant, if rather nervous, anticipation. After thinking about it for a few minutes, she added a postscript:

'I hope it won't be too long before we see each other again.'

30

The journey was the longest Megan had ever taken on her own. When she set out on the main stretch, from Paddington Station in London to Lime Street, Liverpool, her wonderment at the novelties around her began to recede and she felt the first pangs of separation.

She had left. Mrs Pughe-Morgan's house was no longer her home. Wales wasn't her home. She was going to be a resident of England, without anyone or anything familiar to give her comfort or confidence.

They had all gathered at the front of the house to see her off. Mrs Edgar, too overcome to speak, gave Megan a big wax-paper packet of sandwiches for the journey. Griffiths and Jenkin mumbled their goodbyes, then stood by watching her, sadly reminiscent, as old Mrs Foskett kissed her cheek and lectured her, for the third time, on how to look after herself in a big city. Clara, Edith and Dick made shy gestures of farewell as she climbed into the motor taxi.

In the four weeks since she had told Megan she must go, Mrs Pughe-Morgan had remained cool and studiedly aloof. It hurt Megan only because she knew the mistress was causing herself pain. She was making sure that Megan didn't weaken in her resolve, she was making it clear there was to be no turning back. But as Megan took her seat in the taxi Mrs Pughe-Morgan came to the open door and smiled at her with all the old warmth.

'Well, then,' she said, 'it's happened. You've cut the ties.'

'With your help.'

'At my insistence, Megan. The decision was forced on you, but you made it nevertheless. You didn't buckle.'

Megan nodded. 'What if I had buckled? What would have happened then?'

'That question's academic, and this is no time to discuss it. The point is, you're leaving this refuge.' She nodded towards the house. 'Refuge is the last thing you need, the worst possible

293

thing for you. You need challenges.' She leaned in suddenly and grasped both Megan's shoulders. 'Make me prouder than ever of you.' There were tears in her eyes.

'I'll miss you terribly,' Megan said.

The mistress hugged her tightly, then moved back, dabbing her eyes. 'Go on, then, get out into the world. Make something of yourself. And remember to write.'

Megan sat now with her eyes closed, her head back against the rough head-rest as the train rattled north. She saw the house as she had seen it from the back window of the taxi, diminishing, the mistress and staff all standing on the drive, waving. The image made Megan want to cry, but she knew she couldn't afford that luxury.

It was seven in the evening when she arrived at Liverpool. As she stepped down from the train she immediately felt the size of the place, the vibrancy of it. People, hundreds it seemed, were milling around her, hurrying, shouting to one another, setting up random patterns of noise and movement that made her feel dizzy.

Megan walked along the platform with her two bags and stepped through the barrier gate. She looked right and left. This was what it felt like to be truly lost, she thought. There wasn't a landmark in the station, in the city or in the entire country of England that meant anything to her.

She found the taxi rank. The driver of the first cab crossed to her and took her bags.

'Where to, love?'

Megan stared past him, out across the vastness of the city, its winding thoroughfares threaded with cold, alien streetlamps. 'Marefield Memorial Hospital, please.'

They passed along streets crammed with motor buses, carts, cars and bicycles. The pavements were even more crowded. After ten minutes Megan noticed that the pedestrians they passed were becoming poorer-looking, ill-dressed most of them and uniformly thin.

'It's a bit of a rum district, this,' the driver said through the open glass hatch.

'Is the hospital near here?'

' 'Fraid it is, love.' He pointed. 'Right on t'corner there.'

When she had been set down with her baggage and the taxi had driven off into the sooty dark, Megan paused before the tall grey building and felt her spirits, so precariously maintained, begin to sink. It was an awful-looking place. Black iron gates fronted an arched double doorway of scarred and pitted stone; it seemed to yawn, with dim green lights visible at its throat.

Megan entered the arch and the smells assailed her – cooked cabbage, carbolic and something else that might have been ether. Approaching the swing doors with the lights beyond she had her first sight of hospital discipline. Under one of the green-shaded wall lamps a woman in the crisp uniform of a ward sister was shouting at a probationer nurse. Megan couldn't hear the sister's words; there was only the muffled echoing of her gritty voice. Her anger was distinct enough, however. The young nurse looked terrified.

Megan pushed open the door. The sister stopped in mid-sentence and glared at her.

'There's no visiting at this hour,' she snapped. Her face was like a man's, hard-lined and aggressive-jawed.

'I'm not a visitor. I have to see the assistant matron, Miss Cumming.'

The sister narrowed her eyes, while the little nurse beside her continued to cower close to the wall. 'Is she expecting you?'

Megan nodded. 'So I was given to understand,' she said politely.

'Along there. Second door. It's marked.'

As Megan moved away, the sister started up at the nurse again. From outside the door it had looked as if the girl was being reprimanded for a major breach of the rules, at the very least. In fact, she was being bawled at for leaving a water tap running in the sluice.

At the assistant matron's door Megan stopped and put down her bags. She knocked lightly. A female voice told her to come in.

The room was dark, with only the overspill from a desk lamp to illuminate Miss Cumming's face. She was in her fifties, a thin woman in a tight, navy-blue dress with two silver badges on it.

Her face had a Victorian severity – thick eyebrows, a thin mouth and eyes that gave the appearance of believing very little that they saw.

'Yes?'

'I'm Megan Roberts, ma'am. I believe Miss Rawlings from the College of Nursing made arrangements with you on my behalf.'

'Ah.' Miss Cumming sat back in her chair. There was no mistaking her displeasure. 'Indeed she did. The arrangements, as you call them, had more the tone of a royal command. You're obviously someone very special, Miss Roberts. Would I be right in saying that?'

'Well, no . . .'

'Then what prompted someone of Miss Rawlings's stature to approach the matron, in the first instance, with a four-page letter extolling your virtues? And what was her motive in practically insisting that we found you a place in training, when the course was already full?' She leaned forward again, clasping her bony fingers on the desk. 'Our matron saw fit, after some resistance, to accede to Miss Rawlings's . . . ahem . . . request. But I had my reservations and I hold them still.'

Megan shifted uneasily. 'I'm sorry if I've caused any inconvenience to you, Miss Cumming.'

'Affront is what has been caused,' the woman snapped. 'In this hospital, the members of the administrative body don't take kindly to outside interference. London interference in particular. Now *do* tell me, Miss Roberts, why the exalted Violet Rawlings expended so much energy and persuasion on your behalf.'

Megan swallowed hard, wondering what to say. 'Well, I know Miss Rawlings . . .'

Miss Cumming aped dismay. 'You know her? Are you telling me you're a personal acquaintance?'

'We've met a number of times and discussed nursing. Miss Rawlings is a cousin of my former employer.'

'So she was doing a favour for an old friend.' It sounded like an accusation of larceny.

'I count her my friend,' Megan said quietly. 'I'm not sure if she regards me in quite the same way . . .'

'She clearly does.' Miss Cumming pointed to a bentwood chair in front of the desk. 'Sit down.' She was regarding Megan with open hostility. 'Now tell me why Miss Rawlings didn't find you a place in a London teaching hospital. It would have been more convenient there, after all.' Her voice was rich with sarcasm as she added, 'You could have met regularly and had little chats, just like old times.'

'She believed I would get better experience in Liverpool.' Megan also suspected that Mrs Pughe-Morgan persuaded Violet to find an appointment in a region totally different in size and custom from anything Megan had ever known. The idea, if Megan read it correctly, was to make her feel genuinely out in the world.

'That could be complimentary, of course,' Miss Cumming said grudgingly. 'But it doesn't change my feelings in this matter.' She riffled through some documents on her desk and pulled one out. 'Everything we need to know about you, for the present, is written on this paper. Our subsequent opinion of you will be governed by what's added as the months go by.' She squinted at the sheet. 'You are Megan Roberts, you are twenty-six and you have been enrolled here on a general nursing course, with a view to State Registration three years from now.' She looked up. 'Is that correct?'

'Yes, ma'am.'

'Right.' Miss Cumming put down the paper and fixed her eyes on Megan. 'Now let me tell you what that means in reality. It means you will spend three months in training school, learning basic medicine, surgery and nursing skills. Thereafter you'll divide your time between the wards and the school. You will be expected to work hard. Extremely hard. The hours are long, as long as we care to make them when the wards are full. You will be subject to continual and rigid discipline. At regular intervals you will be examined in theoretical and practical nursing. Failure at any stage will either add three months to your training or result in your explusion from the course – the decision will be at the discretion of your tutors. Have you taken that in?'

'Yes, ma'am.'

'Now this is the part you have to remember every minute of every day. You will have no special privileges in this hospital. I frankly don't care how well you're connected, it cuts no ice with me. You will be treated like any other probationer. Miss Rawlings and the whole weight of the College of Nursing will be no shield to you at Maresfield.'

'I understand that,' Megan said. 'I don't expect special treatment, Miss Cumming. I was never led to believe there would be any.'

'Fine. So long as we understand each other.' Miss Cumming pressed a white bell-push on her desk. 'An orderly will show you to your quarters. Breakfast is at six sharp. You'll be shown where the dining hall is.'

Ten minutes later Megan found herself alone in a damp-smelling little room, eight feet by eight. Its walls were painted green and grimy cream, and in places the paint had flaked away, exposing pocked grey patches of plaster. There was a scrap of rug beside the narrow, iron-framed bed; in the corner was an unpainted cupboard which Megan presumed was her wardrobe. There was a jug in a chipped porcelain bowl for washing. The only light came from one dim bulb in an enamel shade.

'This is it, Megan,' she said softly. 'For the next three years this is home.' It would have been easy to cry, even easier to turn around and walk out of the place. But that, she reminded herself firmly, was out of the question.

Getting ready for bed, she was assailed by sentimental memories of bedtime back at home. Her lovely room, the soft country sounds, the feeling of safety, security.

That isn't your home any more.

The reminder gave her as much of a pain as the memories. Megan switched out the light and huddled down in the terrible bed, feeling the alien clamminess of the sheets, hearing the cries and catcalls out on the streets of the foreign city.

She had to be strong; she had to fight and keep on fighting. Minute by minute, as sleep refused to come, she rallied her watchwords around her. They lacked conviction, and finally they dwindled to empty sounds.

Tomorrow, Megan decided, and all the days after, she would be strong and she would fight. Tonight she could do no more than lie there, feeling separate from everything around her and longing desperately for home.

31

In October Mrs Pughe-Morgan sent for Mrs Edgar and Mrs Foskett. She asked them to sit down and had Edith bring in tea.

'I want to read you a letter,' the mistress said. 'It's from Megan.'

'Is she all right?' Mrs Edgar asked anxiously.

'I think you'll be able to judge that for yourself.'

There had been only two previous letters, one written a month after Megan started her training, the other when she was in her tenth week. They had been brief notes and neither had contained much news. She didn't appear to be very happy.

'There's some chatty stuff at the beginning,' the mistress said, picking up the letter and putting on her spectacles. 'I'll skip that. It's the rest that'll interest you.' She smiled at the two women. 'She's been a child of the three of us. I think it's only right you should share this.'

Mrs Foskett was nodding. 'I still fret over her like she was my own,' she said.

'Don't we all,' Mrs Edgar murmured.

'This is what she says.' The mistress cleared her throat and read from the neatly written pages.

'Now that eight months have passed and I've grown accustomed to the environment, I find that many of my first impressions were wrong. Sadly, a lot of my misgivings have been confirmed.

'I work in a female surgical ward at present. We have thirty beds and quite often extra ones are wheeled in to accommodate the overflow. When I am on day duty I work with three other nurses and a sister. On nights I work alone, supervised at intervals by a roving night sister or superintendent. The days are busy – too busy at times, with shifts of occasionally twelve or thirteen hours – but the nights are long and dispiriting.

'I had never imagined how hard nursing could be. Violet Rawlings always tried to impress that upon me, but such pressure isn't easy to convey. Most of our patients, in the early days of treatment, are helpless. We have to do everything for them. There were three days last week when I went without lunch, working from seven in the morning until eight at night, simply trying to keep up with the needs of the patients. I see a great deal of misery. Tragedy isn't uncommon, either.

'I have begun to keep a diary, so that I'll never forget some of the things I have seen. It will also be a reminder, in years to come, of how unsatisfactory our hospital system is at present.

'I have never known such harshness. Although a few people working here do shine because of their dedication and perseverance, in the main they are stupid, vindictive and insensitive to the meaning of care. The place doesn't help; it is old and run down and the facilities are depressingly out of date. The draughty wards with their ancient beds and noisy plumbing – to say nothing of the cracked floorboards and the mice – do not encourage sensitivity.

'There is cruel indifference to many patients' requirements. Medication is too often a daily dose of whatever will keep an old woman quiet for an hour or two. Creatures with diminished humanity observe the barest letter of their duty towards people who are themselves diminished in health, often dangerously.

'Having got all that off my chest, I have to say that, as a person, I have probably improved beyond recognition. I have my grief and my losses in perspective. I am much tougher than I thought; my work involves me regularly in emotional muscle-building and I get tougher by the day. Most important of all, my dedication to my work is total. Far from being discouraged by the neglect and indifference of other people, I've responded to the urgency for more concern and much more skill.

'When I am State Registered, I intend to go further. There's no way I can be content until I have as much ability at my fingertips as I can muster. As for the enthusiasm, I have plenty of that. I was taught how to develop it a very long time ago.'

Mrs Pughe-Morgan folded the letter and put it down.

'That's the old Megan,' Mrs Foskett grunted, getting to her feet.

'I'll confess,' the mistress said, 'I never thought she would ever be quite herself again. Now I have the impression she's roughly twice the person we all believed her to be.' She made a little smile. 'Young Mr Sykes could be helping. She mentions at the beginning of the letter that he visits on some of her days off.'

Mrs Edgar stood up. 'That's fair made my morning,' she said. 'It seems the girl's doing fine, in spite of the terrible place she's working at. Mind you, she's a long road to go yet.'

'And it's better to be strong at the start of it.' Mrs Pughe-Morgan opened the door for them. 'I'll write to Megan tonight.'

'Do send her our love, ma'am,' Mrs Edgar said.

Mrs Foskett turned as she stepped into the hall. 'Have you mentioned to her about the new housekeeping arrangements, by any chance?' she asked the mistress, smiling.

'No, but I will.'

Mrs Pughe-Morgan was smiling too as she closed the door. It would amuse Megan to learn she had so much free time nowadays that she had decided to be her own housekeeper. Perhaps, reading between the lines, Megan would also understand that the mistress couldn't bear to have anyone else do the job, ever again.

On Christmas Eve John Sykes sat waiting, cold and impatient, in the smoky buffet bar at Newcastle station. The train he was waiting for was thirty-eight minutes late already, and it had just been announced that a further delay of ten minutes was likely.

John pushed away the remains of his third cup of tea and glanced across at the mirror on the far wall, checking his appearance in the crazed silvering. He supposed he looked smart enough. His father was continually telling him that his hair was too long for a man practising the law, and his mother usually added that people never trusted persons with bow ties. But John liked his hair to touch his ears, and bow-ties were his only special preference where fashion was concerned. He brushed a wisp of hair from his forehead and returned his gaze to the counter. The waitress was still running her grimy damp cloth along the top. She had been doing that, on and off, for fifteen minutes.

He tried to imagine what the next three days would be like. Christmas held no particularly happy memories for him; it had usually been dull and predictable, a time of social claustrophobia that always made him anxious, by Boxing Day, to be back at work. This year, he dearly hoped, it would be different. Megan would be with them. He could entertain her and take pleasure in her company. He could talk to her in a way that had never been possible on his short visits to Liverpool. And he could try to keep his mother's jealousy from showing.

He had never realized how terribly possessive the woman was until the day he mentioned he had a lady friend. The few girls he had known before had produced sour reactions from his mother, but on this occasion she had reacted as if he had bitten her. She went into a long silence afterwards, a brooding alcove of her mind where she seemed to be re-examining the whole foundation of her existence. For days she was preoccupied and desultory; later, she began to quiz John about his friend, asking questions that sought the kind of answers which would allow her to criticize.

'A nurse?' Her brows had gathered. 'There are some unwholesome elements in that calling. And Welsh, into the bargain. The Welsh are a graceless lot. Barely civilized, most of them.'

Then there was Megan's age. 'Someone that old and not married yet – well, it raises a question or two, doesn't it? I mean, what can be wrong?'

To all of his mother's tiresome, defensive prejudice John had responded with humour. But when he announced that he had invited Megan to spend Christmas with them the old woman's reaction made him suddenly realize the scale of her mother-cat tendencies, and how unamusing they had become with the passing years.

'But she can't come here! It's preposterous! I can't be running round after guests at my age. Besides, I like to know I can trust a person before I leave them alone among my possessions.'

Even John's father, who normally allowed his wife to say what she liked without interfering, had objected to that. He told her she was behaving like a spoiled, petulant child. Which had only made her worse.

'He's inviting some strange Welshwoman into this house! Some nurse or other that's enticed him in his simplicity . . .'

As calmly as he could, John had told his mother that, if Megan was to be made unwelcome in their house, then he would make arrangements to spend Christmas in Liverpool with *her*.

The prospect of living through a Christmas without him had shocked his mother. Another long silence had followed. When finally John asked her what she had decided, she told him huffily that his friend would be welcome to visit at Christmas.

John was on the platform as the train pulled in. In a panic he craned his neck, dodging back and forward as the passengers poured out through the doors. She was nowhere in sight. Women of every age and description were milling past him but there wasn't a familiar face among them. None of them was Megan. In a near panic he ran to the barrier and looked along the length of the train. Not a trace. He turned to go to the other side of the platform and bumped right into Megan.

'Oh, my God,' he gasped. 'You're here.'

'I was invited,' Megan grinned.

'No, I mean, I thought you'd missed the train, or something.'

Megan put a calming hand on his shoulder. 'John, do you want to go for a cup of tea? You're terribly flustered.'

He smiled sheepishly. 'I'm just glad to see you. I'd planned to be much more debonair. As for tea, I think I've had enough of that to last me for a while.' He took her bag and led the way through the barrier. 'The car's outside. It'll take us about twenty minutes to drive to the house.' He stopped suddenly, staring at her. 'My, but you're looking smart.'

'Thank you.' She had on a fashionable cloche hat and a long grey woollen coat. 'Thought I'd make an effort, seeing that it's Christmas.'

'Me too.' John spread his arms and stepped back, showing her his new tweed overcoat. 'Bit of a swell, eh?' He laughed and took her arm in his. 'Megan, I hope you have a splendid holiday. I hope we both do.'

On the way out of the town Megan sat watching the slow sweep of hillside and moor as the houses thinned and gave way to open country. In a sense she was surprised to find herself there. She had agreed readily enough to John's invitation, but she wasn't sure why she responded so easily, without thinking first.

She had been steadfast, after all, in keeping their relationship at the friendly level. She knew the dangers of too much closeness, too much time spent together. John, she was sure, still loved her, although he tried not to show it; Megan had a duty to ensure he remained content with matters as they were, as content as she believed she was.

So why had she come here? Now that her mind was temporarily clear of the pressures of work and study, the answer presented itself at once. She had come because she had instantly liked the idea of spending Christmas with him. The answer brought with it a startling new truth which she shied away from: John Sykes had the power, given time, to make her love him.

'Here we go, then,' John muttered a few minutes later as he swung the car into the drive in front of the house. Megan looked at him, wondering why he sounded so apprehensive.

'Come in, come in,' John's father called from the doorway as they got out of the car. He was a tall man with a face that habitually looked cheerful. 'Come into the warm, my dear, before the Northumberland air immobilizes you.'

Megan felt welcome at once. The feeling continued throughout the introductions and for the first few minutes of idle chatter in the hallway. It was when they sat down in the drawing room with glasses of sherry that Megan began to notice the strain in Mrs Sykes. The woman was maintaining her cordiality with an effort.

'It must be a treat just to get away from the hospital for a while,' John said. 'All that hard labour, all the misery you've to contend with.'

'It certainly is.' Megan sipped her sherry, aware that Mrs Sykes was staring at her like a specimen in a bottle. 'I've been looking forward to the break for months.'

'You didn't wish to spend Christmas with your own family, then?' Mrs Sykes asked. John shot her a look and Megan caught it.

'My family are rather dispersed these days. The last time we spent Christmas together was when I was a child.'

Mrs Sykes seemed to be held by that remark. She sat with her mouth half open, heavily implying that she was mystified.

'I left home when I was thirteen,' Megan explained.

'Good gracious.'

'To go into service.'

Mrs Sykes sniffed and averted her eyes.

'Tell me about your training,' John's father said. 'A long haul, is it? Exacting?'

'Very long and terribly exacting. Three years to State Registration, with probably another three after that. I hope to become a Queen's Nurse – what used to be called a Queen's Jubilee Nurse.'

'And what will you be doing then?'

'Home nursing,' Megan said. 'I've had enough time to realize that's where my real ambition lies. Taking nursing care into the homes of people who need it. The poor people.'

'Indeed,' Mrs Sykes muttered. 'I would have thought *ambition* would inspire loftier goals.'

Megan smiled at her. 'I can think of none loftier,' she said.

Dinner was no less of a strain. Megan sat opposite John, who kept giving her encouraging little smiles as his mother's veneer of friendliness steadily fell apart.

'I take it that in nursing there are no particular educational requirements?' the old woman enquired as she spooned apple sauce on to her pork. 'You did say, didn't you, that you were working by the time you were thirteen? Not a great deal of schooling, such as John has had, for instance . . .'

'I was lucky,' Megan said brightly. 'My employer saw to it that I had a good education. Nothing formal, of course, but very thorough.'

'Reading, writing and arithmetic,' Mrs Sykes said airily. 'Of course, there are so many definitions of an education.'

Megan watched John's face grow red. 'That's true,' she said. 'Mrs Pughe-Morgan, my employer, always held that education was limitless, but that it had certain basic requirements before it became worthy of the name. So I learned mathematics – geometry, algebra, trigonometry – and I studied literature, history, botany, medicine and got myself a fair grounding in the arts while I was about it.'

Mrs Sykes was on the point of trying another tack when John

cut in. 'That's always been one of mother's big regrets,' he told Megan. 'She married rather young, and she was never able to get a real education of her own.'

With Mrs Sykes's stolid silence guaranteed for the remainder of the meal, the conversation was allowed to become light again. John's father turned out to be a wag and kept Megan entertained through coffee and brandy with his anecdotes about the law. John relaxed visibly, scarcely taking his eyes off Megan as the brandy softened him and put a light glow on his smiling face.

As the clock struck ten Mrs Sykes stood up abruptly and announced that she was going to bed. Her husband diplomatically decided he should do the same. 'Christmas Day tomorrow, after all. Got to rest my digestion for the major offensive.'

When they were alone, Megan and John went into the sitting room and sat on the wide sofa in front of the fire. Megan leaned back into the cushions and smiled at the firelight.

'I'm desperately sorry,' John said.

'No need to be. Really there isn't.' She turned her head and looked at him. 'I'm used to dealing with difficult people. My skin's thicker than it looks.'

'I'm sure she doesn't mean to be like that.'

'Oh yes she does. She doesn't want to lose you, John. She thinks I'm a threat in that direction. Of course she means to be that way. It's a valid form of attack, anyway – perhaps if she was more sure of herself she'd be better at it.'

John laughed softly, then he reached out and took Megan's hand. She let him.

'Are you, then?' he asked her.

'Am I what?'

'A threat?'

Megan closed her eyes. 'I told you a long time ago, John . . .'

'I know what you told me. But people change, circumstances shift.'

The thought was clear in Megan's mind. He could make me love him. I would only have to let him, it would be as easy as letting him take my hand.

It hardly surprised her that there was no shocked reaction.

Alun's place was secure in her past, in her heart. He was a glorious part of a separate existence, so betrayal, she now knew, was not an issue.

'I've changed,' Megan said, 'it's true. And I'm still changing. Growing.'

John sighed. 'I can't help myself loving you, you know. So I can't help hoping you might . . .'

Megan opened her eyes and looked at him again. 'For the moment my career has to be everything, John. I set out to get a training and I'll have it.'

'I can wait. My affections don't have anywhere else they want to go.'

'I want to work when I'm qualified,' she said patiently. 'I'm going to.'

'I wouldn't stop you.'

'Really?'

'I think it's a splendid idea.'

She smiled at his dear, kind face. 'Can we just hang on, please, and see how I shape? I don't want to be unfair to you, but I'm not ready yet for commitment to anything but my work.'

'For which I respect you enormously,' He leaned across and kissed her lightly on the lips. 'I promise not to raise the matter again during the holiday. Let's simply concentrate on having a lovely Christmas.' He frowned and added, 'If mother lets us.'

'Don't worry about your mother,' Megan said. 'I can cope with her. Three of her, for that matter.' She gazed at the fire again, her hand curled warmly in John's. The sensation of the kiss was still on her mouth, a delicious tingling that she willed to linger. Lord, she thought, it would be so easy . . .

On the day she left Newcastle, Megan stood in the station with John.

'I won't change,' he said. 'I have the kind of nature that never looks for love, but when it happens, then it's for keeps. Does that sound silly?'

'No. Honesty's never very silly.' Megan touched his arm

impulsively. 'John, I feel sorry for what I'm doing to you. Making you wait, saving my options . . .'

'Your motives are immaculate. I told you, I admire you for it. And you'll be my friend in the meantime.'

'Five years. That's a long, long meantime.'

He grinned. 'With a mother like mine you learn patience.'

'I thought she behaved rather well, after the first night,' Megan smiled.

'You'd have had her jumping through fiery hoops if you'd wanted to. The trouble is, I won't have you around the rest of the time to keep her under control.'

The guard's warning whistle blew. They both caught the same memory, the pair of them on a sunny platform in Rhyl. He looked much happier this time, Megan thought. She crossed and got into the carriage, then leaned out through the window.

'Goodbye, John. Thank you for a lovely Christmas.'

'Thank you for coming.' He kissed her for the second time, then stood waving as the train pulled out. Megan waved until she couldn't see him any longer.

All the way back to Liverpool the thought was in her mind; she could love him, she could do it without prejudice to her conscience or her career, and it would take no effort at all.

Quite the opposite, she thought wryly. By now she knew she was keeping herself from loving John. It was perhaps a greater effort than she admitted to herself, but it was one she could withstand.

'Five years,' she murmured to herself. State Registration, probably midwifery after that, then Queen's Nurse. A tall order, but manageable. When it was accomplished, she would really know the strength of her feeling, the stature of her emotions. And perhaps she would have gained a little more wisdom to help her decide.

32

The orderly had tidied the office, as she did at that time every morning. The desk was polished, the inkstand dusted and the two pots topped up, one with red ink, the other with blue. On an afterthought she stood on a chair and drew her duster along the top of the founders' picture on the wall behind the desk. Before she left she turned the knob on the silver-plated desk calendar, changing the date to 12 June 1925.

Miss Cumming entered at nine o'clock sharp. She sat down behind the desk and unlocked the top drawer. Taking out a buff folder, she set it squarely in front of her, opened it and pressed the bell-push.

The orderly put her head round the door. 'Yes, ma'am?'

'Ask Nurse Roberts to come in,' Miss Cumming said without looking up from the folder.

Megan was shown in a moment later. She was in her dark-blue uniform dress with short, white-ruffed sleeves and broad black belt. Around her neck she had a chain with the filigree Queen's Nurse badge attached. She stood in front of the desk and waited until the assistant matron finished reading.

'Ah.' Miss Cumming looked up and smiled tightly. 'I suppose you've been wondering if I would ever send for you.'

'I tried not to be impatient,' Megan said.

'And we've made every effort to speed matters for you. But the wheels grind slowly, however hard we push.' Miss Cumming put her elbows on the desk and looked at Megan thoughtfully. 'You're still as set on this move as you were a month ago, are you?'

'Every bit,' Megan assured her.

'I must say your request surprised me. I know you like challenge in your work, but this one is going to tax you sorely, I believe. What's your motive, precisely?'

'I've more than one,' Megan said. She found it easy to talk to

Miss Cumming now. The woman's initial hostility had gradually turned to acceptance and ultimately to respect as Megan had steadily proved herself in the wards and clinics, and in her eighteen months of home nursing. 'The first and most important motive is to get back to Wales.'

'You still miss it, do you?'

'That surprises me,' Megan admitted. 'There was a time when I thought ties were cancelled by time. There's one tie I didn't take into account, though. One I couldn't ever break.'

'And what's that?'

'My racial character. There's a rhythm to being Welsh. I'm out of tune elsewhere. It's a very deep instinct, Miss Cumming. I'd have to respond to it sooner or later.'

'Are you not tied to any special part of the country?'

'There's one place I'll always love, the place where I lived and worked until I was twenty-six.'

Miss Cumming looked puzzled. 'Then why not go back there, or at least somewhere near? I'm sure something suitable could have been found.'

'Because going back, in that sense, never works,' Megan said. 'Not for someone like me. I want to feel I'm going forward, if you follow me.'

'Well.' Miss Cumming sighed and looked down at the folder. 'Forward's hardly a word I'd apply to this place. It's static, as far as I can see. Some people would call it primitive. They're going to resent you, you know. It'll be very hard to get yourself accepted.'

Megan smiled. 'That's the challenge.'

'Very well. So what's your other motive for burying yourself in a South Welsh mining community?'

'I'll be able to do a lot of good. It's the very poverty and backwardness of the place that makes it ideal for somebody in my profession.'

'God help you, then,' Miss Cumming said quietly. She tapped the official letter on top of the papers in the folder. 'You know why you're here – I have to advise you that, one month from today, you will take up your appointment as district nurse to the community of Pencwm in South Wales.'

311

'Thank you, Miss Cumming.'

'I'd also like to take this opportunity of congratulating you, Nurse Roberts. I'm not given to being prodigal with my praise, but over the past five years you've acquitted yourself in a way which my report will describe as exemplary.' She frowned for a moment. 'There have been times when your strong individuality has led you into indiscretion – such as the occasion when you called Sister McKee an incompetent, ten-thumbed old menace.'

Megan blushed. 'I'd forgotten that.'

'Four years ago, nurse. You've mellowed since. And old Ten-Thumbs has subsequently retired, thank heaven.' Miss Cumming stood up and extended her hand. 'My very best wishes to you.' She shook Megan's hand warmly. 'Do keep in touch. I'll be interested to know what you make of your new parish.'

That afternoon Megan packed her bags in preparation for her month's leave. When everything was ready, when the dingy little room was cleared and ready to be occupied by another nervous, dispirited novice, Megan stood by the window and gazed down at the street. She had done it very often, and many times what she saw repelled her. That was an ugly street without one graceful feature to redeem it. But it was always so sad, Megan thought, consciously to do something for the last time.

The street had become as familiar as any place she had known. So had the others around, the streets and the people and the awful lives that were thrust on them. Alongside her knowledge of medicine and nursing Megan had gained a keen depth of compassion. Liverpool had contributed its part to her growth. She would miss it.

At two o'clock she took a taxi to Lime Street Station and put her cases in the left-luggage department. She then went back to the taxi rank, climbed into a cab and told the driver to take her to the Palace Hotel.

She waited in the hotel bar with a glass of lemonade on the table before her. She had taken only a couple of sips when John Sykes appeared, sombrely dressed in a dark business suit. He was smiling broadly as he approached the table.

'Megan, it's wonderful to see you.' They embraced for a moment, then Megan sat down again.

'I told you on the phone, John, there was no need for you to come to Liverpool.'

'And I told you I wanted to. Besides, I've got business in Manchester that can be attended to while I'm here. It's less than an hour on the train.' He sat down opposite Megan. 'Somebody had to see you off on your last day here.' He clasped her hand. 'How does it feel, being all qualified and ready to branch out?'

'At the moment I'm feeling amputated. Cut off from all that's been a part of me for so long. But I'm excited, too.'

'Do you have a nice warm sense of accomplishment? That's what I always remember – getting my finals, *arriving*.'

Megan nodded. 'It's nice having bits of paper to confirm you know what you're doing. But I don't feel I've arrived yet. That's still up ahead.'

John hailed a waiter and ordered a pink gin. Turning back to Megan, he produced a small flat box from his pocket. 'For you. To say congratulations.'

'Oh, John . . .' She took off the lid. There was a brooch inside, delicately fashioned in silver and gold with tiny seed diamonds. She had a sudden recollection of childhood and a silver-wire brooch she still kept in a souvenir box. 'It's gorgeous.'

'Put it on, then.'

Megan pinned it to her coat. 'There. How does it look?'

'Splendid.' He leaned over and kissed her cheek. 'I'm proud of you.' The waiter brought the drink. John held up the glass in the gesture of a toast, then sipped from it. 'Now tell me, have you made any plans yet? About where you'll be working?'

Megan looked at the table for a moment. 'It's all arranged,' she said. 'I start in a month.'

'In a . . .' John looked startled. 'I didn't even know you'd made up your mind. You didn't say anything the last time I saw you. I assumed . . .'

'I made up my mind a year ago.' She hesitated. 'About everything.'

John swallowed some more of his drink, then sat looking at her. 'As long ago as that?'

'I said nothing about it because I thought I might change my mind again, after the finals. People often see things differently when the choice they've waited for is actually there, right in front of them.'

'But your plans didn't change.'

'No.'

'Go ahead, then,' John said, his voice low now, his expression serious. 'What did you decide?'

Megan twirled her lemonade glass on the table. 'John, first of all, you have to understand that I considered everything very carefully. I was as honest with myself as I could be.'

'I wouldn't have expected anything less.'

She looked up. 'Well, I'm going to be the district nurse in a place called Pencwm. It's a coalmining and farming community in South Wales.'

'Wales?' He looked devastated.

'I want to go back there.'

'*South* Wales?' John was clearly struggling to be placid and objective. 'Why the south? You know what your countrymen can be like. I noticed it even in Rhyl. They'll be against you on two counts. You're anglicized and you're from the north. God, you're asking for problems, aren't you?'

'I have my reasons.'

'Megan, I'm beginning to think you haven't considered things as carefully as you believe you have.'

She looked at him pleadingly. 'John, please don't be upset, I didn't do any of it to cause you pain –'

'Pain? Who's feeling pain?' He made an impatient gesture and picked up his glass, glared at it and put it down again. 'Bewilderment, that's what I'm feeling. You came to England to get away from your background, to start afresh and do something positive with your life. Now you tell me you're heading back to the hills and valleys practically the moment you're qualified.'

'But I'll be a stranger where I'm going, as you pointed out.'

'That's not the point I'm making. It's that you're going there at all . . .' He drained his glass suddenly, then leaned towards her. 'Do I have to beg you to tell me?'

'About us?'

'Right. About us.'

This wasn't the way Megan had wanted it. She had planned to write to him; not out of cowardice, but so that she could state her case without John being present to discolour her mood or distort her meaning.

'I've never seen you angry before,' she said.

'I'm not angry. Just tell me.'

'Very well.' She looked at him levelly. 'I've decided to devote my life to my work. I've lain awake at nights thinking it out. I've agonized over it. It's a conclusion I can't escape. There isn't room in my life for a partner, John.'

He sat nodding at her. 'I see. Well, you seem to have come to a nice tidy solution there, Megan,' he said bitterly. 'No complications. No commitment . . .'

'Total commitment,' she corrected him. 'To my patients, my job.'

'And you honestly think that'll fulfil you?'

'I know it will.'

'I have my doubts. Strong doubts.' He folded his arms and leaned back in his chair. 'God, Megan . . .'

'I know it seems unfair to you. But I'll tell you this, it would be even more unfair the other way. It'd never work out. You a solicitor, me a district nurse, never seeing each other, expecting so much from the relationship and only getting morsels. As friends we've had lovely times – friendship doesn't expect too much.'

John had sulked into silence. Megan sat opposite, not knowing what else to say. She had finished her lemonade before he finally spoke again. What he said surprised her.

'I suppose you're right, Megan.' He sighed. 'My fantasies about marriage have had their troublesome features. I think deep down I'd have resented you working, after a while. I suppose there would have been a plan buried in me to make you stop, to make you the housewife, the little woman waiting when I got home. You wouldn't have stood for that. There would have been war.' He looked at her with unconcealed sadness in his eyes. 'Even so, it hurts to know that none of it will happen.'

'It hurts me too,' she told him. 'Truly. I could fall in love with

you so easily. But I won't. And you'll learn not to hope in that
direction. You'll be the better for it.'

'You sound like a nurse.' He smiled dejectedly. 'I'm going to
miss those dreams of mine.' After a pause he said, 'Mind you, my
mother's going to be very relieved.'

They both laughed, and the laughter was like the seal on a
firm contract. Friends.

A few minutes later John saw Megan to the door of the hotel.
'I'll stay a while longer,' he told her. 'Probably get a little bit
drunk. Only enough to take away the sting, though.' He dug his
hands in his pockets and squinted out at the busy sunlit street.
'Where are you spending your leave? With Mrs Pughe-Morgan?'

Megan shook her head. 'That idea tempted me. But I resisted.
I'll go back to see them all when I'm settled in my district. I'll be
a visitor from elsewhere then. Somone with another place she
belongs. And I know they understand.'

'You certainly do think things out,' John said. 'So are you
going to be on your own somewhere? It doesn't seem a very
cheerful prospect.'

'I'm going to Eastbourne with Violet Rawlings. A whole
month of sea and sand and swapping professional lore.'

'Now *that* sounds delightful.' He made an effort and smiled.
'Give my love to Violet. Tell her I hope she's kept up her
bridge.' John couldn't keep the dolefulness at bay for long. His
smile died as he reached for Megan's hand; plaintive-eyed, he
put a small kiss on her fingers. 'Look after yourself. Always.'

'You too, John.' Megan kissed his cheek. She gazed at his face
for a second, then turned away sharply. 'Goodbye,' she called as
she hurried down the steps. 'I'll send you my address. Keep in
touch.'

John stood at the top of the steps, nodding and waving. His
eyes were as clouded with sadness as they had been that day in
Rhyl, the other time he had learned he could only be a friend.

Megan caught the train to Eastbourne at four o'clock. She sat
close to the carriage window, watching Liverpool recede.
When it had gone and she had said her last silent 'thank you' to
the city, she thought inevitably of John Sykes.

She thought of what she hadn't told him. A year before she

had realized the thing had happened. All unwitting, she found herself in love with him. It had been a happy feeling, almost joyous, but the pleasure gave way by slow degrees to a torment she couldn't define until much later.

The answer came to her in her sleep, as many answers did. She had sat up, her heart pounding softly with the understanding – she could no longer allow her emotions to stand at risk. She knew where she was weakest; she understood, tragically well, what the loss of a loved one could do to her. So she must make sure it never happened again. She mustn't ever run the risk, however slight.

Her resolution grew from that moment. It had hurt to put John out of her heart, but it took away the torment. Finally, in the aftermath, she felt secure again. Her deeper feelings could remain where they were safe and where they no longer hurt – with her father, with Alun and with Bronwen.

On a humid, overcast day in July, the porter at Pencwm station stood watching mumpishly as four people stepped down from the afternoon through-train. Three of the passengers he knew. Two never used a porter and the third always did, but he never gave a tip. The fourth was a woman in uniform with a tight cap that all but obscured her forehead and hair. The porter decided to approach her before the non-tipper caught him.

'Want a hand with them bags, miss?'

'No, it's all right,' Megan said. 'I was told to wait on the platform until someone came to fetch me.'

'Oh.' The porter narrowed his eyes at her. 'It's a nurse you are, isn't it?'

'That's right. I'm the district nurse for Pencwm.'

The eyes got narrower still. 'Not Welsh, then.'

'Oh, yes. I'm from Drynfor.'

'Where?'

'Drynfor. It's in the north.'

'Oh,' he grunted, turning away. 'The north.'

Megan crossed the platform and looked out beyond the white slatted fence. She saw row upon row of smoky miners' cottages

317

and the mine buildings and tips beyond. It was like a dozen places she'd passed through on the train. But this one was going to be special.

She felt as nervous as she had the first night in Liverpool. Alien territory. No landmarks to comfort her. Megan took a deep breath and made herself smile at the sombre landscape. Conviction was everything. She was here to succeed, and succeed she would, or she'd go down trying.

A mastery of life, Megan . . .

The challenge, she knew, was going to be fierce. But she was equal to it; she was prepared to embrace a life of service to others. So the others had better get used to her.

A thought dawned sudden and bright. It broadened Megan's smile, making her impatient to get out of that station and into the lives where she could do some good. After a long prelude, she thought, a prelude that had been sometimes happy and sometimes desperately miserable, this was her true beginning.